Death
Map

Short Stories by Diana Catt

"Photo Finish" in *Racing Can Be Murder*, Blue River Press (2007)

"Evil Comes*"* in *Medium of Murder*, Red Coyote Press (2008)

"Slightly Mummified" in *A Whodunit Halloween,* Pill Hill Press (2010)

"Boneyard Busted" in *Bedlam at the Brickyard*, Blue River Press (2010)

"Au Naturel" in *Patented DNA,* Pill Hill Press (2010)

"And Through the Woods" in *Back to the Middle of Nowhere,* Pill Hill Press (2010)

"Salome's Gift" in *Murder to Mil-Spec,* Wolfmont Press (2010)

"The Art of the Game" in *Hoosier Hoops and Hijinks,* Blue River Press (2013)

"Raspberry Summer" in *Distant Dying Embers,* The Four Horsemen Press (2015)

"The Circle Effect" in *Decades of Dirt,* Speed City Press (2015)

"The Dark Core" in *Decades of Dirt,* Speed City Press (2015)

"Metaphor" in *Below the Line* (2015)

"The Stuff of Dreams" in *Below the Line* (2015)

"Deeper into the Darkness" in *Below the Line* (2015)

"Framed" in *The Fine Art of Murder*, Blue River Press (2016)

"Framed" reprinted in **The Best by Women in Horror anthology,** *Killing It Softly 2,* Digital Fiction Publishing Corp **(2017)**

"The Final Recall," in *Me Too Short Stories*, Level Best Books (2019)

"The Circle Effect" in *Circle City Crime*, Speed City Press (2019)

"Flashes of Life" in *Circle City Crime*, Speed City Press (2019)

"The Hundred Year Time Capsule" in *Murder 2020*, Speed City Press (2020)

"Which Witch?" in *Trick or Treats, Tales of All Hallows' Eve,* Speed City Press (2021)

Death Map

Diana Catt

Per Bastet

Death Map

Published by Per Bastet Publications LLC, P.O. Box 3023 Corydon, IN 47112

Cover art by T. Lee Harris
ISBN 978-1-942166-80-1

Available in trade paperback and DRM-free ebook formats

Death Map

Acknowledgements

A thank you full of love to my parents, Dwight and Mary Ann Mobley, for their unconditional support and for reading and providing feedback on everything I sent them my entire life. I only wish you were here to see this one published.

To Barry, Mike, Kristy, and Wade — you are always first in my heart! Thanks for putting up with my lifelong writing hobby/obsession and cheering me on.

A special shout out to my critique group, In Mysterious Company. You are all very dear to me and I have enjoyed our years and years of deep discussions and comradery— Michael Dabney, Dave Reddick, Marianne Halbert, Shari Held, Michael Eldridge, Bridgett Kephart, Janet Williams, and the late Suzanne Harding. Where would I be without all of you?

I must applaud the Speed City Indiana chapter of Sisters in Crime for all the emotional support, education, and opportunities for growth I've had as a writer since I joined almost 20 years ago. Thank you, my friends!

Because Death Map has been a long time in coming, a lot of other people along the way have read drafts, provided feedback, or listened to me work out various ideas or problems. Special thanks to the Borderlands Bootcamp 2017 attendees, and 2017 faculty Tom Monteleone, F. Paul Wilson, Douglas E Winter, Peter Straub, what an amazing experience; to Vikki Ciaffone for providing valuable editing; and my walking buddies, Chris and Marianne, for your patience when I rattled on about my characters. To anyone I've missed please know I appreciate all your help and I hope you will enjoy this version.

And finally, so much gratitude to Marian Allen for her superb editing skills and repeatedly telling me she loves the story, and everyone at Per Bastet Publishing — thanks for accepting me into your fold!

Chapter 1

April: Charleston, South Carolina

The plane touched down with a jarring thump that caused a collective "Oh" from the passengers, yanking me from my daze. I'd spent the entirety of the flight from New York City huddled within myself struggling with the tragic news that sent me on this urgent trip to Charleston. Ellen, my best friend since college, had been murdered this morning. Ellen's pre-teen son — my godson — was seriously injured and in the hospital.

I glanced at my phone. Seven hours ago. Seven hours since the news reached me at work and my world changed. Seven hours since Ellen's world had ended and Mike became my responsibility. My hands trembled as I reached overhead to retrieve my carry-on. How could I comfort Mike, let alone foster the twelve-year-old through his teenage years and life beyond? Besides his crippling emotional loss, I had no idea of the extent of his physical injuries. I imagined extensive surgeries, long hospital stays, physical therapy, grief therapy. This kid was important. I couldn't mess up.

The rental car was ready when I arrived. The hospital was downtown, about twenty minutes away. No need for a map; I knew my way around Charleston.

The horizon had rolled up to block out the sun, leaving soft pink and orange swirls decorating the darkening sky. The beauty contrasted with the unnatural aspects of the horror of that morning. For a while, I had clung to a tiny spark inside my heart, hoping that it would all turn out to be a colossal, horrendous mistake. Everything would return to normal. I'd hug Ellen and Mike; they'd laugh with relief, order pizza delivery, take selfies. I would take the red-eye back to NYC, finish the story on the Senator's latest scandal and make the *Morning Star*'s afternoon on-line edition. Just a little bump, but life would return to normal.

That tiny spark dimmed as I remembered the horrific phone call that alerted me to this emergency.

Chapter 2

April: New York City
Seven Hours Earlier:

The newsroom babble and ringing phones faded to background as I focused to fashion the perfect ending for my exposé. The bribe allegations against Senator O'Connell headlined last night's broadcast news, but I had an unexpected angle for tonight's online edition of the paper that would blow the O'Connell saga wide open.

And earn me a by-line.

And name recognition.

And fame.

I gave myself a mental slap. These daydreams of grandeur weren't going to get the story finished. However, I could anticipate going viral for a little longer during a quick trip to the corner café for a double hit cappuccino, then get back on track.

My phone jangled as I stepped away from my desk.

I almost ignored the ring. It seemed a no-brainer, chocolate trumping phone call, until I spotted Buzz Bradley hovering between my desk and the elevator. If I left now I'd be hounded by more of his pesky questions. He popped up everywhere this week, as if stalking me. Or, maybe the *Morning Star* management had assigned him to do a feature on Lila Kincaid, their Supergirl Reporter. Yeah, right.

The chocolate caffeine fix could come later. I swiveled a one-eighty and reached across my desk to answer the phone.

"Lila Kincaid, *Morning Star* news."

"Ms. Kincaid?" It was our receptionist. "I have Ms.

Sophia Jacobsen on hold. Want me to put her through or take a message?"

"Put her through, Dora. Thanks."

"Okay, just a moment."

Curious. Sophia Jacobsen was the elderly aunt of my best friend, Ellen Jacobsen. I couldn't imagine why she'd be calling me. Then, Buzz spoke up.

"Hey, Lila. You busy?"

Great. Morning buzz-kill. "Morning, Buzz," I said, turning to face him.

"Going for coffee?" he asked, persistent as ever.

"Soon as I take this call."

"Mind if I join you?"

"I'm getting it to go."

"I was, um, wondering if you'd look over something I wrote?"

Ah, that explains it. "Sure, I'll take a look. Gotta finish my piece first. If you're in a hurry you might try Clunie."

"Oh, no hurry. It's not due 'til next week. Thanks, Lila. I really mean that. I'll email it over." He jingled some change in his pocket then asked, "Can I help with yours?"

In your dreams, Buzzy Boy. "Another time, maybe," I said. "I'm about done with this one."

My phone clicked and Dora said, "Thank you for holding. I'm connecting you to Ms. Kincaid now."

I waved my hand in the air toward Buzz and turned my back on him, wishing my so-called cubicle had more than a twelve-inch-tall desk separator and actually had a door to close.

"Is that you, Lila, dear?" I recognized the soft southern accent, but the old age tremble in her voice was more pronounced than I remembered.

"Aunt Sophia? This is a pleasant surprise. Are you visiting Ellen?"

"No, dear. The nurse was kind enough to let me use the phone today." She paused a long moment. "I'm afraid I have some tragic news and I need your help."

I walked around my desk and sat down. "What's happened?"

"A police officer came to see me about Ellen."

Ellen in trouble with the police? No way.

"I'm so sorry to tell you this, my dear," she continued, "but our Ellen is gone, and her little Mikey is injured. Seriously, I suppose, since he's in the hospital."

"Gone?" I repeated, as the chill of panic began to inch up from my knees. "What do you mean, gone? And what's wrong with Mike?"

"I can't remember the details. I'm so sorry to be the one to break this news, Lila, dear, but I feel so helpless. You know I can't drive anymore, can't care for a child. Would you check on the boy? Come to Charleston?"

"Of course I'll come. But, Sophia, what's happened?"

"It can't be true," she said. "Perhaps the officer made a mistake?"

I heard the note of hope and let out a sigh of relief. Her dementia, of course.

"I did try to reach Ellen by phone," Aunt Sophia continued, in her precise Carolinian lilt. "But I may not have the correct number. I'm so confused these days. Could I impose on you to help me, Lila, dear?"

"I'll make some calls, Aunt Sophia, and don't worry. I'll help however I can."

She hung up after a quick, "Good-bye, dear," and I sat motionless, staring at the phone. Poor Sophia. She had a history of getting things mixed up, but this was delusional in the extreme. I should call and alert the staff.

Instead, I sent Ellen a text, then followed up with a call that went directly to her voice mail. I left a message for her to call me at once. I tapped my desktop, thinking. Ellen always forgot to recharge her cell's battery. Or maybe she was in the shower, or using the hairdryer and couldn't hear the ring. I called her number again. And again. I didn't have Mike's cell number so I messaged him on Facebook to contact me ASAP.

There were reasonable explanations for a delayed response. Mike was in school where he belonged and couldn't check the Internet. Ellen was busy. After one more unanswered text, I called the assisted living facility and asked for the director.

Mrs. Edgewood knew about Sophia's call.

"I'm very sorry, Lila," Mrs. Edgewood said. "I wanted to speak with you when Sophia called earlier, but she hung up before I could get to the phone. Poor soul's baffled and upset over this news, as we all are."

The newsroom noise vanished, replaced by a pounding in my veins. This was wrong. It had to be wrong. "But, it . . . can't . . . be true. Sophia was confused."

"I spoke to the officers myself. There was an incident."

"An incident? You mean, like an accident? A wreck?"

"No. An incident occurred at their home. It's being treated as a homicide. That's all they told us."

Her words crushed my heart. "My God, no."

"Yes. I'm sorry."

"Wait," I said, afraid Mrs. Edgewood was going to hang up, "wait, please. I can't . . . oh, God, I mean, who's in charge of the investigation?"

"Let me see. They left a card," she said, and provided a name and number.

My hand trembled as I scribbled the information and Mrs. Edgewood continued with more details. Ellen had called 911, but when the police arrived, they found her in the kitchen. Stabbed to death.

Ellen dead. Mike injured. It was too dreadful to comprehend. Increasingly vivid images of Ellen's thin frame lying crumpled and bloody on her kitchen floor flashed through my mind in rapid succession, each spectacle containing new layers of gruesome detail stolen from random slasher movies. I squeezed my eyes shut to dispel these thoughts and tried to focus on what Mrs. Edgewood was saying.

"The officers who came here recognized Sophia's limitations at once and contacted me. I suggested she call you. Other than Ellen, you're the only contact name in her file."

"There isn't any other family that I know of," I said. "I'll be flying down as soon as I can."

"Well, the boy's still alive, but I don't have any specifics on his injuries. I think he must be in bad shape. They've set up a guard for him at the hospital," Mrs. Edgewood continued. "I had the impression he might be able to identify their attacker."

I conjured up an image of Mike lying in the hospital hooked up to life support, with unknown enemies lurking in the shadows, waiting for the chance to silence him forever.

"Please assure Sophia I'll be there soon. And give her my love." I hung up and sat, unable to function, in a sort of fugue state. Some moments later I resumed thinking, but a protective inner force was still in place that kept Ellen's death unreal and at a distance.

Instead, I focused my energy on my godson, what he needed and how I could help. He was alone in the world and suffering after witnessing a horror beyond imagination. And I suspected a police guard at the hospital was no small matter. *Could Mike ID his attacker?*

I'd take a leave of absence and bring Mike up here where he'd be safe. If he'd seen the killer. . . .

Killer. Once formed, the word loomed large and wouldn't go away. I wished I could return to that fugue state. God, I couldn't grasp that Ellen, my best friend in the world, was dead.

I lowered my head to the desktop, trying to get my mind to believe what I'd been told and consider my options. A touch on my shoulder caused me to jump. I whirled upright and met inquisitive brown eyes, magnified to giant orbs by thick glasses.

"Hey," Buzz said. "Everything okay? Anything I can do?"

I closed my eyes, unable to suppress a shudder.

"Thanks, Buzz. But, no."

Although unwelcome, his intrusion motivated me into action. I rose and walked to my editor's office, gave a quick knock, entered, and closed the door on Buzz's curiosity. A wave of Dan McLeish's fruity citrus aftershave assaulted my already anxious stomach.

"I need to take some time off," I announced. "At least two weeks, maybe longer."

"Are you sick?" McLeish asked from his seat behind a massive oak desk. "You look sick."

"No." I paused a moment, not sure if I could voice the words. "I just had some awful news. I need to go to Charleston. Today."

McLeish frowned. "South Carolina?"

"My very best friend was killed there today. And she has a son. Twelve. I need to help him."

McLeish cocked his head and leaned forward. "Accident or murder?"

"Murder." I shuddered. He pointed to one of the leather chairs and I took a seat.

"Details?" he asked.

I struggled to hold back tears and clasped my hands together to stop them from trembling. Twisting my spinner ring usually soothed me, but this was too much for that simple trick. I took a deep breath and relayed the phone call from Aunt Sophia. My voice shook, but I hadn't entirely lost control. I was on the verge, though, and the fall was going to hurt like hell.

McLeish stood and walked over to a coffee maker sitting on top of his credenza. He raised his eyebrows. I thanked him.

"It happened this morning," I said, taking the steaming mug he offered. "Mike saw it all. Ellen's dead. Mike's in the hospital. It's under investigation." I took a sip and my lip ring chinked against the brim. The coffee burned my throat. The cough forced tears from my eyes. "It's up to me to help him. His great-aunt's too old. There's no one else, really, and I care a lot for him."

"Shit," McLeish said. "I'm sorry. You bringing the kid up here?"

"I . . . guess. I don't know his condition yet. I need to get down to Charleston. Today."

"Got anything on the burner?"

I sighed with relief. He was going to agree.

"Just that rumor about O'Connell and the bribe." My voice lost the waver. "I've got a lead on the source of the leak and some strong indications that he was being blackmailed. It's good stuff."

"Up to you," he said. "Finish it first, or give it to someone and leave today." He paused a beat. "Bradley'll take it."

"I think I'll try Clunie." Then, glad for the distraction, I asked, "What's with Buzz lately, anyway? He's been following me around like a pup."

McLeish snorted. "He's been bugging me for a chance to work with you on something. Anything."

"Well, call him off. The last thing I need right now is a shadow."

McLeish refilled his own mug, took a drink, and returned to his leather chair behind the desk.

I took another tiny sip of the too-strong coffee. Gagged again, but didn't tear up. "I'm going to need some time, Dan."

"I know you haven't taken a day off since you started here," he said, "so you can go. Take two, three days even. But look, I need you back as soon as possible." McLeish jabbed the desk with his forefinger while he finished his coffee. Then he waved me out of his office and returned his attention to his computer screen.

I rose from my seat. "Right, Dan. Um, thanks." I'd hoped for a straight out "Take as long as you need," since that's what I intended to do anyway. But, one step at a time. I left my editor's office, passed Buzz lurking in the hall, and returned to my desk to make arrangements for leaving town.

A few minutes after I'd phoned the airport and lucked into a flight leaving early evening, Clunie stopped by my cubicle.

"Hell, girl," she said, "your aura is, like, spiking red all over."

Clunie is fresh out of college and eager to please. She's also the organizer of a group of tattoo junkies called *The Ink Marks* and a self-proclaimed psychic.

"Oh, Clunie, great. I was just going to call you." Maybe McLeish had given her a heads up? I filled her in.

"Jeez, Lila. Hope they find the bastard. I'll hold you and your godson in the light."

I glanced at her thickly decorated eyes and saw sincerity beneath the art.

"Thanks," I said, and handed over the stack of notes that made up the O'Connell file. "My article's about finished." I opened up my laptop and attached it to an email and sent it to her. "You should find everything in here, but text or call if you have any questions."

Clunie gripped the thick collection of documents with both hands and tilted the file toward me. "No worries. I'll email you the copy."

"Thanks," I said again, numb as an automaton. I stood and picked up my backpack. "I've got to run. Have a flight to catch." I dashed out of the office and jostled my way through four blocks of crowded sidewalks to my apartment.

I packed in a flurry and Ubered to the airport. At my

departure gate I sat near the edge of the waiting area, unable to gather a cohesive thought. The ringing of a nearby cell phone jangled my nerves and forced me to face an important call I needed to make. I knew Ellen had me listed as legal guardian of Mike in the event of her death, but I had no idea what I needed to do at the moment. I'd need proof of guardianship before I could deal with his doctors and school officials. I needed a lawyer.

I knew one attorney in Charleston. He was supremely qualified and also a long-time friend of Ellen's. Unfortunately, I wasn't certain any longer how he felt about me. But this was for Mike, not about the failed relationship between Harry and me. I steeled myself and placed the call.

"You have reached Harold Greenstreet." The familiar deep voice on the recording caused a momentary pang in my heart. "Please, leave a message and I'll return your call."

At least I didn't have to speak to him in person. I waited for the required tone then said, "Harry, it's Lila. I'd like to hire you. Ellen's aunt wants me to take care of Mike, so I'll need to get guardianship, I guess. I'm flying down today. Don't bother to meet me, I've already rented a car." I scribbled *call for car rental* on a piece of scrap paper. "The police didn't tell me much. If you find out anything, please call me. I. . . ." There was a beep and the call disconnected.

Oh well, Harry could figure it out. I boarded the plane and found my seat. As we accelerated down the runway, an irrational panic gripped me, increasing with the plane's speed and power. Guardian? Making decisions for another human? I was heading into something way over my head.

Chapter 3

Charleston, South Carolina

I entered the hospital, went directly to the information desk, and asked for Mike's room number.

"He's still in the ER," the attendant said after punching information into her computer. "You family?"

"Yes," I said. It was easier to agree.

"He's in one-twelve. The quickest way back is to follow the blue line on the floor through that door and make a left. You'll go through a set of double doors, then follow the orange line to ER. That way, you bypass the patient sign-in desk. I'll call and let them know you're here. One-twelve is straight past the nurse's station, all the way to the back on the right."

"Can you tell me anything about his condition?"

"Sorry, I don't have any info. Ask at the nurse's station."

I thanked her and followed the blue line, switched to orange, found the ER nurse's station. The nurse at the desk held up one finger at me while she finished her phone call. I waited, shifting from one foot to the other. I looked beyond the nurse's station toward the end of the hall but couldn't spot a police guard. Maybe they'd moved Mike.

People in the know could distinguish the nurses from the doctors, and residents from techs by their uniform color, but I wasn't in the know. I watched the bustle of activity: charts plunked into door file holders or pulled out and quickly scanned before the reader disappeared into the room; lights flashed over doorways; monitors positioned at the nurse's station ticked off information. I strummed my fingertips on the countertop and caught the sweet scent from a bouquet of flowers awaiting delivery.

The nurse hung up the phone and studied me with an appraising eye, one brow lifted. "You're here for the Jacobsen boy?"

"Yes," I said. "How is he?"

"What's your relationship to the patient?"

"Guardian." It wasn't exactly a lie. I had verbal permission.

"Need you to read this and sign at the X." She slid some papers across the counter. I scanned them and signed.

"How is Mike?" I asked again. "Was he seriously injured?"

The nurse gave me a wary look, with a noticeable pause on my hair, then my lip ring. "Do you have proof of guardianship?"

I shook my head. "I just flew in from New York and the paperwork is with the attorney. I can try to reach him if you really need it."

The nurse tapped her computer screen and studied my signature for a moment. "No worries. The police told us to expect you. I know what the boy did was horrible, but he's still a minor and someone needs to take responsibility for him."

My stomach turned. "What do you mean?"

"Haven't you been told?"

I mentally braced myself. I'd been told enough. "I know Mike was injured when his mom was murdered. What else should I know?"

I watched a muscle in her face twitch, her eyes narrow. The room overheated as the walls pressed in on me.

"He arrived covered in blood." The sides of her mouth turned down in a frown and I received that wary look again. "We cleaned him up enough to look for wounds, but found only a few minor abrasions, nothing to account for that amount of blood. He hasn't spoken a word since he got here, either.

Just stares at the light and laughs." She lowered her voice to a whisper. "It's creepy."

I could feel the blood draining from my face and I felt lightheaded. "Laughs? Is he in shock or something? What about a head injury?"

She dropped her gaze and tapped the computer screen again. "Looks like the MD called for X-ray, MRI, urine analysis, CBC, and tox screen. Results aren't all back." She looked back up at me and a touch of compassion escaped her eyes. "Vitals to be checked every hour until further notice. Do you need some water?"

I shook my head but quaked inside. "Who's his doctor?"

"Whitaker. David Whitaker. He's the best," she added and placed a reassuring hand on my arm in a motherly pat. "Dr. Whitaker's in surgery right now, and looks like he'll be there awhile. There's a resident you could talk to, though. Dr. Duffy."

"I'd like to speak with him. Please."

"Her," the nurse said. "Joan. I'll let her know."

"Thanks. Can I see Mike now?"

"Sure. One-twelve, end of hall. Maybe he'll respond to a familiar face. Oh, by the way, the police left a guard. Tell him Angie said you were okay."

The phone rang and Angie picked it up. I headed toward 112, rethinking the implications of a guard.

I hurried down the corridor, anxious to console, but still feeling totally unprepared. A child wailed in room 103, and I detected the low murmurings of a woman's voice, trying in vain to soothe. I hoped I could find comforting words.

As I passed room 106, a red signal light flashed over the door but no sounds escaped. The door to room 107 was open and an elderly man in rumpled clothing, standing next to a bed with a tiny figure under the covers, turned his head toward me.

"Nurse?" he called. "Can you ask the doctor to come in? Nurse?" I ignored him and focused on the room at the end of the hall.

As I neared Mike's room, panic gripped me and I stopped. Who was I kidding? I had barely managed to get myself through the last five years — what comfort could I give a kid? I wanted to turn and run out of there. Before I could bolt, the door below the exit sign opened and a tall, beefy man wearing blue scrubs emerged. He went directly into 112, leaving the door ajar behind him. The bright interior light made a distinct V on the corridor floor.

I resumed my journey toward the door wondering if the man was Mike's doctor or nurse or the guard. I knocked and pushed the door open wide enough to enter. I stepped into the room and my concern over finding the right words to comfort Mike vanished, replaced by confusion and a jolt of fear.

Chapter 4

I stopped abruptly inside Mike's hospital room. The man I'd witnessed entering the room seconds before was kneeling down by the foot of an empty bed. Blood was smeared all over the floor. Enough blood to mean something was drastically wrong.

"What the hell?" I asked. "Where's Mike?" I stepped forward and spotted a figure lying on the floor next to the kneeling man. I leaned in further and Mike's pale face came into view. "Mike? My God. What have you done to him?" I grabbed the man's shoulder to shove him out of the way.

"There's gauze in that drawer," he said. "Hurry."

I yanked my hand back as if bitten. He'd indicated the roll cart and I pulled open the top drawer. Empty. "There's nothing here," I said, panic rising. "Oh, God, it's not here."

"Next drawer."

I jerked open the second drawer, knocking the water jug off the cart onto the floor in the process.

"Yes. Yes. I've got it."

"Tear it open. Quick."

I ripped apart the paper wrapper. "Here." I held it toward him and he grabbed the thick gauze pad with a blood-soaked hand.

"Red button," he said, glancing over his shoulder. "There, above the bed. Hurry."

I followed his nod and found the button and slammed it with all my might. An alarm clanged in the hallway. People came running.

"Non-medical personnel out of the room," someone called, but I was powerless to even process the command. "You." A man clutched my arm and gave a tug. "Step out into the hallway, Miss."

His touch startled me and I instinctively shook off his hand. I took a step toward the door only to meet a stream of ER staff running into the room. I backtracked out of their way and skidded on the wet floor. I grabbed at the nearest object for support. The roll cart slowed my fall, but it skittered away. I landed hard on my back, and my head slammed into the floor.

The impact stunned me momentarily, but helping hands were instantly at my side.

"You okay?" a woman asked.

I started to get up and noticed the blood on my hands. I lay back down. The room was spinning. "Not sure," I said. "I'm bleeding."

"Here you go." It was Angie from the information desk. She handed me a towel, then snapped on a pair of gloves. "Might not be your blood. This room's a mess. If you're not hurt, we need you out of the room. Are you hurt?"

I realized my head was throbbing and there was a pain in my right shoulder. "I hit my head."

"Here, let me check." Angie knelt down beside me.

"No. Take care of Mike."

"Plenty caring for the boy already. Here." Angie gently wiped my face. "You've given yourself a pretty good-sized knot on your noggin," she said, and gave my arm her signature pat. "But I don't see anything to account for the blood. I think you landed in some. . . ." She broke off as she took my pulse. "I'm going to have you lie still right here, out of the way. As soon as we can, we'll lift you properly and double check."

That was fine with me. If I got up, they'd send me out of the room. From this position, at least I could see what was

18

happening.

"Sure," I said. "Just take care of Mike."

With my eyes cleared of blood, I could see I'd landed on the floor beside the empty bed. Mike lay somewhere near my feet, but my view was blocked by a confusion of legs and crouched ER personnel.

Blood smears were everywhere, even on the floor under the bed. It looked odd there somehow, less than random. I lifted my head for a better look. My pulse quickened when I realized it was writing. Someone had written a message in blood. Mike? I could tell it was a long word which began with the letter P or maybe D, but the remainder was impossible to read from my position. Then the comments from the ER team drew my attention away from the bloody message on the floor.

"Pulse's too faint. He's lost too much blood."

I wanted to scoot around for a better look. A little repositioning shouldn't put me in anyone's way. I could stay under the radar.

I scooted myself further under the bed, trying to be unobtrusive yet turn my body so I could see. Then wished I hadn't. My stomach contents roiled and I tasted acidic bile at the back of my throat threatening to break loose.

My godson was lying on the floor by his bed, arms outstretched, and surrounded by blood. Nurses were holding gauze tightly to each wrist and another was cutting away his hospital gown. A bloody scalpel lay on the floor.

I turned away from the sight and puked. Tears streamed down my face. Mike was in serious trouble.

"Clear."

I had to look back. The shout was followed by a tremendous lurch of Mike's body and blood oozed through his wrist gauze and through a gauze on the side of his abdomen. The nurses applied more gauze and tape at each site. The torturous procedure was repeated. Then a third time. The room was quiet, waiting for signs of life.

"I got a pulse. Let's get him to surgery." The entire room reanimated and Mike was whisked out on a gurney within seconds. I remained in my crumpled position on the floor, unable to draw a complete breath. Voices began to swirl around me, disconnected, confusing, a mix of male and female.

"Ma'am?"

Someone touched my shoulder.

"We need to get the police in here."

"Be careful, she fell earlier."

"Wasn't there supposed to be an officer watching the boy?"

The lights in the room grew dim.

"Doctor Duffy, would you mind looking at this woman?"

"You're right. Someone find that damn guard."

"This is the boy's guardian. She fell and may have hit her head."

"She's in shock. Get another gurney in here."

Hands lifted me, then the room slipped into darkness.

Chapter 5

I flew upright and pressed my hands to my eyes but I couldn't block the flood of images. "No, no, no, no."

A monitor beeped and a door pushed open. A vaguely familiar woman appeared at my side.

"Ms. Kincaid, you need to lie back down."

"No," I said again, recognizing an ER room and the nurse. Angie. Her name was Angie. "Why am I here? How long have I been here?"

"Not long. About an hour. You passed out for a moment. When you came to, you were sort of hysterical, so Dr. Duffy gave you a mild sedative. How do you feel now?"

"Numb." Only numb of body; my mind was racing. "Where's Mike? Is he alive?" I remembered way too much.

"Yes. He's still in surgery. Please lie back down."

Relief flooded through me. "I need to see him as soon as I can. He doesn't even know I'm here."

"We'll let you know as soon as you can see him. It might not be until morning." She pointed to my pillow.

Obediently, I lay back and closed my eyes. Big mistake. My mind filled with a vivid memory of Mike lying near death on the bloody floor. Someone had attacked him here in the hospital. My panic returned and I sat upright again.

"How could this have happened?" I asked. "Where the hell was the guard?"

"I don't know how it happened, but there was a guard," Angie said.

"There sure as hell wasn't one when I reached his room."

"Ms. Kincaid, I need you to lie back down. The police are investigating."

I shook my head and felt the hysteria rising again. This nightmare made no sense. First Ellen was murdered, then Mike was attacked, maybe dying. There'd been so much blood. Maybe another round of hysteria and sedation was my only sane response. Then I thought of Sophia. She didn't know I was in Charleston, either.

"I need to make a phone call."

The door to my room pushed open again. My heart leaped when I recognized the man who entered. Then wariness settled in.

"Harry? What are you doing here?" My right hand involuntarily checked the position of my hospital gown on my shoulder.

He walked to the bedside and took my free hand. "I'm so sorry, Lila, about Ellen." The words sounded sincere, but the eyes were cold.

I slipped my hand from his. "Thanks, but. . . . "

"I came in to check on Mike and found out you'd been hurt as well."

I suddenly felt tiny and vulnerable in my hospital gown. I pulled the sheet up over my chest and held it in place. "I'll be fine; it's only a bump."

His gaze rested on my hair, now short, choppy, and maroon. His expression changed from noncommittal to a slight frown. "Well, if you need anything, the doctor and the police have my number."

I should've known Harry would've already taken charge. Ellen and Mike were his friends too, after all.

"I suppose you're the reason they found out I was Mike's guardian?"

He shrugged. "I wrote Ellen's will several years ago. You're executor of her estate, as well."

I shuddered inside, hoped it didn't show. "I was in the room where Mike was attacked. It was horrible." I squeezed my eyes shut. "He was supposed to have police protection. I got there too late." Then I looked up at Harry. "Do you know what happened? Who would have wanted to kill Ellen?"

He shook his head. "I can't imagine anyone wanting to hurt her. She was a generous soul."

"I haven't had a chance to let Sophia know I'm here. I should probably call her."

"It's after ten, Lila. You can tell her in the morning."

Ten? I'd lost so much time. I felt an urgency I couldn't explain and turned to Angie. "If I can't see Mike 'til morning, I need to get out of here."

"Normally, with a head injury, we like to observe for an hour or so. But in this case, they're talking about keeping you overnight," Angie said.

"For God's sake, why? I'm fine now."

"Precautionary. You threw up. You lost consciousness. It happened on our property."

"I'll sign a release or something. That should work, right, Harry?"

He tilted his head and lifted an eyebrow.

"He's a lawyer," I said to Angie.

"Sorry, but it's not up to me. I'll page Dr. Duffy." She glanced at Harry and left the room.

"Maybe you should stay, Lila," Harry said. "You fainted, after all. And you look . . . pale."

"Never mind that," I said, sharper than was necessary. "It's shock or something. You can't imagine how horrible it was. There'd be something wrong with me if I hadn't fainted after seeing that. Did you get a look at Mike's room?"

"A peek. The kid lost a lot of blood." His voice hitched. "It's horrific."

I was ashamed, thinking I was the only one affected by this. Harry was hurting, too. I suppressed a sudden impulse to reach for his hand, and then realized what was needling my mind. "Mike left a message."

"The police will have it."

"Maybe no; it's under the bed. On the floor, written in blood. I've got to make sure they see it before the place is cleaned."

He threw me a questioning glance. No time to explain how I'd managed to see it.

"It might be too late already. Cover for me with the doctor and I'll go get a picture."

Harry shook his head. "You're too . . . messy. Someone will stop you. Stay put and I'll go have a look." He held up his cell phone. "No worries. It's a crime scene, it won't be cleaned yet. I'll get pics."

I watched him head out the door, frustrated as usual by his logic. However, I wasn't going to "stay put." I could ignore the ache in my shoulder and the throbbing in my neck and head. I eased myself off the bed and found my clothes stuffed into a plastic bag in the corner of the room. I dumped them out onto the floor and swallowed hard at the sight. A semi-congealed layer of blood coated everything. My suitcase, with clean clothes, was in the rental car in the visitor's parking lot in front of the hospital. I dug the keys out of the pocket of the ruined jeans and noticed my arms were also caked with dried blood. No wonder Harry called me messy. I checked in the bathroom mirror, and recoiled from the image. My hair was a matted blob. The little room didn't have a shower, so I stuck my head under the sink faucet until the water ran clear. I washed my face and arms as best I could and dried off with paper hand towels. The gown hung loose, but I tied it at the sides, slipped on my shoes, and headed down the hallway toward the ER entrance. No one stopped me, or even seemed interested.

I toyed with the idea of starting the car and driving away. Ellen's house would have a hot shower and she usually kept some wine on hand. And I might have done it, too, if it wasn't for the message on the floor under Mike's bed. If Mike had named Ellen's killer, I wanted a head start on the manhunt. So, I grabbed a change of clothes and shoes from my suitcase and headed back to the ER.

The nurse stood in the hallway outside my room with her hands on her oversized hips. The wary look had returned.

"Sorry, Angie," I said. "Don't scold me. I'll feel better in clean clothes. Did you find the doctor?"

"She said you could go, if you have someone to watch over you."

Harry was approaching us from the direction of room 112. On impulse, I pointed at him. "I'm his guest."

I had to give Harry credit. The only hint of surprise was a minor twitch of his upper lip.

"That's right," he told the nurse. "Ms. Kincaid is staying with me, and I promise to check on her throughout the night."

Like hell he would. I'd bolt the door.

"Okay, then. I'll get the paperwork ready." She headed toward the nurse's station.

"I'll be waiting in the car out front," Harry said.

"Oh, no, you don't." I grabbed his arm and steered him into my room, closing the door. "What'd you find?"

Before he could answer, there was a knock on the door and a woman wheeled a trash can into the room. "S'cuse me, folks," she said. "Housekeeping." She began emptying the room's containers. "Won't be but a minute."

"I'll wait in the car out front." He tilted his head toward the cleaning woman and left.

I let him go. He'd obviously seen something, and I wanted to hear it in private. I plunked the bag with my ruined, bloody clothes into the woman's trash bin. When she left, I changed into my clean clothes, then picked up my discharge papers from Angie on my way out.

"I'm parked right over there," I said as I climbed into Harry's car. "What was the message in Mike's room?"

"Later," Harry said. "Close the door. I'm driving you home."

"Like hell you are. I'm not staying at your place. I'll stay at Ellen's."

He gave me an incredulous look. "You can't. It's still a crime scene."

That jolted me like a punch in the gut. A crime scene. Of course. But I couldn't stay at Harry's. "A motel, then."

He started the car. "No. My house. I signed your release papers. I'm responsible for you tonight."

God, he was bull-headed. But I could be just as stubborn. "It's only a mild concussion. No permanent injury. They're not going to know, or care, where I spend the night."

"You want to know what I found, don't you?"

"That's blackmail."

"Call it what you will, I'll show you when we get back to my house. I've got pictures."

I wanted to know the details more than I wanted to avoid Harry, and he was right; I couldn't stay at Ellen's. I should've anticipated that. Okay, I'd move on to Plan B — get the information, leave, and find a motel. "You still at the same place?"

"Yes." He stared ahead, no longer looking at me.

"I'll drive myself over. You can follow me if you want. Make sure I don't crash or anything. But I need my stuff."

"Fine." He sounded weary. "I'll follow."

I hadn't driven the route to Harry's house for five years,

but I'd never forget the way. I grew increasingly uneasy as I neared his place and had to force out memories of that other time in my life. Just find out what he knew and make a fast exit, I reminded myself.

Ellen had remained friends with Harry after he and I split. Ellen, ever the matchmaker, always tried to work him into the conversation, so I knew he was still unattached. She had eventually quit asking for an explanation on the break-up.

It was my business, my secret.

Even from Harry.

Especially from Harry.

When I turned onto Beaumont Avenue, I nearly succumbed to an unanticipated wistfulness that pulled at my heart. I allowed myself one tiny nostalgic moment and recalled my first trip to this street all those years ago, in the car beside Harry, who was so eager to show off his new house. He was settling in, ready for a family. As it turned out, I wasn't. Couldn't do it.

I shook off the time warp and concentrated on more immediate questions. What was the message under the hospital bed? Who killed Ellen? Had the same person later attacked Mike? It had to be the same person. And what the hell had happened to the police guard?

I pulled up in front of the two-story brick Tudor cottage with its quaint arched entryway. Nothing had changed since my last visit. Except me. The lawn was carefully mowed and the shrubs were precisely trimmed, as always. LED lights outlined the front walk. The ancient live oaks still stood guard at the edges of the yard. In the dark, I couldn't make out the moss hanging from their branches, but I knew it was there. I took a deep breath to ready myself and opened the car door. Lilac and azalea scents filled the breeze. From now on, the beautiful spring of Charleston would be associated with unbearable heartache and horror.

I left my belongings in the rental and watched Harry pull his car into the garage. I met him at the front door. "So, what was Mike's message?"

He unlocked the door without a glance my way. "I could use a drink first."

I followed his icy trail inside, leaving fond memories dead on the doorstep. I wasn't sure a drink would be wise, for a multitude of reasons. Harry motioned me toward a chair in the kitchen. "Sit there. I'll be right back."

"Wait. You've got to tell me what you saw."

He turned and walked away.

Stay put. Sit there. He was good at giving orders. I didn't sit, but watched him continue down the hallway toward the family room at the back of the house. When he vanished from view, I looked around and fell back into the time warp. The kitchen décor hadn't changed a bit, but there was a new painting hanging in the hallway. I walked over to examine it, to focus on the new. Then wished I hadn't.

It depicted a desolate beach, with a storm brewing overhead, dark and menacing. Turbulent waves threatened major destruction. Too depressing to bear close scrutiny.

"Like it?" Harry asked. I hadn't heard him approach and jumped in surprise. I glared, hoping he hadn't noticed my reaction. He was carrying two tumblers and a bottle of Glenlivet and looked at the painting, not at me.

I faked nonchalance. "Feels too sad. Guess it fits today, though." I looked for a signature. "Who's the artist?"

"Local woman. Specializes in landscapes, usually pastoral. This one matched my mood that day, I guess. Here."

I took the glass he offered and returned to the kitchen.

"Nothing's changed much," Harry said, following behind me. "But I suppose you don't remember."

"No." I didn't turn to look at his face, but the silence that followed gave lie to my response.

Death Map

I pulled out a kitchen chair and sat down. Harry poured alcohol into our glasses without meeting my eyes. Then he placed his cell phone on the table in front of me.

"Here's what you wanted to see," he said.

I stared at the image. A word scrawled in a thin red script. "Pinwheel," he said.

I could read it and I knew firsthand the red was blood. I looked up at Harry. He was watching me closely.

"That's what was written on the floor," he said. "Mean anything to you?"

"Pinwheel?" I questioned, though the word was clearly visible in the picture. "I've never heard anyone called Pinwheel. Have you?"

He shook his head. "Might not be a name. Maybe it's a game or a place?"

I pursed my lips. As with everything else that happened today, it made no sense. "Is that all you found?"

"No, go to the next picture. Someone also wrote 'no pain' in blood under the bed."

"Someone? You don't think it was Mike?" I advanced to the next image.

"Actually, I do, but the police found both messages without my help and are checking fingerprints."

I looked from the camera phone to Harry. "What does it mean?"

"I don't have an inkling," Harry said. "Wish I knew."

I knew what I thought it meant. Mike knew Ellen's killer. It was someone nicknamed Pinwheel.

Chapter 6

Obviously, I needed to get into Ellen's house and look through her stuff, especially her journal, for someone named Pinwheel.

Or maybe I'd find a reference in Mike's things. Did he journal, too?

I might have to interview Ellen's neighbors. Maybe someone had seen a visitor at her house. Or, had Ellen met a new guy? Or maybe it was an old boyfriend who was jealous or couldn't get back in the game? All these possibilities flashed through my mind and I couldn't wait to get started.

"I'd like to get into her house tomorrow," I said as I finished my drink. "Think the police are done there?"

"Unlikely." Harry looked toward the window. "I'll call in the morning to check, but even if they're done, you don't want to go in until it's been cleaned."

"I can handle it," I said, not at all sure I could. "I know Ellen kept a journal. Maybe it holds the answer." Then I remembered I needed to stop by the hospital and visit Mike first thing in the morning, then visit Sophia to update her about Mike.

"Maybe," Harry said, turning his stare on me. His gaze was making me uncomfortable. "You've had a long day. Another scotch?"

I felt flushed and the room took a minor spin to the left. Another drink and I wouldn't be driving anywhere. "No. Don't worry, I'm not staying." I stood and carried the glass to the sink. "Thanks for the hospitality. I can call the police myself in the morning to see about getting into Ellen's place."

"Wait a minute," Harry said, coming up behind me at the sink, touching my arm. I cringed and could tell he noticed. "You've got to see Jay-Jay before you go."

Jay-Jay? No way. "You still have him?"

He flashed a proud papa grin. "He recognized your voice on the answering machine and has been talking about you all evening. He'll sulk if you don't say hello."

"I can't believe he's still alive."

"He'll outlive both of us."

"He couldn't have recognized my voice. It's been years since he heard me."

"I always told you he was smart." Harry grabbed my hand and pulled, suddenly as eager as a boy. "Come on. He's still in the family room."

"Can't this wait?" I asked, but I let him lead me down the hall. We entered the dark family room and stood for a moment before Harry flipped a switch. Soft light on an end table illuminated a dark leather sofa and chair facing the opposite wall on which hung a flat screen TV. Between the doorway where we stood and the back of the sofa loomed a six-foot cage.

"Jay-Jay," Harry called softly. "Say hello to Lila."

The cage was in the same spot it had been on my last visit. More swings and perches and toys decorated the interior than I remembered, but the big gray parrot with the striking red tail seated on the nearby perch was most certainly the same. He blinked, ruffled his feathers, and let out a raucous squawk.

I walked slowly to the side of the cage, leaned down and peered in at the bird. He was as beautiful as I remembered.

"Hello, Jay-Jay," I said.

"Hello Lila hello Lila." The parrot added a squawk at the end.

"You are a pretty bird."

"Pretty Jay-Jay." It was the response I'd taught him.

"Does he know any new words?"

"No. He quit cooperating after you . . . left. Maybe you could teach him something new while you're here?"

"He's probably reached his capacity," I said, watching Jay-Jay turn upside down and look at me, eyes unblinking.

"He pulled out a lot of feathers back then," Harry said. "I was worried he was making himself sick over you."

"He's just a bird," I said. "He can't grieve over someone."

"He did, though, I swear," Harry said. "And the vet thought so, too. He was more attached to you than you knew. You saved his life, after all."

"Yeah, but you nursed him back to health. He should be focused on you, not going ga ga over me."

"Ga ga," Jay-Jay said with a flourish of wings.

"See," Harry said. "He's listening to you all over again."

I eyed Harry almost as intently as I felt Jay-Jay eyeing me. He was probably telling the truth. Harry was thoroughly honest. Besides, he couldn't have anticipated that I'd use ga ga in a sentence.

"Okay," I said, "I'll spend some quality time with the bird. Satisfied?"

Harry flashed his boyish grin. I felt a microscopic thaw at the corner of my heart.

"Yeah. That's great, isn't it, Jay-Jay? Lila's back."

"Lila's back," the bird repeated. Another squawk. "Lila's back."

My resolve returned. "Look, Harry, I'm not back, you know. Have you forgotten why I'm even here?" I turned and walked out of the room. Jay-Jay squawked a few more times, then quieted down when Harry turned off the light.

He caught up with me at the front door as I tried to unlock the deadbolt. His hand covered my fingers and resecured the latch. Then he touched my chin and turned my face so I was forced to look into his eyes. They had gone cold again.

"For God's sake, Lila, use some sense. Of course, I haven't forgotten why you're here. Ellen was my friend, too, and this is just as hard for me." His fingers tightened a bit. "Today's been shocking beyond belief, and emotionally you're probably about to crash. You don't have to worry about my intentions. But you're here. Go on upstairs and use the guest room. I'll get your things from the car and bring them up."

My heart picked up speed as I gazed into those steely blue eyes. He was right.

Damn him.

Chapter 7

My cell phone let loose its six AM jingle, wrenching me from a restless, shallow sleep. I cursed and fumbled until I pushed the right button. In the subsequent quiet, thoughts I'd managed to keep at bay for a few hours flooded my mind. Ellen gone. Mike at death's door. All that blood. I picked up my phone and called the hospital.

Mike was still in ICU and still sedated. His small intestine and liver were both damaged by the abdominal stab wound, but the surgeon was optimistic. He'd required four pints of blood. It'd taken additional hours of surgery to reattach nerves, ligaments, and tissues of his wrists, hands, and fingers. He was allowed one ten-minute visit per hour until his condition was upgraded.

I sprang out of bed and headed toward the bathroom across the hall, but stopped in the doorway. I leaned against the doorframe and touched the tender spot on the back of my head. I knew alcohol on top of a head injury often meant trouble. How stupid could I have been? I let out a rueful laugh.

I'd stayed here. Stupid to the max.

Thirty minutes and a hot, hot shower later, I descended to the first floor. The house was quiet and I peeked into the kitchen. The only sign of Harry was the fresh coffee. It smelled great, tasted better. Maybe a truce could work. Or was it the coffee talking?

A squawk from the family room suggested Harry's likely location, but the raucous bird and its master were the last things my pounding head needed. I stayed put, sipped coffee, planned my day. Three major items were on my agenda: visit Mike, visit Aunt Sophia, and get into Ellen's house.

Not much time passed before I sensed Harry standing in the doorway. I looked up and tried out a smile. It didn't work.

"Feeling rough?" he asked.

"The worst."

"Well. . . ."

As my grandpa used to say, that's a deep subject. I snaked my eyes sideways at his undertone. "Well what? What else's happened?"

He let a few beats pass before answering. "A couple things. First, I called the hospital. Mike's still in ICU."

"Yeah, I checked on him already. I'm going in at eight, for my ten minutes of contact. What else?"

"The detective on Ellen's case called me already this morning."

"This early?"

"About thirty minutes ago." Harry walked over to the coffee maker and poured a cup. His back was to me. "He's released Ellen's house."

My eyebrows shot up with my mood. "That's good. I can get started right away on my search." Harry didn't respond. Warning bells sounded louder than the pounding in my head. "There's something else, isn't there?"

Harry sighed and faced me. "He's satisfied they've identified Ellen's killer."

I closed my eyes and said a little prayer of thanksgiving. There would be justice for my friend. When I opened my eyes again, Harry's intense expression was confusing.

"But that's a good thing, isn't it?"

He shook his head and met my gaze.

"They think it was Mike."

Chapter 8

All I could do for a moment was stare at Harry, open-mouthed. I must've misunderstood. But his look said otherwise. "Mike? That's the most ridiculous thing I've ever heard," I said. In my agitation, I rose from my seat, bumped the table and knocked over my mug of coffee. I let out a muffled yowl of frustration, and Harry grabbed the paper towels from the counter. I snatched them from his hands.

"What kind of police force do you have down here?" I asked as I stabbed towels at the mess. "We've got to do something."

"I agree," he said. "You and I are going to meet with him to discuss the evidence." He held open a trash bag. "His name is Turner."

"Great. Let's go." I dumped the towels in with a flourish.

"Except, it's not happening today." He tied the ends of the trash bag together with finality. "Turner agreed to meet with us tomorrow at ten."

"Tomorrow? I don't think so. You never mind, Harry. I'll go see him myself."

"Now, slow down a minute, Lila. He's on his way out of town, that's why the early call. They've got fingerprint evidence. . . ."

"I don't care if they found Mike holding the damn knife. He couldn't have killed his mother, or anyone for that matter." Harry knew Mike as well as I did; he should know the police were way off track. I gripped the back of the kitchen chair in frustration.

"What about the message Mike left at the hospital?" Yelling hurt my head. I lowered my voice to a menacing growl. "Anyone looking into Pinwheel? Or have you decided to ignore that little item?"

"Not me, Lila. Not for a minute. And Turner couldn't explain it."

I reined in a scream. "My God, Harry, I can't believe this."

"I know. Look, I have to be in court this morning, but I can help this afternoon, whatever you need. When the house gets cleaned . . . or even before . . . we can search through all Ellen's papers. We can talk to her neighbors. We'll find something the police missed."

I punched the table again, and then cursed. Pain stabbed behind my eyes. I pressed my fingertips over my pulsing orbs. I didn't know whether to cry or laugh hysterically over the pure absurdity of the police theory. And I felt like crap. "Got any aspirin?"

Harry went to the pantry and retrieved a bottle. "At least Turner's released the house. And here's the name of a good crime scene cleaning company. If you're lucky, you might get a crew in there today." He pulled a scrap of paper out of his pocket and handed it over along with the aspirin bottle. I grabbed them both out of his hand, but couldn't look him in the eye.

"Damn," he said with a quick glance at his watch. "I've got to run. Feel free to make yourself at home. I'll call your cell as soon as I can get away."

He practically ran out of the house. Make myself at home? I had no intention of doing any such thing. I read the number on the little piece of paper and called A-One Cleaners. With shameless pleas and the promise of a significant bonus, I arranged for them to meet me at Ellen's house in three hours. In the meantime, I would pack my belongings back into the rental car and visit Mike, then Sophia.

Death Map

A little later, at the hospital, I checked in at the nurse's station and was given instructions on hand washing policies and what to expect when I saw my godson. They'd brought him out of sedation early this morning during the physician's visit. Mike had been nonresponsive but restless and struggled with his bandages. They'd had to put him back under. No change in treatment was expected until the physician returned in the late afternoon, when they'd try it again.

I washed up at the station nearest his bed area and went behind the curtain. Mike lay on his back, hooked to an IV and to a monitor colorful with lines zigging across the screen. His skin looked white-washed and the equipment in the room dwarfed him. I spent a few minutes watching his chest rise and fall in concert with a gentle background beep. This child had witnessed his mother's death, survived a vicious attack, and now faced prosecution. Persecution, in my mind.

"Hey, Mike. It's Lila. I'm here now, and I'm going to help you. You just get better, you hear? Don't worry about anything." I brushed my hand across his cheek, even though I knew he couldn't respond. I leaned down toward his ear. "I'll be back later. Love you, kiddo. Get well."

I stopped at the ICU desk and made sure they had my cell phone number. Thirty minutes later, I arrived at Aunt Sophia's assisted living home. I paused outside the entrance and peered through the glass doors. There were more people milling about than I remembered from my infrequent visits, but it was still breakfast time. I entered, stopped by the front desk to sign in and learned that Sophia had already eaten and returned to her room. I found her seated in her rocking chair, staring out the window. I kissed her wrinkled cheek in greeting and pulled a chair over so I could sit next to her. Then, as gently as I could, I told her of Mike's latest injury, but not the latest police theory.

Sadness gathered in her dark eyes and she sank deeper into the rocker.

"That poor child," she said, voice barely above a whisper. Then she patted my hand. "Thank you, dear, for coming to help. I know you're suffering, too."

I was crying by this time. Sophia passed me a box of tissues and spoke again. The genteel timbre had returned to her voice. "I outlived my baby brother and now my niece. Shouldn't have happened that way, you know. So many sad days over the years, but . . . none worse than this."

I wasn't sure what to say, but I could relate. My own brother, Bruce, was twelve years my senior. Our parents had died when I was a teen, and I'd lived a couple years with Bruce and his wife, Susie. I didn't fit into their lives and I think they, too, were relieved when I left for college. That's where I met Ellen, and she and Mike became my substitute and chosen family. "Mike's going to get better, and you've still got me, Aunt Sophia," I said. "I'll be your family."

She patted the back of my hand. "Thank you, dear. That means a lot to me."

In the end, it was Sophia who consoled me. "We all die, Lila, dear," she said. "It's unfairly hard on the living. Memories are a poor substitute, but it's all we have. As survivors, we have custody of the memories."

It seemed like an immense responsibility, to hold custody of someone's memory. And so many of my memories involved Ellen. With a shock, I realized no one would hold custody of my memories. By now, Harry would have purged any he had once treasured. I vowed to reconnect with my brother as soon as my life returned to normal.

"Will you help with the arrangements, Lila, dear?"

I shook off my reverie and promised to do my best. I admitted I'd never made funeral arrangements before. Sophia retrieved her Bible from her bedside table and pulled out a sheet of paper.

"I've been polishing up my own arrangements for years now."

Her list included multiple songs and biblical reading selections. I listened as she recited phrases from memory and sang bits of her favorite church hymns. With Sophia's insight and strength, we spent the next hour planning the ceremony for Ellen.

I white-knuckled the steering wheel on the drive from the assisted living home to Ellen's house. I'd omitted telling Sophia about the police's ridiculous theory that Mike was the killer, and now I was second guessing that decision. While I knew it couldn't be true, the police intended to announce their conclusion as early as tomorrow unless there was another suspect. Unless *I* could find another suspect.

What if reporters descended upon Sophia for comment? I should've given the woman the chance to prepare herself, in any event. On second thought, I'd phone Mrs. Edgewood, the facility director, and recruit her to run interference, just in case.

It seemed my only recourse now was to find something that would convince the police to investigate in a different direction. Otherwise, Mike would be branded a freakish killer and Ellen only remembered for the actions of her son. If memories were all Sophia and I had, then I needed to do all I could to uncover and defend the truth.

Chapter 9

I pulled up to the curb in front of Ellen's house, but didn't cut the engine. Her house, with its frilly white curtains and wicker furniture on the front porch, looked normal; impossible to picture as the scene of a horrendous crime. I wondered if the police had found Ellen's stash of journals. She'd taken up the journaling habit in college and had detailed each major and minor event of her life since. If someone named Pinwheel had been threatening her or her son, Ellen would have recorded it. In my opinion, a search for her journals was the logical place to begin.

The normalcy of the scene disappeared, however, when I eased my rental into the driveway. From there, the doorway to the kitchen was visible. The screen stood ajar, with remnants of police tape waving in the breeze, still tethered to the house by one end. I sat in the car, mesmerized by the movement of those flapping yellow tentacles, lost in thought. The cleaning crew pulling into the driveway behind my car nudged me alert. I glanced at the dashboard clock. Time to face Ellen's murder scene.

I grabbed the canvas bag containing my notebook and camera, hopped out of the car, and walked back to the van. "A-One Cleaners" and a phone number were splayed across the side in bold letters. Two women emerged from the vehicle. They were dressed in white disposable coveralls and each had the white circle of a face mask hanging below her chin, ready to pull up into position over nose and mouth.

"Ms. Kincaid?" the smaller of the two said. "We're sorry for your loss. I'm Ethel. This is Mary." I shook hands with both women.

Mary glanced toward the kitchen door. "Let's get started." She opened a jar of mentholated gel and spread a layer under her nose. She positioned her mask and offered me the jar, along with a mask and pair of gloves.

I followed Mary's example and applied the gel, took the personal protection gear, but didn't think I'd need them for my search. I led the way toward the house, removed the spare key from its hiding place under the biggest rock in the flower bed border, and opened the door. The putrid, metallic odor assaulted me as soon as I entered the kitchen.

"Gags," I said, retreating outside, "that's horrible."

The two women, already with masks in place, covered their shoes with blue cloth booties and slipped their hands into gloves. They stepped past me, carrying in an array of cleaning supplies, biohazard trash bags, machines, and hoses.

I tugged the elastic strap of the face mask snuggly into place, pulled on the gloves and reentered the house. The nasty odor was diminished, relegated to the back of my throat. That was, until I spotted the vast pool, thick and dark, in the center of the white ceramic-tiled kitchen floor. Deep burgundy on white tiles, with spatter escaping across the floor to the wall, the table, and the chairs. Endless.

My knees buckled. Mary grasped me around the waist and led me toward the door, where I fumbled to yank off the mask. I drew in a deep breath. Not a good idea. The repeated exposure to the stench, even mixed with menthol, pushed my stomach contents beyond their limits. For the second time in two days, I tasted bile.

Mary handed me a paper towel. "Shouldn't have taken off the mask," she said. "Smell does it every time."

"My God." I blinked back tears. "How do you do this?"

The woman shook her head. "Somebody's gotta help the poor relatives. Might as well be us." She escorted me to the yard before returning to her job in the kitchen.

It took me several minutes, sitting on the lawn and breathing in fresh air, before I considered going back inside. I strongly favored waiting outside until they finished cleaning, but that would mean a delay of my mission. Armed with that thought, I replaced the mask, determined to try again. This time I went through the front door and mentally reminded myself of my goals: find Ellen's killer; salvage Mike's reputation.

In the living room, I spotted pictures of Ellen with her arm around Mike and his latest school picture on an end table. His impish grin was the same in both, and I smiled behind my mask. Sophia had mentioned gathering pictures for Ellen's funeral service. These would be good.

On the coffee table, I spotted a stack of drink coasters. I picked up the top one and touched the raised image of a pink flower and the caption, Desert Rose. Ellen worked part-time for that facility, a shelter for battered and abused women, and I wondered if Mike's violent biological father had found them after all these years. He was the reason Ellen was so committed to Desert Rose. I knew his name but I had no idea where he was now. I needed to tell the police about him.

Maybe her journal would fill in some blanks. I replaced the coaster and turned to search through the rest of the small three-bedroom for clues as to what led up to yesterday morning's violence.

Mike's room was first down the hallway, so that's where I decided to start. I pushed open his door and faced an unmade bed. The TV remote and a game controller were lying on the sheet, while his quilt laid in an untended heap on the floor at the foot of the bed. The TV and game system perched atop the bureau, facing the bed, next to stacks of DVDs and video games.

I ran a finger across the gold label on one of the Little League trophies that lined the top shelf of his bookcase next to the bureau. I'd been to that championship game last year. He'd played his heart out, and Ellen and I had cheered to extremes. I found a photo lying on the shelf next to the trophy. It was of the three of us — me, Ellen and Mike — taken right after that game. Mike's grin spread ear-to-ear and he was standing on tippy-toe, shooting for that ten-foot-tall self-image.

I checked the titles of the books shelved on the bookcase. I spotted those I'd gifted over the years. I pulled out some, flipped through some. Nothing sinister.

Mike's computer sprang to life with a touch of the mouse. An iTunes file filled the screen, ready for music selections. The Internet browser was minimized and I opened it to check the user history. Nothing violent. Nothing unusual for a kid. I tried a couple of logical passwords to open his email account, without any real hope that they'd work.

They didn't.

Next, I searched through Mike's dresser drawers, his closet, and under his bed. Nothing to suggest he suspected a predator or the presence of a predator or that he was a predator himself. No reference to Pinwheel. Nothing to reinforce or change the direction of Turner's suspicion. Nothing. Nothing. Nothing.

I moved on to Ellen's room — tidy, as expected. The scent of ammonia from the cleaning crew in the kitchen pervaded the house. In spite of this tangible airborne reminder of why I was there, I couldn't shake the feeling that I was invading my friend's privacy. The feeling intensified when I found Ellen's purse on her dresser, poised and ready to go. Illogical, of course, but seeing her purse gave me a powerful feeling that she was nearby; the sounds of the cleaning women in the kitchen could have been Ellen moving around in the next room. I could even imagine the resonance of her voice hidden in the noises from the other end of the house and found myself expecting to see her any second. This anticipation pulled my heartache back to the surface.

Damn it, I couldn't get through this if I couldn't control my feelings.

Ellen's purse might contain a clue, so I had to look inside. My hand trembled a little when I twisted the clasp. The contents of the bag were organized into individual compartments — typical Ellen. For me, purses are like a black hole, pulling things in, never giving them back. Once, in college, Ellen attempted to teach me to organize, but eventually gave up, declaring me hopeless.

I flipped through her check book and read the entries, jolted by the familiarity of her precise handwriting. The payment and deposit notations for the past few months all looked routine. I moved on to her datebook. The same efficiency graced every page. Ellen had included everything. If she'd had a stalker or someone had frightened her, she probably would have bolded that information with brilliant warning signs and arrows. Nothing stood out.

After I finished with her purse, I found what I was expecting in her nightstand drawer — her daily journal. If the police had bothered to look, they would've found it. They must have suspected Mike early on and hadn't bothered to check any further. The implication made me angry and I pushed forward, more determined than ever.

In all the years we'd known each other, I'd never once been tempted to look at her daily reflections. I touched the soft cover that had this year written on the spine and shut my eyes tight to hold back tears. But, if anything had been written down that would clear Mike, it was likely here.

I sat on the edge of the bed, started to open the volume, and then hesitated. These were Ellen's private thoughts; her view of things and events. It was bound to be different from my memories of the same events. I felt a rush of trepidation and took a deep breath. I could do this. I opened the book, selected an entry dated one month ago, and began to read.

Sometime later, Mary from A-One Cleaners poked her head into the bedroom and pulled me back to the present.

"We're done," she said. "Want to inspect?"

I closed the journal and carried it with me to the kitchen, glad for a break. The room no longer displayed the aftermath of violence, but I knew I'd never be able to entirely block out the gruesome memory of the death scene.

"Thank you so much for coming out today," I said as I handed over my credit card.

"We're glad to help. Your friend is in our prayers. Hope she gets justice."

I closed the door behind them, and turned to see Mike's face staring out from a photo on the refrigerator. Those dark eyes implored me to figure out the truth of what had happened in this room before it was too late.

I'd made it through the last month of entries in the journal without finding a reference to Pinwheel. However, three days before her death, Ellen recorded a frightening encounter at her house, with the spouse of one of the victimized women staying at Desert Rose. I moved from the kitchen to the living room and reopened the journal to read the passage again.

Gordon Anderson is creepy beyond belief. He appeared out of nowhere, threatening to "make someone pay" for turning his wife against him. I've seen the result of his anger. I witnessed Katie's arrival at the shelter, battered and desperate, so I believed him. I'm worried about how he found me. The screen door seemed insubstantial as the only thing separating me from his intense, raging presence — violence nearly erupting. Mike heard the commotion and joined me at the door. Anderson switched tactics to include Mike — "wait until someone takes away someone you love." Terrifying. Stan pulled into his drive next door, thank God, and Anderson left. I can still see the raw hatred in his glare when I close my eyes.

Chapter 10

But Ellen hadn't called the police. Maybe that was the biggest mistake of her life. I could see the expansive front porch through the living room window, and tried to picture the man standing there, issuing threats. The image made my blood run cold.

Ellen's last entry was brief.

Claire is trying to figure out how Anderson found me. Mike doesn't want me at home alone. I don't want to be home alone either, for that matter. Maybe Harry can help.

Harry? Why hadn't he mentioned this? Maybe he didn't know. How did Ellen think Harry could help? Stay with her? I felt a sudden pang of jealousy, then laughed at myself. She meant legal help, of course. Of course.

I knew Claire was Claire Hampstead from Desert Rose. Claire was both Ellen's boss and friend, and I'd met her many times over the years.

The shelter's mission was to provide a secure sanctuary for women and their children on the run from a violent situation. Its address was a closely guarded secret, but after ten years, many people around the city knew the location. Gordon Anderson must have found the shelter, and then followed Ellen home.

Or, this incident could reflect a more serious breach in the facility's privacy policies. Would someone working there release staff addresses? Maybe Anderson wasn't the only one looking for someone from the shelter to punish. I needed to call Claire, see what she thought about this possibility.

I figured I'd find Claire's phone number in Ellen's records. I headed down the hall toward the guest room. I'd spent so many weekends here over the years that her guest room had become my home away from home. I had spare clothes in the closet and a toothbrush in the adjoining bathroom. The guest room also doubled as Ellen's office.

Ellen's desk and computer were in one corner. I turned on the computer and searched around for a contact list or a file on Desert Rose, but apparently, electronic records keeping was not one of Ellen's skills. Out of curiosity, I opened the Internet connection and pulled down the favorites file. What appeared were the links to my short list of published articles. Oh, Ellen. My most loyal fan.

I gave up on the computer, opened the desk file drawer, and hit pay dirt. The drawer held a column of neatly alphabetized, old-fashioned, individual folders, including one labeled Desert Rose.

One look into the organization's file reminded me that Ellen was the staff representative on their board of directors. I found copies of all the minutes of their board meetings for the year, in addition to copies of receipts and event announcements. A donor's list of several hundred names caught my attention because fourteen of the names and addresses were highlighted yellow. I skimmed the list. Harold Greenstreet was among those highlighted.

Harry. Turning up again. I noticed I was twisting my spinner ring. Why did thoughts of Harry make me so edgy? Of course he'd be on the donor list. I almost laughed, thinking of Ellen working from beyond to force me to communicate with my ex-fiancé. And Clunie would jump all over that idea as proof of a psychic connection.

Thank you, Ellen, but while Harry's legendary logic and my intuition made us a formidable investigative team all those years ago, I'd see what I could discover on my own, first. But I knew that for Ellen and Mike's sakes, I would excavate the deepest fathoms of Harry's orderly brain, if necessary.

I returned to the file and found Claire Hampstead's cell phone number and placed the call.

"This is Claire," she said.

"Hi, Claire. It's Lila Kincaid. I met you several times with my friend, Ellen Jacobsen."

"Oh, Lila, my God, it's just horrible news. I can't believe it." Her voice shook. "We're all either crying or staring off into space in plain shock. If there's anything any of us can do, please ask. We want to do something to help."

"Thank you, Claire. There might be something. Did you know Ellen kept a journal?"

"She did? I didn't know."

"Yes, and she was obsessive about writing in it. I thought I might find a clue in her recent entries that might lead to her killer."

"You don't think it was random, then? You think she knew who it was?"

"I don't know, but I found an entry I wanted to ask you about. Pertaining to some Desert Rose violence that followed her home?"

I heard a sudden intake of breath before she answered. "Yeah, Ellen told me, of course. Gordon Anderson. About a month ago, he showed up here and tried to break down our door. He was threatening to kill his wife and anyone who turned her against him. We called nine-one-one, but he got clean away. Completely disappeared from the area."

"No arrest?"

"No. His wife wouldn't press charges, but we filed a complaint. Then he pounded his way back to our attention four days ago. His wife barely escaped with her life this time. We alerted the police, expecting him to show up, but he didn't follow her here. Instead, he showed up at Ellen's house."

"And now Ellen's dead. Have you told the police about Anderson?"

"Of course. As soon as I heard, I contacted them. Detective Turner asked me lots of questions. They're checking into how he found Ellen's home address."

Not checking hard enough, I thought. "What does he look like?" I asked. "This Anderson guy, I mean."

Claire provided a physical description. I hoped I could find a witness in the neighborhood who would place the creep here yesterday morning when Ellen was attacked. Then I remembered to ask Claire about the list of names Ellen had in her Desert Rose file at home. Turned out the highlighted names were the ones Ellen had agreed to contact for the next fundraiser.

I looked at the list with renewed interest. Money made a good motive for murder. I stared at Harry's name, bright yellow. I'd bet he could fill me in on these other people on the donor list. Plus, I hadn't thought to ask him when he saw Ellen last. Or what they had talked about. Or . . .

"I'll do whatever I can," Claire said, stopping my train of thought right before a major wreck; I knew in my heart Harry could not be a suspect any more than Mike.

"Detective Turner's a good man," Claire said and her voice broke. "I can't imagine what this place will be like without Ellen. She was an anchor to these women. And then to die like that after helping so many other victims of violence. . . ." Her voice trailed off.

The irony was not lost on me.

"Oh, one more thing, Claire," I said. "Does the word pinwheel have any special meaning for you?"

I heard a quiet laugh. "How'd you know about the pinwheels? From Ellen, I suppose."

I started. Not only had I found a violent man, but a pinwheel. *How did the police miss this?* "I don't know the details," I said. "Can you fill me in?"

"It was all Ellen's idea. Last month she started the project. Each woman or child crafts a paper pinwheel and writes things like their fears or their goals, or names of loved ones, whatever, on the blades. Then they watch it spin freely in front of a fan, or outside, if the wind's blowing. It's supposed to represent release. We have a row of them mounted in the back yard."

I could see it now. Someone from Desert Rose had a goal of "no pain" written on their pinwheel, and Mike had spotted the pinwheel in the hands of his mother's murderer, either at home, at the shelter, or in the hospital. It made perfect sense.

"Did Mrs. Anderson make a pinwheel?" I couldn't keep the excitement out of my voice.

A moment passed before she answered. "Why?"

"It's important, Claire, in finding her killer. Could I look at Ellen's records on the pinwheel project?"

She was quiet again for a moment. "I'm sorry, Lila, but we are strict about confidentiality."

"But if there's a clue. . . ."

"I'd like to help, but my hands are tied. I loved Ellen and I want to find her killer as much as you, but it'll require a warrant to search through our records."

Whoa, I wasn't going to rat out anyone to their nosy neighbors. I was looking for a killer. Why didn't this woman understand?

"Claire, Mike wrote down the word pinwheel. I think he was trying to name his mom's murderer."

"But Mike was never here. He never saw any of the pinwheel projects."

"Maybe he didn't see it at Desert Rose. What if someone was carrying a pinwheel that had been made at Desert Rose? Why else would he write pinwheel? It must tie in somehow. It's such an obscure term."

There was another pause from Claire. "Look," she began, after a moment. "I'll call Turner and tell him about the pinwheel project. But I'm sorry, Lila, I can't let you see them. I hope you understand."

I didn't understand at all. These were merely crafts, for God's sake. It wasn't as if I wanted to interview the women or put their pictures in the paper. Or put their lives at risk. I closed my eyes and sighed, resigned. Well . . . okay, so maybe I did understand. I couldn't chance putting their lives at risk. At least Claire was going to call Detective Turner.

"Could you call him today, Claire? It's important, or I wouldn't ask."

She agreed and I hung up, buoyed by the possibility of a suspect other than Mike.

I reviewed what I'd jotted down from Claire's description of Gordon Anderson. He was tall, 6'2 or 6'3; blond; quite handsome by Claire's standards; and built like a linebacker. The day he'd appeared at Desert Rose, he was wearing Dockers and a dark Polo shirt, and driving a red Porsche with a dented passenger door.

Hopefully, one of Ellen's neighbors had witnessed her encounter with this guy on the porch or, better yet, could put him in Ellen's neighborhood the morning of her death.

I checked the time. Two in the afternoon. The clock was ticking down toward Mike's public accusation.

Chapter 11

I closed the Desert Rose file and returned to Ellen's journal entry from three days before her death. After my conversation with Claire, Gordon Anderson's behavior on Ellen's front porch seemed even more frightening. In my mind, I pictured an angry blond Adonis crushing a pathetic hand-made pinwheel in a thrashing fist. I had to convince Detective Turner to look in Anderson's direction.

I closed the journal and carried it with me to the living room. I stared out the front window at the surrounding neighborhood. I had met a few neighbors over the years. Waved at others. They were a friendly group. Someone out there must have seen something. Or someone might know something totally unexpected about a pinwheel. And I couldn't forget the possibility that maybe someone out there *was* Pinwheel.

My cell phone rang. I answered without looking at the number, assuming it was Harry. It wasn't. Clunie's voice bubbled into my ear as she rattled on about the status of the story she had taken over from me on Senator O'Connell. But all I could think of was the cell phone. I hadn't seen Ellen's or Mike's cell phones anywhere in the house. And I hadn't thought about checking the call history of the land line. Clunie paused and I knew I'd missed a question.

"What'd you say?" I asked. "Sorry, I totally missed that."

"Hello? Have you heard anything I've said at all? You'll want to know this."

"Sorry, what?" I was pretty sure I didn't want to know.

"O'Connell's dead."

She had my attention now. "You're kidding. What happened?"

"Your source had it right about the potential for blackmail, totally. He was taking bribes to award or extend government contracts. Both, I mean, actually, and who knows what other nefarious enterprises he had going. Anyway, he's history now, and so are his secrets."

"Wow. Suicide?"

"Wow is right. But not suicide. The police haven't released the details, but this thing is freaking me out. I sensed a bad energy with this case as soon as you gave me the file. Like it was burning my hands."

I never knew how to respond to Clunie's psychic references, so I did my usual murmur thing.

"Seriously, Lila. I don't know if I can work on this anymore. There's a black aura around everything."

Damn. If she dropped the ball, McLeish would probably order me back. "The bad stuff's over, girlfriend. You just need to follow up on all the contracts the Senator approved and see if they're reasonable or not. It should be easy to spot something suspicious." I almost suggested she ask Buzz to help, but caught myself. No need for desperate measures. Yet.

"I guess." She didn't sound confident.

"You can do it," I said. "I've seen your work. You're awesome."

"Thanks," she said, sounding more like herself. "I don't suppose his killer would come after me for looking into O'Connell's voting history over the past couple of years. It's public record after all."

"For sure," I said. "If what my informant said was true, something related to government contracts that O'Connell approved was blackmail-worthy." I paused a second, then added, "Probably doesn't have anything to do with his murder. I'd go back at least five years, but hey, I don't want to tell you how to do your research. It's your story now. Call me with an update, okay, Clunie? Sorry, but I've gotta go."

As soon as I hung up, all thoughts of O'Connell vanished. I turned on Ellen's satellite TV and checked the land line call history under the main menu. I wrote down the twenty numbers on display. Then I ran back to the file drawer in her desk and pulled out the file with her phone bills. All her records for both cell and land line phone accounts were there up to the latest bill, including the number for Mike's cell phone. I called it from my own cell. I heard the ring in my ear then pulled the phone away, hoping to locate the phone ringing in the house. Then the unexpected happened.

Someone answered Mike's phone.

A deep male voice said, "Hello?"

I couldn't respond immediately, other than produce a startled squeak.

"Who is this?" he said, with gruff authority..

"How'd you get this phone?" I demanded with equal force.

There was silence. Then the man spoke again. "I have your number, Ma'am. I'll be able to trace you. This phone is part of an ongoing police investigation, and you might as well tell me who you are and why you are calling."

The police. Of course.

"This is Lila Kincaid," I said. "I'm executor of Ellen Jacobsen's estate, and I was trying to locate her property. Do you have Ellen's phone, too, or should I keep looking for it?"

"It's here. And they'll both stay here until the case is closed. If you have a problem with that, you can contact Detective Turner."

"No, no problem. Thanks." I hung up. Damn. I wanted to see who Ellen and Mike had called recently, since their last bill. Harry could probably get that information with some of his lawyerly mumbo jumbo. But, for now, I still had the latest calls made from the house line. I began dialing those numbers.

Harry showed up as I finished the last call. I explained what I'd been doing.

"Any luck?" he asked, looking over the names and numbers I'd jotted down.

"No. I only reached five real people, and the police had already contacted them. The rest went to voice mail."

"So, the men in blue did some investigating after all."

"Appears so. But I think they missed this." I pulled out Ellen's journal and showed him the entry about Gordon Anderson. Then I gave Harry the description I'd gotten from Claire at Desert Rose and her rendition of Ellen's pinwheel project.

He whistled a low note. "Ellen should have called me about this. I would have slapped a restraining order on Anderson, with pleasure. Damn, Lila, this might be what we're looking for."

He pulled out his phone and called his assistant. "See what you can find on Gordon Anderson." He supplied Anderson's physical description and type of car.

I held up a finger and Harry asked his assistant to hold.

"There's someone else I thought of. Ask them to discretely check on the whereabouts of Mike's father, Chase Hampton. He used to live here in Charleston. Ellen dated him right before college, but he was abusive and she got away. I don't think he even knows about Mike's existence, but it's worth a look."

Harry nodded and relayed the request. When he hung up, he gave me the once-over with a slight frown. "You might not get much cooperation out of these neighbors with that new look of yours."

Death Map

I glared at him but removed the lip ring. Then I fished a scarf out of my backpack, wrapped it around my hair, and stomped across the yard.

As I turned to walk up the sidewalk of the house next door, I saw Harry head out in the opposite direction.

Canvassing the neighborhood sounded easy but it was a frustrating experience. No one I spoke with remembered ever seeing a red Porsche in the area, or a person who might be Gordon Anderson; not even Stan, the neighbor whose return home, according to Ellen's journal entry, scared off Anderson. No one remembered seeing anything unusual the day Ellen was killed, or noticed recent visitors to Ellen's house. No one reacted to the word pinwheel.

I was depressed, but not defeated. Ellen's journal implicated Anderson by her vivid description of his threatening behavior, and proved he knew where she lived. He seemed like a very good bet. I intended to offer him up to Turner in the morning.

Harry had a little better luck. Ellen's neighbor to the west, Mrs. Engels, was home the day Anderson and Ellen had had the confrontation on the porch. She gave an accurate description of Anderson and his red Porsche, including plate number. My elation vanished when Harry added that she had also provided this information to the police officer canvassing the neighborhood following Ellen's murder.

So, they knew about Anderson, but they wouldn't have known about the pinwheel project at Desert Rose. Anderson was still a viable suspect in my mind, and I intended to sway Detective Turner.

Harry headed back to his office with the promise to get Ellen and Mike's recent cell phone records. He phoned a few minutes later to remind me of our early morning meeting with Turner, and to see if I felt like a late dinner or a drink. I declined with the excuse that I wanted to read more of Ellen's journal.

That part was true. I didn't mention I could concentrate better if Harry wasn't around.

Chapter 12

The next morning, Harry picked me up at Ellen's and drove us to the police station for our appointment with Detective Turner. On the way, he destroyed my best theories.

His assistant had discovered that Chase Hampton had died eight years ago in a knife fight in a bar in Raleigh, and Gordon Anderson was currently confined to county lock-up, and had been there since the day he'd confronted Ellen on her porch. Both perfect alibis. Still, I couldn't wait to confront Turner. Mike a killer? Preposterous. Except I'd feel better if I had an alternate suspect to offer.

"Look out," Harry muttered under his breath as we entered the front door of the police station. I looked. A young man stood in the corner of the foyer watching our approach.

"Mr. Greenstreet? May I have a word?"

"No comment, Ronan." Harry turned his back to the man and pushed the button on the wall to announce our arrival.

Ronan persisted. "Are you here about the Jacobson kid who killed his mom and then tried to commit suicide?"

I wanted to belt the arrogant bastard. I didn't realize I had gone so far as to make a fist until Harry took hold of my hand.

"The case is still unresolved," Harry said. He maintained a calm expression. I'm sure I presented quite the opposite. "And I can't comment at this time, except to say that I'm helping in the investigation."

A disembodied voice cracked with static on the intercom. "Name."

"Greenstreet and Kincaid to see Detective Turner."

We heard a buzz from the door. Harry pushed the door open and let me enter. As I passed through, I glanced back and saw Ronan scribbling in a notebook. I recognized the familiar earmarks of a reporter. Harry made sure the door closed behind us before we proceeded to the security screening area.

We were escorted to Detective Turner's tiny office by a police officer who could fit right in with Clunie and her *Ink Marks* buddies. He told us sit, wait. There were two wooden, straight-backed seats on the visitor's side of the desk.

We sat.

We waited.

I fidgeted, but at least my knees didn't press into the desk like Harry's did. My chair was so close to Harry's that our shoulders brushed with my every squirm. My disloyal shoulder tingled at each touch.

"Thanks for stopping me from flattening that reporter," I said.

"We're in a police station, Lila. I couldn't let you slug him."

"Maybe later, huh?"

He didn't reply. I looked around the office. Institutional floor tile, painted concrete block walls, one window fitted with a noisy air conditioner. No frills. The desk had a phone, a calendar, wire bins labeled "in" and "out", and stacks of manila file folders stuffed to overflowing.

"Where do you suppose your reporter pal got that idea about Mike?" I asked.

"Not my pal," he said. "But I was wondering the same thing."

We were interrupted by the arrival of a tall, stoop-shouldered man. His gray hair and lined face made it difficult to estimate age. Mid-forties was as likely as mid-fifties. "Mr. Greenstreet, good morning. And you must be Ms. Kincaid?"

"Yes."

"Thank you for seeing us, Detective," Harry said.

Handshakes all around. So civilized, yet he thought my godson was a murderer.

"I need to know what you've been doing to find Ellen's killer," I said.

Turner met my gaze, unflinching. "You have my condolences, Ma'am," he said. "I understand you were very close to the victim."

"She was my best friend. Her son is my godson."

Turner let out a deep sigh. "Yes, Ma'am. And I hate to be the one to break the news, but we're convinced that the boy was responsible for his mother's death."

I thought I'd steeled myself for that conclusion, but it hit like a fresh gut wallop. I shook my head. "Someone tried to kill him, too."

"We don't think so."

"What's your proof?" Harry asked.

Turner took a file folder from the top of the pile and laid it in a clear spot on his desk. He opened the folder and took out a document. "When Michael was admitted to the ER at 7:45 AM, he was uncooperative with the attending personnel," Turner said, reading from the document. "The boy was secured to the bed with restraints, blood was drawn, IV started, and a guard posted. Let's see, at 8: 06 PM a lab technician came to the room to draw another blood sample. The lab tech admits she may have forgotten to secure the boy's arm before leaving."

Turner looked up from the report. "In her defense, they don't put restraints on boys very often. Then, the guard made an unauthorized decision to leave his patient and escort the tech back to the lab."

I shot a glance at Harry. That explained the missing security guard.

Turner returned to the paper in his hand. "The lab tech's fingerprints were found on the strap which was supposed to be on the boy's right arm, the arm she took the blood from.

Michael's prints were on the left arm restraint and on the leg straps. Only Michael's fingerprints were found on the scalpel."

Detective Turner glanced up again and waved the document. "There were no other fingerprints on those surfaces."

"There were a lot of people helping him," I said. "There should be more fingerprints."

"The ER personnel wore gloves."

"Maybe the perpetrator wore gloves," I said. "Did you think of that?"

The detective gave me a sideways glance. "Of course." He continued reading aloud. "'Pinwheel' and 'no pain' were written in blood on the floor of room one-twelve, under the bed. Fingerprint analysis proves the words were written by Michael Jacobsen."

"In an attempt to identify the person behind all this," I said.

He tipped his head in my direction but continued to read from the report.

"Nothing could be determined from footprints at the scene, due to the heavy traffic of ER personnel smudging the floor with the victim's blood during resuscitation attempts. Hallway security cameras show the security guard leaving the room with the lab tech at 8:12 PM. No one entered the room until a resident, Dr. Martin Bradly, entered at 8:48 PM, followed a few seconds later by you, Ms. Kincaid."

I digested this new fact. There was a security camera. How had someone entered and left the room without getting caught on camera? I needed to get back to the hospital and take a closer look at the layout of room 112.

"I have more," the detective said. "I have Ms. Jacobsen's nine-one-one call."

My heart skipped a beat. I looked at Harry. "Why didn't you tell me?"

"I didn't know, Lila."

"He didn't know," Turner confirmed.

The detective retrieved a recorder from within his desk drawer and pushed a button. I recognized Ellen's voice — agitated, urgent.

"I need an ambulance. Something's wrong with my son."

"What is the nature of the emergency, Ma'am?"

"It must be a seizure or something. It's like he's catatonic. I can't get him to the car. I need an ambulance."

"Are either of you injured?"

"He must have hit his head or something. We're at 4657 Hiawatha Drive."

"Is your son bleeding, Ma'am?"

"No."

"I'm dispatching an ambulance now. Could I have your name?"

"Ellen Jacobsen. Please hurry."

"Is your son conscious, Ma'am?"

"Sort of, but he's . . . like a zombie."

There was a loud clattering sound, like Ellen dropped the phone.

"Are you there, Mrs. Jacobsen?"

"Mike, stop. What . . . no! Michael!"

Detective Turner stopped the recording. Ellen's final scream echoed in my soul and sent chills up my back.

"The ambulance arrived ten minutes later," the detective said, "and the EMTs found Ms. Jacobsen dead at the scene. Michael was sitting at the kitchen table covered in blood. A bloody knife was on the table in front of him. His prints and Ellen's were on the knife. He didn't respond to the EMT's questions, and they brought him to the ER."

I was stunned into silence. Never, even in my wildest nightmares, had I considered that Mike would hurt his mother, or anyone else, for that matter. Never. But the recording seemed to prove otherwise. Yet, I couldn't get my mind to accept it.

Harry cleared his throat. "Ellen said Mike was zombie-like, in a trance. What would cause that? He didn't use drugs, that we're aware of."

"We don't know yet," the detective said. "His blood alcohol level was zero. We've found no evidence to indicate drug use, but the tox results aren't back."

I was the one in a trance, now. This conversation had taken an unreal, nightmarish turn. I wanted to lash out at someone. Harry was closest.

"I thought you were their friend. You sound like you believe him."

His face darkened momentarily, then softened. "I believe Ellen," Harry said. "You heard the tape. That *was* Ellen."

Yes. It was Ellen. I couldn't explain it, but there had to be an explanation. Other than the one the police had chosen. There had to be something they had missed. I felt like letting loose with a scream, but screaming wasn't going to help. I needed facts. I needed to stay in control.

"I'm sorry, Ms. Kincaid. If it weren't for the nine-one-one call, I'd be looking for someone else. I'd never have picked that kid to do something like this. But as it is . . . Let me get you some water. Or coffee?" He slid a box of tissues across his desk.

I blew my nose and dipped my head. "Coffee."

"Greenstreet?"

"Yes, thanks," Harry said, and his arm went around my shoulder. I shrugged him off.

"I'll be a few minutes," Turner said and left the room.

I sat with my fist pressed against my mouth, eyes tightly shut, trying to regain my composure. To his credit, Harry didn't say a thing.

Chapter 13

While waiting for Turner to return with the coffee, my mind circled the damning information in a frenzy of disbelief and confusion. By the time he returned and handed me the Styrofoam cup, my flurry of questions boiled down to one — *why?*

If this was true, there had to be a motive.

Detective Turner couldn't offer a reason. "I'm sorry, Ma'am. We're looking into the situation. We thoroughly examined both crime scenes, but didn't find anything that would point to a motive. We're hoping the lab work on the boy's blood or Ms. Jacobsen's autopsy will tell us more. Unfortunately, Michael's not able to answer questions at the moment."

"But he left clues," I said. "Those words under the bed must be clues. Why would he go to the trouble of writing them? They must be important."

"I agree with your logic, Ma'am," Detective Turner said. "It would be satisfying if we could understand why the boy did what he did. But the truth of the matter is, we may never know. We will be closing the case once the lab results are back. Might be another week or so. I hope you understand."

I glanced toward Harry. He was nodding, but I couldn't let it go. "Have you talked to any of Mike's friends to see if they've any ideas about what pinwheel means? It could be a person, but I don't know, what if it's the name of a new drug or something? His friends might recognize it."

"Hmm. That's an interesting idea," Detective Turner said. "We have compiled a list of his teachers and a few friends to see if they could provide a clue as to the state of the boy's mind before the incident. I had an officer interview the teachers yesterday. They all thought very highly of Michael, and were unable to conceive that this had actually happened. We haven't been in contact with his friends yet."

"Did pinwheel mean anything to the teachers?"

"Nothing remotely related to the killings."

"I met a friend of Mike's last summer," I said. "I'd like to find him. Maybe he'll tell me something he might not tell one of your officers. I can't remember his last name, but his first name was Philip."

"Well now, you know, Ma'am, I believe we have a Philip on our list. Let me check my notes."

Turner shuffled through a stack of files on his desk. I craned my neck to see.

"Here it is. Philip Donnelly, age twelve, resides at Seventeen Cracker Wood Lane."

I recognized the last name. "Yeah. That's him." I felt an enormous surge of hope that this boy would have the answer. I was like a drowning woman spotting a rope. If only the rope was attached to something solid, or at least something still afloat.

Turner read off the phone number and I copied it down. "I expect you will keep me informed should you learn anything useful from Philip Donnelly?"

I furrowed my brow. I couldn't promise this man anything.

"Of course she will," Harry said. I glared at him. "Could we look at the crime scene pictures, Detective?" He turned to me. "You don't need to, Lila."

"I saw both places in person," I said. "I think I can handle it."

Death Map

Detective Turner offered Harry two envelopes, each stamped *Crime Scene Photos* with the location written below. Harry opened the one with Ellen's address first, and scrutinized each picture carefully before passing it on to me. I thought I'd prepared myself for the images, but seeing Ellen's body was more appalling than anything I'd conjured up in my most outrageous horror-movie-inspired imaginings. I stopped looking after the third picture and moved to the window. The small air conditioning unit was blowing and I positioned myself so that the full force was striking my face. The cold air went a long way toward quelling the disturbing sensation in my stomach. My spinner ring was practically twirling of its own accord.

Detective Turner reached into a desk drawer and pulled out a box of snack crackers. "Have one, Ma'am," he offered. "They always do the trick for me."

I nibbled on a cracker but stayed near the air conditioner. Harry was quiet while looking through the photos from Ellen's home, but I noticed his usual dark complexion had an unhealthy cast. When he finished, he placed the pictures back in the manila envelope and switched to the images taken of Mike's hospital room.

"What about this other message, Lila? No pain. Can't be referring to himself, not with this much blood loss."

"Maybe he was wishing away the pain," I said. "Or maybe he was referring to Ellen. That she didn't suffer any pain." I still couldn't get the idea out of my head, though, that Mike was referring to his attacker.

"Well, Ma'am, he may have believed that, but I can show you her face. It was distorted in pain — she felt those stabs all right."

I reached for another cracker, not sure I could get through this, after all.

"I'm afraid that we will never know exactly what went through that boy's mind," Turner continued. "His doctor tells me he may not remember a thing, even if he becomes responsive to questions." I felt him watching me closely. I couldn't look at either man.

"I'm not sure there's anything to learn from these pictures, Lila," Harry said, placing the last one back in the envelope. "Thanks for your cooperation, Detective."

"I've been thinking that maybe you're looking too hard for a scapegoat in this case," Turner said. "Insanity can be very difficult to detect. Even specialists can be fooled about a person's mental state."

He picked up the envelopes, tapped them on the desk to send the pictures to the bottom and returned them to the file folder. "With the nine-one-one call and the fingerprints on the knife, we have the case pretty well wrapped up. Unless additional evidence comes to light, the investigation will be over when the tox screen is finished. Like I said, about a week."

He stood, so we did, too. There wasn't anything else I could say.

Harry continued to talk, but I was only halfway listening. "The family is planning to hold Ellen's funeral service on Monday," he said. "Will her body be released in time?"

"Most likely," Turner said. "Your funeral director can make the arrangements with our office."

Harry thanked the detective again and led me from the tiny room. I felt cold, and gripped his arm for support. It couldn't be over. I'd been so sure. But *why*? I still didn't know why my sweet godson would turn on his mom. And without a why, I couldn't buy the police's conclusion.

Chapter 14

"No sign of the reporter," Harry said as we passed through the front lobby of the police station.

I didn't respond.

When we reached Harry's car, my brain kicked back into gear, and I asked Harry to drive me to the State Laboratory. He didn't question the request, just gave a thumbs up, and we rode the next fifteen minutes in silence.

He parked in the visitor's spot in front of a small brick building, and we followed the sidewalk through a sandy front lawn consisting of stubbly clumps of grass, broken palm fronds, and struggling rose bushes. Desolate. A mirror of my mood. I stopped and caught Harry's eye.

"Thanks," I said. "I'm going to find out why this happened." He gave me a quizzical look. "I think there's more going on here than Turner suspects," I added.

He opened the front door and held it for me. "We know the boy. Of course, there's more going on."

His simple statement reinforced my resolve. I lifted my chin and marched into the lab.

In contrast to the desolate exterior, the interior of the state lab glistened with high-tech brilliance. We met with Dr. Adele Sims, the state chemist. She listened to my concern that Mike had been given a new drug that might not show up on a routine test.

"I've never heard of a drug called pinwheel," the chemist said, "and my list of slang terms is updated almost daily." Her brow furrowed into a deep line. "Why don't I tell you what we can do here?"

She proceeded to explain the standard protocol.

"A normal blood sample contains many components. In order to visualize any abnormal or foreign component, we build a profile of what's present in the test sample and compare it to a similar profile of normal blood. We use two techniques to separate the components in a blood sample. One technique involves separation by size, while the other separates by electrical charge."

I was following her so far. Sort of.

"Typically, the information we get from these two procedures is enough to distinguish an abnormality and most drugs or poisons can be readily identified."

"What if it's something new?" I asked. "Could it be missed?"

Her eyebrows pulled together. "Of course. But, if there's a reason to suspect the presence of such a compound, the procedure can be adjusted to increase the sensitivity of the test. It can get expensive and time consuming, and it's not usually necessary."

"I think, if I understand what you're saying," I said, "you have the ability to do a more exhaustive analysis than what a typical tox screen calls for, right?"

She shrugged noncommittally. "If there's a chemical in the boy's blood that shouldn't be there," Dr. Sims said, "and we search hard enough, I believe we can find it or rule out the possibility."

She quoted me a price. I gulped down my surprise and considered backing out. But if I didn't try, I knew I'd regret it. I signed the necessary paperwork accepting financial responsibility for the search, and left a hefty deposit.

The ride back to Ellen's house was less tense. I was emotionally drained by the whole morning's experience and needed a diversion. Harry must have felt the same way. He reminisced about a cookout he'd attended at Ellen's recently, going into great detail about who else was there and funny things that happened. I drank it in, allowing myself to picture Ellen, alive and happy, throwing a party.

"I've got pictures," Harry said. "Lots of pictures from over the years. I'll bring them over and you can use them for the funeral service, if you'd like."

I squeezed his hand in thanks as I exited the car.

I paused in the kitchen doorway at Ellen's, momentarily seeing the gruesome images from the crime scene photos. The ammonia smell from the cleaning crew hung in the air, and I opened the window over the kitchen sink. I caught myself listening for familiar sounds of life from the house, but faced only oppressive silence. I fought back a sense of panic that I was running out of time. The nine-one-one tape was damning, but it didn't begin to explain *why*.

I hoped Mike's friends would have some answers. I telephoned Philip Donnelly's home, expecting to leave a message on their machine, but a woman answered. I introduced myself to Mrs. Donnelly and explained how I'd met Philip last summer at the Jacobsen's.

She replied in a soft Southern drawl, full of pain. "Ms. Kincaid, I'm so sorry. Ellen was the sweetest woman. And Michael? The poor boy, is he recovering? This must be terrible for the child. If there's anything we can do, please let me know."

"Thank you, Mrs. Donnelly. Mike's still in intensive care, and I'm afraid there's a long road ahead. I'm calling because I'm trying to reconstruct the days before the attack, and I wondered if Philip could help."

"I kept Philip home from school today. He's just so traumatized by it all. I don't know what he can tell you, but you're most welcome to stop by."

I followed the woman's directions and located the Donnelly residence without any difficulty. I parked on the street and walked up the sidewalk. I caught the sticky-sweet scent of the magnolia blossoms which bordered the path. Philip greeted me at the door. Instead of the smiling, open-faced kid I remembered, he looked shy and distraught, with red, swollen eyes. I hugged him and felt my own eyes fill with tears. He led me into the living room, introduced his mother, and then sat on the edge of an overstuffed armchair, looking miserable. I got straight to the point.

"Philip," I said, "the police are going to be talking to you and some of Mike's other friends about his activities these last few days. Their questions might seem insulting to that friendship, but try not to let it make you angry. It's just something they have to do. They don't want to assume one thing and miss something else."

Philip didn't answer, only stared wide-eyed at me, so I continued. "I'll go over some of the questions they might ask, but remember, you and I both knew Ellen, and you know I love that boy. So please understand that I'm trying to find the truth. Think about it as trying to eliminate any weird possibility, okay?"

Philip gave a slight nod.

"Did Mike say anything about anyone quarreling with his mom lately, or someone who might've upset her?"

"No," the boy replied. "I've been thinking about that all day. There wasn't anything."

"Great. Now, how about in the past? Did Mike ever get upset or seem worried about his mom?"

Philip thought for a moment. "Sure, sometimes, I guess. But nothing big."

"Was he grounded a lot?"

"No, that hardly ever happened. His mom was cool. But even if he was grounded, which, like I said, hardly ever happened, he'd only be mad for maybe a second. Then he'd grin and say something like 'Guess I shouldn't have done that', whatever it was."

Philip was quiet for a minute, and then added, "As for being worried about his mom? He'd worry sometimes about her getting married, or then worry that she wouldn't. It's hard to explain. We don't talk about it much."

I glanced at Philip's mother. She watched her son closely, sympathy spilling over her face. I wished I could've conducted the interview alone with Philip. But at least Mrs. Donnelly only listened, didn't try to influence the boy's responses.

"Okay, you're doing great. This one might be hard. Did you ever notice drugs at the Jacobsen's? Ever see anyone using drugs over there?"

"Drugs?" Philip shot a quick glance toward his mom. "Are they saying he used drugs?"

"The tests aren't back yet," I said. "But you'd be surprised?"

"Well, yeah," Philip said. "We don't do that. Mike doesn't do that. And his mom sure didn't."

"Could someone have given him something without him knowing?" Mrs. Donnelly asked her son.

"What do you think, Philip?" I asked. "Could that have happened?"

"I don't see how." He glanced at his mom again, then back to me. "Of course, there's kids that do drugs, but we're never around them. And I don't think they'd waste their drugs by slipping Mike something. Why'd anyone do that?"

I smiled. The kid made a good point.

"Has Mike picked up any new friends lately?" I asked. "Or had his mom?"

Philip shook his head. "I don't know about his mom, but no for Mike."

"Just a couple more questions. Do you know anyone in a cult, like satanic worship or voodoo, witches or vampires, anything odd like that?"

His eyes got huge. "No, are you kidding? Why would you ask that?"

"It's only a question. Does Mike seem overly interested in it?"

"He likes scary movies. No more than the next guy, I guess."

"Does pinwheel mean anything to you?"

"Pinwheel?" he asked. He looked confused.

"Yeah, maybe a nickname for someone?"

"No . . . but," he thought for a moment, "no."

I caught the hesitation. "But? But what?" He knew something, I was sure.

"It's nothing, really."

"Please, Philip. Anything could be important. Even the smallest comment. Please tell me."

"Well, okay, but remember, I warned you it was nothing." A pink tinge spread across his face. "It's just that, on the last day, you know, the day before it happened to his mom, I mean. Angela, this girl at school? Well, she had on white pants and a red T-shirt with a white sorta stripe thing across the middle, you know?" He waved his hand across his chest in a flash. "And one of the guys, I think it was Kevin, said she looked like a candy cane."

Philip's blush deepened and he stared intently at the pattern of the throw rug in front of his chair. I could imagine the sort of comments that would follow that comparison.

"Then Mike said she'd look like a pinwheel," he continued, "that is, if you spun her around and around, sort of end to end, you know. Kind of weird, I thought."

"That's it?" I'm sure I looked disappointed.

He thought for a minute. "Well, he said the world needed more red, and then he just laughed. I thought he meant more girls like Angela in shirts like that, so I laughed, too. It didn't mean anything. You know, talk." He held out his hands, palms up. Beseeching me to understand.

"Does Mike like Angela? For a girlfriend?"

"Everyone likes Angela. She's real popular, you know? Cheerleader and all. But Mike's got a thing for Jillie."

I digested that for a moment, and then Phillip asked, "Why'd you ask about a pinwheel?"

I don't know why it took me by surprise. I should've anticipated the question. But I couldn't explain to a twelve-year-old about the blood.

"Mike wrote it down," I said. It was true . . . whitewashed, but true. "I think it might be a message, but no one can figure out what it means."

Philip couldn't think of any other time the word had come up. "I want to visit Mike at the hospital," he said with another quick glance at his mother. "Mom thinks it would be best to wait a few days. I called last night, but the nurse wouldn't let me talk to him. Can you get me in?"

His eyes were large and glistening.

"He can't have visitors just yet," I said. "But pray for him, and I promise I'll let you know the minute he can. But it might not be anytime soon."

"It doesn't even feel real," Philip said. His lip trembled.

"Why don't you get the pictures?" Mrs. Donnelly asked. Philip's expression lightened and he pulled a bulging photo album off the book case in the corner of the living room.

I stayed a while longer, looked at pictures, and reminisced with them about fun times with Mike and Ellen. It felt good. Finally, I thanked Philip and his mother and headed back to Ellen's.

Alone in the car, I reflected on Philip's version of the pinwheel conversation at school. None of it made sense. As much as I wanted to deny Mike's role in the whole mess, the evidence was overwhelming. What could have happened to the wonderful, normal kid I had known?

I let my mind wander and pulled up more happy memories with Ellen and Mike. Despite these thoughts, or because of them, a wave of grief descended upon me in the solitude of the car. The horrible unfairness of my friend's death overpowered me, and I slammed my hand on the steering wheel. Tears flowed steadily down my cheeks as I pulled into Ellen's driveway.

In the kitchen, I put some water on to boil and collapsed into a chair. My hands were trembling and I needed to eat. When the water boiled, I fixed hot tea and instant soup, and gathered myself to face the many tasks still ahead.

I spoke at length with the funeral director about arrangements for a service on Monday, then called to update Sophia. Next, I arranged to meet with Mike's teachers and classmates at his school on Tuesday. Finally, I consulted with Ellen's bank manager and her insurance agent in my role as executor of her estate, and provided Harry's office number for legal documents to be faxed over. When I eventually let the phone rest for a few minutes, a call from Harry came in and invited me to dinner. My stomach growled, and I realized Detective Turner's crackers and a bowl of weak soup were the only things I'd eaten all day. I agreed to dinner.

On the way to the restaurant, I described my conversation with Philip.

"That's strange," Harry said. "Mike actually used the human pinwheel image at school? Better tell Turner."

"I'll call him tomorrow. I totally ran out of time today."

"So, there was a group of kids gathered around during that conversation? Someone else could have overheard the comment."

"Yeah. I told Philip I'd like to reconstruct that entire day and he agreed to talk to as many classmates as he can to see if they remember any contact with Mike."

"You're leaving it up to the kid?"

"Well, yeah. The preliminary, anyway. I'm going to the school on Tuesday to talk to them myself."

"Give them a chance to get their story straight, you mean?"

I bit back a retort. Even if I were a team of twenty, I couldn't expect an independent interview from all the kids without them discussing it among themselves. Not with cell phones and texting.

"I'm aware of human nature. I'm doing what I can." I simmered the rest of the way to the restaurant.

The pleasant atmosphere and promise of real food helped my mood. The place had a pianist softly playing in the corner and a small dance floor. The bread was hot and fluffy, the salad crisp. By the time my entrée arrived, I'd asked Harry if he'd be able to say a few words at the funeral. So, he started to reminisce about Ellen. I was doing okay with this, no fresh tears, but then he switched the memory train.

"Remember when we met?" he asked.

I didn't answer, but of course I remembered. Harry'd been a third-year law student and I was a junior majoring in journalism at Columbia. I was covering a major court case for the *Columbia Daily Spectator* when I first saw him. He was assisting the prosecutor and seemed a lot more approachable than the attorney — as in closer to my age and incredibly handsome — so I'd asked him for an interview.

"You were an idealist," Harry added. "And you haven't changed much in that regard."

"You were, too," I said, despite my resolve to avoid that topic. "You can't deny it." My thoughts jumped to the Truman murder, the case that resulted in our becoming a couple. "You were so sure Ms. Sparks was innocent, I couldn't help but get on board."

Harry smiled. I felt myself blush. I'd gotten on board, all right. Harry and I had been inseparable from that time until my graduation. But I didn't want to dredge up those memories.

"You're still a champion for the innocent, right?" I asked.

"Sure, but you won't find me chasing smugglers or drug kingpins anymore. I'm not a risk taker at heart."

I heard the implied "like you are". And while it was true I was a risk taker, I couldn't take the risk of continuing down this memory lane. But damn, seeing Harry up close and personal . . . .

Physically, he hadn't changed much. In fact, he was even more handsome now, with the extra few pounds. Every time I looked up from my meal, I met those steady, smiling, blue eyes. Those eyes held a wistfulness that pulled at my heart.

I needed to direct the conversation away from our past. "I'm thinking of selling Ellen's house to raise funds for Mike's defense," I said. "He can't live there alone, anyway. I suppose he'll come live with me once this is all over." I buttered a chunk of bread and placed it on the edge of my plate. "As executor, can I do that?"

Harry took a bite of his entrée, chewed a moment, washed it down with a sip of wine. I could see him calculating his response. Finally, he nodded. "You can do that. It's probably a good plan. He's going to have high medical and legal bills."

"Thought I'd auction off household items he won't need. Store his things and some heirlooms."

"Good plan. I'll get you some numbers."

I sighed. "Don't. I can manage this. I only wanted to verify it's within my power."

Harry held up both hands. "Not a problem. Yes, you can do it and yes, you're more than capable. I'm not trying to interfere here."

"Fine," I said.

We finished eating in an awkward silence. Then, Harry pushed aside his plate, took my hand and escorted me to the dance floor. It was a slow song and he held me close. I plunged headlong into a time vacuum. The years simply vanished. They disappeared as completely as if they'd never happened, and Harry and I were still a couple. My feelings for this man were as deep as ever. I knew it. But he didn't need to know it, and my feelings wouldn't change a damn thing about why we split or why we couldn't reunite.

"I like your hair this way," he said. "Makes you look adventurous."

My hand automatically brushed up my short, spiky do. The drastic change hadn't been my choice; chemo demands its own fashion. But I had beat the odds — survived with my short hair, my commemorative tattoo, my sterile future. I knew Harry's plans and I no longer fit. "Things change," I said, with a shrug.

Harry whispered into my ear. "I've always felt, somehow, that we weren't finished. Do you think we could give it a second try?"

The spell of the moment broke with a stabbing pang. I stopped dancing and pushed myself away. "No," I said. "Don't even try it, Harry. It's not going to happen." I left the dance floor, grabbed my purse and called a cab. This time, my tears weren't for Ellen.

Chapter 15

I sat in the front row at the funeral service with Ellen's Aunt Sophia on one side of me and Harry on the other. Yesterday, the local paper had tagged Mike as the primary suspect in his mom's death and from the whispering around me, the shock ripples were still reverberating through the community. And sure enough, I spotted the reporter I'd seen at the police station, Ronan, seated in the back row. It's what reporters did, I knew, when there was a sensational murder, but I still wanted to hit him.

I held Sophia's hand as resonating strains of *How Great Thou Art* echoed. When the song ended and the preacher took the podium, I had trouble focusing on his message. When I sensed Aunt Sophia stiffen beside me, I tried to pay attention.

"Young Michael is a troubled boy, hounded by demons too fearful to comprehend." My head snapped up.

"No," I muttered. "No, he's a good kid."

Aunt Sophia gripped my hand even tighter.

"We know of God's unlimited capacity for forgiveness," the preacher intoned, "but we, too, must forgive this child and help him live with the consequences of his actions."

I rose to my feet. "No," I said. I heard a collective intake of breath from the crowd. Harry had also risen and placed an arm around me.

"You don't even know him," I said to the preacher. "He's not troubled."

There was a moment of silence from the room, and then

a crescendo of whispers enclosed me. The preacher placed his mouth close to the microphone to be heard above the rumble. "It's true, I don't know the boy. But I say again, we must not judge him. Only God can judge his actions."

I wanted to scream. Then Sophia struggled to her feet to stand beside me and sent me a weak smile. "We know him, dear," she whispered. "We love him."

It was a strange moment, with the three of us standing in front of the other mourners. Harry, tall and distinguished; Sophia, tiny and elderly; and me, petite and punk. Maybe it was our triple solidarity, or maybe it was a spiritual connection with Ellen, but I felt something pass through me in that instant. It was a flow of love and peace that enveloped me and calmed my heart. Was this the kind of thing Clunie was always going on about? Channeling, or karmic brouhaha, or cosmic anomaly? By whatever name, it felt real.

Suddenly, it didn't matter what anyone else thought. My conviction about Mike was reinforced by this unexpected, surreal link that I couldn't explain and absolutely couldn't ignore. I returned Sophia's smile and let Harry ease me into my seat. I promised myself to give Clunie a call to sort out this sensation. Soon.

The preacher finished his remarks, and then Harry took the podium.

"Thanks, everyone, for coming today. Ellen Jacobsen was a long-time friend. This woman was, first and foremost, a loving mother, prepared to sacrifice everything for her son. Here's a little example of their relationship. A mere two weeks ago, Ellen had a cookout at her home. Several of you were there." He sent pointed looks to a few in the audience. "She and Mike talked non-stop about their upcoming trip to the coast. He'd already researched the history of the area and had a list of places for snorkeling, crabbing, and even found a map for pirate treasure. Their enthusiasm was contagious." Harry smiled at the memory, then directed his smile at Sophia.

"Likewise, Ellen cared deeply for her aunt, Sophia Jacobsen. She was also a loyal friend to Lila Kincaid and to so many in this community." He paused and looked around. He had a talent for connecting with people on an emotional level. I'd seen his flair before, when he appealed to a jury. And when he appealed to me.

"Some of you might not know this," Harry continued, "but Ellen worked tirelessly on behalf of abused women and championed women's rights." He finished by reminding everyone to be open-minded, and remember our love for Ellen, and reach out to help Mike.

My heart ached in response to his tenderness.

Later, following the brief graveside service, Harry, Sophia, and I made our way back to the car in silence. The ceremony provided some comfort, but I feared it was merely a temporary fix. I wouldn't have true closure on Ellen's death until I followed through with my conviction to find out what happened to Mike.

I tried to reach Clunie several times that afternoon and into the evening for her take on the otherworldly feeling I'd experienced during the funeral. I left several messages and waited impatiently for her to call back.

Chapter 16

I woke Tuesday morning to the persistent ringing of my cell phone. I rolled out of bed and eventually located it my jacket pocket. The caller ID said Morning Star Dan. I leaned against the bedroom wall and answered the call from my editor.

"Kincaid? You coming in today?"

"Good morning to you, too, Dan. No, I'm not coming in. I'm still in Charleston."

"What the hell for?" He sounded more gruff than usual. "Case is solved, isn't it? Funeral's over?"

"The funeral's over, but the case is not solved. At least not completely. The autopsy report isn't finished."

"Just a formality, from what I hear."

"Who's your source?"

"Buzz looked into it for me. Called some local reporter name of Ronan. And before you use the estate as an excuse, hire a realtor to manage it, whatever. I need you here."

I sighed. And I'd thought a Buzz out of sight was a Buzz out of my hair. "Look, Dan. I've still got another week of vacation time. No one else is trying to find out why Mike did what he did, and I need to know."

"One week, Kincaid. One week, then you'd better get your butt back to your job while you still have one." He hung up.

I stared at the phone in astonishment. He'd just threatened me with my job. Damn him, anyway. How could he do that to me? I stamped my foot. To hell with him and his job. I did a quick mental inventory of my finances. I could afford to go a month, maybe six weeks, without a pay check. But, hell, I liked that job. He'd given me one week.

Could I figure out Mike's motive in one short week?

Chapter 17

I had a meeting scheduled for Tuesday afternoon at Mike's school. Harry insisted on participating, so I spent the morning drafting a script of sorts to make sure we covered everything with the teachers and students. Last Friday, I'd personally contacted the school principal, Mr. Avery, for help with my idea. He was more cooperative than I'd expected. He agreed to let me interrupt the regular day's class schedule and review Mike's last day with his teachers and classmates as a group.

I met Harry in the school parking lot. Mr. Avery met us at the door and escorted us to the gym. There was an assembly of twelve adults sitting together near the bottom of the bleachers and about fifty students clustered at the top. Mr. Avery indicated the adults.

"I notified the parents," he told us. "There might be one or two more show up, but all the teachers are here." He pulled a portable microphone out of his pocket. "Ready to start?"

My hand shook and I couldn't take the microphone. I hadn't expected a room full of teenagers would make me nervous. And now I'd become the guardian to one.

Harry covered for me. "Thank you, everyone, for giving up your valuable time. I'm Harry Greenstreet, a local attorney, friend of Ellen Jacobsen and now an advocate for her son, Mike. I know all of you are shocked and disturbed by these recent events, and I appreciate your meeting us here today. This is Lila Kincaid, also a family friend, as well as Mike's godmother."

I lifted my hand in greeting. Harry's last sentence echoed in the silent gymnasium. I sensed tension in the air. Maybe it was sadness, maybe fear. I tried to calm myself and portray a detached, impartial investigator. These people knew Mike; lived in the same community. I spotted Philip sitting near the top of the bleachers, and hoped the boys sitting around him were also Mike's friends.

"As Mr. Avery has explained," Harry continued, "we're searching for clues to try to determine Mike's frame of mind on the last day you saw him. We think we might be able to do this by examining his activities that day."

A girl coughed, then blushed as all eyes turned toward her. I wished there had been another venue available. A classroom would have been more intimate, encouraging conversation. No one spoke, even to ask a question. And who could blame them?

I decided to dispense with the microphone and moved closer to the bleachers. "Why don't we try this? We can start with first period, and move through sequentially to the end of the day." I consulted the list Mr. Avery had supplied. "Mike had English first period with Mrs. McNairy. Is Mrs. McNairy here?"

A short, stout woman sitting in the front row waved her hand and stood. Smooth rosy cheeks dotted a face topped by a pillow of white hair. Tiny dark eyes were magnified by thick silver-rimmed glasses.

"Would you start us off?" I asked.

Mrs. McNairy consulted her agenda. In a loud, authoritative voice, she described her lesson plan for the day, described where Michael sat in class, and relayed what she remembered of his participation that day. He had turned in the paper that was due. She had assigned chapter reading, and there had been a disturbance from two girls who were passing notes. It had nothing to do with Michael. Mrs. McNairy added that she had graded his paper and he received a B. The paper was up to his usual performance in her class.

When I asked, several students raised their hands as having been in that class, but no one volunteered any additional information.

I continued down the class schedule, asking each teacher in turn what Mike did that day. When we reached Mike's fourth period, Philip stood up. He was the first student to say anything, and he looked nervous. He had everyone's attention, and recounted an abbreviated version of the incident in the hallway where the pinwheel was mentioned, then sat back down. I looked over the students seated in the upper rows, hoping someone else would speak up.

Several kids glanced at each other; a few elbow nudges passed through the crowd. I waited, trying to make eye contact to encourage a response. Finally, a boy stood and admitted that he had been with Mike and Philip during that conversation. Then another student said he'd overheard them, adding a little bit about who was near the scene. A girlfriend of the student who had worn the attention-getting red striped shirt remembered the boys laughing and watching her friend. Eventually, it sounded pretty much like Philip's original version.

I saw Mrs. McNairy watching the principal during the discussion.

Mr. Avery coughed slightly and stepped forward. He admitted that he usually patrolled the hallways between classes, and he might have been in the area at the time, but he denied overhearing the conversation.

It didn't add anything to my investigation, but the discussion broke the ice. Several boys stood as a group and mentioned sitting by Mike at lunch. They talked over each other in their excitement. I slowed them down and got them to speak one at a time.

A tall, black-haired boy went first. "I tried to get Mike to trade his Jell-O for my carrots. I mean, he wasn't eating it and lunch was about over."

A heavy boy in an AC/DC T-shirt laughed, then looked embarrassed as the sound echoed across the gym. "Yeah, he was just staring at it," he added.

The tall boy said, "Mike looked up at me like he didn't know what I was talking about, then he said, 'I like red. I really do like red.'"

The heavy boy snorted. "Then you said, 'That's because you're gay.'"

There was an uncomfortable snicker among the boys and the heavy boy said, "It was funny at the time. Everybody laughed, we got yelled at by Mrs. Kasper, and Mike went ahead and ate his Jell-O. Then the bell rang." He sat down, and the others followed.

Mike's last period of the day was gym class. He'd told a classmate that nothing hurt anymore. The boy told the story and shrugged it off as Mike trying to act tough. I shot a glance at Harry. No pain? Coincidence, or a connection to his final blood message? Harry sent an almost imperceptive nod my way as he scribbled notes.

By the time we wound up the session, Mike's last day at school was fleshed out. But I didn't see how a sprinkling of odd remarks was going to help the boy's case one bit.

Chapter 18

Tuesday evening, I sat in front of my computer wondering what to do next. I seemed to be at a dead end. I spent my time either at the hospital waiting for Mike to recover enough to talk to me, or waiting at the house for someone to call in with a tip, or better yet, the solution. My last week of vacation loomed ahead and my investigation was going nowhere. Soon, I'd have to make a choice: continue this search and lose a great job, or go back to work and maybe never know what was behind Mike's ruin. At this rate, I could very well lose the job and still never find the answer.

I sent an email to Clunie to call when she had a chance. Then, to fill my time, I turned to Google and entered a succession of key words, beginning with *pinwheel* and moving to *drugs called pinwheel, new illegal drugs, poisons, environmental poisons,* and *environmental contaminants.* After nearly twenty minutes of fruitless searching, I found an article reporting detectable levels of steroids and other hormones in the water supply across the country. That couldn't be good.

I followed up with an Internet search on steroids and hormones to see their side effects. A frightening list appeared. Aggression, dizziness, headaches, and nausea came up, also psychotic disorders, peptic ulcers disease, hyperglycemia, edema, hypertension, and a whole list of conditions I didn't recognize. I went to the journal web site for the scientific paper cited in the news release to see where water samples had been collected. Charleston's water supply was not on the list.

I printed off a copy of the journal article and the news release to show Dr. Sims at the State Lab.

I spent the rest of Tuesday night reading more of Ellen's journals, all the while waiting, hoping, for the phone to ring. I gave in to my curiosity and turned to Ellen's entries from five years ago, the time of my own critical life event, even though it couldn't have a bearing on Ellen's death.

I found what I was looking for — Ellen's concern over my break-up with Harry. Her frustration when I refused to explain. I became the Great Withholder. After six months between visits, I became the Workaholic. When I showed up at Christmas, thin, wan, unhealthy-looking, her concern turned to drug abuse.

She was wrong.

Hell. I should've told her how sick I was.

Chapter 19

The first thing I did Wednesday morning was drive to the State Lab. I pulled into the parking lot as Dr. Sims walked her bike through the front doors.

"Hi, Lila," she said, hanging her helmet on a wall peg. "You're out early."

"Couldn't wait." I handed her the information I'd printed out yesterday. "I found this on the Internet."

Sims glanced at the title and gave a nod. "Yeah, I've read this. Interesting stuff."

"What do you make of it?" I asked. "Could there be drugs in the water here?"

She flipped through the pages and read the concluding paragraph. "The way I read it," she said, "the drugs were found because of huge improvements in detection technology. The authors emphasize the levels in the water are extremely low and probably wouldn't show the side effects you're worried about."

"Could they be cumulative? I mean, if you drink a lot of water over a number of years, would the drugs accumulate in your body?" I asked.

"Some, I suppose, but you might have to live a long time before any side effects show up. Look, I know one of the authors on this paper. They're doing round two of testing right now and she asked for a sample of our city water. I can check with her, see if they've found anything unusual in our area. But, in Mike's case, the blood analyses we're doing will

95

show any detectable drug, regardless of the source."

"Wait a sec. So, you are worried about our water supply?"

Dr. Sims frowned. "Always. Water quality is critical to the success of any civilization. Safeguarding it should be, and is, a priority." She glanced at a photograph on her desk. "I have three kids. We invested in a water purification system for our home years ago. Recommend it to anyone who asks."

My stomach dropped. Could Ellen have been saved by something as simple as using a water purification system? The horror must have been visible on my face.

"Oh, don't freak out," Dr. Sims added quickly. "I don't worry if my kids drink from a fountain at school. At least, not yet."

Before I left the lab, Sims checked on the status of the tests she was doing on Michael's blood. There was nothing new showing up yet, but she had another check point tomorrow morning and would call me with the results.

The next morning, things took an interesting turn. Dr. Sims called. She'd found something curious in Mike's blood. She faxed me the report and asked me to call her back as soon as I had it in hand.

The page inched out of the printer, bottom first. I read the figure description as the bottom portion of the graph appeared. The diagram consisted of a line with numerous sharp peaks and valleys. One peak had an asterisk, but no other explanation.

I called Sims. "I don't know what this means."

"Don't get your hopes up just yet," Sims said in a rush. "It's something unusual, for sure. But I wanted to give you a heads up that I'll have to purify it before I can tell you more. This'll take a while. Couple of weeks, maybe."

Damn. More waiting. I needed action.

Chapter 20

The waiting was unbearable.

My investigation moved at a snail's pace. No one phoned in a tip. Clunie hadn't returned my messages. And I expected the chemist's finding would likely turn out to be nothing.

It was already Thursday. McLeish expected me back at work on Monday. So, I decided to head over to Turner's office again and have another go at the crime scene photos.

I sat in the detective's tiny office and updated him on Tuesday's meeting at the school. Then, Turner handed over the envelopes containing the crime scene photographs and offered coffee.

I managed a small smile and a nod. He left the room and I released the clasp on the envelope marked with Ellen's home address with my eyes shut, heart pounding. I inhaled deeply, and peeked at the top picture. If I concentrated, it was barely possible to study the images without thinking that it was my best friend's body lying there. One by one, I worked my way through the pile, scrutinizing the background of each print, not sure what I hoped to find. My focus was so intent that Detective Turner's return caused me to jump.

"I'm sorry we couldn't uncover a reason for the boy's behavioral change," Detective Turner said, handing me the coffee.

"I haven't given up," I said.

"I appreciate that, Ma'am. But sometimes it's impossible to find an answer. In fact, there's been an increased awareness in the number of cases nationwide, where an apparently normal child will become mentally unbalanced and commit an unspeakable crime. In too many of the cases, the motive is unsatisfactory."

"Care to expand on that, Detective?" I appreciated a breather from the horrific images.

He folded his hands together, with his long, freckled, index fingers touching at the tips. "The number of violent underage offenders in general is on the rise. Usually, their actions are drug related, or there's a history of violence in the home, or easy access to handguns. However, there've been some instances where no external cause can be determined, and these bear a striking similarity to the Jacobsen case."

I jolted to the idea that other experiences paralleled Mike's.

"Do you think you could get me a list of those unusual cases?" I asked.

"Well, Ma'am, even if I could, I'm not sure what good that'd do at this juncture."

"Maybe I could see how the families handled it, or theories people came up with. I don't know. But, with that list of cases, could you also include some details on each?" I asked.

He looked pained, but too polite to turn me down cold, I hoped. "I couldn't possibly fit a search like that into my schedule today. Besides, what are you looking for, Ma'am?"

I didn't know. A survivor support group? A miracle? Something to do to keep me sane? Finally I said, "If I look at enough of these cases, I might recognize a pattern, some common denominator that could explain how normal children turn into killers."

"I expect the *Morning Star* archives would be an excellent source of information."

I sighed. I couldn't help myself. The crime scene photos

were devastating, Mike's situation looked hopeless, and now Detective Turner's comment brought home the uncertainty of my job's future. I automatically turned my spinner ring.

"Ma'am?"

I shook my head. "You're right," I said. "Even if I don't go back to the paper, I have great contacts there. Plus, there's probably tons of stuff online. Still, nothing is as good as your database, I'd bet."

Detective Turner met my gaze. "I didn't know you were contemplating not returning to the paper. I can't promise anything, Ma'am."

"Well, you did bring up the idea."

He raised a shoulder. "That I did." The detective finished his coffee, excused himself, and left me alone to continue looking at the crime scene pictures.

An hour later, I'd finished looking at the vivid images without inspiration. I was beyond frustrated, and now the fishing expedition inspired by Turner's comment, though bleak, sounded better than nothing. I decided my next move would be to search the *Morning Star* archives while I was technically still employed. I'd see what I could access from here, then maybe try to persuade Clunie to help by searching the archives in person.

As I was putting away the pictures, Detective Turner pushed open the office door. He bore a file folder and a grim expression. "I printed a list. This is only a start, but it'll give you an idea of what's out there."

I was dumbfounded and said so.

"Well, Ma'am, you were right about our database. And it's only a list of dates and locations. I can't give out details on the juveniles. You'll have to track down the investigating officers for specifics." A slow smile graced his features. "But I included those IO names as well."

I took the file and didn't resist the urge to give him a hug.

Harry phoned later in the morning and suggested lunch. I agreed and met him at Little Jack's Tavern. After we were seated and placed our orders, I recounted my conversation with Detective Turner.

"I'm about two hours into the search," I said. "There's a lot of juvenile crime out there."

"Lila." He paused long enough for me to suspect bad news. "You'll simply be wasting your time. That whole thing about good kids going berserk for no reason? It's a crock. It's always drugs. I hate to say it, but someone needs to point it out. Mike's at the age where kids start experimenting. Parents are always shocked. Kids always lie."

That stung. It was as if his beautiful eulogy meant nothing. The cloud I was riding turned to swamp gas.

"Sims is going to find it," he added. "And then you'll track down how Mike got it and whoever made it to begin with. You'll have plenty to investigate."

What could I say? Harry always presented his argument as if there was no room for doubt. But if his version was reality, that would make mine a pipe dream. Yet it was the police detective who started me down this path.

"I don't expect you to understand," I said with a sigh. "It's lot of work, yes. And maybe it'll only make me feel like I'm doing something positive. In any case, I can't just sit around and wait, hoping a clue will drop out of the sky. Investigating records is something I can do. Something I'm trained to do."

"Will you have time? Getting Ellen's place ready to sell will take some work."

"The auction house is sending a crew over to take inventory and arrange things for sale. They're thinking it'll take a couple weeks. I'll lock myself in Ellen's guest room, I suppose. Stay out of their way. Just wish she had faster Internet service."

"I do. The fastest available in the city. Why don't you set up in my library and stay in the guest room? You'll have more privacy."

My heart pounded. Harry's offer made sense. I could get a lot of work done, fast. And he didn't even know about McLeish's pending deadline. Living in the same house with Harry would offer a much different distraction than an auction company crew, but I had already survived one night there. If I lost my job, I might be there awhile. Could I survive awhile? I was ping-ponging with myself. I had to make a decision.

"I'll be working," I said. "Don't expect me to be a guest you have to entertain."

"I'll stay out of your way."

"I don't know how long it will take. This research may be time consuming."

"Stay as long as you need."

So, I became the live-in guest of the former love of my life, the Honorable Harry Greenstreet.

Chapter 21

My suitcase rested on the dresser in Harry's guest room, still packed and ready to relocate if this experimental living arrangement didn't work out. My phone was fully charged and ready for incoming tips. Harry's library was quiet, as promised, and I dove into my research. A cursory check of the Internet, the *Morning Star* files, and the FBI's stats on *Crime in the United States* overwhelmed me with the sheer number of cases where the offender was younger than sixteen. I'd had no idea there'd be thousands of hits. Limiting my search to the last three years decreased the numbers somewhat, but it was still a daunting database.

When my phone finally rang and I saw it was Clunie, I welcomed the break.

"Hey, girlfriend," Clunie chirped. "Isn't it amazing about our case?"

I was so focused on Mike, I'd forgotten about the O'Connell murder. Didn't think it qualified as "our" case anymore, though.

"Find a suspect?" I asked.

"You haven't been following it? I've had three articles in the last week. Front page, no less. I owe you big time, girlfriend."

"Three? Fantastic. I'll look them up."

She laughed. "Saw you'd called. What'cha need?"

Only a few days ago, I had wanted to discuss spiritual sensations with a gifted friend. But, so much had happened.

Today I needed Clunie's other gift — her technical skill as a researcher. I explained my current project and the logistics problems; how I wanted to narrow down the numbers, use key words to search through the masses of data for cases similar to Mike's.

Clunie's view was the opposite of Harry's.

"I so get it," she said. "Focus on a minor chakra, like patala. It can screw over a totally normal prana."

"Clunie," I sighed. "I don't know what that means, but I'm sure none of those words will be in the files."

"Maybe not, but if we eliminate anyone with past disciplinary problems, gang affiliation, or history of violence in the home, we'll be a lot closer to someone like your boy there."

"Yes, that's it, exactly," I said. We agreed on which files we'd each concentrate, then I couldn't help myself and added, "Are you okay with this project? You know, psychically?"

"Like, shift made to orange. Yeah."

"Hell, Clunie. Translate please."

"It's a good strategy, girlfriend."

Chapter 22

The next morning, I started the day with a visit to Mike's bedside. His unresponsiveness was heart wrenching. The doctors, however, were cautiously optimistic and planned to move him from ICU to a post-surgical ward as soon as a private room opened up, probably by that evening. The police guard sat in his room reading the paper, a reminder of what the boy might be facing for years to come. Possibly even if I discovered a reason for his behavior change.

As I was leaving the hospital, Harry phoned. "Turner requested a meeting," he said. "Can you meet us at the café across the street from my office?"

I made it there in ten minutes. Harry waved at me from their table in the corner. They already had a carafe of coffee and a cup waiting for me.

"How's Mike?" Detective Turner asked.

"No change," I said. "The guard is a waste of county funds."

Turner's mouth twisted to the side. Then he asked me if I'd looked into any of those other cases he'd mentioned yesterday. I forced my thoughts out of my gloom and met his gaze. He was watching me closely, seriously. Harry piped up that I'd been on the computer all night.

I took a sip of coffee, then answered. "There's so much out there. I pulled out over a thousand. Enough to give someone nightmares."

"I had no idea," Harry said.

"That's why I wanted to speak with you," Turner said. "I spent quite some time searching the FBI database after you left yesterday, using my clearance to access files people in the public sector would not be allowed to view. I found about, oh, seventy-five or so cases for you that you might not have found otherwise. The list is in my car."

My coffee forgotten, I said, "Wow, that was above and beyond." Two surprises from this man in two days. Why would he do this?

Turner looked grieved. "It's my wife. She taught Michael in Sunday school, and she's distraught with guilt that she didn't pick up on a problem. Like you, she's not wanting to let go of hope that something will turn up to vindicate the boy. I promised to do what I could."

I raised an eyebrow. *Thank you, Mrs. Turner.*

"I'm trying to narrow down the numbers by removing anyone with a prior record," I said. "Can I tell that from your data?"

Turner spooned sugar into his coffee. "You can tell," he admitted.

"That'll bring down the numbers fast," Harry said.

I narrowed my eyes at him over the bottom of my coffee cup as I downed the last drop. "Well, thanks for the effort, Detective. Now, I need to get back to my search." I followed Turner out to his car and retrieved the file, glad I'd enlisted Clunie's help to weed through it all.

I slept fitfully during the next two nights, haunted by dreams that mimicked the horrors I was researching. Newspaper articles might describe an incident in general terms, but Internet sites often included pictures and accounts filled with gruesome details, which became distorted in my dreams.

On Sunday, I heard back from Clunie. Between the two of us, we brought the original daunting number down to a manageable twenty-two cases.

Death Map

Twenty-two. We'd actually uncovered twenty-two cases similar to my godson's. I could understand why no one had bothered to connect them. They were similar due to age and gender — all ten-to-fifteen-year-old boys — but also because of what was missing. No prior record. No history of any personal, school, or family trouble. Unless someone was desperately looking for a connection, there was no reason to pool these few cases out of the thousands nationwide. I was desperately looking for a connection.

Monday morning, McLeish's deadline arrived, but I persisted in my quest. Since I could still access the *Morning Star*'s archives, I assumed the old battle-axe had relented and I maintained my employee status. For the moment, anyway. Could be, he hadn't yet registered my absence. I rated my chance of staying under the radar as nil and phoned McLeish, hoping to convince him I was on to something.

"Good morning, Dan. It's Lila."

"Good. I want you to take that Robinson fiasco at the Art Museum. Get back to me by two." He hung up.

I hit redial.

"Don't hang up, Dan. I can't do the thing at the Art Museum. I've got something I'm working on already."

"Lila? Where are you?" I heard his suspicion.

"I'm on to something here, Dan. It's going to be big. I just need a little more time. A day or two. A week at the most."

"A week? Are you still on vacation?"

"No. I'm working on a story. I'll have a draft for you by Wednesday."

"Tomorrow. I want that draft tomorrow." He hung up.

I allowed myself a wry grin and a momentary sigh of relief. Not much of a reprieve, but it was something. One more day, which I might be able to stretch into two. I returned to my gamble of a project and reread my notes. A handful of cases connected only by a host of negatives? My momentary relief was replaced by realism. This was pathetic. I was trying to turn nothing into something. Shift to orange, Clunie had said.

Orange, my ass.

Chapter 23

Detective Turner had suggested that I might need to contact the investigating officers to get specifics on each boy. I had twenty-one IO names, so I spent the remainder of Monday afternoon on the phone attempting to reach them.

The majority of calls went to desk clerks or answering machines. With the few that I spoke to in person, I first verified the information Clunie or I had dug up from our varied sources. Then, I asked about changes in the child's behavior, like whether the child had said anything unusual or odd in the days immediately preceding the crime. After the third variation of "WTF", I changed tactics.

Asking if it was merely a matter of time before the child got into serious trouble, or did this action totally surprise, well . . . bam! It was the home run question. Every person the IOs had interviewed had been surprised.

Every one.

Even though it was only from a subset of the cases, this similarity allowed me to start my article for McLeish. By eleven, physical and emotional exhaustion set in. The weekend of reviewing the specifics of horrific crimes took its toll, and I called it a day.

In the middle of the night, after three days of intensive research, I woke up in a sweat. The nightmare vividly replayed in my mind. Ellen and I were shopping at a mall. I held up a sweater to show her, and then she was standing in front of me, covered in blood, staring blankly, a grisly crime scene photo zombie.

I jumped out of bed, turned on the lights and paced the room, trying in vain to dispel the memory of that ghastly image. I was too agitated to go back to sleep. I crept downstairs to the kitchen, brewed a cup of tea, grabbed an orange and headed toward the family room. Jay-Jay sprang to life when I switched on the lamp. I fed him orange pieces, watched CNN news and succeeded in distracting myself.

As Tuesday's dawn broke, I caught the aroma of fresh-brewed coffee floating into the family room from the kitchen. Harry settled in beside me on the sofa a few minutes later, bringing me a cup.

"Morning," he said.

"Hope the TV didn't wake you," I answered.

"That's okay. How's Jay-Jay today?"

"Hungry. Lonely. Demanding."

"And you? How are you today?"

"Just demanding." I sent him a tiny smile.

The newscaster was joking with the weatherman about the hat chosen for his on-location report. It was shaped like Sesame Street's Big Bird. It deserved a joke.

"Maybe too demanding on yourself," Harry said.

I didn't reply.

"Looks like it'll be beautiful all week," he added, as Big Bird Hat pointed to the weather map.

"Hmm," I said.

"Want a change of scenery today? We could go out for lunch. Drive to a place I know out in the country."

My heart gave some weird kick in reaction to his suggestion. Where was that coming from? "Thanks, but no," I said. "I'm making good progress and I need to finish."

"Care to tell me what you're finding?" Harry asked.

"Ah, no, not yet."

"Okay. When you're ready, I'll be here."

I wasn't ready in any of the ways the tone of his comment

implied. I sensed his eyes on me but I focused on the flat screen. My pounding heart told me to get out of there.

"Well, at least I'll enjoy the great weather for my hospital trip," I said. "Then it'll be back at the computer." I tried for detached, and thanked him again for the coffee; then went upstairs, dressed, and fled to the hospital for my now-routine visit. I spent my ten-minute allotment watching my ward sleep and hoped he dreamed of a happier past.

Return calls from investigative officers trickled in during the morning, and case details began to fill in. I eliminated an additional eight cases from my list and emailed McLeish to expect a big report tomorrow. Unfortunately, fourteen cases didn't sound big; it sounded random. I'd set out to find cases that were connected by a list of negatives, and it had worked. But, interestingly, there were some unexpected similarities — they'd all occurred within the last two years, the perps were all male kids, the majority of whom had committed suicide after the murders, and all had been considered normal — good kids, even — prior to the event. But did it mean anything? Would it help Mike?

Only three of the fourteen boys were still alive, one being my godson.

A second child, Clarence Luke, had committed his crime only six months ago in a small town named Milton, Louisiana. He had killed his grandmother and a local preacher. The report said the boy claimed to have received a message from the Lord. I wondered if that was enough to eliminate him from my list. Perhaps the child was insane. The witnesses, however, consistently described him as a good child, a normal child. I wasn't sure, but I decided to leave the Luke boy on my list.

The third living child was institutionalized in Taylock, Montana. Steven Oaks had shot and killed his parents and his fifth-grade teacher for no apparent reason. He was also overwhelmingly described by everyone as a normal boy before the killings.

Interviewing Mike was not happening at this point, but maybe I could question the other two. But one was in Louisiana and one was in Montana. Impossible to do in person in a single day, on my limited budget, even if I could somehow get permission to visit them.

Out of curiosity, I found a road atlas on one of the shelves in Harry's library and opened it to the big map of the United States. I found Taylock, Montana easily and I dotted it using a fine-tipped red marker. I couldn't find Milton, Louisiana on the US map, so I went to the page for that state. Milton was a tiny spot in the road. I circled it on the state map, estimated where it would be on the US map, and put a dot there. Then marked Charleston. No real easy way to get to either location from here. If I had time and money, I'd do it. In fact, if I had time and money, I'd go to each of the fourteen locations. That thought made me find the other towns from my list and dot them on the map, as well. Most were small, and I had to go the individual states, then approximate them on the US map. It took way too much time, but once started I couldn't stop until I found them all.

My phone rang while I was placing the final dot, for Toomsboro, Alabama, on the US map. I answered quickly, expecting it to be another investigative officer returning my call. Instead, it was Harry.

"Hey," he said, "I was thinking of taking Sophia out for an afternoon treat and thought I'd give you another chance to say no. Want to take a break and join us?"

"That's a nice idea," I said. "I am feeling a little brain fog coming on. A break might work better than a nap." I set the red marker I was using down on the map and found some scrap paper to write down the address for the Kaminsky's Dessert Café.

When I reached out to pick up the pen again, I noticed it covered up several of my red dots in the western-most states. Harry was spouting directions into my ear on how to find the restaurant, but I wasn't listening. I moved the red pen a bit, rotated it, slid it along a line. The implications of what I was seeing took a moment to sink in. Then, it nearly made my heart stop. The adrenalin rush swept the need for sleep or food right out of my mind.

"I can't make it, Harry. I'll text you later." I was talking fast. "Tell Sophia I'll come by and see her soon." I hung up the phone without giving him a chance to reply.

The red pen was hiding eight of the fourteen cases that were clustered in the northern mid-west. Moving the pen illustrated how they were positioned in a more-or-less straight line. With mounting excitement, I shifted the pen to the other six red dots I'd made on the map. They were all located in the south, and also in a straight line.

I tried to make sense of what I was seeing. The connection between the cases up to now had been little more than a list of negatives. Suddenly, I had evidence of a positive, tangible connection. The southern cases fell nearly in a straight line east to west from Charleston, South Carolina, to Mesquite, Texas. The northern cases were also aligned east to west, from Duluth, Minnesota, to Taylock, Montana.

I paced the room trying to think. What could this mean? Fourteen kids, normal by all accounts, undergo an apparent psychotic break and commit bizarre, murderous acts, and the only connection was geographical? My mind whirled, searching frantically for a link between these locations. I couldn't think of anything. But this had to be more than a mere coincidence.

Was Harry right about the drugs? Had I found the distribution path of some new drug the police hadn't recognized? Or was I right, and it was something entirely unexpected? Like a truck traveling down these roadways and intermittently leaking a toxic chemical? Or maybe it was a mail route or delivery truck route carrying terrorist biohazard-contaminated packages? Or maybe someone had tampered with food or pharmaceuticals delivered along these routes, like the Chicago Tylenol murders. What about a radiation leak that moved downwind, west to east?

I reviewed the dates of each case to see if there was also a chronological order associated with the geographical connection. No. They had all occurred within the last two years, but the dates appeared in random order along the two routes. I needed more information. I needed to go see for myself. Talk to people myself. Spend all my money on a hunch.

Interlude One

Last January: Taylock, Montana

Georgie Crow awoke to the scrape of the snow plow on her driveway. Tom, from Snow Movers, Inc., always did her drive first, and he liked to get an early start on his neighborhood rounds. The weather forecast must have been correct, but how much had they gotten? Enough to call off school? She wasn't going to complain, but the school officials wouldn't usually declare a snow day until five-thirty, and Tom's version of an alarm clock started at five.

Georgie decided to put the time to good use. All the papers were graded, but she still needed to enter the data online. She turned on her coffee maker and her computer.

Steven Oaks' paper was on the top of the pile. Steven was a typical fifth grader; spent more time thinking about sports, video games and movies than math. She glanced at his file in her records and noticed she still hadn't entered his make-up homework score from his last absence.

Georgie sighed. She wished her school's computer system was a little more up-to-date, so parents could log into their kid's file to view the progress report at will. Steven's mother would love that option. She was always sending in notes to make sure her son was on track. Too bad more parents didn't put that much effort into their child's education.

Georgie finished entering data by the time the school called. It was good news — a two-hour delay. She turned her attention to the TV and the local weatherman, cheerful and animated in front of the Montana map. Three inches had fallen during the night, more expected throughout the day, watch for more school closings as the day progressed. Not so great.

Georgie enjoyed her extra-long morning at home. She did a load of laundry and watched *Dial M for Murder* on TCM. She called her mom in Tucson, and compared weather.

Later, at school, Georgie greeted the students as they entered her room. Steven Oaks didn't reply to her, "Good morning," and she gave him a closer look. The boy's clothes were splattered with blood-red drops and he didn't meet her gaze.

"Steven, are you all right?" Georgie Crow asked. "What's happened?"

TAYLOCK, MONT. (AP): An unexplained shooting incident at Taylock Elementary School this morning has claimed the life of fifth grade teacher Georgia Crow, age 31. The alleged shooter was an 11-year-old student in Ms. Crow's class. The student, whose name is being withheld at this time, is reported to have turned the gun on himself after allegedly shooting Ms. Crow. He remains in critical condition at University Hospital. The police are investigating a connection to two bodies discovered this morning in a south side home.

Chapter 24

Tuesday: Charlestown, South Carolina

I waited in Harry's kitchen, studying the map. The two horizontal lines in striking red that connected the locations of the final fourteen cases meeting my inclusion criteria tickled my imagination. I pictured skulls and crossbones drawn in along the lines to capture everyone's attention. I heard Harry pulling into the garage and bounced up to meet him at the door.

"Okay, I'm here," he said. "What's so urgent?"

"Look at this! I've found something."

Harry tossed his overcoat and briefcase across the back of a kitchen chair, loosened his tie and took the map I waved in front of him.

"What's this?" he asked.

I pointed to the bold dots I'd marked on the map. "These are the locations of fourteen cases very similar to Mike and Ellen's. See how they line up?"

Harry studied the map. "Fourteen cases? That's all?"

"I sifted through hundreds, thousands probably. These are all that fit my profile."

"And exactly how did you end up with these?" he asked.

"Right, right. Okay. There's no motive, no prior history of violence, but a very gruesome death scene."

"That's . . . not much." He furrowed his brow and studied the map.

"Wait, there's more. The murderer in each case was a juvenile boy. It happened within the last two years. And, most committed suicide."

I stopped to take a breath. Harry tilted his head and raised his eyebrows. I quickly added, "Fourteen might not seem like many by itself, but then, when I decided I needed to go to each crime scene personally, I found this." I pointed to the atlas. "The biggest connection of all."

Harry continued to stare at the map. I watched him impatiently, knowing his legal mind considered all the implications. Finally, I couldn't stand it anymore.

"Well?" I asked. "What do you think?" I was practically jumping up and down.

"Could it be coincidental?"

"Oh, come on. How could it be a coincidence? There's got to be a connection."

Harry tipped his head to the right, turned the map to the side. "It looks that way." He studied the page a few minutes longer. "But I'd place money that if you picked any five cities in a straight line, you'd find violent crimes and get a map looking like this."

My mouth dropped open for a second, then I snorted. "Only if you look ass-backwards," I said. "Which I didn't. I got there from the other direction, altogether."

Harry chuckled, then belly laughed. "God, I've missed you, Lila."

I glared. He wasn't supposed to have missed me. He was supposed to have moved on.

"Are you going to publish it?" he asked.

I reacted from the gut. "Publish it? Now? I don't know anything else yet. I think it's too soon."

"But, if this is true, then people should know, and law enforcement should be told. You could be withholding evidence."

"Evidence of what? All I have is what's already in their files. I've got to fill in the story before going public."

Harry looked at the map again, then back at me. "How

long do you think it'll take you to visit each town, then locate and interview friends and relatives? Weeks? Months? You don't have a clue what you're looking for." He returned the atlas to me and pointed at it. "If you go public with this now, maybe more cases fitting your profile will turn up. Or someone might recognize the significance of these routes in some way you can't imagine. It'll still be your story, Lila. You're the one to discover the link."

"It's not that. Really. It's only . . . oh, I don't know . . . I guess I don't want to give families false hope — or worse, false fear. I need more facts."

"What if it happens again?" Harry asked. "And along those routes? Publish now and you might prevent additional killings. Prevent more suffering. Have you thought of that?"

It was a strange role reversal. Reporter holding out for more facts, lawyer pushing to publish. I sighed. "I've been thinking about nothing else all afternoon."

"Have you even shown this to Detective Turner?"

I shook my head and looked at the map. While the dots connected to make two straight lines, a lot of space remained in between points. I didn't want more dots filling up the lines. But what if I was wrong? What if it was only a crazy, improbable coincidence? On the other hand, what if I was right? Harry had a valid argument.

I had to publish.

"How about this," I proposed. "I'll convince McLeish to run this in tomorrow's paper, then, as soon as it's going to print, I'll text a copy of the map to Turner. Sound okay?"

Harry smiled and arched an eyebrow. "And, no one's going to scoop you. He won't even see it until morning."

I bowed. "Now, if I'm going to New York tonight, I'd better make my travel plans."

I ran out of the room to use my phone upstairs.

A little later I glanced up at Harry's knock on my open door.

"Yes," I said into the receiver, one eye on Harry and holding up my hand, "the eight o'clock to New York will be perfect. Can you book me on a flight out of New York tomorrow morning then, for Dwight, North Dakota? How about Fargo? Sure, that works. Great. Thank you."

I ended the call, suddenly wanting to celebrate. I jumped up from the bed and shocked us both by giving Harry a big hug.

"It's all arranged," I said. "Clunie's picking me up at the airport in New York and McLeish will wait for me at the office, then I'm off to do the on-location interviews. Keep an eye on Mike and Sophia for me, okay?"

Chapter 25

Tuesday: New York City

I found Clunie waiting for me in the arrivals pick-up zone at LaGuardia. Her black hair fell in choppy waves around her smiling face and she sported a new swirly web tattoo on her beckoning hand. I gave her a hug.

"Thanks for meeting me," I said. "Like the new tat."

"Oh, yeah, the guys voted it best of the week," she said. "I was inspired by O'Connell's web of deceit."

By "the guys" Clunie meant *The Ink Marks*, most of whom were associated with *The Morning Star*. They met frequently to explain and dwell on the meaning behind their tattoos, while drinking lots of alcohol. I have often declined offers to join the fun. My single tattoo is hidden from the world and not a subject for some cathartic group Rorschach test. I know why it's there and that's good enough.

We climbed into her car and she continued, "He was such a crook. I've tracked at least seventy small companies that were in his pocket. I'd never heard of any of them."

She started listing companies and I zoned out.

"Golden Donuts, Fresh Veggies, Amalgamated Recovery Products, Wizard Sewer Cleaners. Crazy, huh? I mean, who cleans their sewer?"

She didn't need an answer and I didn't have one anyway, so I changed the subject. "Thanks for your help with my research."

"No problem, Lila. My karmic joy magnified like awesome since you passed on the Senator story. I still owe you. Can I see your map?"

I'd told her about my death map when I'd called earlier asking for a ride from the airport to McLeish's office. I opened the atlas and pointed out the highlights. She traced the red trail on the map with a blood red fingernail. Then her hand started to quiver and she curled it into a fist, then started the car.

"Be careful, girlfriend. There's evil on this route."

She shifted into drive and pulled out into traffic.

"Any news on your godson's condition?" she asked.

"No change. Tomorrow will mark two weeks. His doctor's moving him to an extended care facility." I stared out the window at the city skyline. Would Mike ever get to be a normal kid again? I dared not plan on moving him into my apartment, finding a school. "His prognosis is poor, but I'm hopeful."

I didn't sound hopeful and Clunie, bless her, let it ride.

The flight time had given me the opportunity to prepare my pitch to McLeish and punch out the article I hoped he would publish. When I entered the building, I sent the article to my designated office printer. As promised, my editor was waiting in his office when I arrived, the map and notes that I'd sent to him before I left Charleston were spread out before him.

I placed the finished article on his desk and paced the floor while McLeish read. When he put it down, he looked at me so intently I stopped pacing.

"You're certain of these facts?"

It was more of a statement than a question, so I only nodded.

"And you've talked to the investigating officer in each case?"

I launched into my argument. "No, not all of them. Like I say in the article. I arrived at these cases by process of elimination." I ticked off the criteria on my fingers. "First, there was no apparent motive. Second, the kids were, by all accounts, totally normal. And third, the killings were excessively violent and bloody. It wasn't until later that I noticed the geographical pattern. I've checked and rechecked my thinking. There's definitely something weird going on with these routes."

He picked up the map and studied it for a moment. "I like it. We'll run it tomorrow." He made a call to the copy room and ordered space for the article.

Yes. I silently rejoiced. I hadn't expected it to be that easy, but I knew this map would grab everyone's attention. Hopefully, Harry would be right. Someone out there might see the connection that eluded me.

If there was a connection.

I couldn't get that nagging thought out of the back of my mind. I thanked McLeish and then remembered I intended to turn a copy of the map and data over to Detective Turner.

McLeish raised a shoulder. "Probably a good idea," he said. "It'll keep you on good terms with the locals."

I turned to leave his office, but paused when he called out after me.

"This is going to bring in lots of letters and phone calls, you know. If you're taking off again tomorrow, you'll need to find someone to cover here for you."

I glanced into the pressroom. The place was nearly deserted. Buzz Bradley, though, was at his desk, watching me emerge from the boss's office.

"Bradley's already been in on this story, somewhat," McLeish said, following my gaze. "See if he'll cover at this end, okay?"

Buzz? He's got to be kidding. "What about Clunie?" I asked. "She helped gather the research."

McLeish shook his head. "I've got her on something else." He shouted, "Bradley, over here."

My heart sank.

"Yes, boss?" Buzz was at the doorway in two beats.

"Fill him in, Kincaid." A copy boy pushed past me to get to the editor and McLeish waved us out the door.

I sighed and motioned Buzz to follow me. I led the way toward his desk. He rushed ahead of me and punched at his keyboard, clearing off his computer screen while trying to cover up whatever was lying undone on his desk. *He must think I'm after his current story.* The thought almost made me smile.

I glanced at Buzz's desktop, spying an open notebook next to the computer. Too bad I couldn't read upside down. Buzz slid the notebook into a drawer.

"Home from Charleston?" he asked. "Finally get enough Southern hospitality?"

"Nope, just missed your pretty face," I said. "McLeish has volunteered you to help me with a story."

He pulled the notebook back out of the drawer it had so hastily been thrust into, never taking his eyes off me.

"No kidding?"

"Sad, but true. One thing though, before I tell you the details," I said, folding my arms across my chest, "I want you to understand that Clunie's my first choice to work on this story. The big guy picked you, but I won't have someone trying to sabotage my job behind my back."

Buzz's mouth dropped open. "Nobody'd do that to you, Lila."

"Well, I know you were in contact with that reporter, Ronan, from Charleston, trying to stir up shit with McLeish, and it didn't work. I'm still here. McLeish wants you on this for some reason, so listen up."

I described my initial theory and the journey through hundreds of cases until there were merely fourteen that resembled my friends' situation. Then I showed him the map that was going to be in the next day's edition and gave him a copy of the article that would accompany it.

Buzz let out a low whistle. "Wow, that's weird. Sure it's not coincidence?"

"Reasonably certain."

"So what do I do?"

"Take calls. Read the mail," I said. "I'll check in daily and we can go over everything. I may want you to do follow-up if something interesting comes in, okay?"

"Sure, Lila, it's your show."

"Damn straight," I said. "And don't forget it."

I suspected he was hatching a plan already. Was this some sort of McLeish punishment? But, then, how could Buzz mess up opening the mail?

Chapter 26

After detailing specific duties to Buzz, I returned to my apartment and tried to sleep. I had an early flight to Fargo, North Dakota, and would only get five hours if I fell asleep right away. But I was too restless. I closed my eyes and my thoughts churned between the excitement of my discovery of the map, to my fears regarding the meaning of the map, to my fears for my ward's future. How could I care for a twelve-year-old when I traveled so much? What would I do if he didn't return to normal?

When I accepted that sleep was out of the question, I pulled out my case files and read them over again. It hadn't been hard to choose which crime scene to visit first. The case against Manny Karlsson was eerily similar to Mike's. I had interviewed the Dwight County sheriff, Matthias Karlsson, over the phone. Manny was the sheriff's nephew.

Sheriff Karlsson had been hesitant to discuss the case until I explained my theory about a possible external factor affecting the children's behavior. Then his response surprised me.

"I knew it!" he said. "Something was messing up that boy's mind. He was worried about it himself, too, but didn't know what to do."

"How do you know that?" I'd asked.

"I got a letter from Manny the day after the murder. I wish to God it'd arrived earlier," he said softly. "Maybe they'd all still be here."

"What'd he say in the letter?"

Instead of telling me, Sheriff Karlsson texted me a copy. I reread the letter.

Dear Uncle Mats,

Something is wrong with me. Something in my mind. Mom says it's nothing, just becoming a teenager. She can't understand, or she'd be very worried. I'm worried. I have these sharp pains in my head, and I sometimes hear things. The worst is the terrible, terrible thoughts. I'm really scared. Can you talk to mom for me? Please help me, Uncle Mats!

Love,

Manny

It was poignant, indeed. I understood the sheriff. He needed to have a reason — and here I was, offering the hope of one.

Chapter 27

Wednesday Destination: Dwight, North Dakota

When I deplaned at the airport in Fargo, North Dakota, Wednesday morning, a man towered above the gate attendant and held a small sign card bearing my name. I smiled. There were fewer than thirty passengers getting off at this stop.

"Hi," I said. "I'm Lila Kincaid." We shook hands.

"Matthias Karlsson. Nice to meet you. Hope you don't mind, Ms. Kincaid," he said with an aw-shucks grin on his weathered face. "I'm not busy today, and well, truthfully, I've been anxious to speak with you. Thought I'd save you having to rent a car."

"Thank you, Sheriff. I don't mind at all."

He tossed the name card into the trash and touched the thick gray hair over his forehead in a salute to the gate attendant. "Did you bring any luggage?" he asked me.

"Only this carry-on," I said. "I've got a room for tonight near the airport. I fly out again tomorrow morning bright and early."

"Think you can get everything done in one day?"

"I'm flexible. If I need another day, I'll change flight plans."

"I thought you might want to interview Kurt and Dawn's neighbor. She found their bodies and knew the family real well. Her son was a good friend of Manny's."

"Okay," I said. "Do you think I could speak with their son, also?"

"I'll arrange it. I made copies of that article you emailed over and passed it around to some interested parties, including our county coroner. He wants to meet you, by the way. Also, I set up an appointment with Manny's aunt on his mother's side. She was one of the last people to speak with him. Hope you don't mind going for a walk with her. She's kinda fanatical about those walks, I think. But anyway, you'll go right by where he was found."

I agreed again. The drive to Dwight would take about forty minutes. The sheriff traveled this far in order to talk with me, but he was quiet as we headed out of town. His thumbs beat rapidly on the steering wheel.

"Want to tell me about that day?" I asked, trying to prompt a conversation.

The sheriff glanced over at me and gave a slow nod, but continued to play his nervous thumb melody for another minute. Finally, he launched into a description of the afternoon his brother and sister-in-law were found murdered.

"A call came in from Sherry McIntyre. She sounded hysterical and I couldn't understand what she meant. I thought she was describing a wreck. She kept sobbing, 'They're dead. They're dead. There's blood everywhere.'"

His thumbs continued to beat on the steering wheel as he talked. "Eventually, I realized Sherry was talking about a kitchen. My brother's kitchen. So, I rushed out to Kurt and Dawn's place as fast as I could. They were both dead at the scene, but Manny, their thirteen-year-old son, was nowhere to be found."

I could sense his agitation increase with the slight increase in the car's speed. The sheriff stared straight ahead. "At first," he said, "I feared the boy'd been abducted and was in danger or dead also. We found bloody footprints leading from the kitchen to the outside stairs and through the grass. But as the investigation progressed, evidence against my nephew mounted. There was only one set of footprints, and they were probably Manny's. Also, his shotgun was missing. It didn't seem possible. He was a great kid, Ms. Kincaid, but we were forced to conclude that Manny murdered his parents and ran away."

"I'm sorry for your loss," I said. It sounded inadequate. Then silence filled the car and I stared out the window, thinking about his version of events and how it compared with the account in my file.

Gradually, the view from the car window seeped into my consciousness. There was no traffic to speak of, or houses, for that matter. No trees, but miles of wind farms. The turbines sprang up from tall, lush prairie grass, often surrounded by cattle. Every now and then I'd spot an antelope visible only for a moment before the ground dipped behind another rolling hill and it vanished from sight. This was my first trip through the plains, and the scenery was unexpected. Alien, but beautiful in a way all its own.

We pulled into Dwight, North Dakota. The tiny town seemed to have been randomly plopped down in the middle of nowhere. There were all the small-town features that I recognized from my own upbringing in the Midwest: barbershop, tanning parlor, pizza joint, churches.

Next to the school stood the community center, which the sheriff pointed out housed his office. He pulled to a stop in front of the adjacent building. The sign on the door identified it as the office of Clifton D. Elliot, M.D.

"Let's visit Doc Elliot first," Sheriff Karlsson said. "I told him we'd stop by. He's the coroner."

The receptionist escorted us into the doctor's private office. I sat in a comfortable cloth-covered chair in front of a mahogany desk. The sheriff paced the room.

"Doc, this here's Ms. Kincaid, the New York reporter I told you about," the sheriff said as a man with ram-rod posture entered the room.

I stood and greeted the physician. I tried not to stare at the dime-sized black age spot that disturbed the smooth surface of his bald head. "Dr. Elliot? Nice to meet you. I understand you're the town's physician and coroner."

"Yes, Ms. Kincaid, I have that dubious honor. Please, sit back down. Mats, quit pacing and sit down, too.

"Now, Ms. Kincaid," Dr. Elliot continued, after seating himself behind the massive desk, "I know our sheriff here has explained about the letter he received from his nephew, but let me assure you that extensive toxicology was performed and nothing turned up. What was left of his brain looked normal at autopsy."

"Have you read my article, Dr. Elliot?"

His heavy sigh sent coffee-soured breath my way. "Yes, Mats provided me with a copy, and I agree the way those cases line up's peculiar. But I'm not convinced that statistically. . ."

"Well," I interrupted, "my editor had a statistician check it out last night. He tells me that the geographical data *is* statistically significant. If we were looking at highly populated areas, it'd be a different matter. But these cases run across sparsely populated parts of the country."

"Still," the doctor said, "Manny wasn't murdered. He committed suicide. It's hard to imagine someone or something forcing him to do that. I'm not sure what you're out here looking for, but it's not going to do anyone here any good to blow this way out of proportion. It might give your career a boost, but have you considered at what expense?"

"Now, hold on a minute." I stood up. "I have a personal connection to one of the crimes on that map. I'd never use that horror to further my own career."

"Don't get your dander up, young lady. That's it, sit back down there. Surely you know as well as I do that as soon as this paper hits the stands today, I'll be getting calls from frantic parents. Ridiculous, but they'll be calling."

"I know," I said. "But maybe they should be frantic. This

132

whole thing is scary. But this is not about me. It's about my godchild. He turned into one of the murdering lunatics."

The doctor leaned back in his chair, folded his arms across his chest and looked from me to the sheriff.

"I'm sorry, Ms. Kincaid," he said. "I really wish I could help. And you, too, Mats. But I don't have any more information about Manny Karlsson than what I reported at the inquest."

His gaze, heavy with certainty, bounced from me to the sheriff and back again. There was nothing more to learn here. The sheriff and I left.

"I'm sorry about that, Ms. Kincaid," Sheriff Karlsson said when we reached the car. "I hope he hasn't changed your mind about looking into Manny's case."

"Hell, no," I said. "Every coroner I've interviewed over the phone so far has felt about the same as your Doc Elliot. If anything, they've made me more determined than ever. I'm going to find out what connects these cases, clear the names of these kids, and put the blame on whoever or whatever is responsible. The neighbor's next, right?" I got into the passenger's seat.

"Right."

He headed the car out of town, toward the home of his brother's neighbors, Sherry and Mabry McIntyre.

"Have you been out there since the murders?" I asked.

"A time or two. Not often. Not if I can help it."

The sheriff was quiet until we pulled into a gravel driveway. Dust rolled up from the tires and swirled around my window, settling in at the base of the glass to form a pattern of little waves. I thought it was similar to the way the information on the cases settled in to form a pattern. But was it meaningful, or just a layer of dirt? I considered my attitude at Doc Elliot's. I had sounded so confident, almost haughty. But what if I was wrong? What if there was nothing connecting these cases at all? I wasn't worried about the embarrassment of a retraction, although it would be tough. I glanced at Sheriff Karlsson. I was worried about promising too much to people who needed an explanation.

I peered out the window at the two-story white farmhouse, neatly perched on a small rise at the end of the drive. Tiny red buds covered the two small trees in the front yard. The house overlooked miles of undulating grassland being grazed by cattle. Off to the side of the house was a pond and two red barns, a silo, two rusty green tractors and various pieces of farm equipment I couldn't identify. Sheriff Karlsson opened his car door and stepped out. I did the same, and immediately crinkled up my nose at the acrid odor that greeted me.

"The smell is silage, the rumble is the turbines," he said. "You get used to it."

A woman in jeans and a floral tee came out of the front door of the house and walked over to greet us.

"Hi," the woman said. "I'm Sherry."

"Lila Kincaid," I answered. "Thanks for seeing me."

"Well, when Matthias asked, I didn't hesitate. This whole thing has been horrible, like a nightmare where we never wake up. We can't imagine what could've made Manny go off crazy like that. Matthias seems to think you'll figure it out."

I glanced at the sheriff, who was watching me.

"I'm going to try," I said. "Would you mind telling me about Manny? What sort of kid he was? What he liked to do for fun? That sort of thing."

Sherry pushed back a strand of blond hair.

"Sure, but let's go inside. Have some lemonade."

She led us through a side door into the kitchen and motioned for us to take seats around the table. A ceramic rooster, beak open in silent crow, centered the table. Mrs. McIntyre remained standing and began her story.

"The Karlsson house is about a quarter of a mile that way." She pointed out the window over the sink. "They were our closest neighbors. Next ones are about ten miles further out. Mabry, my husband, and I grew up with Kurt and Dawn. And with the boys being the same age, we got to see each other a lot. Manny was over here, or our David was over there, nearly every day from the time they were big enough to ride bikes that far."

I pulled my notebook out of my bag. This woman was going to give me better stuff than Doc Elliot.

"He was a good boy," Sherry said. "Liked hunting, fishing, riding horses, same as my son. Never was any trouble out of that one."

She turned, reached up into the cabinet over the stove, and brought down three glasses. "I remember the last time he was over here," she continued. "It was only two nights before it happened. Mabry had promised to take a day off from the mine as soon as it warmed up a little, and take the boys camping along the river. They couldn't talk about anything else.

"It was cold that morning," she continued. Her voice shifted to a huskier tone. "It'd snowed some in the early morning hours, but there was a hint of spring in the air. My daffodils were just poking up through the ground. I seem to remember hearing two shotgun blasts coming from that direction the evening before." Mrs. McIntyre gave a slight nod toward the kitchen window. "But I never gave it any thought. Manny and Kurt were often target shooting, you know. This here ain't the city, Ms. Kincaid. All the ranchers have guns. We need 'em, and learn how to use 'em early. Have to be able to control the coyotes and prairie dogs."

She put big chunks of ice in the glasses and poured lemonade out of a brown stoneware pitcher. The ice cracked like shotgun blasts echoing across the field on a cold evening.

"I'd been trying to reach Dawn by phone for an hour, but no one answered. I could see her car in the drive, so I thought she must be working outside and couldn't hear the phone. I didn't suspect anything was wrong. Not at all."

I followed her gaze out the kitchen window. The Karlsson house was easily visible across the empty landscape. No car in the driveway today.

"So, I decided I'd go on over there and visit her in person," she said. "I had to return a book of her's I'd finished reading, anyway."

Sherry McIntyre turned away from the window and wiped off the kitchen counter with a blue and white checkered dishtowel. There couldn't have been a spot of dirt left on that counter top, but she kept wiping. Then she turned to look at me, wringing the towel between her hands. Her voice shook when she finally continued.

"I pulled into the drive, not thinking anything was wrong. Until I spotted the back door standing wide open. That wasn't right, you know? It was too cold yet to leave the door open. I started walking faster up to the house, calling out Dawn's name."

Mrs. McIntyre stopped speaking momentarily and closed her eyes. Tension was visible in the lines on her face.

"They were there," she continued, nearly whispering now. "Dawn and Kurt, or what was left of them, anyway. I screamed, And screamed. I couldn't help myself, or them. I ran to my car, but had left my cell at home. Somehow I drove home and called the sheriff. I don't remember doing it, but I know I did."

The kitchen went quiet except for the occasional chinking of ice in the lemonade glasses.

"I can still see the blood splattered on the walls whenever I . . . well, it's hard to sleep." Her voice cracked and she swallowed.

Matthias moved across the kitchen and put his arm around Mrs. McIntyre. "I'm sorry to make you go through all this again, Sherry."

She wiped her eyes and nodded curtly. "Well, Mats, I go

through it in my mind every day. Saying it out loud isn't any different. Hope this time, it'll help."

"I hope so, too," I said. "Is it possible to speak with David? I'd like to know if Manny said or did anything out of the ordinary those last couple of days."

"He's out in the barn. I'll go call him."

Mrs. McIntyre left the kitchen and I jotted down a few more notes. I noticed out of the corner of my eye that the sheriff had moved over to stand in front of the kitchen window. I glanced up at him. He was staring out across the pasture toward his brother's house. He stood there staring, silent, until Mrs. McIntyre returned with her son.

David was blond like his mother, almost as tall as the sheriff and built as solidly.

"David," I said, "I'm sorry. I know this'll be difficult. Could you tell me about the last few days of Manny's life? Can you remember anything unusual about them?"

"It's been over a year, you know," the boy said, looking thoughtful. "I don't know. He was about the same as always, I'd guess."

"Your mom mentioned a camping trip. Did you spend some time talking about it? Was he expecting to go?"

"Sure, why not? Oh, I see. Yeah, we talked about it. He was even going to buy a new sleeping bag. Don't know why. His wasn't that old, and still in good shape. Said he'd sleep better in a red one. I never knew him to be so particular before, come to think of it."

"How'd he get along with his parents?"

"Okay. They never had any big problems. Ever. His folks were super nice people, and he thought so, too. I don't know why it happened."

"Did he smoke or drink?"

David glanced up at Sheriff Karlsson, then met my eyes.

"Never. Look, I don't know what happened. He was just

like me." He paused, then repeated softer, "Just like me." The boy shook his head slowly. "And look what he did. No one ever thought such a thing could happen here."

He stopped speaking and his mother put an arm around him.

"I'm sorry," he continued. "I wish I knew more, but I can't help you. I wish I could explain why he did it, but I don't know."

"Only one more question, David, and I'll be done," I said. "Sheriff Karlsson received a letter from Manny. It didn't arrive until after the killings, but in it Manny wrote that he was afraid something was wrong with him. Did he ever mention anything like that to you?"

"No." David paled and turned on Sheriff Karlsson. "Why didn't you tell me? What did he say was wrong?"

"There wasn't any more to it than that, son," the sheriff said. "He mentioned sharp pains in his head. Did he ever complain of headaches?"

David thought for a moment. "No." He turned to his mother and I saw pain in his eyes. "Why didn't he tell us if something was wrong? Maybe he was too sick to know what he was doing."

She tightened her arm around him. "Maybe," she whispered, then turned to me. "I hope you can find an answer, Ms. Kincaid."

She and I both.

Chapter 28

My next interview, also pre-arranged by Sheriff Karlsson, was with Madeline McGuire, sister of the murdered woman, Dawn Karlsson. Madeline worked as a teller at the local bank and was one of the last people to talk to Manny before his killing spree. She had also found her nephew's body.

By the time the sheriff drove me back into town, the bank was closed. "There she is," Sheriff Karlsson said, pointing to a woman standing inside the bank's doorway.

"You say she found Manny's body while she was out hiking?" I asked.

"More or less," the sheriff replied. "I'll let her tell you about it. Sure you don't mind a walk?"

"I'd love a walk."

The woman came out the bank's front doors, checked the lock behind her, and then walked toward the sheriff's car. She wore a jogging suit and carried a gym bag.

"Hi, Mats," she said.

"Madeline, this is Ms. Lila Kincaid, from New York. She wrote that article about the Death Map that I showed you."

"Hi," Madeline said. "Nice to meet you. Mats said you'd be up for a walk."

"I'm ready."

"Guess we'll take my car over to the trail. Want me to drop her at your office when we're done?"

"That'll be fine," he said. "About an hour, then?"

Madeline smiled her assurance.

"Thanks, Sheriff Karlsson," I said, and followed Madeline.

"You know, Ms. Kincaid," Madeline said, once we were settled in her car, "that map of yours makes us all a little nervous."

"Call me Lila, please. And I'm a little nervous about the implications, myself. And I'm sorry for the loss of your loved ones."

"Thank you. So, I guess you're here to pick our brains for ideas?"

"You could say that. By the way, I'm glad you suggested exercise. I've done nothing but sit all week."

"Well, this isn't anything strenuous, and it has fresh air as a bonus."

"The sheriff tells me you go jogging every day. How do you find the time?"

"I'm desperate. My youngest child is already two and I can't lose this last ten pounds." Madeline patted her abdomen. "So, I started this new exercise routine. Every afternoon after work, I hike around the high school cross-country track. Usually, I pick up my three kids from day care and take them along."

"Three kids? Wow. That must be a circus."

Madeline laughed. "For sure, especially when you throw in our dog."

"So were the kids with you the day you found the body?"

"No, thank God," Madeline replied. She parked the car and we got out. "We start over here." She pointed her head toward a grassy track. "And I didn't exactly find the body."

Madeline started jogging at a slow pace. I kept even with her, thankful I'd worn sneakers on this trip. Madeline explained how the track was laid out as two loops. A smaller, half-mile loop near the school encircled the soccer field and the football practice field. We started and finished on it. The larger, one-mile loop, due west of the smaller loop, encircled a tract of undeveloped, school-owned property that was bisected by high-intensity power lines. Undulating prairie bordered the large loop to the north and west, and the old railroad tracks to the south. At two points along the path, the backs of farmhouses could be seen, but otherwise anyone using the larger loop was almost invisible to the world.

"As much as I love to bring my kids out here," Madeline said, "I can't jog when they're along. So, I come out occasionally by myself to relax and unwind."

"I don't have time for anything like this," I said, already noticing a change in my breathing. "I usually try and sort my life out in the shower. Most of the time, I just end up waterlogged. When exactly does this 'walk' become a walk?"

"Soon. So, you want to know about the day I found the boot?"

"I thought you stumbled over the body out here," I said. The words came out in short bursts. No doubt about it, I was officially out of shape. I needed to quit talking if I wasn't going to totally humiliate myself and pass out or something.

"Well, it wasn't exactly the whole body," Madeline said.

"Care if I record this?"

Madeline shrugged. "Go ahead, if you'd like. I don't have much to tell, though. I remember it had been a tough day at work. I had to count my money drawer three times to balance. That never happened before, and I was stressed to the max." She waved a hand over the top of her head.

"A solitary trip around the track was definitely in order. I rushed to pick the kids up before the day care closed. Then went home, fed Joe — my husband — and the kids, and returned to the track."

"What time was that?"

"After seven. It was getting dark and Joe insisted I take a flashlight and our dog for company. But don't worry," she added in response to my furtive glance over my shoulder. "Nothing would attack us during the day. Besides, since that night, I always carry my gun."

I noticed she slowed her pace the more she talked. With luck, we'd be walking by the time I had to come up with the energy to ask another question.

Madeline continued with her story. "By the time I reached the track, night had fallen, with a cloudless sky and a full moon rising. A beautiful night. I could see well enough to jog the smaller loop, and Thunder, that's our black lab, tagged along behind. I always focus on rhythmic breathing: three breaths in, three out; three breaths in, three out. Concentration is key. I don't allow myself to look up the trail any farther than my next immediate steps. If I even look ahead to calculate how close I'm getting to the corner, I'll feel the pain, wimp out, and stop.

"I still can't jog the big loop," Madeline admitted, slowing to a walk and holding her hands on her sides, breathing big gulps of air as we reached the end of the small loop. "You seem to be doing okay, though."

I gasped. "You've . . . been talking. Makes a difference."

"Well, I slowed to a walk right here that evening." Madeline continued walking, but looked around. She pointed to a spot ahead. "About there, Thunder ran off the grassy trail into the brush to follow some animal smell. I knew he'd pop back out onto the trail before long, to check on me . . . you know, usual dog stuff."

I'd never had a dog, so I didn't know. We rounded the corner, entering the big-loop portion of the track and were immediately faced with a steep climb. Neither of us spoke until we crested the hill.

"Only steep spot in the county," Madeline said, "and I

still can't jog it."

"Thanks for that," I said, words interspersed with breaths.

We walked in silence for a few more minutes, recording only my mouth-breathing.

"Manny was my only nephew," she finally said. "My older sister's boy. A great kid. My own kids loved him and looked up to him. I'm trying to keep the details of the murder from them. We just say they all died in an accident. I dread the day when they hear the specifics. Small town, you know. Bound to happen."

"It's too gruesome for kids to understand," I said.

"Well, I don't understand it, either. Kurt, my brother-in-law, brought Manny to the bank every week. That morning, Manny made a deposit to his savings. He seemed entirely normal."

"So, he had a job?"

"With Kurt on the farm. Got a paycheck every week."

"But he was depositing his money, not taking any out for a getaway?" I said.

"Yeah. I said the same thing to Mats. I don't think it was premeditated at all. If he planned to kill his parents and run away, he would've cleaned out his savings. He had enough to travel a long way and make a new start, if that's what was on his mind."

"Did he say anything unusual at all?"

"No, nothing. Just his usual 'See ya later, Aunt Maddie. Say hi to the kids.'"

"How much time passed between his disappearance and your finding the body?"

"About two weeks, and I didn't exactly find the body."

"What exactly did you find?" I asked.

Madeline returned to her story of that fateful walk. That night, the combination of eerie shadows from the moonlight and the scurrying noises from the brush along both sides of the track had made her jumpy. She never noticed that much movement going on in there during the daytime. Most noises were probably nocturnal rodents. No comforting explanation was on hand for the occasional big rustle. She contemplated the list of possible predators in the area. There were always reports of coyotes, and occasionally someone would claim to've seen a wolf or mountain lion. She wondered where Thunder was, but didn't want to shatter the night noises with her voice. She turned on the flashlight and held the handle in a death-grip, imagining how satisfying it would feel to smack it into the side of a predator's head.

"I've always had a vivid imagination," Madeline said. "Then, as I neared the final turn on this big loop of the track, I saw Thunder's silhouette on the trail ahead of me, sitting, waiting.

"I sort of whisper-called to him, not wanting my voice to attract the attention of anything bigger than a mouse. Thunder held a large object in his mouth. He saw me, stood up and trotted along the trail ahead of and away from me.

"I called to him again, louder." Madeline said. "This time he stopped, turned back to look at me, dropped what he was carrying, and waited with his tail wagging until I was almost within reach. Then he grabbed up the thing and ran off ahead. I ran, too, and finally caught up with him at the junction of the two loops. I stopped and leaned down to pet him. I guess I was still feeling jumpy, because I wanted to hold onto his collar to make him walk beside me the rest of the way. Canine comfort, you know. Works wonders." She glanced at me and her mouth twitched downward.

"It was then I recognized the thing Thunder'd been carrying. It was a boot. He'd dropped it in the tall grass and it was lying on its side. I could see a black smooth sole, pointy toe and chunky heel — a cowboy boot. All the men in this area wear them."

"Was it Manny's?" I asked.

"It was. But I didn't know it at the time. Anyway, I held onto Thunder's collar and used my foot to kick the boot off the path into the brush, scolding Thunder about trying to drag the thing home. As the boot rolled over, I noticed a cloud of bugs lifting into the air, revealing something white sticking out the top of the boot, before they settled back down. I leaned over and shined my flashlight on it for a closer look."

She crumpled up her face. "I was hit with the most disgusting odor I've ever smelled in my life. That's when I realized what was still left in that boot."

"Oh, my God," I said. "How awful."

"Yes. Well, I practically dragged Thunder back to the car where I dialed nine-one-one on my cell. I shook so badly I could barely get the correct numbers punched in. I was practically incoherent, out of breath, trembling. It was so grotesque, I couldn't quite explain it over the phone. The dispatcher did his best to calm me down, told me to remain in my car, a unit was in the area and could be at the high school parking lot in five minutes. He kept me talking until the officers arrived."

Madeline stopped walking and looked questioningly at me. "Care to do the small loop again? I've got a little more to my story."

"Was that two miles already?" Disoriented, I looked around and spotted Madeline's car parked directly in front of us. "Wow. Uh, sure, if we just walk."

The grim lines around Madeline's mouth slipped into a hint of a smile but returned as we continued walking and she resumed her narrative. "I'd calmed down a bit by the time the police car pulled into the parking area, four or five minutes later. The dispatcher'd asked me questions that made me realize the wearer of the boot couldn't have died that day or the leg wouldn't be in that state of decay. Also, I'd not met anyone on the path and there'd been no other cars parked in the area, so, the dispatcher reasoned it was unlikely that a killer was on the scene. All the same, as soon as I hung up with him, I called Joe. He took the kids over to our neighbor's and came right over.

"The police officers were friends of Joe's, and I could tell they didn't totally believe my story. They wanted me to show them where I'd seen the boot. I wanted to wait until Joe arrived, but they were impatient and said he'd be able to find us. I put Thunder on his leash and led them as far as the point where my flashlight beam picked up the boot lying at the edge of the track. Once the officers spotted it, I wasn't going to walk any closer. It looked evil, the way it lay there with all that writhing going on inside. Thunder seriously wanted to get it again and it took all my strength to hold him back, which helped to distract me a little, I guess.

"One officer, Mark Reynolds, tipped the boot into an upright position with his foot. I heard his disgust when he saw what was inside. Mark pulled out his mobile radio and notified Mats.

"About then I heard Joe. He was on the trail, calling my name. I yelled back and ran to meet him when he came into view. The officers walked over to us, greeted Joe, and told him what they'd seen. A leg and foot stuck in a boot."

"Did they suggest it was your nephew's?" I asked.

"Sure. Manny was the only missing person in the area that we knew of, so naturally his name came up."

"Did you help search for the rest of the body?"

"Oh, hell, no," Madeline said. "I was so shook up they let me go home. Joe drove me, then he came back later and helped with the search."

We walked in silence for bit. Then Madeline said, "Why are you doing this story?"

"My godson is one of those on the Death Map. I guess I need an answer."

We walked in silence for a few minutes before Madeline responded.

"Feel the wind blowing through the grass?" she asked. "It's cleansing, don't you think? In the summer you can smell honeysuckle and there'll be a hint of wild rose. I love it. I don't come here after dark anymore, but during the daylight, I can almost forget about that evening."

"It is beautiful out here," I agreed.

"Are you married, Lila? Have kids?"

"No."

"Boyfriend?"

"Not at the moment." Then I heard myself tell this woman I'd met less than one hour earlier, all about Harry. Secrets I hadn't even told Ellen. Why I didn't have kids, couldn't ever have them.

"Tell him," she said.

Maybe Harry and I should go for a long walk.

Chapter 29

Thursday: Toomsboro, Alabama

I included Toomsboro, a little town in Alabama, on my Death Map because of the horrendous crime committed by twelve-year-old Victor Allen. I used my travel time from North Dakota to Toomsboro to ponder the similarities between Manny Karlsson's case and what I already knew about Victor Allen's. I recalled my previsit phone conversation with Officer Andie Compton of the Toomsboro Police Department. Officer Compton had been the main investigator on the Allen case. Although a year had passed since the brutal murder/suicide, the detective was clear on the details.

"We did a damn good job investigating," Officer Compton told me. "Don't get much opportunity to use our skills here, but we have 'em, don't think we don't. The boy's steps were detailed in blood at the scene. Stabbed his sister, then sliced the throats of both parents. Killed Mom in her bed, Dad on the sofa.

"Took the boy awhile to die," she added. "We found him, wrists slit, sitting on the floor next to the sofa. Lots of blood. Blood tells the story plain as anything."

Officer Compton had been unwilling to scan any documents for me but agreed to let me read through the Allen case file if I came out in person; so, when I reached Toomsboro, my first stop was police headquarters. As promised, I had as long as needed to read the file, take notes, or even photograph, as long as the file remained at the station.

Victor Allen had been an above-average student, active in

a variety of school sports, and well-liked by everyone. I knew as much from newspaper accounts of the murder/suicide. He fit all the necessary criteria to make it into my select little group of crimes.

Even with Officer Compton's warning, I was shocked by the graphic crime scene photographs. The kid must have bled completely out. After looking at all the images, I took a bathroom break for a cold splash of water to the face. I almost didn't recognize myself in the mirror. I looked grim and exhausted, but I was as determined as ever.

Officer Compton lingered in the hallway as I emerged from the restroom.

"Looking for me?" I asked.

Officer Compton glanced from me to the restroom door and back. "Wasn't sure how you'd take those pictures."

I took a deep breath. "It was tough, no doubt about it. I'm fine, though. Thanks."

Compton answered a beep on her shoulder mic and moved on down the hallway. I returned to my task. Several letters to the editor, neatly clipped out of the local paper, were included in the Allen case file. I glanced through them, noting the level of community shock and horror. I was surprised, however, by one letter urging the introduction of yearly mandatory psychological testing for all students above the fifth grade due to the "growing problem in our country of psychopathic children."

Officer Compton had written a comment in her report regarding the letters to the editor. *Rumors of kids turning into psychos right and left. Fear level's rising among the civs. Intervention recommended.*

The residents were fearful. Worried about some unknown factor causing Victor Allen to crack. And what kind of intervention was Officer Compton suggesting? I felt a stab of guilt. What if all I accomplished was to resurrect that fear?

I gulped. Too late now for second thoughts. I made a note of the contact information of everyone the police had interviewed, and returned the file to the police officer.

"What'd I tell you?" Officer Compton asked. "We were damned thorough."

"Yes, you were," I agreed. "Except, I didn't find the boy's autopsy report. One was done, wasn't it?"

"Of course." Officer Compton smiled for the first time since I'd arrived. "We can investigate, but we can't file for shit." She walked over to a file cabinet, which had a foot-high pile of folders stacked on top. She rifled through them. "Here you go."

I took the document and read it closely. Tox screen was negative for drugs and alcohol. But there was a log-in number for blood and tissue samples that had been saved.

"I'll just snap this and I'll be done," I said, holding up my phone for the pic. "Thanks for your help. Oh, one more thing. You recommended intervention to prevent a panic among the civilians? What kind of intervention did you have in mind, and has anything been done?"

Officer Compton lost the smile. "Superiors didn't care for my suggestions. Just make your copies and be on your way."

I left the police station, checked into the only motel in town, installed my laptop and began my calls to all the police contacts. Since there weren't any close relatives remaining, I'd decided early on to go to the school, as I'd done in Charleston with Mike's teachers and fellow students. I phoned the Middle School and the principal agreed to allow a meeting with some of Victor Allen's teachers at the end of the school day in the teacher's lounge. I also reached the mother of Doug Spencer, one of Victor's friends, and arranged to meet with mother and son after school at their home. I felt a sense of déjà vu and suspected this would be the formula for my on-site investigations here on out.

I had an hour to spare before my meeting at the school. Not enough time for a nap, but time for a call to check on Mike's condition. As I feared, no change. Then I ventured over to the small café adjacent to the motel. Coffee and an omelet did wonders to revive me.

At the school, I was surprised to find the faculty lounge packed with teachers and staff. Each person held a photocopy of my Death Map article which, having been picked up by the Associated Press, had appeared in today's edition of the local paper. I introduced myself and was immediately bombarded with questions regarding the safety of the other children in the community and their families, the pros and cons of the proposed mandatory psychological testing, and theories as to what possible connection there could be between the locations listed on the map.

I listened to all the questions and comments. It struck me as significant that my article surprised no one in this room. I remarked on this, and one of the teachers tried to explain.

"After the Allen family incident, someone pointed out the increasing number of violent crimes committed by youth in America. Of course, we're all concerned. This is a small community, and almost everyone knew the Allens. Victor was your typical normal, happy kid. There was no warning sign. If it could happen to him, well, we don't know who could be next."

I saw heads nodding in agreement. "But you were thinking that way before my article appeared. Why?"

Another person stood up, nodding to several teachers in the group. The room grew quiet. The man introduced himself as recently retired from teaching science at the high school. "Ms. Kincaid," he said, "I'm responsible for this thinking in the community. I wrote a letter to the editor about this topic because I'd recently noticed a trend, maybe in the last couple of years, of increasing psychotic behavior among kids. After

Columbine, teachers are acutely concerned. I was pushing for mandatory testing so we might be able to recognize warning signs, protect our children and our community."

Heads bobbed, murmurs traced through the group.

"I'm also looking for warning signs," I said. "Something you might not have recognized. Look, I know it's been a long time, but can anyone remember anything at all about Victor, the last few days before the murders?"

Several teachers spoke up about Victor's excellent attitude and behavior in class. He was never a problem. Then the school nurse spoke.

"Victor stopped by my office, it was one or two days before the incident, and he complained of a severe headache. The lights were hurting his eyes, so I had him lie down on the cot with a cold cloth to cover his eyes. I called his mom and got permission to administer Tylenol. After about forty-five minutes he felt well enough to return to class."

"Did he do or say anything unusual?" I asked.

"No, not specifically." She paused and looked embarrassed. "He did compliment me on my appearance, though. Such a nice boy."

"What did he say?" I asked.

"Well, it was something odd, like 'You look very soothing today, Mrs. Beacher.'"

"Soothing?"

"Yeah. It was an odd word to choose. But, that's not exactly right. Let me think for a minute." She sat back down.

Victor's English teacher had saved his last assignment and brought it to the meeting. It was a paragraph on The Scarlet Letter which she read out loud. Victor referred to the story as The Red Letter at least three times.

"That's it," the nurse blurted out, jumping to her feet. "I remember now. It was my red sweater. Victor said, 'That red sweater is very soothing.' Yeah. That's it. And it was odd because I had him down in the chart as color blind. I even made a note to myself to ask, but, of course, I didn't get the chance."

I couldn't believe it. Red? I flipped back to my notes from Manny Karlsson. He'd wanted a red sleeping bag. And Mike had made a couple of red references. There was the Jell-O and the T-shirt/pinwheel thing. A tingle of cautious excitement ran through me. I didn't know what it could possibly mean — this red connection.

Chapter 30

By the time I returned to my motel room, I had gleaned as much from Toomsboro, Alabama as I could. I wracked my tired brain to try to connect the color red to this map. It wasn't happening. I gave up. My early morning flight to Arden, Mississippi, left little time for sleep, and I still needed to check in with Buzz in the pressroom at the *Morning Star*.

"Hi, Buzz. Had much response to the story?" I asked when he answered my call.

"You mean our 'Death Map' story?" he asked.

Duh. What a jerk. "Of course. Has anyone phoned? Emailed? Faxed?"

"I've spoken to no less than sixteen people claiming to have caused this by telepathy or some other form of psychic intervention. Want me to follow up?"

"Just file them, last resort stuff. Anything else?"

"Only a couple other dumb suggestions. But since AP picked it up, a reporter from every town with a local rag has a hard on over this."

Exactly what I'd hoped for.

"And I've got emails to make you scream," Buzz continued. "Four new cases and each might fit on our map. One would be hard to prove, but I included it anyway. It's from a county coroner who was suspicious about an accident at an auto repair shop. Seems a cutting torch somehow got into the hands of a teenager who managed to blow the whole place up. Anyway, Linton, North Dakota, is right on the northern line of our map, so I'm sending it along. Glad I could make your day."

I instructed Buzz to forward the emails, along with a list of all suggested connections, no matter how dumb. I hung up and suppressed a sigh. *Our story? Our map?* Surely, he didn't expect a byline for opening mail. Next, I checked my voice mail.

"Girlfriend, your map is humming with black rainbow vibes. Call me soon."

I got her meaning this time, but a call back would have to wait a bit.

Three messages from Harry. Wondering where I was. No change in Mike. Wondering when I'd get home. I started to call him back, then hit the disconnect button. That last one about home didn't sit right. It wasn't my home. I didn't know what to do about Harry.

The ping of an active inbox interrupted my musings. I read the stuff from Buzz with care, and recognized two cases I'd already discarded from my original list because they didn't entirely meet my criteria. The other two cases, however, were new.

I read Buzz's final email, with the list of suggestions of factors that might connect the cases on my map. Nothing reasonable. Nothing related to the color red. I turned my attention back to the two new cases.

Using my US road atlas, I located the towns where the newly discovered incidents took place. Linton, North Dakota and Middleton, Montana, both rested on the trail I had etched across the northwestern United States, precisely as Buzz had said.

The email from Middleton, Montana was unusual for a couple reasons. First, the boy involved in the bizarre killings was alive and hospitalized. This put him into a small subset of boys I might actually interview. Also, the victims had not been human. The boy, Eddie Hammersmith, had gone on a dog-killing spree. He'd killed fourteen dogs in one afternoon before he was captured. The dogs belonged to friends and neighbors, and many of the dogs were familiar with this boy. He had simply walked up to each animal in its pen or on its leash in the yard, petted the dog, and then slit its throat with a hunting knife.

I placed a call to the police officer who had handled the case.

"It was definitely strange," Officer Crane said. "I can't believe you think this case could be one of your Death Map cases, though. It was only them animals he killed, don't you know."

"Yes, I realize that," I said. "But it is certainly not normal behavior."

"That's true, what you say there," the police officer said. "Our paper ran your article, you know, because Middleton's on that route and people's interested. I just can't believe I'm talking to the writer. You're famous, don't you know?"

"Thanks," I said. "We received a letter from Josh Waters suggesting that this boy might fit our profile."

"Yeah, I know Josh," Officer Crane said. "He lost a dog in that mess."

"Do you know the boy? Eddie Hammersmith?"

"Yes, as a matter of fact, I do. Went to school with his older sister, you know? I always thought Eddie was a normal kid. Until all this happened, that is. I guess he's a little crazy after all."

"Could you give me his home phone number?"

"Gonna interview the parents over the phone, are you?" Officer Crane asked. "Because I'm thinking they won't be wanting to discuss this with the paper."

"Or we could let them decide," I said. "We might be surprised."

I called the number Officer Crane reluctantly provided.

I reached the boy's dad, Irvine Hammersmith. After I introduced myself, he immediately passed the phone to his wife.

"Mrs. Hammersmith," I began.

"I read your article," the woman interrupted, "our boy ain't one of those murderers."

"Yes, ma'am," I said, "but his case is similar in many respects."

"No, it's not. Don't call again." The woman hung up with a slam.

Damn. A call back wouldn't get me anywhere. But I had a gut feeling that the Hammersmith case belonged on my map. It might be worth a trip up there.

I opened the email for the other new lead that Buzz supplied. It was from the coroner in Linton, North Dakota. However, before I could dial his number, my cell phone rang. Harry's name appeared. I wavered, thinking my voice mail could handle it, but I gave in and answered after the third ring. Answering didn't signify a commitment.

"I've received some interesting news," Harry said, after a quick greeting. "That chemist, Sims, has finished her analysis of the odd thing she found in Mike's blood sample."

"That was quick," I said, glad I'd chosen to take the call. "So, what is it?"

"The report calls it a chemical closely related to the neurotransmitter family of molecules, whatever that means."

"Did Sims give any explanation?"

"Not exactly," Harry said. "Except to say that it's unusual. I've notified Mike's doctor, and he's looking into it, too. Dr. Sims says it reminds her of a presentation she saw at a meeting a few years back. She sent the name of a scientist who might give you more information." Harry paused a moment. "Here it is. You ready? Dr. Sven Peterson, from the Biochemistry

Department at the University of Toronto." He read off a phone number. "Sims thought you might be interested in following up on it."

"Interested?" I laughed. "This could be the break I'm looking for."

"Well, keep me posted," he said. "Jay-Jay misses you."

I hung up, smiling like a goof about the chemistry news. Maybe a bit of the smile was about Jay-Jay missing me. I couldn't rule that out.

Instead of calling the coroner in Linton about his email to *The Morning Star*, I called the University of Toronto in search of Dr. Peterson, only to discover that he no longer worked there. He'd taken a job with Manchester Chemicals, Consolidated, in California. The secretary then put me in touch with Martin Archer, who'd been a post-doc working with Dr. Peterson and took over his faculty position.

Dr. Archer was very helpful. He knew exactly which presentation Sims referred to, and offered to email me a copy of the abstract that had been published solely for the attendees of the meeting.

"Dr. Peterson was the only one in the lab working on that project," Dr. Archer informed me. "He was looking at a number of petroleum byproducts and their effects on rats. He hadn't gotten too far along, but his research was noticed by a big US company that snatched him up. They made their offer so good he couldn't pass."

"Do you know what he found in those studies?" I asked.

"No, but he was very excited about the last series of experiments he ran before taking the new job. I've been watching for the data to be published, but it's never come out, and it's probably been six years now."

"Is that unusual?"

"Not if the findings didn't hold up with more testing. I get a Christmas note from Sven each year, but he's never mentioned that project. Must've been a dud."

I thanked Archer for his time, and then tried the California number for Dr. Peterson. I only succeeded in reaching his secretary and learned he was out of town and not due back for three days. I made a notation on my calendar for when to call Peterson.

While I'd been on the phone to California, the promised email from Dr. Archer arrived. I tried to read the scientific abstract, but quickly got lost in the terminology. I forwarded it to Harry and to Sims at the state lab. Maybe she could explain it to me in simple layman's terms.

I glanced at the clock. I had to head out early for Mississippi but it wasn't too late to call Linton, North Dakota. My return call to Clunie could wait until tomorrow.

Interlude Two

Last October: Linton, North Dakota

The sparks rained down like orange, glowing confetti. They hit the concrete floor of the garage and danced across the room. Anna Bennett marveled at the mechanic, in his drab, grease-spotted work clothes, standing at the center of the shower, seemingly unconcerned about any danger and unaware of the beauty he was creating. A cool breeze flowed through the open side door of the garage, and the radio was tuned to a rock and roll oldies station. Anna had expected a dull morning, but this wasn't too bad. A curious black dog meandered into the garage after the spark show ended, and greeted Anna and her son, Kyle, while they waited for their car's turn to be repaired.

Anna watched the mechanic pull off the old muffler and discard it onto a growing pile out the back door of the garage. She was sitting in the corner holding a magazine, but couldn't focus on reading. Instead, her attention was drawn to the mechanic as he chose a new muffler and tailpipe from the storage shelves. Her thirteen-year-old son was showing an extraordinary interest in the proceedings, as well. He had moved closer to the elevated car and was staring blankly at the cut pipe, still glowing hot red.

"Kid needs to get out more," the mechanic called to Anna as he began to weld on the new muffler.

"Kyle," Anna said, "come over here and sit down."

The teen shuffled back to the waiting area. The mechanic finished with the car, lowered the hydraulic lift and backed the repaired vehicle out into the driveway. Then he drove Anna's car onto the lift and began to remove its ruined muffler.

Kyle seemed mesmerized by the cutting torch, the way the blue flame turned bright, blinding orange-white as it contacted the metal. He edged closer to the heat, until his face took on a glow and his body was directly under the sparks.

"Kyle," Anna called from the makeshift lounge area in the corner. "Come back over here, out of the way. You'll bother Mr. Majors."

Kyle didn't respond.

"Kyle," she called, with more emphasis this time. "Get over here."

Anna Bennett rose from her seat and approached her son, putting her hand on his shoulder to get his attention. He jumped, as if startled by the physical contact. He startled Anna, in turn, when he grabbed the cutting torch out of the mechanic's hand.

"Hey, what do you think you're doing?" Mr. Majors demanded.

Kyle didn't answer, but turned the flame on the mechanic, who was standing directly under the car. Then he whirled around and aimed the torch at Anna, standing behind him. Her clothes burst into flame. She screamed and tried to beat out the flames with her hands. She heard the mechanic yell, "No, no, not there!" and glanced up to see another shower of sparks erupt from the undercarriage of the car. Kyle was spinning around, laughing maniacally as the sparks rained down around him.

LINCOLN, ND (AP): An explosion ripped apart the garage of Majors Mechanical, a local business. The owner, Patrick Majors (47) and a customer, Kyle Bennett (13) were killed in the blast. Anna Bennett, mother of Kyle, sustained third degree burns to

the majority of her body and remains in
critical condition. Examination of the
scene suggests flames from a cutting torch
ignited the gas tank of a car undergoing
repairs. The coroner ruled the explosion
an accident.

Chapter 31

The email from the Linton coroner was brief, listing the date of the incident and the names of the victims. I phoned the Linton police station first to track down the investigating officer. I waited a full twenty minutes for someone to return to the line with the information. Turned out there was no IO assigned because the coroner, Dr. William Nichols, had ruled it an accident. I reread the letter from Dr. Nichols to the *Morning Star*. Apparently, he wasn't satisfied with his own ruling. I called him next.

"Dr. Nichols?" I asked and introduced myself. "We received an email from you earlier today regarding an accident involving a boy named Kyle Bennett."

"Yes, yes, of course," the man replied in a high-pitched, squeaky voice. "Kyle Bennett, his mother, Anna Bennett, and a mechanic, Pat Majors, all were victims of an explosion a few months ago. Mrs. Bennett survived. Yes, yes. That's why I sent an email to your paper. We sit smack dab on that Death Map of yours."

"So, it's location, then? Nothing else?" I asked. "The police report says you ruled the deaths accidental."

"Yes, yes, well, I might be wrong, you know," Dr. Nichols said. "It was tragic, yes, tragic. I knew all three parties involved, you see. Majors worked on my car for years. Excellent. He would never be so careless as to cut a hole into a gas tank with a torch."

"Is that what caused the explosion?"

165

"Yes, yes. We found the boy still holding the cutting torch. Very odd, to say the least. Very odd, indeed. But mind you, no reason to think it was not accidental. At least, no reason that I could document."

"What, then? You sensed something wrong?" I asked.

"Well, yes, yes, I did. And the more I think about it, the stranger it becomes."

I waited for Dr. Nichols to elaborate but finally prompted him. "Dr. Nichols? Are you still there?"

"Yes, yes. Sorry. I was thinking about Anna Bennett. She's a teacher here, and very well thought of. Unfortunately, she can't remember anything that took place immediately prior to the explosion. Head injury, you know. Not unexpected. Her son, Kyle, was quite the athlete. I think he played almost every sport at our small middle school. Everyone knew them and liked them. Kyle wanted to play sports in high school and be a teacher like his mom. He'd never expressed an interest in auto mechanics. I can't fathom why the boy had the cutting torch. No, no, I can't fathom it."

"Are you considering changing your verdict?"

"Oh, no, no. That would never do."

"Well, thank you, Dr. Nichols. I appreciate you bringing this case to my attention, but I can't include it on such little. . . ."

"But I haven't told you the part that's been bothering me," Dr. Nichols interrupted. "You see, the explosion threw all three clear of the garage. Consequently, they did not burn like the rest of the place. That saved Anna, but not the other two. My concern has to do with the burn marks on the clothes of both the mechanic and Anna. They had been on fire *before* the explosion."

"So, how do you explain it?"

"I don't have an explanation to fit what I know to be fact about these three people. Majors was experienced and very safety conscious. Kyle had no interest in auto mechanics. Majors and Anna Bennett both had burn marks on their clothing which was inconsistent with the explosion. Then I read your article. What if something happened to Kyle? Something like whatever drove those other boys in your article to commit murder? There is no proof, however. No proof."

I couldn't add Kyle to my list if it was merely a tragic accident. I needed proof of intent. Too bad the mother couldn't remember details.

"Dr. Nichols," I said, "could I speak with Mrs. Bennett?"

"I'm afraid she's not up to an interview as of yet. This has been extremely distressing for her, as you might imagine."

"Could you ask her a question, then?" I pushed.

"Yes, yes, I suppose I could. Depends on the question, though."

"Fair enough. Ask her, please, if her son said anything unusual the day of or the day prior to the accident. Especially if he reacted oddly to red."

"Red? The color?" Dr. Nichols asked.

"Yes. I can't explain, but would you ask?"

"I can ask, but of course he wouldn't have. You see, the boy was color blind."

Chapter 32

Friday: Arden, Mississippi

My sense of déjà vu vanished when I reached Arden, Mississippi the following day. A small group of adults bearing signs reading, "We Teach Love, Not Hate," "Freedom of Religion for All," and "Let Them Rest in Peace," huddled in front of the police station. They eyed me suspiciously as I found a parking space. I walked past the slogan-chanting group and entered the building's tiny waiting area. A placard directed me to push the bell at the front window and wait for an attendant. I pushed and wondered vaguely what local issue had prompted the picket. I heard the outer door open behind me and turned, expecting to see a uniform. Instead, a middle-aged man I'd seen among the demonstrators entered. He bore down on me, anger spewing from his eyes.

"I demand that the *Morning Star* retract its prejudicial and unfounded attack on the downtrodden and abused members of society," the man said, spitting out the words. I took a step backward as the attendant window slid open behind me.

"What's going on, Reverend?" the woman at the window asked. "You can't be bothering people in here."

The man didn't answer, but continued to glare at me.

"I'm sorry," I said to the Reverend. "You must have me confused with someone else." I turned to the woman. "I'd like to speak with the investigating officer on the Russell Johnson case." I passed her my business card.

"I think I can find someone who was on that case," she said. "Be just a minute. Reverend, you'll have to hold it down or take it back outside." She closed the window and disappeared from view.

"You here from that New York paper?" the reverend asked, narrowing his eyes.

"Yes, the *Morning Star*," I said, holding out my card.

"I don't want your card." Anger, like a fiery sermon, streamed from him and he thrust a newspaper clipping in front of my face. I expected to see my Death Map article, but instead it was a letter to the editor of the local paper. The writer was blaming Reverend Bertram of the Tabernacle Christian Church for having put evil thoughts into the head of the Johnson boy.

"So, are you Reverend Bertram?" I asked.

"Yes, I am." He tilted his chin upward and continued to glare.

"Well, Reverend, I didn't write this letter."

"Of course, I know that," he said, snatching it back. "But we object to any more nonsense being written about this tragic affair."

"Did you read my article?" I asked.

"No, not exactly." His preacher accent slipped a beat. "A member of our congregation works here and told me you were coming." He squared his shoulders. "I will not see the facts blurred by rumor."

I swallowed a sarcastic reply. "I totally agree," I said instead. "Believe me, I'm only interested in finding the truth." I pulled a copy of my Death Map article out of my bag. "Look, Reverend, I'd like you to read this. It'll give you something to think about while I speak to the officer in charge of the investigation." The minister took the paper, holding it by one corner as if it would contaminate him. "Then perhaps we can discuss facts," I added with a smile.

I watched his face as he read. His scowl gradually relaxed and the sharp edges of his features reshaped into a frown. He glanced at me, then back at my article. He studied the map for a considerable time, then lowered his head and appeared to be saying a prayer.

I heard the window slide open behind me, and turned back to the woman.

"Ms. Kincaid, the detective you wanted to speak with is out on a call right now. Should be back in about thirty minutes. Want to see someone else, or wait?"

"I'll wait, thanks."

There were four chairs in the tiny waiting area. I raised an eyebrow toward Reverend Bertram and waved toward the chair. "Shall we?"

His deep brown eyes, full of sadness now, met mine. "I'm afraid I've been misinformed, Ms. Kincaid," the minister said. "Can we start over?" He smiled and extended his hand.

"I'd like that." We shook hands and moved to the chairs. "Okay, Reverend Bertram, why would someone write that letter to the editor about you? What's your connection to Russell Johnson?"

"My son, Marcus, was one of the victims of Russell Johnson's shooting spree. Fortunately, he survived, but others were not so lucky."

"Could you tell me what happened?"

"Well, the Johnsons belong to my congregation," Reverend Bertram began. "Russell and his family also lived next door to us. Russell and my son, Marcus, walked to school together every morning, along with Vestalee Jacobs, who lived two doors down across the street. The three children had just started fifth grade at Arden East Middle School. Marcus told me, and the police, and anyone else who would listen, all about the walk to school that fateful morning."

I activated my recorder and Reverend Bertram continued with his story.

Interlude Three

Last September: Arden, Mississippi

"Get your math done last night?" Vestalee Jacobs asked the boys as they walked along the edge of the street, kicking small pieces of gravel along ahead of them.

"Yep," Marcus Bertram said.

Russell Johnson, who usually couldn't keep his mouth shut, didn't say anything, just kept kicking rocks. Marcus didn't think much about it at the time.

"My momma says I gots all the answers right," Vestalee said.

Neither boy replied. Marcus hated it when Vestalee bragged. She was smart, but she didn't need to go on so about it.

They were walking down Harding Avenue. Marcus loved this street. It was lined with empty shells of abandoned warehouses and factories. There were weeds growing tall around rows of shattered windows, giving the buildings an exciting, scary look. Kind of like the place in his video game, where enemies with mega weapons were always hiding, ready to ambush. His heart pounded every time he looked at the place. The broken walls and security fences lying violated on the ground beckoned him to explore. One of these days, he'd do it. He and Russell talked about it almost every day. They were going to vanish into one of the buildings and totally skip school. Of course, it would have to wait until Vestalee wasn't around. Else she would tell as soon as she got to school, and then they'd be in big trouble. But wait 'til she was sick or something. Then they'd do it for sure.

They listened to the train whistle, tried to guess which of the many sets of tracks would come to life with signal lights flashing and wooden arms dropping down to barricade their progress. Marcus could tell it was the second set of tracks, and that was great, because they would have to wait and if the train was long enough, they might get to be late for school.

They ran the next block to the tracks so they could wave at the engineer, and then tried to decipher the graffiti decorating the boxcars. After a few minutes, Marcus noticed that Russell wasn't playing the game. Instead, he stood in front of the flashing signal light. Just stood there.

"Hey, ain't you never seen a light before?" he yelled at Russell.

Russell didn't answer or even look his way. Marcus gave a mental shrug and turned back to the train because Vestalee squealed that SlyBoy's tag was coming.

The train ended abruptly and the crossing guard lifted. The flashing lights turned off their beacon, but Russell appeared to be in a stupor. Marcus was almost across the tracks before he noticed that his friend wasn't following. He nudged Vestalee and pointed back toward Russell.

"Hey," Vestalee called, "come on, Russell. What's wrong, dude?"

Russell didn't answer, but started walking toward them.

The last set of tracks they had to cross didn't have a signal light; the only train that traveled that route was a train carrying scrap metal from the one remaining factory in the area to a recycle center a few blocks away. The train was never very long, but traveled down the tracks at a snail's pace. The engineer blew the warning whistle repeatedly as the train crept closer to the intersection. Cars would continue crossing the tracks in front of the approaching train until the last possible second. Marcus knew they could make it across the tracks and back about a jillion times, but they stopped and waited, enjoying the rare chance to be delayed by two trains the same morning. Today, they'd be late for sure.

After the train passed through the crossing, Marcus noticed that Russell had moved behind one of the waiting cars and was staring at its taillight. He nudged Vestalee and pointed again toward Russell.

"Russell," Vestalee said, with a note of irritation in her voice. "Quit fooling around! You're gonna get runned over."

The driver of the car released his brake to advance across the tracks and Russell responded as if a spell had been broken. He moved out of the street and joined his friends for the final three-block walk to school.

Since they were tardy, the three had to report in at the office. Two trains proved the bomb of excuses. Marcus followed Vestalee and Russell to their first period class, already in progress. Marcus saw Russell reach into his backpack but he didn't think nothing about what Russell was doing. Figured he was getting his homework or something.

But it wasn't homework. The room exploded with the sound of gunfire. Marcus didn't see his teacher get shot, but he heard the students in the class start screaming. Vestalee ran toward Russell, then another explosion of sound knocked her to the ground. Marcus watched Russell slowly turn toward him. Russell was smiling when the hot white pain tore through Marcus's shoulder. Marcus didn't see the next shot, when Russell turned the gun on himself. Russell died immediately. The teacher lived two days longer; Marcus and Vestalee survived after a long ordeal in the hospital.

ARDEN, MISS. (AP): Tragedy struck this morning in the form of an apparent murder/suicide at Arden Elementary School. Russell Johnson (11) shot and killed his teacher,

Mr. Arctus Samson (33), then himself, with a weapon he brought to school in his backpack. Two other students were injured in the incident and were life-lined to St. Jude's Hospital in Atlanta, where they are listed in critical condition. The gun used in the shooting is of the same caliber as a weapon registered to the boy's father. The incident is currently under investigation.

Chapter 33

"And I thank the Lord every day that my son and that young girl survived," Reverend Bertram said, finishing his account.

"How's your son doing now?" I asked.

"He's recovering. It's been traumatic for all of us."

"And the girl, Vestalee?"

"Almost back to normal. Her version of that morning jibes with my boy's."

"What do you think caused this?" I asked.

"We've got no idea what happened to that child," the minister admitted. "He was always a good kid. You know, the sheriff asked Marcus if he remembered Russell doing anything or saying anything odd, and the only thing he could think of was Russell staring at those lights."

I again felt the tingle of excitement, like I was on the edge of a discovery mere microseconds beyond my understanding. "Anything special about the lights?"

"No. It was only the signal lights at the train tracks, and the brake lights on a car."

"Red?"

"I suppose so. Yes, must have been. Is that important?"

The attendant at the window interrupted at that moment because the investigating officer had returned to the station. I rose to go. "Thank you, Reverend Bertram. I don't know yet, but it might be very important."

The minister rose, apologized for his earlier attitude and shook my hand again. I followed the attendant.

The remainder of my visit to Arden slid back into the realm of déjà vu: I read the police report, interviewed the investigating officer, teachers, parents and friends of the children involved. And, although I had no clue of its significance, I added another child to the list of those fascinated or obsessed with the color red.

Chapter 34

Friday night at the hotel on the outskirts of Arden, I reviewed the weird comments the kids on my Death Map list reportedly made about the color red. My godson, Mike, in Charleston, commented on red Jell-O and a red shirt; Manny Karlsson in Dwight, North Dakota, mentioned a red sleeping bag; Victor Allen from Toomsboro, Alabama, liked a red sweater and called The Scarlet Letter The Red Letter; Russell Johnson from Arden, Mississippi stared at red lights. Then there was the kid from Linton, North Dakota, who was color blind. *Wait a minute.* I checked my notes. The nurse from Toomsboro thought Victor Allen was color blind. *Was this something?*

I pulled up Google and searched for frequency of color blindness and found it wasn't rare at all, seven to ten percent of males were color blind. I had fourteen boys on my map. Statistics would expect one or two of those to be color blind. Damn. Dead ended, again.

I diverted my Google search to Dr. Sim's finding of a neurotransmitter-like molecule in Mike's blood and pulled up tons of information on neurotransmitters. I got excited to learn these molecules were involved in signals to the brain. I got bogged down with science real fast, with terms like cholinergic receptors and myelin sheath popping up. But it made sense in my mind, anyway, that bad things would happen if the normal signals in the brain were affected. Bad things, like uncontrolled thoughts and actions. Bad things, like normal kids becoming killers.

This was interesting stuff. I wondered if it would be worth changing my road trip to include a visit to Dr. Peterson in San Francisco to discuss neurotransmitters with him in person, as opposed to a phone call. I had one more town on the southern Death Map route scheduled to visit on this leg of my trip. The Luke kid from Milton, Louisiana was one of the boys still living, and I didn't want to skip a chance to interview him. I checked the available flights from around Milton to San Francisco. Nothing direct, but could be done. I made the arrangements and texted Harry my updated schedule.

A text from Clunie came in before I headed to bed. Verbatim: *black shift to red and yellow spikes around O'Connell. See tomorrow's story about votes on construction contracts.*

She was nothing if not cryptic, and I dreamed of the dapper Senator demanding his name on the sides of buildings and bridges.

Interlude Four

Five Months Earlier: Milton, Louisiana

Clarence Luke was in charge of his world when he rode his bike. The prized possession had arrived at Christmas, a gift from the preacher at his grandmother's church. Grandmother said it was because he was such a good helper to Reverend Mason, always sweeping out the church and straightening up the social hall on Sunday afternoons.

Clarence surely did like that preacher. He made good sense. Always told him to stay in school, work hard, and listen to his grandmother and to the Lord. Clarence worked hard in school and always did what his grandmother asked. He hadn't heard much out of the Lord though . . . until yesterday.

Clarence lived with his grandmother, Lacy Luke, in a small three-room house near the edge of town. A narrow dirt road ran along State Road 16 for about a mile, linking their home and the Milton East Side First Baptist Church. Clarence rode his bike up and down that dirt road, pretending to race cars along the highway. He loved it when they honked at him. Sometimes other kids from the neighborhood would join him, but they didn't all have bikes, so then he would have to play something else.

Yesterday had been Sunday, and after a morning of church services, Clarence and Grandmother walked home. Grandmother fixed a delicious Sunday dinner while Clarence played outside. Reverend Mason came for dinner that day, as he usually did on Sundays. After dinner, he and Grandmother visited while Clarence, also as usual, rode his bike back to the church to sweep out the meeting room and straighten up the social hall. It was in the social hall that Clarence first heard the Lord's voice.

"You've done a good job," Clarence heard a voice say.

"Huh?" he said, glancing around. He had believed himself to be alone.

"Who's there?" he called out. There was only silence in reply.

Clarence got spooked and dropped the stack of song books he was arranging on the shelf, ran outside and jumped on his bike. As he peddled at top speed, he heard the voice again.

"You ride like the wind!" the voice praised him.

He stopped in the middle of the dirt road and whispered, "Is that you, Lord?"

"It'll be fine," the Lord assured him. "There'll be no pain."

Clarence grinned at the sky and resumed his ride home.

"Grandmother," Clarence called as he approached the house. "Grandmother, guess what happened."

Since there was no one in the living room or kitchen, Clarence headed back outside, calling for his grandmother. A few seconds later, she emerged from the house in her bathrobe.

"You sick, Grandmother?" Clarence asked her.

"No, honey. Now, what's wrong?"

"I heard the Lord talking to me, Grandmother," he told her, waving his hands in the air around his head.

Within moments, Reverend Mason emerged through the squeaky screen door and joined his two parishioners on the porch. "And what did the Lord say to you, young man?" the preacher asked.

"He said I done a good job, that everything was fine, and ain't nothing gonna hurt me," Clarence said with a beaming grin.

Death Map

Grandmother and Reverend Mason smiled warmly at each other. "You are a good boy, Clarence Luke," the preacher agreed.

"Why don't we go inside for some lemonade," Grandmother suggested. "I can finish changing out of my Sunday-go-to-meeting clothes." She winked at Reverend Mason and they all went into the kitchen.

The next day, the Lord spoke to Clarence Luke again. The command seemed unusual, but after all, it was from the Lord . . . and He promised it wouldn't hurt.

```
MILTON,  LA  (AP):  The  members  of  the
Milton East Side First Baptist Church held
a  spontaneous  candlelight  prayer  session
for  their  leader,  Reverend  Thaddeus  Mason
(45),  and  parishioners  Lacy  Luke  (44)  and
Clarence  Luke  (10).  The  three  are  reported
to  be  in  serious  but  stable  condition  at
Memorial  General  Hospital  with  unspecified
injuries.  The  incident  is  currently  under
investigation.
```

Chapter 35

Sunday: San Francisco, California

I deplaned, along with fifty or so fellow travelers, onto the airport tarmac. I inhaled the brisk air, savoring the salty taste in the misty breeze caressing my face and the strange, sweet scent of flowers unidentifiable to this Eastern seaboard native.

This was my first trip to California, and my expectations included crowds of beautiful people in swimwear, earthquakes, and lots of sunshine. So far, I had the sunshine, but the cool temperature precluded swimsuits and the ground was steady at the moment.

I hailed a taxi and went directly to my hotel. I had sent a text to Dr. Peterson requesting an informal interview for tomorrow, and he'd set up a late morning appointment. Today, I needed to check in with Buzz and Clunie back in New York at the *Morning Star*, and with Harry in Charleston. I started with Buzz, wanting to get the expected irritating conversation out of the way first.

"Hey, Lila."

"Hi, Buzz. What's new?

"Nothing. Seems the hype is slowing down. There's only a couple things I'll scan and send you. I haven't talked to any of these people, just so you know."

Hmm, well that certainly didn't ease my mind. When Buzz goes out of his way to deny something, red flags pop up. "Sure, Buzz. Whatever. Send them along."

He sent the documents immediately, and I read them over.

Included were several follow-up articles and letters to the editor that had appeared in newspapers along the Death Map route. Lots of speculation and concern about serial killers, poisons, unidentified drugs — nothing new or unexpected.

Except for one article.

The reporter speculated, accurately, as it turned out, on the names of the kids associated with the crimes on my Death Map. He'd also identified the Luke boy, the Oaks boy and my godson as the only living members among the potential perps on the map of violence. Could this be the person Buzz wanted to assure me he hadn't spoken with?

I dreaded the thought of reporters descending on any of these kids, but especially Mike.

I called Harry next. "Harry," I began, without preamble, "can you protect Mike and Sophia from reporters?"

"Like you?" he asked.

Smart ass.

"Yes, like me," I said, with an edge. "I got in to see the Luke boy in Milton yesterday without any red tape. It shouldn't be that easy." That interview still disturbed me. The boy had eagerly described the voice of God directing his actions. And the aural assurance of "no pain" continued to overrun his comments throughout our conversation. Echoes of those identical words scrawled under my godson's hospital bed resounded achingly in my mind.

"I've already taken steps," Harry said. "Mike's not responding to anyone yet, anyway, so no chance of an interview there. But, you know, I can't prevent interviews with the police or hospital personnel."

"I know," I said, fighting the impulse to blame Harry for pushing me to publish earlier than I'd wanted. His argument that I'd get a tip about a connection between the cases hadn't panned out, and the odds of anything coming in by this date were dropping fast. Time had already bypassed the collective attention span of the general public. But I held my tongue, I thanked Harry for his efforts and ended the call.

My fun call was next.

"Hey, girlfriend," Clunie said. "Where are you today?"

"Sunny San Francisco," I replied. "And I finally had a chance to read your pieces on the O'Connell murder. Congrats. But what was that text about last night?"

"It's getting weird, with ever-changing auras. I'm still analyzing his past voting record. It's like a series of nightmare cue ball breaks. After each event, interested parties scatter into separate pockets."

"Follow the. . . ." I started.

"Money, yeah. I know," Clunie interrupted. "A yes vote is pretty straightforward, but I can't always tell who benefits from a no vote."

"Can you narrow it down to decisions where his vote was the deciding factor?"

"Working that. There's lots to research, but readers have moved on and so has McLeish."

Man, didn't I know that feeling.

"Another link popped up yesterday, though, with its slew of angry dudes and dudettes. S&S Construction filed a federal suit against O'C, claiming he somehow diverted stimulus infrastructure funds into his new yacht and new winter home. Money, money, filling the web for sure."

"That might take a while to unravel. Think a special prosecutor might be on the horizon?"

"Calls are out. McLeish will be an auroch." She laughed.

I laughed and said good-bye as I Googled the definition of auroch . . . an extinct wild ox. What a perfect description of our boss in angry mode.

Monday morning, at the appointed time, I took a taxi to Dr. Peterson's office. The impeccable landscaping and building design screamed big bucks. The lobby featured a two-story fountain in the center of an oval pool surrounded by flowers. An elaborate chandelier of multicolored lights hung overhead. The combination of colors and splashing water droplets created a fairy-tale glitter on the surface of the water. I tried not to gape on my way to the security desk, thinking of the bare bones *Morning Star* offices. *I'm sure I'd be more efficient if we had a fountain.*

The security attendant didn't flinch at my hair color or piercings. Instead of pulling his gun, he asked for my name and driver's license. He checked his list, then issued me a visitor's ID badge. An escort to Dr. Peterson's office on the fifth floor was provided. There, I gave my name to the secretary in the reception area.

"Dr. Peterson?" the secretary spoke into the phone. "Dr. Lila Kincaid is here."

"It's Ms. Kincaid," I said, smiling at the secretary. "I'm a reporter from. . . ."

"A reporter?" she turned pale and drew in a breath. "I can't believe they let you by security. I'll have to get someone back up here to escort you out."

At that moment, a man's face appeared in the doorway behind the secretary. He looked at me for a second, and then broke out in a warm smile. "Lila! You made it. I'm so sorry I wasn't able to meet you at the airport." He walked around the secretary's desk and gave me a welcoming embrace. "Play along," he whispered near my ear.

I hugged him back and smiled into his eyes. "It's okay, really, I can take care of myself," I said.

Dr. Peterson turned back to his secretary. "Nora, forget she's a reporter. Lila's the daughter of my best friend. Fresh out of college. I've been trying to convince her for at least six months to come visit and enjoy the beauty of California. Right, Lila?"

"Absolutely," I said, trying for a young college-age inflection. "And no lie. It's totally rad here."

I'm not sure I pulled it off.

"Cancel my two o'clock. I'm going to spend the rest of the day showing Lila the sights. Here," he took the appointment book, "let's cross her off and put in 'personal time.'" He marked through my name with a felt tipped marker.

Nora frowned at the mark on her date book, then tilted her head and smiled at us. "Well, have fun," she said.

Dr. Peterson put his arm around my shoulders and led me to the elevator, which opened immediately.

"What was that all about?" I whispered.

He kept his arm around me once the doors closed. I began to feel uncomfortable. He bent down toward my ear and I tried to edge away.

"Security camera," he said softly. "I'll explain soon. Try to look natural."

I forced a smile and glanced quickly around the interior of the elevator. There it was — a tiny camera in the corner. The security here was tight. *He'd better have something important to tell me after this elaborate charade.*

When we reached the main lobby, Dr. Peterson steered me to the security desk. "We have to sign out," he said.

"I can't wait to see the Bay Bridge," I said as we approached the desk. I felt ridiculous. A poor cousin to James Bond.

"Please sign here, Dr. Kincaid." The guard indicated a line in the logbook. "I'll take your visitor's badge, as well. Thanks, and I hope you enjoy our city."

"Thank you." This time I didn't correct the title.

"Will you be back today, Dr. Peterson?" the guard asked.

"Probably, Mike, but it'll be near the end of the day."

"Have a good afternoon, sir."

We left the building and Dr. Peterson whispered, "Do you have a car?"

"No," I said.

"Okay, mine's over this way."

Once on the road, I turned to Peterson. "Now, will you explain what that was all about?"

Dr. Peterson dropped the smile and pressed his fingers to his temple. Worry lines creased the somber face. "Got a call from Martin Archer yesterday," he said. "He mentioned your interest in the report I presented six years ago. I'm sorry about all the subterfuge, but it's impossible to talk to anyone from the press at work."

"I'm not after any big company secrets." I said. "I just wanted to know about some research you did before you started working here."

"Let's stop for some coffee, or maybe it's dinner time for you?"

"Sure, I'm hungry."

He drove to a small Mexican restaurant a few blocks away. A television in the upper corner by the front door was tuned to a Spanish soap opera. The few customers glanced our way as we entered the *taqueria*, but they quickly turned back to the soap. Peterson led the way to a small table in the back, away from the group watching TV, and sat where he could see the door. No one inside was speaking English. A waitress came by and Peterson placed an order in Spanish. His eyes kept flicking to the entrance as he folded and unfolded a napkin.

"Why are you interested in ARP 2728?" he asked when the waitress was out of ear shot.

"I'm interested in whatever was in a presentation you made six years ago." I pulled my notebook out of my purse. "Was that ARP 2728?"

"Why are you asking about it?"

"Didn't you see my Death Map article? It was picked up by the syndicated press and ran nationally."

His brow furrowed. "Missed it, sorry. I can go weeks without picking up a paper."

I pulled a copy of my article out of my bag and passed

it across the table to him. I watched him read through it. He finished, turned the article face down on the table, and then looked expectantly at me.

"What does this have to with me?" he asked.

"A chemical turned up in the blood from one of the kids that committed crimes associated with that map. It's still unidentified, but the chemist called it, oh, hang on a minute." I flipped back a page in my notebook. "Neurotransmitter-like. She remembered seeing your poster describing a chemical that she thinks is very similar to what was in this kid. I'm hoping you can tell me for sure."

Dr. Peterson was quiet for several minutes, lost in thought. Meanwhile, our huevos rancheros arrived and he began to eat, still not saying a word. I watched him think and nibbled at my food.

"I had a grant from the Canadian Department of Energy," he said at last.

I placed my tape recorder on the table between us, raised my eyebrows. He motioned for me to push the record button.

"It was for examining health risks of petroleum byproducts," he continued. "I was getting supplies from various refineries and processing plants around the US and Canada and comparing processing techniques for the amount of hazardous materials they produced. One of my test procedures involved exposing rats, either by aerosol or by subcutaneous — that means under the skin — injection, to the different compounds or chemicals that I purified from these samples."

He paused, gave me a questioning glance. I nodded, so he continued.

"One set of results proved to be very interesting. I found a molecule that induced erratic behavior in juvenile males — some were very irritable and violent, while others were simply lethargic — and I saw the effect only in young rats.

This same substance had no effect on adult rats whatsoever. I labeled it ARP 2728, and presented these results at a poster session at the International Biochemical Society's conference in Montreal nearly six years ago."

He took a drink of water. He glanced around the room and at the entrance before continuing in a lower voice. "Within days after returning home from the meeting I was offered this position with Manchester Chemicals. Apparently, one of their chemists had been at the meeting and was interested in my poster. The offer was a surprise. I hadn't been looking for a new job. At first I didn't consider it, but they kept sweetening the offer until, well, I couldn't turn it down."

He took bite of his meal, and scanned the room again.

"Did you notice anything else about the behavior of the test animals?" I asked. "Anything to do with colors?"

"Colors? That's a curious question. I didn't notice anything, but then again, I wasn't looking. Hmm, that's interesting." He took another bite of his meal and stared across the room toward the television. "I did some preliminary studies trying to localize the chemical's site of action in the young rats. It appeared to accumulate in the brain at three locations, one of which was near the vision control region, but I was never able to do any follow up."

"Since this company hired you because of the work you were doing with ARP 2728, surely you've done something with it since coming here."

Dr. Peterson watched a couple enter the restaurant and take a seat nearby. I followed his glance. They weren't paying any attention to us.

"That's the weird thing," he said, lowering his voice. "I suspect I was hired to *prevent* me from doing any further research on ARP 2728."

"What?" I asked.

"Can't be sure," he said. He stopped speaking again and forked around with his food. He didn't eat it. Minutes passed before he looked at me again. This time his eyes were narrow slits.

"When I tried to publish the rat studies," Dr. Peterson said, poking the tabletop with his index finger, "Manchester's legal department blocked it, even though the work was done before I ever came here."

He shook his head and continued.

"I argued I had a moral obligation to publish, inform others about the potential hazards. They wouldn't back down, and suggested my moral obligation had been met since I'd informed both ARP and the Canadian Department of Energy."

His shoulders sagged. "They convinced me, I guess, with a big bonus. Felt like pay-off money."

I tapped my lip ring. "That doesn't make any sense. Why would they care whether or not you published your earlier research?"

He frowned and shook his head. "As I said, I think the main objective in hiring me in the first place was to get control of my research. I'm pretty much out of research altogether now. Certainly nothing to warrant the extravagant salary I make. More importantly, all samples and notes pertaining to ARP 2728 that I brought with me have disappeared. Stolen. But with the security around that place? Someone inside. Had to be."

"So, no one's following up on your studies?" I asked.

"If they are, I don't know about it. There was a guy who used to drop by all the time to ask about my protocols and results. Then, after my materials turned up missing, he didn't come around much. Now I never see him. I figured he'd lost interest, but maybe not . . . ." His voice trailed off.

"Would you look at this report? It's what was found in that boy. Can tell me what it is?" I asked.

He took the paper I slid across the table toward him and studied it.

"My God," he whispered, "it's identical. But that can't be possible, there's no way it could be—" he broke off mid-sentence. I let him think.

"I only found ARP 2728 in samples from ARP," he resumed a minute later. "That map of yours . . . those points are other kids, right? Have you checked their blood for this molecule?"

I slowly shook my head. Only two boys, other than Mike, had survived. How could I get samples of their blood? How could I check blood from the dead kids? I remembered seeing on the police report for Victor Allen that blood and tissue samples were collected. Were there samples still in toxicology labs somewhere? Why hadn't this occurred to me earlier? So much time wasted. This could be the tangible connection I needed.

Meanwhile, Peterson was still talking. I forced myself to pay attention. "They had a novel way of processing the petroleum byproducts from a refinery in Midland, Texas. There's got to be some connection between this boy and that company. Did he live near Midland?"

"No," I said. "South Carolina. What do they use these petroleum byproducts for, anyway?"

"Could be in anything. From tape to antihistamines. The list of possibilities is amazing and growing daily. The main thing is plastics, I think. But I don't know about this particular product. You'd need to call the company."

"ARP?"

"Yes. Amalgamated Recovery Products."

"Do you have a contact person at ARP?"

"Used to," he said. "I'll have to search my memory, 'cause that information disappeared with paperwork and samples. Well, that's not quite true. I think there's one set of samples in a freezer back in Toronto. Archer could find it."

"Maybe I could compare it to the blood?"

"Sure. It was in a chest-style -80° Celsius freezer. I'll clear it with Archer. You might want to request a new sample from Amalgamated for a comparison. Maybe they've altered their protocol. It's been six years, after all."

Peterson bit his lower lip, then added. "I sent my report to their chemist, but his name eludes me. Tyler or maybe Tayler? It will come to me. Their PR department should be able to give you a list of what the petroleum byproducts are used for, and possibly a list of the companies they sell to. This stuff gets into plastics, textiles, paint, lots of stuff. Maybe it's leached into the water supply from landfills."

I stared at him in horror. It could be everywhere, anywhere. But my map indicated a specificity. "If it is in the other kids I've identified along this map," I began, "why would it be limited to these routes? Any ideas? Wild speculations?"

"Wild speculation? Okay, off the top of my head, let's say it's leached out of plastics from landfills. Maybe look at land fill practices along those routes for differences from neighboring states? Better yet, check soil, water, even air samples for this molecule. I don't know . . . finding it could be a long shot."

He strummed the table top. "I'll give it more thought and get back with you on that. I'd like to know what they're using it for, or if they've sold the processing protocol."

"Right," I said. "You said you suspected the theft of your research on ARP 2728 was an inside job. Is there any way you could find out if someone has followed up on any of your original studies? I need to know as much as possible about this chemical."

Dr. Peterson went silent again. I was afraid for a moment that I'd asked too much. When he finally spoke, his voice was angry, but the anger wasn't directed at me.

"I've been manipulated," he said. "There's a lot of money behind this . . . this . . . cover up. Thing is, I can't figure out Manchester Chemical's angle. They've succeeded in quashing my research and burying my report on the dangers. They must have an interest."

"Do they do business with Amalgamated Recovery Products?"

His face took on a determined look. "I'll find out," he said. "If this chemical is responsible for turning those kids into killers, then, ultimately, I'm responsible, too." His voice softened. "I should've done more to report the dangers."

I reached over and turned off the recorder. I pulled out a business card with my office address and phone number, e-mail address, fax number, and cell phone number. I flipped it over and wrote Harry's name and number on the back.

"This is my lawyer, and I stay in touch with him. If you can't reach me at one of the numbers on the front, try to get the information to him."

He went silent again and poked at the remainder of his meal. I waited, anticipating more questions. I didn't have to wait long.

"Tell me," he said, "why'd you ask about colors?"

"Several of the boys made weird comments about red." I gave him the specifics. "Each time, it was strange enough to be remembered later by friends or teachers. If it were only one instance, I wouldn't think anything, but it seems like a repeating theme. Maybe not a coincidence."

Peterson sat up straight and placed his fork down on his plate. "Actually, it might be extremely important."

"How's that?" I switched the recorder back on.

"Well, the gene enabling us to visualize the color red is X-linked, meaning that males, who only have one copy of the X chromosome, manifest red color vision defects more often than females."

"So?"

"So . . . and I'm just brainstorming again here . . . perhaps these boys had a defect in how they perceive the color red and somehow this chemical restores their vision to normal.

Imagine being able to see red in its full richness for the first time. Enthralling."

"Oh, my God," I said. "I was told two of the kids were color blind. But, you can't convince me that suddenly being able to see red would turn someone into a killer."

"No, of course not. It's not that simple," Dr. Peterson said. "But, there's a lot of similarity in how different sensory organs are regulated. In fact, it's been proposed that genetically defined variations in perception may lead to alterations in behavior. Exactly how that might come about is unresolved at this time."

"Whoa, wait a minute," I said. "You totally lost me."

"Sorry, let me try again. As we transition from child to adult, a lot of our genes are shut off as they are no longer needed, and others will get turned on. Let's suppose when ARP 2728 is around, a gene that should be turned off remains on, maybe even is amplified. Let's say this chemical's effects are restricted to boys undergoing puberty, as it was restricted to young rats in my studies. Perhaps a number of sensory genes are also affected by the presence of this chemical. Maybe the boys see new shades of color, maybe they hear voices, maybe smells are intensified, or maybe their sensitivity to pain or pleasure is altered. Anyway, certain genes influence our behavior and the regulation of these genes is intricately connected to the regulation of the genes for our senses. So, a substance that alters our sensual perception may influence our behavior as well."

"That seems too strange," I said.

"Oh, not at all, really. Think about it. Take smells, for instance. Some make you sick — like a baby's dirty diaper. Some make you hungry — like a turkey roasting in the oven. Or some can make you sexually aroused — like perfume or pheromones."

"And those smells can influence your behavior," I concluded.

"Actually, our advertising industry is pretty much dependent on the connection between our senses and our behavior," he added. "The science lags behind somewhat, but psychophysics is combining with genetics and making remarkable headway."

Dr. Peterson picked at his food again, then slid his plate away.

"I'm sorry, Ms. Kincaid, but I can't sit here and pretend to eat. I need to get back to Manchester and see what I can learn about any additional research on this chemical. Too much is at stake to be hanging out here any longer."

I offered to pick up the tab and take an Uber back to my hotel. He let out a breath, shook my hand and left, almost colliding with the waitress on his way to the front door. An hour later, when I reached my hotel room, I tossed my purse on the bed and sat in the cushioned chair at the table in front of the heavily curtained window. I stared at my blank computer screen thinking about my discussion with Peterson.

He'd seemed sincere, but he could've been lying. He'd been in on the initial research of the ARP chemical, and had subsequently been hired by Manchester. Maybe his surprise was because I'd tracked him down and confronted him.

One thing he'd said, though, made lots of sense. I needed to look for that molecule in blood from the Luke kid and the Oaks kid. I supposed Harry would know the legal steps I needed to follow to have a blood sample sent to Sims at the Charleston lab, so I sent him an urgent message to that effect.

And, just as urgent, I needed to look deeper into the history of Amalgamated Recovery Products, Manchester Chemicals, and Dr. Peterson.

Chapter 36

My current travel plan had me leaving San Francisco the next morning, but I was anxious to pursue the blood testing idea. If it sped up the sampling process, I would willingly return to Milton, Louisiana tonight to try to get permission for a sample from the Luke boy, and resume my site visits with a trip to Taylock, Montana for the Oaks boy. I clicked on my computer and checked my e-mail for a reply from Harry about the best way to proceed.

I had an email from McLeish in my inbox. Strange. He usually preferred to yell orders over the phone. I opened the message and read his short, terse statement. He should've called and told me in person.

Buzz was dead.

He'd been mugged in an alley a few blocks from the *Morning Star* office, during his lunch hour, today. I was stunned. I'd spoken to him today, this morning, probably right before he'd gone to lunch.

There was too much senseless death in the world.

I read the email a second time. McLeish wanted me back in the office for a few days to go over Buzz's files on the Death Map story and, if I still had more traveling to do for the story, to find a suitable replacement on that end. Cold, even for McLeish.

I called the airport. There was a seat on a flight out of San Francisco tonight, scheduled to arrive in NYC about three

AM. I sent a text to Clunie. Maybe she'd be available to take over Buzz's role.

Chapter 37

Tuesday: New York City

On the flight back to New York, I listened to my tape of Peterson speculating on visual and auditory signs that might appear in someone exposed to this chemical, then made a chart of what I knew about the kids on the Death Map route. Manny Karlsson, Dwight, North Dakota, wanted a red sleeping bag, and reported hearing things. Victor Allen, Toomsboro, Alabama, liked a red sweater, referred to The Scarlet Letter as The Red Letter, but was color blind. Russell Johnson, Arden, Mississippi, stared at red lights. Mike Jacobsen, Charleston, South Carolina, talked about red Jell-O and a red pinwheel. Clarence Luke, Milton, Louisiana, heard voices. Kyle Bennett, Linton, North Dakota, was color blind. And they were all killers. After a thought, I included Eddie Hammersmith, Middleton, Montana, the dog killer, because he was alive and could provide a blood sample.

All these bizarre, disconnected comments took on new significance after my discussion with Dr. Peterson about sensory detection and behavior. If only I could find that same molecule somewhere else along this map—from a person or from the environment. I hoped I could convince McLeish this was a worthy pursuit.

McLeish had promised to deliver a company car to the airport short-term parking garage and leave the keys with his pal in airport security. When I saw the car, I was appalled. He had left me the old jalopy that Buzz always drove. McLeish didn't possess an ounce of sensitivity.

It was raining gently when I emerged from the airport parking garage, and I turned on the wipers. The rain seemed to pull the smog out of the air to settle in a greasy smear on the windshield. And, of course, the car was out of wiper fluid.

I drove into the city and parked in front of the corner building that housed the *Morning Star* offices. Circles of light dotted the empty sidewalk in front of the building. By three-thirty in the morning, the daytime panhandlers had vacated the area and were typically replaced by a different breed of homeless, those I looked upon as more unpredictable and possibly dangerous. Tonight, the rain dictated that this nocturnal population would stay out of sight. In addition to the city street lights, our building had a bright light at the front entrance that served to discourage sleepers. I parked in the loading zone in front of the building and dashed inside.

Night security buzzed me in and I signed the log book. I took the elevator up to the fifteenth floor. The corridor leading toward the *Morning Star* offices was dimly lit, and not much light passed through the glass door to the newsroom. It always appeared eerie this time of night, illuminated by the dim glow coming from rows of computer terminals maintained overnight on screen-saver mode. I unlocked the door, flipped on the overhead fluorescent lights, and the room took on the appearance of day — minus the noisy bustle of reporter activity. Two faces peered out of the big window of a walled-off area located at the back of the room. The night-time skeleton crew obviously conducted their business from the break room. I couldn't blame them; the majority of third shift activity was taking place across the street in the building that housed the printing presses. By comparison, this place was a tomb.

I waved at the guys in the break room and turned toward Buzz's workstation. I opened his file drawer and spotted a file labeled "LK Death Map." I pulled it out and leafed through its contents.

Death Map

Within seconds I realized Buzz had been holding back information; there were several letters that he had not sent to me, or even mentioned. I read over the letters, relieved that they didn't seem important; probably why Buzz hadn't forwarded them. I glanced at his notation of date of receipt and felt a stab of annoyance. I'd spoken with him at least three times since he'd received these. He should've at least told me they'd arrived and he considered them unimportant. It was typical Buzz behavior.

My annoyance shifted to suspicion. What else had Buzz kept from me? Damn it. I couldn't even yell at him now.

I sighed and pulled open his center desk drawer. It was probably worth my time to search through his desk. I stared at the black leather-bound notebook lying there. I'd seen it a million times. It was Buzz's private journal, which he always carried with him. So why was it in his drawer? Why hadn't he had it on him when he was mugged?

I opened the journal to the entry he had made this morning — well, technically by now it was yesterday morning — his last entry before he was murdered.

I'm convinced this lead is important. If A.R.P. wants to distance itself from the construction crew working on the D.M. route, they must have had prior knowledge of the involvement of one of their employees in the murders. Will meet with G.M. today — 12:30 pm.

This was interesting. Buzz was investigating on his own, and had arranged a meeting that was to be held at about the time he was reportedly being mugged. Maybe his death was more than a random mugging? Could G.M. be his killer? Or, more likely, Buzz simply chose a dangerous spot for a meeting with this G.M. person. But what exactly was the lead he had been following? A.R.P. rang a faint bell but I couldn't place it.

Then I remembered. I hadn't actually seen it written, but

ARP was how Dr. Peterson identified the test samples from Amalgamated Recovery Products. They were the supplier of the petroleum byproduct that Peterson had tested for the Canadian Department of Energy. A chemical in an ARP sample matched the chemical Dr. Sims found in the blood samples. Maybe Buzz had stumbled on something, after all.

Then there was Buzz's reference to a construction crew along the Death Map route. There seemed to be a lot Buzz was keeping from me. I flipped back through the journal to the day the map had been published and began to read all of Buzz's handwritten accounts of the recent events:

Mon. — L.K. asked me to work with her on the D.M. article. Finally, being recognized for my talents! Get to have first crack at all the feedback from the article. Chance to show up L.K.!!!

I winced. Damn McLeish. I hadn't wanted Buzz to begin with.

Tues. — Phone calls began almost as soon as the issue hit the stands. Lots of nutty responses. Will separate into MY FILE and L.K. FILE.

I looked again at the file I'd pulled out of his file drawer. It was labeled "L K Death Map." Apparently Buzz had another file somewhere. I looked through the file drawer at each tabbed folder. Nothing labeled "My File." I continued to read in the journal.

Wed. — Received confession today from hypnotist J.C. Claims to have traveled the D.M. route about five years ago, hypnotizing young boys at random and placing the suggestion that they go berserk when they hear the phrase 'extra cheese, please.' Seems unlikely at first glance, but who knows. Should be fairly easy to check J.C.'s whereabouts five years ago.

I sighed. I knew all this information.

Death Map

Thurs. — J.C.'s a phony. Worked as a pizza delivery guy from six years ago until six months ago. Never delivered beyond 42nd Street; used his mom's car; never took a vacation. Mom claims he practices hypnosis all the time, but as far as she knows, he's never gotten it to work on anyone. Scratch J.C.!!!

I scanned a week's worth of unimportant entries before finding something interesting.

Wed. — Interesting letter today with photocopy of the northern route of the map. Not taken from my article, but overlaps exactly. Sender claims he was on a road construction crew working that route six years ago. Also claims the crew went south for the winter months. Need to contact job foreman for names of crew and see if southern sites line up with D.M.

I stopped reading. His article? That conniving little jerk. Someone else had a map of the northern route, and Buzz hadn't told me. If he weren't already dead, I'd have strangled him myself. This could be the key to the whole puzzle. I read the next entry.

Thurs. — Reached a reluctant foreman J.G. Managed to get names/addresses of workers on job. Maybe have name of killer. Shall begin phone interviews today.

I needed to find that other file. Surely, that was where Buzz had put the letter containing this second map. I searched through his file drawer again, this time ignoring the label on the file tabs and looking at the contents of each folder. Nothing. I looked through his desk drawers, even checked to see if anything was taped underneath the drawers. Again, nothing.

Maybe Buzz had taken it home. I wracked my brain to remember anything personal about Buzz, like where he lived, or if he had a roommate. It was hopeless; I hadn't paid that much attention to the guy. Then I noticed the large pad covering the desk top. I smiled to myself as I lifted a corner and spotted a file folder hidden there. I slid the file out from under the pad and checked the tab. "My File." *Yes.*

I opened the file and leafed through its contents. There were several sheets of notepaper with Buzz's handwritten notations in the margins and an envelope addressed to "The *Morning Star*, Attn: Death Map Investigation."

I opened the envelope and took out the two sheets of paper it contained. On top was a letter. I scanned the signature, didn't recognize the name, and read the letter.

To whom it may concern,

I worked as a member of a road construction crew for Meyers Construction six years ago. Our work route matches your map of those murders reported in the paper the other day. You asked for information concerning the area or anything that might seem connected.

Well, we were there, so I guess it's connected in that way. However, I did not notice anything remarkable along the route which could lead to the murders you described. Besides, it was so long ago. But it seems to me that if we were using this route, there must be lots of others doing it too.

Sorry I didn't write sooner. The birth of my second child interrupted my plans to contact you right away. Maybe you already know this by now.

Sincerely,
Zeke Waggoner
Equality, IL
618-765-4422

I read through the letter again and felt my pulse race. This had possibilities and raised more questions. How closely did Waggoner's work route actually match the Death Map? What kind of construction had they done? Could one of the crew have returned to the area years later and somehow influenced the boys along the way?

Death Map

Buzzy Boy had apparently come up with several of the same questions. His journal entry mentioned he'd gotten a list of names of the road construction crew and had started phone interviews.

The second piece of paper in the envelope from Zeke Waggoner was a photocopy of a small US map, crisscrossed with the major highways — the kind that was in the back of my date book. An additional line had been penned in. The added line matched the northern route on my Death Map. Of course, Waggoner could've simply created the line after reading my article in the paper.

But Buzz did have a list of names. Maybe there *had* been a work crew along that route. I looked at the pages in the folder again and found a faxed list of names and addresses with Buzz's cryptic notations handwritten in the margins. This must be the employee list he was investigating.

The unexpected ring of a desk phone made me jump. It seemed to be coming from my workstation. Who would be calling me at this hour? I walked down the aisle to my desk and answered.

"Kincaid here."

"You back?" McLeish barked.

"Don't you ever sleep?" I asked. I absentmindedly tucked the papers back into the file and put the file into my bag.

"I asked Matt Barnard to let me know when you showed up again. I thought he could fill in for Buzz, so I asked him to hang around."

"Well, see, I need someone on days. I'll get Clunie,"

"Matt'll adjust. Ask him. He's interested." McLeish hung up.

I frowned; boss man was doing it to me again. I didn't know much about Matt, but I'd lay out my expectations and see what he said. It would save me a lot of headache if he switched to day shift for this project. I left my cubicle and walked back down the aisle toward Buzz's. I'd almost reached it when I heard a "zing" and a computer on the desk in front of me shattered.

I whirled around as I heard more zings and chunks of plastic began flying through the air around me. I'd never been shot at before, but that's what was happening. I dropped to the floor and crawled under the nearest desk. The computers on the desks above me fragmented, sending glass and plastic fragments flying around the room. It didn't make sense! Why would someone shoot up the newsroom in the middle of the night?

Since I was near the break room, I yelled for Matt. He didn't answer. He had to still be around somewhere, since his phone was probably still hot from informing McLeish I'd arrived. I didn't have the break room number in my cell phone, so I reached up and felt along the desk until I found a phone. The shooting slowed, but I didn't dare sit up. Instead, I pulled it down to the floor next to me. I punched the direct line to the break room but there was no answer. There had been two people in there when I had arrived. How long had it been? Twenty minutes? I hadn't seen anyone leave. They could've been shattered like the computers. Or, and this thought freaked me out, they could be doing the shooting. I shook my head. That made no sense. I dialed 911 and reported my situation. The police and an ambulance were dispatched.

The room went eerily silent, and I realized the shooting had stopped.

"Matt?" I yelled out again. "Are you guys okay back there?"

Still no answer. If they were injured, there might be something I could do for them until the ambulance arrived. Hoping the gunman had left, I rose up enough to peek toward the front door before standing upright. I saw the door open, and watched a man enter the newsroom. EMT's don't wear ski masks and arrive bearing flaming Molotov cocktails. The man looked directly at me and threw the flaming bottle high into the air in my direction.

Chapter 38

"No," I yelled as I turned and ran toward the emergency exit at the back of the newsroom. I heard the bottle break and caught a whiff of kerosene. The flames whooshed behind me as the desks, all topped with stacks of files, old newspaper, and magazines, easily caught fire. The shooting began again, and I dropped to the floor. I crawled as fast as I could along the rows of desks to the side exit. I kept my body low to the floor and reached up to push on the door handle. The door buzzed as it opened, and I crawled out into the safety of the stairwell.

I shoved the door closed and leaned against it, my heart a rapid-fire staccato; my body on adrenaline alert. This was crazy. What had happened to Matt? And the other guy in the break room with him? Were they dead? I tried to reopen the emergency exit door, but it had locked automatically from the inside. *Shit!*

I thought my *Morning Star* key might work, and I searched through my purse for a second before changing my mind. The room was on fire, there was a shooter in there, and I didn't have a weapon. But I had my cell phone. I could call McLeish. I continued rummaging through my bag and found my cell phone. Of course, no signal penetrated the stairwell. I tossed the phone back into my bag, and then noticed the smoke seeping out from under the door. This was no place to loiter.

I turned and ran down the stairs, my thoughts flying faster than my feet. Who the hell would shoot up the newsroom? And why?

I rounded the fourteenth-floor landing. They had seemed to be aiming at me. But was that deliberate or circumstantial? Surely, they wouldn't have been after *me*.

My thoughts were disjointed, pulsing ideas as my feet pounded the steps.

Two steps at a time, jumping the last three. Twelfth floor. No one even knew I would be there tonight. Except McLeish. And Matt Barnard, and probably the other guy in the break room. And Clunie. Would they tell anyone else? No reason I could think of.

At the tenth floor, I recalled a threatening letter I'd received last year. Turned over to McLeish. Old news. No interest to anyone now. Not me. They weren't after me.

By the eighth floor, I considered recent events. New threats? The Death Map story? Buzz hiding info. Buzz's desk exploding first during the attack. Could Buzz's desk have been the target?

My mind reeled at my next thought and brought me to a halt. What if I'd been right that Buzz's death might not be a random mugging? If Buzz had stumbled onto something, he could've walked right into a trap. He might not've realized the information was important or dangerous.

I looked back up the stairwell. The only sound was my labored breathing. No footsteps following me. I could smell the smoke, however, and tried my cell phone again. Still no signal.

I was at the sixth-floor landing before it dawned on me that I should be hearing footsteps. Surely a fire alarm had gone off in the building by now. I hadn't heard anything in the stairwell, but would I hear the alarm in the stairwell? I didn't even know how many people were in the building at this hour.

I tried the door on this landing. It was also locked. I pounded on it with my fist and waited. No answer.

"Fire," I yelled. No answer. I spotted a fire alarm box and pulled the handle, then continued my downward flight in step with the ear-splitting alarm.

My thoughts continued to whirl. Had the front door security guard let in the shooter? Was the security guard involved, or a victim?

I passed the fifth floor. Something else. Had to be something else. Some other gripe against the *Morning Star*. Not my story. Yet, if Buzz had been murdered . . . and they'd wanted to destroy his files . . . burning down his workplace would do that.

Fourth floor. Buzz's death; shots fired at me on the same day. Too much of a coincidence? Working on the same story. *Oh, God. Buzz's death was not an accident.*

I reached the second floor. I wanted to scream at Buzz. Too damn secretive, trying to take over the investigation. Had he caused this fiasco? Now the answer had gone up in flames with his journal.

Then I remembered the file I'd been reading when McLeish's call had interrupted me. I stopped my flight down the stairs and looked in my purse. There it was. Buzz's "My File." It was safe.

One more flight and I'd also be safe, also have cell signal. I jumped down the last four steps.

I started to open the outer exit door when the image of rats leaving a sinking ship popped into my mind. And one little punk rat about to be picked off by a sniper waiting specifically for her. I stopped running and leaned against the wall next to the outer door. My adrenaline pumped, and my body continued to tremble. I tried to think clearly about my situation. Was there safety or danger on the other side of that door?

If someone wanted to destroy Buzz's files for some other reason, I was probably not a target. Even though the masked Molotov cocktail thrower had tossed the weapon toward me, he hadn't followed me down the stairwell. Didn't try any harder to get me. But then, Buzz had been keeping secret leads related to my story; there *really* might be someone waiting for me on the other side of the door.

I tried to calm myself, tried to believe this attack had nothing to do with my Death Map story at all. It was an act of violence against the paper, nothing else. Buzz's death was a random act, nothing else. The man was not shooting at Lila Kincaid, or throwing a fire bomb at Lila Kincaid specifically, he was targeting a random woman in the hated newsroom of the hated *Morning Star*.

I jumped at the sound of a door opening somewhere up the stairwell, momentarily increasing the decibels of the alarm. Then thundering footsteps and echoing questions approached. I flattened myself against the wall and let a few individuals exit the building ahead of me, blending into the midst of the small crowd.

The flow of the exiting group, maybe thirty at the most, stopped under the corner street lamp. As one, we looked back at the building for evidence of smoke or flames. There were exclamations of horror as a top floor window shattered and flames shot out into the night.

I stayed in the middle of the group, listening to the chatter. No one seemed to know about the attack on the newsroom. I must be the only one from the uppermost floor. I needed to call McLeish, find out if he'd heard from Matt again, but I didn't want to risk being overheard. The shooter could be standing next to me in the crowd.

I slowly worked my way through the assembly toward the company car. I rounded the corner of the building and realized I couldn't get to it. A fire engine was pulling up in front of it and another had the car blocked from behind. As I wondered how close a cab could get to the building, I kept an eye on the firefighters unrolling their hoses. I saw a fireman hook the end of a hose to a fire hydrant and turn on the water supply. The hose stiffened with the weight of the rushing water and began to bounce erratically in his grip.

With one gyration, the hose bounced solidly off the hood of *Morning Star's* company car. The explosion was instantaneous. Flames streaked upward, cutting into the black sky. Flaming car chunks twisted wildly, rising into the night, falling back to the earth, initiating tiny fires where they landed. Everyone within a fifty-foot radius, myself included, crashed to the ground with the released energy wave.

The people who had vacated the building burst into motion, screaming and running away from the firefighters and the burning remains of the car. The firefighters nearest to the car were protected by their gear from the shower of fire that followed the explosion. Two police officers standing in the middle of the street behind the car were not so lucky. The flames engulfed their uniforms faster than I would have thought possible. The firefighters responded instantly to extinguish the flames.

I stared in horror. The car Buzz had driven, but that I was driving tonight. My workplace. Buzz's desk. Buzz. An invisible target weighed heavily on my back. I felt vulnerable simply being in the vicinity. All my instincts told me to run, to get away as fast as possible. Instead, I rejoined the relative safety of the few remaining bystanders and sent Clunie an SOS. I gripped my bag with throbbing hands and felt the bulk of Buzz's private file.

Could it hold the answer?

Chapter 39

I edged through the crowd without focus until I heard my name. My heart jumped as I turned in the direction of the voice. Through the vibrant flashes of the red emergency vehicle lights I recognized Clunie's dreadlocks and tattooed arms waving at me.

In a moment she was at my side with a hug. "Hey, girlfriend. I got your message," she said. "This is insane, like crazy."

I leaned in close to her ear. "Someone shot at me," I said, panting hard. "And blew up my car."

She stared intently at my face for a second. "Come on." She grabbed my hand. "Let's book."

I let her pull me down the sidewalk, away from the smoke and acrid fumes. Her sandals *thwap-thwapped* as we passed the police barricades. My mind kept circling around the events of the evening. We met a few people running toward the fire, but after a block the street emptied.

"Someone shot up the office," I managed to say. "I got out."

"Wait," Clunie said. "We're almost to the car. Tell me then."

I glanced around and gripped my bag tightly to my chest. As we ran, I imagined eyes staring at me from the dark corners between buildings.

"I'm over here," she said. "It's as close as I could get." She pulled a key fob from her pocket and pushed the button. Headlights came on and locks popped.

Once in her car, safety belt latched, the intense shaking started. "I need to call McLeish," I stammered, fumbling with my phone. I kept dropping it onto my lap, then the floor, trying again and again. He needed to know where I was. I needed to know about those guys from the break room.

Clunie watched me struggle then pulled a small cooler from the back seat and handed me a bottled water, a protein bar, and a tub of honey.

"You're in shock," she said, taking my cell phone. "Drink. Eat something sweet. I'll dial."

She started the car, turned the heater on high and called our boss. I heard his gruff voice say my name and she handed me the phone.

"Lila?" he repeated. "There's a fire at the office. Some kind of attack. I'm on my way in."

"I know," I said, my voice trembly. "I was there."

"What? What the hell happened? Where the hell are you now?"

"Someone shot up the place, then set it on fire," I said. "Right after I spoke to you. Matt and someone else were in the break room. I don't know what's happened to them." My voice hitched. "I don't know if they got out. I'm in Clunie's car right now." I took a big drink of the water.

"Clunie? Was she there, too? Did either of you see who did it?"

"She wasn't inside, just picking me up. I saw one man wearing a ski mask, but there was at least one other person there. A lot of gunfire. More than one shooter."

"Who the hell would do this?" McLeish asked.

"I hoped you'd know. But it might have to do with Buzz."

"Buzz? He's dead, for God's sake. How could it have anything to do with Buzz?"

I took a big breath and then a bite of the protein bar. "The shots." I paused and chewed. "And the initial flame." I washed it down with another drink. My voice steadied. "Were aimed at Buzz's desk. I'm thinking maybe he was murdered, not mugged." I noticed Clunie's grip tighten on the steering wheel. I put McLeish on speaker.

"Explain that leap," McLeish demanded, sarcasm heavy.

I felt Clunie tense. She put the car in drive and pulled away from the curb.

"I found Buzz's notes," I continued, speaking both to McLeish and Clunie. "He was keeping stuff from me, running an investigation on his own, and I think it got him killed."

"Notes? You think they wanted to get rid of his notes? Is that what you think?"

"I failed to mention that Buzz's car was also blown up. That had to've been deliberate."

"Which you were driving, as I recall. You could be the target, Lila, not Buzz."

"I'm aware of that, Dan." I glanced behind us for a tail and then shot a look at Clunie. The flower tattoo on her neck at the base of her right ear stood out in stark contrast to the sudden paleness of her skin. Her wide eyes met mine, then flicked to the rear-view mirror before returning her focus on the road ahead.

"Where are you with your investigation?" McLeish asked.

"Well, I'm following a lead to a company called Amalgamated Recovery Products." I heard Clunie's sharp intake of breath and checked behind us again for a tail. Nothing. "Buzz was looking into a company called Meyer's Construction." This time Clunie squeaked. I looked at her and her eyes were about to bug out. "Buzz opened a letter," I continued, "from a guy who worked the same route as my Death Map. Buzzy Boy failed to share that little tidbit with me."

I resisted the urge to launch into a litany of expletives. The little shit might still be alive if he'd let me know what was going on. I might not have wandered into the middle of a shooting. Matt and the unnamed guy in the break room might not have been put in danger. The more I voiced the details, the more certain I became. "He got hold of a list of employees from that company," I continued. "I got out with it. His journal's another issue. I read a little before the shooting began, but it's ashes by now."

There was no response from McLeish for a moment. Finally, I spoke. "You still there, Dan?"

"Yes. I don't suppose you can recreate any of that?"

"I'll try. Mostly right now I'm worried about those guys in the break room. I didn't see them exit the building. They might not have made it."

"The other guy with Matt was probably Rick. New guy. Last name is Stewart."

I swallowed hard to get the rest of the story out. "The whole room was shot to pieces, then torched."

"Okay," McLeish said. "Write it up. Need it in one hour. I'll find out what happened to the other two. The boys from the pressroom have already called me. They'll hold a spot for you on the front page. I guess they have great pictures. We should have the morning edition out as close to usual time as can be done."

I swallowed hard. Damn, McLeish must think I have nerves of steel. But writing would help me focus, calm my pounding heart.

"Okay," I said, "I'll get right on it." I hung up and turned to Clunie. "Now, you. Spill it."

Her voice trembled this time. "I know them," she said.

"Who? The shooters? The guys in the break room?"

"No," she said, shaking her head. "Amalgamated Recovery Products and Meyers Construction."

Chapter 40

Since my laptop had been blown to smithereens, Clunie let me use hers to write up the attack on the *Morning Star* offices and send it in. She also gave me the list of companies she'd compiled that were linked to legislative decisions where Senator O'Connell's vote was key. And there they were: Amalgamated Recovery Products and Meyer's Construction. No wonder she looked so frightened in the car. Her Spidey senses had blazed.

It was obvious to both of us that if Buzz's death wasn't a mugging but a murder linked to his investigation of Meyers Construction, we were dealing with a very dangerous enemy. Maybe an enemy also linked to Senator O'Connell's murder? Could we dare hope to find a solid connection between ARP and Meyers Construction related to the Death Map?

Clunie scoured her notes on the pieces of legislation where these companies had an interest, looking for an association between them other than the Senator. I wished I'd saved Buzz's journal. But at least I had something that might provide a clue. I stretched out on the sofa, opened the manila file folder I'd rescued from his desk, and began to read.

I awoke as the sun peeked through an opening in the curtains and shone on my face. I was lying at an uncomfortable angle across the sofa pillows with papers from Buzz's file strewn around me and a letter gripped in my hand. I checked the clock as I tried to stretch the kinks out of my neck and shoulders. Ten o'clock. I'd only gotten five hours of sleep. I felt like I had a hangover.

My first thoughts were about the tragedy at the office and the uncertainty concerning the fate of Matt and Rick. It only now occurred to me that the phone call from McLeish probably saved my life. If I hadn't walked over to my office to answer the phone, I would've been standing right next to Buzz's desk when the shooting broke out. I didn't like that notion one bit. I stood up, went to the bathroom and stared at my reflection in the mirror.

"They got Buzz, his notes, and they almost got you," I said to my image. "Now, you've got to get them." My bravado was as impressive as my ruined make-up. I took a quick shower, then returned to Clunie's living room. She was up and making coffee in the kitchen.

"Sorry to wake you," I said.

"No worries, girlfriend. I couldn't sleep, either."

I found my cell phone and placed a call to Charleston. Harry sounded sleepy when he finally answered. I heard Jay-Jay squawking "Hello" in the background, which placed Harry in the family room. I wondered if he was sick or something, home at ten in the morning. I filled him in on the overnight events, including the destroyed journal I'd only briefly glanced at and the file I'd managed to escape with.

"Jeeze, Lila," he said, sounding wide-awake now. "You'd better lay low for a while. Let someone else follow up."

"Are you kidding me? I'm finally getting close. I can feel it."

"You're feeling the danger, you mean."

"Yeah, well, there's no way I'm turning it over to anyone else."

"Where are you staying? Not home?"

"No. I'm not suicidal. I'm at Clunie's. She's a friend from work."

"Stay there. I'm coming to get you."

"You don't need to play the hero, Harry. Anyway, you don't want to become a target, too."

"That won't happen. No one knows about me. I've not been mentioned in any of your articles."

"Neither was Buzz."

"True. But Buzz was actively investigating. Look, Lila, I'll fly up, rent a car and drive you back down to Charleston."

I thought about that suggestion. Maybe they wouldn't trace me down there. And I could use some help. Besides, I needed to see Michael, and interview Dr. Sims again.

"Okay, I'll come back to Charleston," I said. "But you don't need to come galloping to my rescue. I'll see if McLeish will get me a car and I'll drive down. I should be there before midnight if I get started soon. And thanks, Harry."

I called my editor. "Dan, it's me."

"How are you holding up, kid?"

"I'm okay. What did you find out about Matt and Rick?"

"The security guard found them. They'd made it to the other exit before they collapsed. Smoke inhalation. They're hospitalized, but should be okay. Good article, by the way," he said. "Have the police interviewed you?"

"No. Do they need to?"

"I told them you were on your way out of town on assignment. They just said to check in after you get back."

"Thanks. I'm thinking I need to get out of town again as soon as possible. If someone's after me, I'll be safer with your help."

"Someone's definitely trying to stop your investigation. We had a call."

I swallowed hard. "Who was it? Did they mention me?"

"Anonymous male. But, yeah, he ranted about you. Buzz. The office."

"Did you tell the police?"

"Sure. They took notes. Asked if we had any more information on the Death Map. I told them no but we're looking. Do you have any idea who this guy could be?"

"No, but there's some good stuff in Buzz's file. I want to pick up where he left off. He was following up a lead about a construction crew that had worked the Death Map route exactly."

"Why didn't I know that?"

"Yeah, well, you picked Buzz. Nevertheless, Clunie had actually heard of this same construction company and another lead I was following. Both companies were on her list related to Senator O'Connell. We haven't figured it all out yet."

"Well, stay on it. But for God's sake, be careful."

"Can I get a car? I'm afraid to use mine, or even go to my apartment."

"I'll rent one for you, put it in my name."

"Thanks. And I'll need another laptop."

"Consider it done. It'll be in the car. I'll have it delivered to Clunie's."

Time for one more call. I phoned Dr. Archer in Toronto to have him locate the samples that Dr. Peterson had left behind in the freezer. He wasn't in yet. I left word with his secretary that I'd call back later. I hung up with a vague sense of unease. The secretary had said Archer was always in early and she sounded a bit concerned. I scowled, annoyed that paranoia had seeped into every aspect of this investigation.

Chapter 41

I'd been on the road for almost two hours. Clunie's parting gift, some sort of protective crystal, swung on its leather strap from my mirror. The trip from New York to Charleston so far had been a blur. The monotony of the highway allowed my mind to return time and again to the deaths of Ellen, Buzz, Senator O'Connell, and my own brush with death in the newsroom. There were too many emotions at play here — disbelief, horror, sadness, shock, and even guilt. My sane self knew I had to shake off this melancholy. There were still at least ten or eleven hours of driving time ahead of me, and I couldn't whine and cry to myself all the way. I needed to do something. I spent the next half hour trying to recall all that I remembered from Buzz's destroyed journal and logging it into my tape recorder.

When I'd exhausted my memory, I decided it was time to speak to the man who claimed to have been working the northern Death Map route six years ago. Zeke Waggoner. I glanced at my watch. One PM. That meant noon in southern Illinois, if I had my time zones right.

I took the next exit and pulled the car into a Quick Mart parking lot to look up the number. I didn't mind driving and talking on my hands-free set, but it was impossible to look through my files while doing eighty. First, I needed coffee — a big coffee. I ran into the store, grabbed a cup of caffeine and a bag of strawberry licorice sticks and returned to my car. I located the number for Zeke Waggoner of Equality, Illinois, written carefully under his scrawled signature at the bottom of the letter he'd sent with the map. I punched in the number on my cell phone and then continued down the road.

A man answered. I could hear a child jabbering in the background. I clicked on my tape recorder, and asked to speak to Zeke Waggoner.

"You got him."

"Mr. Waggoner, I'm Lila Kincaid, a reporter for the *Morning Star.*"

"Well, what d'ya know. I'd given up on anyone calling me," he said. "I thought maybe you'd decided there was no connection after all."

"Actually, your map just came into my hands yesterday. I'm definitely interested. You mentioned in your letter that you were working a job along that route. Can you tell me a little more about that job?"

"Sure. I was working for a construction company — Meyers Construction, it was. We were paving sections of blacktop with a new type of asphalt. Supposed to be more weather resistant, you know, not break apart so easily in those harsh winters they have up north, or in the high temps down south."

"How many men were in your crew?" I asked.

"Eight regulars, and two locals to direct traffic."

"So, the core crew was together for the entire job?"

"Well, at least up north. They went south, somewhere near Texas, at the end of the summer — October, I think — but I quit then. There was a girl back home I was interested in, which worked out, by the way. Most of the others planned to keep on. I wondered about their southern route," he said, "about whether it matched with the rest of your map."

"I'd like to know that, too," I said.

"I can give you some names. And I have a number for the foreman, Jack Gambone. I'll bet he's still with the company."

I had to wait for a couple of minutes while he found the information, and I wondered about asphalt. Asphalt was one of the things Dr. Peterson had told me used petroleum byproducts. Could asphalt be the connection between ARP and Meyers Construction? When Waggoner came back to the phone, I patiently repeated the contact information out loud for the tape recorder.

"Tell me, Mr. Waggoner, have you ever heard of Amalgamated Recovery Products?"

"No, I sure haven't. Do they work along that route, too?"

"Maybe. And you say no one from the *Morning Star* contacted you? Buzz Bradley, maybe?"

"No, never heard from anyone 'til you. You know, Ms. Kincaid. This whole map of yours is really scary. I hate to think I was so close to something related to all those killers and not known about it."

Well, Zeke Waggoner, I thought, maybe you know more than you realize.

"Yeah," I said, "it's a scary thing. Thanks for sending in your information."

Even scarier was the possibility that I might now have a confirmation of how ARP 2728 had reached the kids. All I needed was a link between Meyers Construction and Amalgamated Recovery Products. My mind raced ahead. If Meyers bought asphalt directly from ARP, that would cinch it. But I could imagine several other scenarios. ARP might not have made the asphalt themselves, but sold the refinery byproduct containing ARP 2728 to an asphalt producing company. Or they could have sold the technology to a third company. Or another asphalt company could be using a similar process, independently producing the same dangerous chemical byproduct. Assuming ARP 2728 made it into the asphalt at all. Could Dr. Sims test the asphalt for the neurotransmitter-like chemical? Thoughts were flying through my mind faster than I was speeding south.

The highway stretched out before me, gently winding through hills covered with dogwoods and redbuds in bloom. I fired up new theories and reshaped old ones.

Had I stumbled upon a serial killer? Could someone familiar with Meyers Construction use the chemical to contaminate the area? Maybe the water supply along the route? If so, how would it have been accomplished? Could some sort of chemical time bomb have been set in place to go off years later, long after the person responsible had left the area?

Was this the same trail that Buzz had been following? Waggoner had said they were pouring weather resistant asphalt. What if the company sent someone back on a regular basis to inspect the stuff? He would follow the same route. My pulse quickened at that idea. Had Buzz thought of this angle? Had he questioned an inspector?

I reminded myself that Buzz's investigation had probably resulted in his death. I needed to find out who he questioned, what he learned, or what someone thought he knew, and keep myself alive during the process.

My journey to South Carolina took me through Washington D.C. I tried to bypass the city traffic using the I-495 outer loop, but it was jammed there, too. I didn't mind the slow-moving traffic, though; my thoughts were focused on my next call. Without pulling over, I dialed the number Zeke Waggoner had provided for Meyers Construction.

"Hello," I said, "I'm Mary Appleby, reporter for *Scientific Innovations*, a new e-zine devoted to current technological advancements. I've been told that your company recently completed a test of weather resistant asphalt with the potential to save millions each year in road repairs. Do you have a PR representative willing to be interviewed?"

"You'd better speak with Mr. Meyers. One moment, please."

"George Meyers," a deep voice announced over the line moments later.

Could he be the G.M. mentioned in Buzz's journal?

I started my tape recorder and repeated my cover line. Mr. Meyers was definitely interested in free press.

"Yes, Ms. Appleby. Your information is correct, except the dollar amount could reach into the billions. The new stimulus package calls for infrastructure repair and this technique qualifies. But we're only the contractors laying the asphalt, not the manufacturer. My men did an excellent job and now that the test period is over, we fully expect to be awarded a contract to continue paving."

"Why don't you tell me about your company?"

"Sure thing. We're a large road construction company based here in Texas. But we do jobs throughout the United States."

"How many people do you employ?"

"I have fifty-three full-time office employees, thirty foremen, and about three hundred construction workers — although that number fluctuates, depending on the number of contracts we have working at any one time."

"I thought I might get a photo of the crew that installed the test asphalt," I said. "Maybe actually doing a job? It wouldn't have to be the same asphalt, I guess, unless there's something distinguishing about it that would be noticeable in a photo?"

"We're not pouring the test stuff right now, but it looks exactly like any other asphalt. Let me check with my secretary real quick here and I'll see if that same crew is still together somewhere. I like to keep the same men together, unless there's a personality conflict. If they like who they're working with, they'll stay with me longer."

He was back on the line a few minutes later.

"Actually, Ms. Appleby, those guys are scheduled to start a job in Raleigh, North Carolina. They should be in the area for about two weeks. If you're in a hurry for a photo, though, any crew would work; they all use the same equipment."

"I like to be authentic in my reporting," I said. "Besides, I'd like to interview the actual crew, for a more firsthand account of the project, you know, how the stuff handled, did it behave differently, smell differently, anything at all."

"I have no problem with you talking to the men. I'm sure they'll tell you they wouldn't have known the asphalt was anything special if we hadn't told them."

He gave me the address of the job site in Raleigh, the foreman's phone number, and the start date.

"So how does this asphalt differ from the regular stuff?" I asked.

"Well, the actual formula's a secret that even I don't know."

"But surely some government agency requires a formulary."

"Well, we have the Safety Data Sheet information on file."

"Could I get a copy of it to compare with the one for standard asphalt?"

"Don't see why not. After all, you could access the same information from the state's Department of Transportation. Sure, what's your fax number?"

"Could you just text a shot of it to me?" I supplied my cell phone number.

"You realize this merely lists the chemical components, not the formula?"

"I'm sure my readers will be fascinated by a comparison," I said. "And thanks, Mr. Meyers. I'll be stopping by the construction site in Raleigh to snap a few pictures. I'll let you read the article before publication, if you like."

"Wonderful."

"Oh, one more thing," I said. "Is there a report filed with some government agency on how these surfaces have withstood summer heat and winter freezing as compared to regular asphalt?"

"Yes, of course. The company that makes the product is trying to prove its superiority. You see, government contracts are usually awarded to the lowest bidder, if all other things are equal. However, if it can be shown that a product is vastly superior and will save money in the long run, then the picture changes. If the product can be considered unique, without direct competitors, things are no longer equal. See the rationale?"

"Sure. It means the company will likely be awarded big government contracts, and there's lots of money at stake. Do you have a copy of the performance record, or the name of the company doing the inspections?"

"I'll have to look that up. I have their final report somewhere here in the file."

"Okay. What states are involved?" I asked.

"If you can hang on a sec, I'll find that for you."

He came back on the line a few moments later and read through a list of states and hearing dates. The first few states were the same ones included both on my Death Map and also in Mr. Waggoner's work log. I continued checking off the states as he read off their names. The remainder matched the southern path of my Death Map exactly. I fist pumped the air and wanted to shout out.

I forced my attention back to Mr. Meyers, relieved that anything I might have missed would be on the tape. He was saying he'd found the name of the inspection firm; it was Sky's-the-Limit Evaluations out of Oakland, California.

"Oh, before you go, Mr. Meyers, I didn't get the name of the asphalt supplier."

"Oh, sorry. Manchester Chemicals, Consolidated."

Well, well. Now that was a surprise. Peterson's current employer. Was all his discussion about Amalgamated Recovery Products an attempt at misdirection? Was Peterson the only ARP connection?

"Thank you again, Mr. Meyers. I'll send you a preview of my article."

"Goodbye, Ms. Appleby. It's been a pleasure."

I thought about Manchester Chemicals and wondered if they were on Clunie's list, too. They seemed like the next logical target to tackle.

My recollection of Peterson's ARP reference reminded me of my earlier call to Dr. Archer. Traffic was still at a crawl, so I scrolled down the recently called numbers on my cell phone and dialed the Toronto number. I hoped Archer was in by now. He was, and I briefly explained my conversation with his former colleague and described the freezer box where the samples could be located.

"You spoke with him yesterday?" Dr. Archer asked.

"Yes," I said, "I flew out to San Francisco and met with him."

"Then you were probably one of the last people to speak to him," Dr. Archer said.

The car seemed to close in on me. Fear poked its ugly head into my heart.

"What? What do you mean?" I asked, nearly in a whisper.

"He was killed in an accident late last night," Dr. Archer said. "They say his brakes must have failed and he plummeted over a cliff and into the ocean. They haven't recovered the body, but he didn't stand a chance, I guess. It's such a shame. He was a true genius and a super nice guy."

I suddenly felt cold. Another death associated with this story. Ellen, Buzz, Senator O'Connell, and now Dr. Peterson. Not to mention all the victims along the Death Map routes. Was someone following me, killing everyone I worked with on the case? Oh, God, I needed to warn Clunie. And what about this guy, Archer? I hadn't told anyone about him. Should I warn him or would he think I was being superstitious?

"Yes," I said, "he was a super nice guy. I'm sorry, Dr. Archer. Listen. I think I should warn you. There have been several, well, mysterious deaths since I began this investigation. I haven't told anyone about our conversations, and I haven't been to see you, so you probably don't have anything to worry about."

"Wait a minute. Are you suggesting Sven's death was mysterious? I'm sure the police ruled it an accident."

"I hope it was," I said. "And I hope I'm being overly cautious."

"I'm sure you are," Dr. Archer said. "I guess, since Sven told you exactly where to find the samples, he wouldn't mind if I send them on. What's your address?"

"Thanks, Dr. Archer. Please send them directly to Dr. Sims, Senior Chemist, South Carolina State Laboratory, Charleston, SC."

I needed to warn Sims to expect the samples from Archer. Then, with a chill, I thought maybe she needed a warning of another type.

Chapter 42

Wednesday: Charleston, South Carolina

I pulled up in front of Harry's house a few minutes after midnight and rubbed my weary eyes. I struggled to force them open again. Harry must have been watching, for he appeared at the front door as soon as I pulled to the curb. He sprinted out to the car.

"I think you should park in the garage," he said.

I signaled an okay and backed up so I could pull into the driveway. I slid the rental into the empty stall next to Harry's car. He was opening my car door as the heavy garage door lowered behind us, blocking out the streetlights. I stepped out of the car and he pulled me into his arms, holding me close. I pushed back automatically. I hated sympathetic gestures. He let go.

"Are you sure you're okay?" he asked.

"Yes, Harry, I'm fine. Just tired. It was a long drive."

"I'm sorry about that reporter, Buzz," Harry said. "You're convinced it's connected to your story?"

I didn't answer, only motioned my conviction with my head.

"Come on inside, "Harry said. "You need to relax after that trip."

He opened the backseat door of the car and picked up my new laptop case. "No suitcase?" he asked.

I winced. "My suitcase blew up with the car and I couldn't risk going home for more stuff." I followed him from the garage through the connecting door to the kitchen and perched on a stool at the counter. "I'll stock up in the morning."

While he poured us each a scotch I asked, "How was Mike today?"

"Still no response to anyone, but there's a new development. He's running a slight temp, so they started an antibiotic."

"I'll go see him first thing," I said. "Thanks for keeping tabs." I looked at my drink and swirled it around in the glass. "Did you find a way to get blood samples from the other two kids?"

"Yep. I'm pretty sure the samples are on their way to Sims by now."

"Oh. Okay. Thanks." I knew I didn't sound excited enough by the wary expression on Harry's face. "There's been another death," I said by way of explanation.

Harry stared. "Another killing on the map?"

I downed the rest of my drink. "No. Dr. Peterson," I said. "The scientist I went to California to speak with about that neurotransmitter-like chemical. His brakes failed and he went over a cliff."

Harry looked sick. "Holy shit, Lila."

"Yeah. I know. It was ruled an accident, but he'd been alarmed about my questions and intended to ask questions of his own. Now, I'm worried about Dr. Sims since I've had blood samples sent to her. Am I crazy? Could there be a cover-up so vast that they would find out about the bloodwork?" I waved off the suggestion of another drink. "I'm too tired," I said. "I need a good eight hours of sleep and some time to think. Can we put off any more discussion 'til morning?"

He frowned and studied my face. "I want all the details over breakfast," he said. "I'll make something special, give you an energy boost."

"Sounds great. Thanks." I took my laptop and headed for the stairs. "I only ask that you have lots of coffee."

I looked at the guest room bed longingly, but bypassed it for the adjacent library. It took only a few minutes to plug in my laptop, log in, and get connected. I knew from my cell phone pings that emails had arrived throughout the day, and I opened up my account. Harry appeared at the library door with a sweat suit for me to sleep in. He said good night and returned downstairs to lock up.

The top message, sent earlier that morning, was the SDS information from George Meyers on the chemicals found in the test asphalt. I forwarded it to Dr. Sims at the state lab. The next message had been sent yesterday, during the wee hours of the morning, while I was hiding from bullets in the *Morning Star* office. It had only been midnight in California. It had been sent from Dr. Peterson, shortly before he took the drive that had ended his life. I read the message:

Dear Ms. Kincaid,

I have had some small success in my inquiries. I remembered the chemist's name at ARP was Travis, but I suggest you look into the past of our CEO, Grant Montallvo. He seems to have a personal interest in the topic we discussed. He is powerful.

Be careful,

Sven

Grant Montallvo. Another candidate for the G.M. mentioned in Buzz's journal.

My exhaustion suddenly vanished. I pulled up the web site for Manchester Chemicals. There was a short bio of the CEO, Grant Montallvo. He was a native of Midland, Texas and had attended University of Texas at Austin, earning a Master of Science degree in Chemistry and a Master of Business Administration degree. He was currently on the boards of the American Oil Chemists' Society and Materials Research Society. He was married with two children. Before taking over at Manchester Chemicals, he'd been CEO at none other than Amalgamated Recovery Products. Now I was getting somewhere. ARP in Midland, Texas popped up too often not to be significant in this mess.

It was almost one in the morning, but I called out to Harry.

"Harry, I've got to go to Midland. Today. Know anyone with a private plane I can charter?"

I heard his footsteps coming toward the room. He stood in the doorway with his hands on his hips.

"Are you crazy?" he asked. "No. Lila, you need to stay here for a few days. Let someone else investigate."

"And get them on the hit list, too? There've been too many deaths already. I can't bring anyone else in on this."

"Lila, please. . . ."

"I'm going, Harry. With or without your help."

I recognized his expression. He didn't like it, but he'd help.

Chapter 43

Despite the hour, Harry used his connections and found me a flight to Midland, Texas, for late in the afternoon. I was initially frustrated by the delay, but in the morning, I was glad for the opportunity to sleep in. The drive from New York and the previous night's excitement had worn me out more than I cared to admit.

Morning sunlight filtered through the lacy curtains in Harry's guest room, creating a dappled pattern of light and dark on the creamy carpet. I felt rested and safe. The terror from the attack at the *Morning Star* seemed remote and intangible, unable to penetrate my protective cocoon of blankets.

I lay in bed and stared at the ceiling, lost in thoughts about the test asphalt project, ARP 2728, and Dr. Peterson's concerns. I decided to listen to the phone conversations with Zeke Waggoner and George Meyers of Meyers Construction I'd recorded on my way down from New York. Meyers had mentioned Sky's-the-Limit Evaluations as the asphalt inspection company, so I got up and ran them through an Internet search. No hits. That seemed odd. Who escaped Google detection these days?

I considered the implications of such a company. If they sent the same person to inspect all the sites, that person would have the opportunity to interact with or poison anyone along those routes. The motive could be as straightforward as pure evil and the need to kill. But what about the means? Could this person somehow expose the individual kids to ARP 2728? Was that the connection between the killings? I hoped the blood samples reached Dr. Sims soon.

According to Peterson, the neurochemical that Sims had found in Mike's blood was identical to the molecule found in his sample, ARP 2728. Manchester Chemical produced the special asphalt using a product from ARP, and their contractor, Myers Construction, poured that asphalt near each murder scene along the Death Map routes. Then I remembered a thought that had occurred to me on the drive down here: The chemical found in sample ARP 2728 might also be in the asphalt. South Carolina was one of the states where the new asphalt had been tested. Could Mike and the other children have been exposed to that chemical through the asphalt?

I tried to recall anything I knew about asphalt. I knew nothing about its chemical properties, except that maybe it contained tar, whatever that was. And it was hot and smelly when it was being poured. Then it was rolled until flat and smooth. Then it hardened. At least I thought that was the general idea. Could the chemical have been aerosolized while the asphalt was at its hottest?

What if the chemical got into the water supply? Maybe it continued to leach out of the asphalt every time it rained, or got too hot, or froze. I bounded out of bed, eager to contact Dr. Sims to see if she could run the same analysis on water and asphalt samples.

I dressed and headed down to the kitchen and found Harry's note. He'd let me sleep in, made a pot of coffee, a stack of pancakes, and bacon. He'd catch up with me before my flight. I poured myself a cup, nuked the food.

Next, I phoned Dr. Sims and alerted her to the additional blood samples coming from individuals on my Death Map route, and the frozen petroleum byproduct sample with ARP 2728 coming from University of Toronto.

"I need to caution you, Dr. Sims," I said. "Some people involved in this investigation have been attacked or even killed, and I suspect it's part of a cover- up connected to this chemical."

Dr. Sims was quiet. I could hear papers shuffle. "I'm not stupid, Ms. Kincaid," she said. "I see the significance of finding the same chemical in all these samples. You know we're a forensics lab that works closely with law enforcement around the state. We get samples every day that are part of unspeakable crimes. It's nothing new to us."

"Well, I just felt. . . ."

"Relax. You did your due diligence . . . and I appreciate your concern, Lila. You watch your own back, though, okay?"

"I will, thanks. Hey, I've come up with a theory that this petroleum byproduct may have been used in an asphalt and leached into surrounding water. Is it possible to run the same analysis on a water sample and maybe a chunk of road asphalt?" I asked.

"The water will be easy," she said. "I'm not too sure about the asphalt. Can you get a sample before it hardens?"

"No. This is specially formulated stuff that was poured years ago."

"Well, bring in a chunk and I'll give it a go. I can try a few different solvents, maybe something will work."

"Thanks, and I have a favor to ask." I paused, not exactly certain how Sims would take this request. I wished now I'd gone to the lab in person. I had better luck gauging a response in person rather than over the phone.

"In case that same neurotransmitter-like molecule shows up in the other blood samples," I said, "can you make sure the results don't get released to anyone other than myself or Mr. Greenstreet?"

"Lila, it might be obstruction of justice or something like that, perhaps withholding evidence, if I don't call in the authorities. I could be in big trouble."

"Listen, I'll check with Harry about your responsibility in reporting these results, but please, please, at least don't tell any reporters," I said. "I promise to tell the cops everything as soon as we get all the data together. Please?"

"I'm going to speak to our attorney, as well. I may have to inform the authorities, but I won't talk to other reporters, if that makes you feel any better. And of course, I'll work on those additional samples."

"Fair enough. Thank you, Dr. Sims."

"And Lila, in my experience, the faster we get an answer to the authorities, the faster the danger from a cover-up will pass. Hurry up with those samples."

I hung up the phone. I hoped we were doing the right thing. She was giving me time to get samples of that test asphalt and water runoff for analysis. But to do that, I needed to know exactly where the asphalt had been placed. I phoned the state highway department next, glad now that my flight to Midland wasn't until later in the day.

I spent the following hour either on hold or being transferred from one office to another before I found someone who could help, but finally uncovered the location of the test strip of asphalt near Charleston. The test area was within a half mile of Ellen and Mike's home. All my instincts told me I was on the right track.

I searched Harry's garage for some tools, then jumped in my rental car and drove out to the mile marker that signaled the start of the test patch of highway. I turned off the road onto a farm lane and parked. I grabbed Harry's hammer and chisel and a plastic baggie I had retrieved from his kitchen and walked over to the edge of the blacktop.

It was a warm, humid, sunny morning and the heat rose from the asphalt in waves. Majestic pine trees lined this section of the road, and I had multiple opportunities where no cars were in sight. I knelt down along the edge of the road and began chiseling away at the asphalt.

Death Map

It wasn't easy. My struggle with the rock-hard surface resulted in damp beads on my upper lip and sweat rivulets running down my back. Eventually, I loosened a chunk about the size of a candy bar. I wished I'd asked Sims how much she needed for analysis. Oh, well. The road wasn't going anywhere. I could fetch more anytime.

A ditch ran along each side of the road along this stretch. It was about a foot deep and bone dry. I'd hoped to get a sample of water which might have run across the asphalt, but it didn't appear to be possible at this location. However, this test section stretched for twenty miles. I got back into my car and drove slowly along the route, looking for a body of water positioned near enough to the road that it might get contaminated if anything leached out of the asphalt. About five miles along the way, the ditches deepened to six feet. I stopped the car and climbed down the embankment, alert for snakes. The weeds grew thick at the bottom but again, there was no standing water. The ground was damp, however, so I scooped up some of the moist dirt into another baggie.

Another mile down the road I found a pond in a pasture not too far from the road. If the water runoff theory was correct, a sample from that pond might have some contamination. I parked the car, climbed the fence and collected a sample, half expecting a gun-toting farmer to appear any minute.

I delivered the samples to Sims and also asked her to compare the copies of the three Safety Data Sheets that I'd forwarded — one filed with the state of South Carolina by Manchester Chemicals for the test asphalt, one already on file with the state for regular asphalt, and the SDS sheet I'd received directly from George Meyers of Meyers Construction for the test asphalt.

I left the lab and headed toward Harry's. My morning's accomplishments had worked up my appetite. I detoured into a McDonald's drive-up for a burger, and glanced at my reflection in the rear-view mirror. The dirt-streaked face and sweaty hair made me laugh. Luckily, I had enough time to purchase some clothes, get back to Harry's for a shower, and still catch my flight to Midland.

Chapter 44

Wednesday Afternoon: Midland, Texas

I arrived in Midland, home of over ten thousand active oil wells and numerous major oil refineries, in the early afternoon, local time. I'd used my flight time to plan out a course of investigation. I needed to find out all I could about Amalgamated Recovery Products and about the men Sven Peterson had mentioned in his final email, Grant Montallvo and a chemist named Travis. I'd checked Google yellow pages for addresses for Amalgamated Recovery Products, or any Montallvo still living in Midland. Amalgamated and one Montallvo were listed. I called the ARP and they confirmed that Grant Montallvo had relocated to California.

There was still one Montallvo in the area. Maybe they knew Grant. I took a taxi from the airport to the Montallvo residence, and asked the driver to wait. As I walked up to the house, I caught the essence of refinery on the breeze.

A tiny woman, on the cusp of a century, answered the door. Her glasses magnified pale blue eyes peering from within folds of wrinkles. Her snap-front, flowery-print dress showcased a jeweled watch pinned on the chest. Her thin, white hair was perfectly coiffed, and she greeted me with a puzzled expression.

"Mrs. Montallvo?" I asked. "I'm looking for Grant. Is he here?"

The woman's face broke into a big smile. "Is he coming home today?"

"I'm sorry, I don't know," I said. "Does he visit often?"

"As often as he can," the elderly woman said. "He's a very important man. Very busy, but always finds time to visit his mother."

"Were you expecting him today?"

"No, not today, I think. He hasn't called. He always calls from the airport when he's coming over. I'm sure the phone hasn't rung today." She looked over her shoulder. "Do you hear the phone ringing?" She turned then and started to close the door.

"Wait," I said, grabbing the door. "The phone's not ringing, Ma'am. May I come in and talk with you about Grant?"

Grant's mother suddenly looked wary. "I thought you knew Grant," she said. "Who are you? What's wrong with your hair?"

I should have worn my scarf. Too late now. "I know a friend of his," I said. "Are there any other friends he would contact when he comes to visit?"

"He always comes to see me first," she said. Then she frowned. "Glenn never comes by . . . I don't know why. He was always perfect as a boy. I haven't seen Glenn in such a long time." She was no longer looking at me.

"About Grant, Mrs. Montallvo," I said softly. "Could he be visiting one of his friends?"

A look of distaste clouded the old woman's features.

"Well, if you mean Frank, he's dead, thank goodness." She looked worried and lost for a moment before she added, "For real dead, not like my Glenn."

I nodded encouragingly. "Is there anyone else Grant would visit while he's home?"

"Well, there's Timmy. You must know Timmy Jones. He married that cute little girl from next door, Linda Goodson? Remember them? Everyone knew Timmy and Linda. But they had a falling out over Glenn. You're a friend of Grant's, aren't you?" she asked, eyeing me warily again.

"Of course," I said. "I'll go find him and make sure he

comes to visit you, okay?"

The old woman smiled brightly. "Thank you, dear. And tell him I want to see Glenn, okay?" That faraway look returned to her eyes and she shut the door in my face.

I glanced at the house next door. Linda Goodson-Jones, eh? There was a car in the drive and the yard was full of toddler-sized toys. I held up my index finger to signal the taxi to wait one moment longer and walked over to the neighboring house.

"Hi," I greeted the young woman who answered the door.

"Hi, yourself," the woman said.

"I'm looking for information on someone who used to live in this neighborhood. Linda Goodson? Married a Timmy Jones?"

"Sorry. You might try next door. Mrs. Montallvo's been here forever."

"Thanks, but she just sent me over here."

"Well, she's a dear, but getting a little dotty, if you know what I mean."

"She lives alone?

"Someone comes in every afternoon. Home health, I suppose. And her son comes by almost every week."

"Grant, right?"

"Yeah, you know him?"

"Well, that's the thing. He's the one I'm really trying to track down. Mrs. Montallvo said he had some friends who once lived here that might know how to reach him. And she mentioned another friend, Frank?"

"Poor dear. Hang on, Grant gave my husband some cell phone numbers in case there's an emergency. Let me find them."

I waited on the porch, watched my taxi driver reading a book. The woman returned in a few minutes with a business card.

"Sorry, I can't find a pen, hope you have one. Here's a post-it." She handed me the card and paper.

I read the information on the card. Amalgamated Recovery Products, 200 W Main Street, Suite B, Midland, TX. Grant Montallvo, CEO. (432) 996-4400. Another number was hand written on the back: Frank Travis (432) 788-6662.

Travis. Of course, I had a pen.

"Maybe this is the wrong card. It says Frank Travis on the back?" I asked as I scribbled down the number.

"Oh, sorry. That won't do you any good. Frank passed a while back." She grabbed back the card and disappeared again into the house.

"Here's the one with Grant's cell phone number."

"Mrs. Montallvo also mentioned her son Glenn? Does he ever come by?" I asked.

"Sorry, I've only met the one. But, now that you mention it, I remember my husband telling me there was a tragedy with a child next door. Died young. Very sad. Maybe that's who she was talking about. Moms grieve forever, you know."

Chapter 45

As my cab made its way to the address for Amalgamated Recovery Products, I did a quick Google search for Frank Travis. The old lady was right, Frank was "really" dead. Hit-and-run dead. He'd been a chemist for ARP. Seven years dead end.

The secretary at the front desk accepted my stand-by alias, Mary Appleby's business card.

"I'd like to speak with Mr. Montallvo."

"Do you have an appointment?"

"No."

"I'm sorry, but he's rarely at this facility and not in today. Would you like to make an appointment? Or maybe someone else could help you?"

"How about Frank Travis?"

"Frank?" She put her hand to her mouth. "I'm so sorry. I guess you don't know. Mr. Travis passed several years back." Her eyes misted over. "It was a big blow to us."

"Oh. I'm sorry for your loss. I must have been looking at outdated information. He was the chemist here, right? Developed the weather-resistant asphalt?"

"He was in on it, yes. But Manchester Chemical owns that product now." She pulled a tissue out of her drawer. "In fact, Mr. Montallvo and Frank founded Manchester Chemicals. Mr. Montallvo is their CEO."

Oh, wow! It was tying together. Had Buzz gotten this far? I needed to be careful.

"Isn't that nice," I said. "I've heard it was the miracle product of the century. I was hoping to interview your chemist about ARP's contribution to that asphalt formula."

"Maybe Jill Chesney could help. She was Frank's secretary, and is now the executive assistant to Mr. Montallvo. I'll see if she has time for an interview."

"Maybe another chemist would be the right person . . . ."

"No," she cut me off. "Jill can handle your questions."

Jill Chesney agreed to see me. I was escorted to her office a few minutes later, where she waited, seated behind a large cherry desk. She looked up as I entered and simultaneously closed a folder over a newspaper clipping. She slipped it into a desk drawer and rose to shake my hand. Chesney was at least five foot ten and very thin. She exuded efficiency in every movement.

The interview didn't go well. Ms. Chesney admitted to having worked for Mr. Travis and now for Mr. Montallvo. She also admitted that the men had been close friends as well as business associates. But when I asked about the weather-resistant asphalt formula, the woman clammed up, and I was asked to leave the premises.

Maybe that wasn't very smart.

I jumped when Chesney's door slammed behind me on my way out. The secretary looked up, startled.

"Is everything okay, Ms. Appleby?"

I thumbed toward the closed door. "I think I made her mad." I started toward the elevator, then turned back to the secretary. "How well did you know Mr. Travis?" I asked.

The secretary glanced at the closed door. She pulled a post-it note from the pad by her phone, wrote something on it and handed it to me.

"You may find out more about Mr. Travis here," she said in a hushed voice.

I thanked her and left the building. I hailed a taxi, and

then glanced at the note. It contained two names — Brian Reese and California Dreaming.

Brian Reese turned out to be the owner of California Dreaming, an *haute cuisine* restaurant located in downtown Midland. I thought he pulled off the spiky bleached blond hair style, making him look a young fifty. He dressed in silk paisley, two macramé necklaces, tiny loop earrings, and Levi's.

Since it was still too early for the lunch crowd, Brian agreed to an interview. We sat in a semi-private booth, separated from the main dining area by a hanging row of lush ferns. There were more ferns perched on tall stands by the sides of the booth. California Dreaming inspired tropical thoughts.

"I'm looking into the death of Frank Travis," I said, without preamble.

"What kind of interview is this?" he asked, looking again at my Mary Appleby business card. "Frank had nothing to do with my restaurant."

"Well, I'm investigating some odd business dealings Amalgamated Recovery Products may have been involved in," I said. "I couldn't get answers there, but someone gave me your name as a possible resource."

"I bet you met that homophobic bitch, Chesney," Brian said casually. "Absolutely hated me."

"So, you knew Mr. Travis?" I asked.

"Let's continue this in my office," Brian said.

I followed him to the back of the restaurant. The aroma of pesto landed a solid hit as we walked through the kitchen door. Brian's office bloomed with plants of every size and variety.

"Wow!" I said. "How do you do it without windows? I can't even get ivy to grow on my desk."

He flipped a switch by the doorway and the tiny area flooded with soft purple.

"Grow lights," he said. "Have a seat." He switched the room back to fluorescent white, automatically poured us each a cup of coffee, and took a seat behind his desk.

"Smells good," I said. "Thanks."

"Cinnamon hazelnut," he said. "Try it. Tastes even better. So, I can't imagine why someone gave you my name. I know nothing about Amalgamated."

"But you did know Frank?"

"Yes."

"Very well?"

He sighed dramatically. "Frank didn't like people to know, but I guess it can't hurt him now. We were a couple. We had a longtime relationship. Six years. So, yes, I knew him very well."

"I'm curious about his business dealings with Grant Montallvo," I said and saw his wince at the name. "I take it you don't like Mr. Montallvo?"

"No. I most emphatically do not. He manipulates people. Such an evil man. He absolutely mesmerized Frank. He's why we split up."

"Montallvo is homosexual?"

"No. Well, I don't know. Maybe. He's married, but that doesn't always mean anything. I don't know if he and Frank, well, ever developed more than a business relationship. Actually, Frank claimed to have become involved with a woman, thus our break-up. I didn't believe him for a moment. It was Montallvo he lusted after.

"The part I hated," Brian continued, "was that bastard knew exactly what Frank wanted, what he needed. He seduced Frank for his own gain. Poor Frankie. He had a major blind spot with Montallvo's motive."

"Which was. . . ?"

"Frank's formula."

"Formula for what?"

"Well, it's a big secret. I can't tell."

"Frank is dead. Like you said, it can't hurt him now," I said.

"Um, right. I guess I could tell if I actually knew what it was, which I don't."

"You mean to say that in all those years Frank never talked about it with you?" I asked.

"No. He couldn't, you see. Company policy."

I didn't buy that for a second, but I let it drop for now and redirected the questions to Frank's death. "Anything unusual about how he died?" I asked.

"A car ran him off the road. He hit a tree. He died. Happens daily around the world."

"Witnesses?"

"Yeah. A bunch of people. Never caught the other driver, though. They found the car, which had been stolen, but the driver got away."

"Did Montallvo get the formula?" I asked.

"I guess. Yeah, he must have. They'd already started a second business together in California, and Frank was moving out the next week. He'd stopped in to let me know. He was excited about the move, I remember. He planned to stay with Montallvo at first, till he found his own place, but I thought he hoped it would be permanent."

"Really? Wasn't Montallvo moving his family with him?"

He sighed. "I know, I know. I sound like a jealous hag."

I wondered if a revolutionary asphalt hinged on that move.

"Poor Frankie," he continued. "His timing was always a little off. Convenient for Montallvo though, I guess."

Yes, wasn't it, though?

"I remember I was kinda surprised," he added.

"Surprised? About Frank and Montallvo?"

"No. Actually, that the deal with the formula was still on."

"What do you mean? Had there been a problem?" I leaned forward.

"Yeah, there'd been something wrong at one point. But, you know, I wasn't seeing Frank very often at all by that time, and I figured they must have worked it all out. I didn't ask. He seemed so happy, and I wanted him happy."

"Back up a sec," I said. "So, there was a problem with the formula. Can you remember about when Frank first mentioned that?"

"This was all six, seven years ago," he said with a shrug.

"Well, was it before or after your break-up?"

"Let's see. After. Definitely after. He'd called because he needed someone to talk to. So, that makes it a few weeks after Christmas." His voice picked up a notch with excitement. "I remember thinking I was glad he hadn't gotten this news before the holidays."

"News? Who from?"

"Don't know who it came from, but someone outside their company for sure. That was his whole problem, you see. He didn't want to tell anyone at work because he thought it meant his formula was worthless."

If his formula was worthless, am I at a dead end?

"What'd he do?"

"Don't know," Brian said. "The next time I saw him was when he told me he was leaving town. Then he died."

Six or seven years ago? It must have been the report by Sven Peterson on the studies he did with ARP 2728 suggesting the byproduct was dangerous. If Frank never told anyone before he died, then that was the end of my hunt. But, no. Someone knew. Someone had bombed the *Morning Star*. Someone had blown up the car I was using. Someone may have killed Buzz to kill this investigation. Maybe someone killed Frank to kill the report?

The phone on Brian's desk jangled. He excused himself and took the call. I busied myself reviewing my notes. The guarded tone of Brian's voice made me pay attention to his words while I pretended to read.

"Not now," he said. "I wish you hadn't done that. Well, I don't care. Go ahead and tell him."

I thought he was going to slam down the phone.

"What?" he said. "Coming here? No way. Well, wait a minute. Yes, I would like to meet with him. Here, at my restaurant, at two-thirty."

He hung up and I noticed the gleam in his eye.

"Guess what?" Brian said, raising an eyebrow. "How'd you like to meet Grant Montallvo in person?"

My heart beat faster at the idea. "I would, very much so."

"Well, believe it or not, that was Ms. Chesney proclaiming that Mr. Montallvo is coming to Midland tomorrow and will be in this restaurant at two-thirty. He would like reservations for two and an audience with me. I think it would be most entertaining to include an interview with you on the afternoon's agenda."

Chapter 46

At two-twenty-eight in the afternoon, Texas sunshine blazed without a cloud for protection. My taxi sat sideways in the street, blocked in by the delivery truck that had struck us in the side and forced us into a line of parked cars. The taxi driver yelled simultaneously at the truck driver and into his radio at the dispatcher. I'd never make it by two-thirty for the meeting between Brian Reese and Grant Montallvo.

An eight-block walk to the restaurant would be a breeze, if there'd been a breeze. I paid the driver and headed north on foot, staying on the shady side of the street.

Before leaving the hotel, I'd called McLeish at the *Morning Star* and told him about my new leads. He'd seen the promise of this afternoon's meeting, too.

"Find out about the formula and who knew about the testing done by Peterson," McLeish said.

I agreed; that was exactly what was uppermost on my mind anyway. But McLeish was crazy if he thought Montallvo would blurt it out to Mary Appleby. I needed to be smart about this. My plan involved getting Montallvo and Reese to reminisce about Frank, then I'd bring up Frank's formula, and throw in that Frank revealed to Reese about the bad test results. It would be throwing Reese under the bus, but I wanted Montallvo's reaction.

I was starting to notice sweat in the small of my back when I spotted the California Dreaming sign shimmering at the end of the block, on the opposite side of the street.

Finally, air conditioning. I checked my watch. Not bad; only ten minutes late.

I started across the street at the corner light and could see Brian standing at the front glass window watching my approach. I recognized the silhouette of the tall, thin Ms. Chesney, standing behind Reese. She obviously knew more than she'd let on in my interview with her yesterday, or this meeting would have never been arranged. I wondered if she recognized me. Well, duh. She saw me yesterday, and how many tiny women with maroon spiky hair do you run across in the average week? I resisted the urge to laugh and wave, and wondered about Montallvo. Late? Canceled? Chickened out? I doubted that last was likely. From what I'd learned about him, he didn't seem the type to chicken out on anything.

The blast struck without warning. The large window where Brian had been standing blew out across the street into a sparkling spray of a thousand shards. The force of the explosion bent my body backward and my feet rose into the air. I had zero time to react. I landed hard on the ground, thrown ten feet from where I'd been in the crosswalk. I felt the gritty pavement embedded in the side of my face. I tried to get up, but couldn't raise my head. Broken glass from the shattered restaurant windows rained down around me, and cars came to a screeching halt. Brian Reese's body lay in my line of sight. I watched his pink silk shirt turn bright red and saw the sunlight reflected in the jagged edge of glass protruding from his chest. Then he faded away to black.

Chapter 47

I awoke in a hospital bed and saw Harry sitting in a chair by the window.

"Harry?" I asked, groggily. "What's going on?"

"Hey, kid," he said, rising quickly to stand by my bed. He took my hand. "How're you feeling?"

"Like I got hit by a truck. Did I?"

"No, not a truck. An explosion. Someone planted a bomb in a restaurant downtown. You had the bad luck to be on the street nearly in front of it when it blew. You're going to be okay, mainly sore for a while."

"Downtown? Where, Charleston?"

"No, Midland, Texas," he said. "Remember? You used your sexy wiles to force me to help you get here so you could follow a lead on that Death Map story."

Death Map. Midland, Texas. Yeah. I was supposed to meet someone and that someone was not a good guy.

"But you weren't in Midland, were you?"

"No. The accident happened yesterday afternoon. The doctor found your business card in your wallet and contacted the paper. Your friend, Clunie, contacted me. I got here late last night."

"Oh, man, sorry for being such trouble. Maybe you could . . . Oh!" I winced. Moving was torture. Merely sitting up threatened to send me into the black oblivion that had held me captive for twenty-four hours. I gave up and lay back down.

"What's wrong with me? I hurt everywhere."

"Nothing's broken," Harry said, "but plenty of deep tissue bruising. And you had some glass embedded in your forehead. They put in a stitch here and there."

My hand automatically went to my forehead, where I traced the outline of the bandage. "That doesn't sound too bad."

"Could've been a lot worse. They assure me the plastic surgeon did an excellent job. You'll hardly be able to tell in a few months."

"Anything else I need to know?" I asked.

"Well, you lost consciousness and have a minor concussion. Your doctor was concerned that you'd stay out of it for so long. And, of course, I told him about your recent concussion in Charleston. I guess he'll be as pleased as I that you've come around."

"Great," I said. "I need to please my doctor. I suppose that accounts for why I can't remember anything."

I tried to focus, recall what the hell happened. Then I had a thought. "Hey, would you look for my purse?" I asked. "My tape player should be in there."

Harry complied and left the room to ask at the nurse's station. A few minutes later, he returned with my bag.

"May I?" he asked, and opened it as I grunted impatiently.

He rewound the tape a bit and hit the play button. I listened closely and recognized my voice asking someone about Montallvo and a formula. When the next voice came on, my memory flooded back like a tsunami. Instantly, I saw Brian's pink shirt turning blood red. I pressed my hands to my eyes.

"You can stop it now," I said. "I remember. Most of it, anyway. I was going to meet that last guy who was speaking — Brian something — at his restaurant. He was having a meeting with Grant Montallvo at two-thirty and invited me to sit in and ask questions."

"At the place that blew up?"

"It must've been. Was it called California Dreaming? I remember seeing Brian. Oh, what was his last name? Reese, that's it. I saw him at the window, and then seconds later he was lying in the street looking very, very dead."

Harry had his forefingers pressed together on his top lip, unsuccessfully hiding a frown. "And you were supposed to be there?"

"As Mary Appleby. And I don't think anyone but Brian knew I was going to be there," I said. "If the bomber had known I was going to be there, he would have waited another ten minutes and been rid of me, too."

"He?" Harry asked. "He who? This Montallvo character?"

I raised a finger. "Bet ya fifty bucks he wasn't inside when it blew."

"Who is he?" Harry asked.

"Not totally sure yet. His name has come up in connection with a lot of bad stuff — Peterson's last email mentioned him. He's CEO of the company that makes the famous asphalt. I think he's mixed up in these Death Map murders. I can feel it."

"Better tell me what you've found out," Harry said. "If you're up to it, that is."

"To tell you the truth," I said, "I'm starving. And I have a killer headache. Can I get out of here and get a cheeseburger?"

"They're just waiting on you to wake up, I think," Harry said. "To see if there was any damage to that unstoppable brain. You gotta quit getting knocked out."

"Hazards of the job, my editor would say. Well? You're a lawyer, I'm awake, get me out of here."

"How about I get you a cheeseburger and we ask the doctor to look you over one more time," Harry said. "You still have a lot a talking to do."

"Oh, all right," I said. "I'll take it loaded."

Harry left in search of the cafeteria, and I looked around the tiny room. I hated being in a hospital. I located the bed's positional controller strapped to the safety railing and succeeded in putting myself in an upright position. Since this hadn't sent me into a blackout, I tried standing. I moved as slowly as possible. If Harry hadn't assured me it was only bruising, I would've been afraid that I was risking internal punctures with each movement, it was so painful. But I couldn't afford to be a wimp. I managed to reach the bathroom.

The shower had intense pressure, and was hot — stimulating, invigorating. I pried up the bandage on my forehead and peeked in the mirror at the stitches. There was too much swelling and bruising to predict how it would turn out. I'd just managed to ease into my clothes when Harry returned with the sandwiches.

"They'll have to re-cover those," Harry said, looking at the bandage hanging loose on my forehead.

"Wounds need fresh air to heal. My mother always told me that," I replied, taking the carryout bag from him and settling, very slowly, back onto the bed. I'd exhausted myself, but he didn't need to know that. "I remember seeing someone standing next to Brian right before the explosion."

I bit into a cheeseburger and wiped the dripping sauce off my chin with the edge of the bed sheet. "I thought at the time it must've been that Chesney woman from APR, since she was the one who'd arranged for the meeting between Montallvo and Brian Reese."

"Um-hum," Harry mumbled, eyeing the sauce stain on the sheet. "I brought you the local paper. She was there, all right, but it doesn't say why."

"Killed in the blast?" I asked, taking the paper from him.

"Um-hum," he said again, unwrapping his sandwich. He ate his lunch while I read the article.

By the time the doctor arrived, I had gingerly worked the

tangles out of my hair and told Harry everything I'd done and learned since arriving in Midland. There was not a thing wrong with my memory, and I informed the doctor to that effect. Just a few stiff muscles and a headache. I'd gotten off easy, and now I wanted to be released.

The physician bandaged my forehead again and prescribed a cream to rub on the stitches and scabs. He agreed that I could go home, if I promised to rest and see my own doctor if the headache worsened. I promised, keeping my fingers crossed behind my back. My doctor was in New York, and I was headed to Charleston.

"There's still the police investigation into the bombing to consider," Harry said, as we waited for my release paperwork.

"Do they want to speak to me?"

"Well, right now they think you only happened to be passing by. But you've got information that could implicate Montallvo."

"Only that he was supposed to be there. I guess you're right, though. I'd better talk with them. Montallvo could've been in the building, and no one knows about it."

I didn't think so, though. Reese had been standing by the window looking for someone. He certainly hadn't been in the middle of a meeting.

"Right," Harry said. "I'm sure the police will consider all possibilities, including that someone meant to kill you, since you were supposed to be there, also."

"That's crazy, Harry. News flash. No one knew I was going to be there."

"Reese knew. And now it'll be rather difficult to find out if he told anyone."

I recognized Harry's unconscious smirk face and I made a mirror image. Maybe difficult to find out, but not impossible.

Chapter 48

Harry worried too much. And it didn't earn him any brownie points. He hovered over me on the way to the Midland police station. I insisted he stay in the waiting area.

The police didn't keep me very long. I'd braced myself for a major grilling, but it didn't happen that way. They listened to my account of the taxi accident and how it caused me to be late for my interview with Reese and Montallvo. I didn't mention that they expected me as Mary Appleby, not Lila Kincaid. I described seeing Reese and Chesney at the window as if waiting for me, or perhaps for Montallvo. I even suggested Montallvo might have been already seated inside the restaurant and might have been another victim of the blast.

The officer didn't comment. I was relieved, on one hand, that he didn't ask any questions about the purpose of my interview. On the other hand, I didn't think he took me seriously. His lack of interest astounded me. When I suggested it was odd that Chesney was on the scene, his only comment was that California Dreaming was a popular place for lunch and they were extremely lucky there weren't more people there when it blew.

"Do you have any information on the type of bomb used?"

"No comment," he replied.

"Are you thinking someone had a grudge against Reese?"

The officer sighed. "We appreciate your coming in, Ms. Kincaid," he said, "but we're not giving out information to the press. We'll contact you if we need you again."

The whole come-clean-to-the-cops thing proved a waste of my time. They weren't interested in me or what I suspected. Besides, I hurt everywhere and it would be easier to simply forget about what the police thought and go lie down somewhere.

"You know," I said, trying to control my voice, "if this had nothing to do with Montallvo or me, it'd be nice if you'd let me know. Otherwise, I might be in danger."

The police officer gave me a there-there-little-girl smile.

"This is merely a typical case of post-traumatic response," he said. "You were seriously injured, Ms. Kincaid, through no fault of your own. You want desperately to find a reason. I see it all the time. Be assured it's merely a coincidence. Off the record, this is currently considered an accidental gas line explosion. You should go home, rest, recover, and move on with your life."

Oh, right . . . well, duty done. I had tried to get him to see my suspicions. I took his verbal head pat and returned to the lobby where Harry paced.

On the flight back to Charleston I started in again on Montallvo.

"The guy gives me the creeps," I whispered to Harry. "His friend and partner gets a report that his billion-dollar formula is dangerous, then is mysteriously killed. Why would he set up a meeting with Brian Reese after all these years, if my visit to Amalgamated didn't trigger something? I think he's trying to get rid of anyone who can link him to these Death Map killings."

"It's only a guess," Harry said. "You don't have a bit of proof."

"Hell, I know that," I said.

"And you don't actually know that Montallvo set up the meeting at the restaurant," Harry said.

I sighed. There was that lawyer thing again. All about the facts. "I know, but Brian was speaking with Ms. Chesney. She was supposed to be setting up the meeting on behalf of Montallvo. Now she's dead too, so I can't confirm that, either." Unless she wrote it in her appointment book. I planned to contact that sympathetic secretary at Amalgamated to check. Chesney must have overheard her talking to me. Put two and two together.

"What if someone else is setting up Montallvo as the fall guy?" Harry asked. "Maybe someone connected to Amalgamated?"

That was an interesting angle. I thought about that possibility for a few minutes.

"Hmm, there could be someone else," I admitted. "Someone does inspections of the test asphalt periodically. I haven't been able to track them down. If there's only one person doing the inspections, actually going on location, I mean, that would place him in the vicinity of the Death Map murders. There's the opportunity. What's the motive?"

"Serial killers don't always have an obvious motive. But what about means?" Harry asked.

"ARP 2728. It contains a chemical that does a number on rat brains. Thing is, since it turned up in Mike's blood, I've been assuming it's in the test asphalt. I suppose though, it's possible this mystery person has access to the chemical and somehow gets it to kids along these routes."

"You think this inspector, someone you haven't identified yet, was associated with Amalgamated Recovery Products at some time?"

"Possibly," I said. "Or associated with the research done on the chemical."

"That brings us back to Sven Peterson, who's now out of the picture permanently," Harry said.

"What about an assistant of his? Or, that person at Manchester Chemicals who showed an interest in Peterson's research." I was getting excited now. "And we've circled back to Grant Montallvo."

"Whoa there, Lila," Harry said. "I know you believe Montallvo's guilty, but you need facts, not suppositions."

I knew I didn't have any hard evidence yet to tie Montallvo to any of the murders: Buzz, Matt, Peterson, Reese, or Chesney. And now, without Reese, there was nothing to suggest that Montallvo had ever heard about the biochemist's report on ARP 2728. I needed something concrete, like finding a copy of Dr. Peterson's initial report on ARP 2728 in Montallvo's files. I decided to go back to California and try to get some information from Peterson's co-workers. I made the mistake of saying this out loud.

"Damn it, Lila. You need to rest. You've been unconscious, for God's sake. Twice in as many weeks. That takes a toll on a person. You need to take a few days off."

I couldn't answer. I felt an intense sense of urgency and didn't have the strength to mount an argument at the moment. In my mind, the murder of Brian Reese was a sign that Montallvo, or someone, was desperately trying to cover his tracks. He surely knew by now someone had been asking questions at Amalgamated. Personally, I was relieved that someone had been Mary Appleby.

Chapter 49

Sunday: Charleston, South Carolina

I woke up the following morning feeling stiff and sore all over. Maybe Harry was right. Again. Maybe I should stay in bed for a day or two. What would it hurt? I'd nearly dropped back to sleep when the house phone rang. I couldn't ignore it because of the racket downstairs from Jay-Jay squawking "Hello" over and over. I knew he'd keep it up until the ringing stopped. I rolled over and picked up the bedside extension and mumbled, "Hello."

"Ms. Kincaid?"

I recognized the chemist's voice.

"Good morning, Dr. Sims. It's Sunday, isn't it? Do you work on Sunday?"

"Yeah, I'm in for a few hours this morning. Could you stop by? I have something you need to see."

I eased myself out from under the covers and sat on the edge of the bed. I used my right thumb and forefinger to apply pressure to my eyes. It didn't help the pain behind them at all.

"I'll be right over," I said, and hung up the phone.

I popped some aspirin, glancing longingly at the bottle of prescription painkillers; that form of relief would have to wait. I took a hot shower, grabbed a quick cup of coffee, and drove over to the state lab.

Sims met me at the door to let me in. She paled when she saw my face.

"What happened? Are you okay?"

"I'm not as bad as I look. I think."

Her eyes narrowed. "Is this the sort of thing you warned me about?"

I frowned and gave a short nod.

"Oh, hell. Oh, hell." She glanced out the door, up and down the street. "Have you spoken to the police? You need to go to them, get protection."

"The police interviewed me, but didn't see a connection. That's why your results are so important. We need proof."

"Come on, let's go to my office. You look like you're going to collapse." She led me into her office and I took a seat. I saw her glance from me to a framed photograph. She turned it so I could see her standing with a man and child. I felt a fist in my gut.

"I didn't really take your danger warning seriously," she said. "I'm not going to put myself, or my family, or my co-workers at risk." She opened my file. "There's a discrepancy here, Lila, that I think should be brought to the attention of the authorities at once." Her eyes roved my bruised cheek and forehead. "Especially now."

"What sort of discrepancy?"

"You know that asphalt sample you brought in? It doesn't match the SDS info that's supposed to represent it," she said. "I decided to check our analysis technique on some asphalt from the road here in front of the lab and it matched the appropriate SDS sheet perfectly. I'm required to notify OSHA about this."

"What will they do?"

"Depends. It could be an honest mistake on behalf of whoever formulated that test asphalt, or it could be a deliberate omission. OSHA will follow up."

I drew in a quick breath. "The chemical from Mike's blood? Did you find it in any of the samples?"

She bobbed her head several times. "The same neurotransmitter-like molecule is in both the extra blood samples you had sent here, but not in your soil sample or the water sample."

I stood. "It's in the blood? Just like Mike's?"

"Exactly like Mike's. It's time to notify the police."

I sat back down, stunned. I wanted this result. I had hoped for this result. But it knocked me cold. Mike and the Luke kid and the Oaks boy had been poisoned by a manufactured contaminant that affected their behavior in a dramatic and bizarre way. The public needed to be alerted, and the truly responsible party held accountable. I wished I had a handle on how it had gotten into them.

"I was so sure it would be in the asphalt," I said. "Wait, you didn't mention the asphalt. Was it negative for that neurotransmitter molecule, too?"

"The asphalt analysis was inconclusive," Dr. Sims said.

"What does that mean?"

"I had to use a solvent to liquefy the sample before analysis. I ran a control sample using the same solvent on one of the positive blood samples. Unfortunately, the solvent masks our ability to detect the chemical in the blood sample. So, I can't say for sure about the asphalt. But, the chemical's definitely not in the soil or water."

"How about the ARP 2728 sample from Toronto?"

"Oh, yes. That arrived yesterday. I have the test running now." She looked at her watch. "It should be finished, actually. Let's take a look."

She led the way into a little room on the left. A pen attached to a robotic arm was making a red trace across an advancing graph paper. Dr. Sims picked up the leading edge of the paper and studied the markings.

"Well, well," she said.

"What?" I asked, standing on tip-toe to look over her shoulder. "What do you see?"

She pulled a similar paper out of a file folder, looked at it a minute and smiled.

"Bingo," she said. "It's the same."

Peterson had been right. I let out a breath I didn't realize I'd been holding. "You're saying the same chemical in the boys' blood is also in ARP 2728, but didn't show up in the water or the soil?"

Dr. Sims nodded.

"And the test asphalt has different components than what is listed on the SDS form, but you can't say one way or another about the chemical?"

"That about sums it up," Dr. Sims agreed.

"So," I continued, "how did these kids get exposed to the chemical?"

"Well, that's the big question, isn't it?" Dr. Sims said, looking at the graphic profile in her hands. "All I can say from my data is that our current technique doesn't work on the asphalt sample."

Double damn. I'd been so sure. Even with this negative result, I couldn't quite give up my pet theory. "Do you think it's worth checking asphalt from other sites?"

"No," she answered. "Since the solvent's the problem, the chemical wouldn't show up in the other samples, either. But, I can try other solvents, see if I can get the control to work. It's up to you, of course. Too bad you can't get a sample of the asphalt before it hardens. Or ingredients from the manufacturer."

Hmm. That might be possible. Again, I thought about the secretary at ARP's office who had been sympathetic to my questions about Frank. Maybe she could help. If I explained to her that the asphalt formula as analyzed by Dr. Sims didn't match the SDS form her company filed, maybe she could locate some additional samples. I wondered if she was the one responsible for typing up the SDS form. Maybe she'd want to prove it wasn't sloppy record keeping on her part, or prove that she wasn't involved in any sort of intentional deception.

What if I was wasting my time with the asphalt? Or what if I'd collected the sample from the wrong road altogether?

"I think I'll collect samples of the test asphalt from a couple more sites, in case I was given wrong information about where to get this sample. You keep working on finding a suitable solvent. Also, if I collected the wrong sample, can you wait and confirm with these extra samples before reporting to OSHA about incorrect SDS information?"

"I'm running a literature search for a suitable solvent, as we speak," Sims said. "How soon can you get me those other samples?"

"I'll get started immediately," I said. "But it could take a few days."

She frowned. "One more sample confirming this SDS is in error is all I'll need," she said. "Then, I'll have to report it to the authorities. But I'm calling Detective Turner today about the blood samples."

Chapter 50

I returned to Harry's house, took a pain pill and rested on the couch for a few minutes, letting the drug take effect, easing my pain. When I woke up three hours later, the day had almost passed me by. I felt like kicking myself; there was too much to do to sleep through my recovery.

I reached Harry on his cell phone and updated him on Sims' latest findings and her intention to pass the results along to Turner. I also called the physicians for the Luke boy and the Oaks boy and informed them of Sim's finding. Because of this new information, they each asked more questions about Mike's symptoms and revealed a little more about their own patients. I prayed one of these doctors would have an idea as to what to do with Sim's information to help all the boys.

I didn't want to publish this finding until I figured out how the chemical had reached the boys. I still suspected ARP or Manchester Chemicals had a role, but had to admit there were other possibilities. Harry offered to let me use one of his clerks to gather information on the locations of the other test sites.

Over the next three days, I weaned myself off the painkiller and, with the help of Harry's clerk, assembled the complete record of the exact locations of the test asphalt in each participating state for the purposes of collecting samples. Then, I called employees of the state highway departments from each state on my list and arranged to have samples of the test asphalt sent to Harry's office.

Three days of light duty had been good for my recovery, but frustrating in other ways. The crew that had poured the test asphalt along the Death Map route were scheduled to be in Raleigh this week, and I didn't want to miss them. I made a quick call to Meyers Construction to confirm the schedule in Raleigh, and then booked a flight and a rental car for Thursday.

My last day of rest, Wednesday, proved a bittersweet anniversary. After one month, Mike's condition hadn't changed, but my insistence on extensive analysis of his blood had led to the discovery of that mysterious neurotransmitter-like molecule of unknown origin. Because of this, Mike's doctor wanted to try a new medication. I spent the morning sitting with Mike, talking with his physician and nursing staff. Then, I ate lunch with Sophia and took her with me to put fresh flowers on Ellen's grave.

Chapter 51

Thursday: Raleigh, North Carolina

Raleigh greeted me with the season's brilliance. Vibrant bougainvillea blossoms decorated landscapes. Pear and magnolia competed for the most fragrant tree. Cumulus clouds with dark gray shadows underneath inspired hope of an approaching rain to dispel the heat. Since I was going to a construction site, I wore the jeans, T-shirt, and cheap sneakers I'd purchased before leaving Charleston. I'd wrapped a bandanna around my forehead to protect my injury from dirt. I took my camera; a fanny pack with my wallet, notebook and pens; baggies for collecting asphalt samples; and a phony plastic badge hanging from a lanyard identifying me as Mary Appleby of *Scientific Innovations*.

This road repair project involved a section of the eastbound interstate. The traffic had been funneled down from three lanes to one and crawled single file for at least seven miles. Massive sections of concrete formed a median to separate and protect the workers from traffic. I drove the length of the construction zone, trying to spot the main action. For sure, I didn't want to walk seven miles in this heat. The majority of the work was taking place about two miles into the work zone. On my second pass, I pulled off the road through a break in the concrete barriers, onto the grassy median between the east and westbound lanes and drove as close to the work site as I could. My approach had attracted some attention, and a man in overalls, boots, and a hard hat marched toward my car as I came to a stop.

"You can't be here," he yelled over the noise of the machinery, waving his hands to indicate his meaning.

I held my reporter's badge up to the windshield, then shut off the car and got out.

"You with Meyers Construction?" I asked, flashing a smile.

"Yeah. So what?"

"So, Mr. Meyers invited me out here to get photos of your crew. I'm Mary Appleby, *Scientific Innovations*." I extended my hand.

"Miss Appleby? Well, Meyers did say someone might drop by. I guess I didn't expect it to be a — that is, today," he said, looking me up and down. "Well, sure. I'm Jack. You can take pictures. Interview the guys too, I guess. Let's get you a hard hat, though."

I followed Jack over to a red four-door pickup truck parked near the concrete barrier. Dirt swirled through the air, and the fumes from the hot asphalt overpowered my senses. He dug through the equipment in the back of the truck and pulled out a battered yellow hard hat. He banged it against his leg a few times until dirt quit falling out, and handed it to me. The bandanna had been a good idea.

Jack led the way to the edge of the newly poured asphalt which was still radiating heat waves. The dump truck pouring the mixture and a machine spreading it moved away from us.

"I'm interested in the test asphalt that was used about six years ago," I yelled above the machinery noise. "Your boss said that most of the crew involved in that project are here on this job site. Were you part of that work?"

"Yeah, I was," he yelled back. "I forgot about that. Wonder how that stuff is holding up?"

"Very good, I've heard. Jack, what's your last name?" I asked.

"Gambone. Jack Gambone."

Death Map

I checked my notes. There he was. Mr. Gambone had been foreman when Zeke Waggoner was with the crew.

"And you are what? Security? Checking out wandering females?"

He laughed.

"Foreman. Go ahead and get some pictures. I'll let you speak to the crew, but not 'til they take their breaks. We got a schedule to keep."

I snapped pictures of the heavy equipment. I had passed road construction crews countless times, but never knew what the machines were called. The big thing with a roller on the front and a smaller roller in the back stopped, and the driver climbed down. A woman climbed in and the machine started rolling again. Mr. Gambone motioned for the driver on break to come over, and introduced him as Phoenix Morgan, a longtime member of his crew.

"Miss Appleby would like to interview the crew that was working the test asphalt project from a few years back. You were on that job, weren't you?" he asked Phoenix.

I watched Phoenix Morgan closely. The man was certainly handsome. He towered above me, probably six-four or six-five. He had to be approaching sixty, but had a body that any thirty-year-old would envy. *Good God, look at that chest, and those arms.* The man clearly had the muscle to do damage, but if someone had poisoned these kids along the Death Map, they wouldn't necessarily need muscle, just brains.

I heard him say, "Yeah, I was there," and I returned my eyes to his face. He was watching me watch him, and a suggestive grin curved his lips. My face grew hot.

"Did you drive that same machine on the test job?" I asked, trying to get control of the interview.

"The compactor?" he asked, still smiling. "Some. We rotate equipment so everyone gets a break, and it doesn't get too boring. Not all crews do that. But it works for us."

"The same crew is together all the time?" I asked.

"Pretty much. We have a few changes every now and then."

"How about for the test asphalt project? Is most of that crew here?" I asked.

"Now, why would y'all want to know that?" he asked.

"I'd like to speak to the actual crew and see if they noticed any difference between the test asphalt and the usual stuff. You know, like how it handled, smelled, set up, that sort of thing."

He had stopped smiling and was watching me closely as he lit a cigarette. I wondered if he'd noticed the connection between the job locations and the Death Map, as Zeke Waggoner had. Did he suspect I had an ulterior motive?

"Couldn't tell any difference," he said. "I wouldn't have known it was a test if they hadn't told me, except for the fact that we only did small sections at each place. That's not usual for us. We usually get big projects like this one."

Then he smiled again. "We got to see a lot of the country on that trip, I recollect. But the places are pretty much a blur. Long time ago."

He drew on his cigarette and seemed to be thinking.

"We worked up north," Phoenix said after another puff, "oh, about six, seven years ago, late spring through fall. It was turning too cold for us to be pouring the stuff 'bout the time we wrapped it up and moved south. Went to Texas after that, worked our way east over the next few months."

He took another draw on his cigarette and met my eyes.

"If you're around this evening for a drink, I might remember more about those locations."

I took a moment to study his face before answering. Was this a come-on, or did he actually have some info about those routes? I had no choice but to go ahead and meet him.

"Where're you staying?" I asked.

"Day's Inn. The whole crew's there. It'd be best if we met somewhere else, though."

"I don't know the area," I said.

"There's a quiet place over on Elm. We can talk. It's an Italian place called Mario's. I'll be there at eight."

He tossed the cigarette on the ground and walked off toward the portable johns. I watched his back and considered his comments. His tone had been matter-of-fact, not flirtatious. I hoped he had something worthwhile to tell me. Maybe there was actually something odd about the test asphalt.

Would he implicate one of his co-workers? What if he wanted to lure me into a trap? I couldn't help thinking of how I suspected Buzz had met his end. Maybe Phoenix was going to relay my questions back to Montallvo, and another bomb would be waiting for me at the restaurant. I touched the tender area on my forehead and closed my eyes. I was getting gun-shy, all right. My only danger tonight would probably involve an unwelcome pass after a few drinks.

Chapter 52

By late afternoon, I was exhausted. My head pounded, I was incredibly grimy, with the smell of asphalt clinging to my hair. I sent Harry a text message that my plans had changed and I'd be spending the night in Raleigh. I cursed myself for not bringing a change of clothes. I should have realized I would reek of tar. It was a plus, in a sense, that I didn't have to sit next to someone on the plane while in this condition. I'd noticed a mall and hotels near the airport, so I headed that way.

The shower and clean clothes revived my spirits immensely. I called the airport to change my flight to the following day. The only flight available left at the ungodly hour of six AM. I spent two hours replaying my interview tapes and taking notes. By seven-twenty I was starving. I put up my notes, washed my face, ran my fingers through my hair, and dialed the front desk for directions to Mario's.

Phoenix Morgan was already seated with a menu and a beer when I arrived at eight o'clock on the dot.

"Thanks for meeting me," I said as I slid into the booth opposite him.

"I'm glad you could make it, Ms. Appleby," Phoenix said.

"No problem," I said. "And call me Mary."

"All right, Mary, if you call me Phoenix." He handed me a menu. "Their specialty is lasagna, and it's outstanding. I highly recommend it."

I agreed and Phoenix placed the order.

"You implied you had some information on the test asphalt you didn't want to discuss at the job site," I said after the waiter left the table.

"First, you tell me why you're so interested in the stuff," he said.

"Fair enough. The analysis of the test project is wrapping up, and the government will be deciding soon on whether it will choose to use the new product for future road construction. It could mean big bucks for the company that developed it, and the taxpayers want confirmation their stimulus money is being used wisely. Any problem with the asphalt needs to be brought to light before the decision is made."

"Well, my information is not about the asphalt, exactly," Phoenix said. He tilted his beer bottle from side to side. "It might involve something strange with one of the crew."

"Strange?" I repeated. "How so? And who?"

"The who is, well, it's me."

I looked at him in amazement. Was he going to confess to the killings?

"What's this all about, Phoenix?"

The man sat upright, toying with his beer bottle, and seemed to exude the same self-assurance I had sensed in him earlier at the job site.

"I've always considered myself a fortunate man," he began. "I work hard, get to travel around the country, meet lots of beautiful women."

Here he paused, looked up from his beer, and smiled into my eyes. My expectations dropped to a new low. This was a come-on, after all. I sighed.

"Damn it, Phoenix. I made special arrangements to be here tonight to interview you. This had better be more than a proposition."

"Don't worry, Mary," he said. "I have a story. But, like I

said, I enjoy meeting beautiful women, and you certainly fit that category."

I eyed him suspiciously. *Not reassured.* "Go on."

"Okay, I'll stick to the subject. I probably should've called that New York paper, the *Morning Star*. They wrote the story. You might not be interested."

I could hardly keep the excitement out of my expression. He knew something about the killings, after all.

"What story do you mean?" I asked.

"The one about the Death Map. Surely you saw the article. It was about kids suddenly going berserk and killing people, and the article showed how the locations of the killings lined up on the map. I didn't see the connection at first, until I read the names of the victims. You see, I recognized two of those names. Now, what are the odds of that? I mean, I've met a lot of women, but not that many."

This wasn't what I'd expected. So, Phoenix Morgan knew two of the victims of the Death Map killings. I suspected the odds of that happening would be very low, indeed. But what could it mean? I could hardly sit still.

"How well did you know these victims?" I asked.

"Well enough to recognize their names when I saw them in the paper," he said. "I mean, I didn't know them too well. I dated them each a few times, and I called Ellen two or three times after we moved on."

I sucked in my breath. Had I heard correctly? Ellen Jacobsen was the only Ellen on the list of victims. Was he saying he knew *my* Ellen?

"Ellen?" I asked. My voice cracked but he didn't seem to notice. He was intent on his story.

"Yeah. And the other woman's name was Georgie. Georgie Crow. Ellen lived in Charleston, South Carolina, and Georgie lived in Taylock, Montana. Both of those towns were on the map in that article. Then I got to looking closer at the other towns on the map, and I'd been in every one of them."

"Wow," I managed to say, my voice almost a whisper. "Like you said, what are the odds?"

"Don't you see?" he asked. "I was in each of those towns when we were laying the test asphalt. And now, here you come around asking questions of the crew that worked those same routes. I ask you, what are the odds of that? I figured you were the one I needed to tell."

I tried to think about what this revelation could mean, but I couldn't get past the fact that he had known Ellen. She must have liked him, or she wouldn't have gone out with him more than once. I tried to remember back to that time. Had Ellen mentioned him? Surely not by name; I would have remembered the name Phoenix. Then, with a jolt, I realized that was about the time I'd been all wrapped up in myself, dealing with my cancer, shutting Ellen out of my life. Had Ellen dated a madman who had somehow influenced her son years later?

"When did you last speak with Ellen?" I asked.

"Years ago," he said. "It must be five or six years now, I guess."

"Did you meet her son?"

"Yeah. His name was Mike. He was about six or seven then. Cute kid. Seemed wary of me, I remember, but I guess that's only natural. How'd you know she had a son?"

"I read the article, too. It was the son who killed her."

"God. I missed that. He seemed like an okay kid. But he would be about twelve or so now. Kids change."

I tensed involuntarily. *No. That's why I'm here.* "Do you remember anything unusual about Ellen or her son?"

Phoenix looked at me out of the side of his eyes. He toyed with an unlit cigarette and thought for a moment before answering.

"We went out to dinner one night. Another night we went to dinner and a movie. I took Ellen and her son to the job site to look at the machinery one Sunday afternoon. I thought

Mike might get a kick out of sitting in the compactor." Phoenix smiled at his memory. "He did, too. It was a fun afternoon. But we finished the job soon afterwards, and moved on."

Our food arrived and he stuck the cigarette behind his ear. He took a bite of garlic bread and stared thoughtfully at me.

"Sometimes I meet a woman and start to wish I could settle down, raise a family, you know? Have a normal life. Ellen stirred those feelings in me. That's why I remember her so well. But I tried the settling-down thing a couple of times. Doesn't work for me. It's just as well I moved on."

I didn't answer. I knew if I tried to speak right now, I'd choke up. I wanted to leave the topic of Ellen and move to a less painful one, but I couldn't do it. He'd known Ellen. This whole conversation had a dreamlike quality, with every turn presenting something unexpected. I wanted to tell this stranger of my own connection to Ellen and Mike, but dared not speak. I tried to eat, hoping the lasagna would distract my thoughts and calm me enough to say something, but I could barely swallow.

He had known her. Ellen had spent time with him. Mike had spent time with him. Was it possible they'd be alive today if they'd not met this man? Or, if he'd kept the relationship going, would he be dead now, too? But this man also admitted knowing another victim. Was Phoenix Morgan the connection? Could he be responsible, somehow? I knew I needed to ask about the other victim. I needed to focus my attention on Georgie Crow if I was going to get through this interview. I needed to try and remember some details about Georgie's case.

I sipped my iced tea while I tried to recall what I knew about Georgie Crow. The woman had been a teacher at the Middle School in Taylock. A student, Steven Oaks, had shot his parents at home that morning, walked to school, gunned down Ms. Crow, and wounded himself. The shooter was twelve years old and not related to his teacher. I had researched the shooter, analyzed a blood sample from the shooter, but didn't know much about the victim.

I tried my voice.

"Tell me about Georgie," I said.

"Not much to tell," Phoenix said. "I met her at a grocery store. She was recently divorced and reluctant to get involved with anyone." He paused and took a swig of his beer. "We only went out a couple of times. I had her number for a long time, but it seemed pointless to call, so I never did." He thought a moment, eyes on distant memories. Then his face hardened and he refocused. "I recognized her name on that list, though. Georgie Crow. An unusual name for an unusual woman. Can't believe she ended like that."

"This was in Taylock, you said?"

"Yes." He shook off the gloom, resumed his machismo. "We did the typical dating stuff. Dinner, movie, bars."

"Did she have children?"

"No. Maybe that's why I didn't get the settling-down urge with Georgie. You know, we might be on to something there. I do like to see women caring for their young. Do you have children, Mary?"

I ignored that question.

"You mentioned you let Michael Jacobsen sit on the compactor. Did you or your crew often let youngsters onto the job site?"

"No, not often. I got the idea from one of the other guys. He said it would impress a woman if you paid attention to her kid."

"So, it happened occasionally, you think?"

"Probably, but I only did it a few times. Why do you ask?"

"I ask questions for a living, remember? Also, I'm curious. Did you take Georgie to the job site?

He laughed. "No, it only seems to appeal to youngsters."

His eyes began to twinkle. "Or am I wrong? Would you like to see the construction site by moonlight?"

"The moon's not out tonight," I said with a slight grin. "But I see your point. You did say you took kids to the site a few times. Remember any other names, not on the list?"

"Nope. Not likely to, either. I've been at this a long time."

"Do you know if any of the others who worked that job recognized any names listed in the Death Map article?"

"Well, you see, I didn't mention it to anyone else. As far as I know, none of the other guys took much notice of the story."

I tried a bite of lasagna again. This time I could actually taste it. I was glad Phoenix had recommended the dish; it was very good. Phoenix was also eating his dinner, and we were quiet for a few minutes.

I considered the man's story. Was he setting up an alibi of some sort? Or was he trying to defuse suspicion by admitting a connection and making it sound plausible and innocent? Maybe it was plausible and innocent. He struck me as trustworthy, but, then, Ellen must have trusted him. How important was it that Mike had actually been on the construction site? I wondered if I could possibly backtrack the movements of the other kids to see how near they'd been to the construction sites? That sounded like an impossible task. Who would know? Phoenix mentioned that another crewmember had given him the idea of taking a date's kid to the job site. I asked him for the name.

Phoenix watched me thoughtfully for a moment. "Why do you want to know?"

"Call it a hunch. Like you said, knowing two victims from that news story seems highly unlikely, but it is very real. What if there's more of a connection than you know? It could make an interesting story."

Phoenix was quiet a while longer. Finally, he said, "No. I can't remember."

It was the first time since meeting this man that I felt he was lying.

"Would you mind mentioning the Death Map story to the other men who were on that job, and see if anyone recognizes any names?" I asked.

Phoenix continued looking intently at me.

"That might not be a good idea," he said. "We'd have reporters looking into everyone's past. People don't like that."

"I think you told me about your link with the victims because you suspect there's some connection between your crew and the killings. Maybe not a direct connection, but something, and you want me to find out. Right?"

Phoenix tilted his head. "I suppose so," he said. "It does seem to defy the odds."

"Well, if you don't help, I'm going to have to call each one of the men who worked that route and see if they remember anything. They might tell you before they'd tell me."

"You're just looking for a story. You could totally mess up someone's life. If he were married, for instance."

"I'm looking for the truth," I said, then realized how that sounded coming from Mary Appleby. I took a deep breath and decided to come clean with Phoenix. So, I told him everything — my true name, my love for Ellen and Mike, how my search for an explanation for Mike's actions had led to the Death Map discovery, the connection with Amalgamated Recovery Products, and how Zeke Waggoner's letter had led me to Meyers Construction and this crew. The number of deaths that seemed to be following me around.

Phoenix listened, watching me from hooded eyes. "I remember Zeke. He didn't stay with the crew very long."

"Right," I said. "Now you tell me that Mike was actually at the job site, not merely in the general area. That might've been how he was exposed to the chemical."

Phoenix thought for a moment before responding. "Didn't you say that the chemical wasn't in the asphalt sample you took from the road?"

"We can't say that just yet. There's a problem with the analysis technique. The chemist is still trying and I'm getting samples from other locations to verify."

"Well, it seems to me that if it was in the asphalt, then me and all the other guys on that job would've been exposed to that chemical every day for about a year. None of us has turned into a killer that I know of."

"Yeah," I said. "I don't have it all figured out, yet. I'm still gathering info, but you've provided the first evidence of a direct connection between two victims along the route. It has to mean something."

Phoenix took the cigarette from behind his ear, and played with it a bit. "Okay, I'll ask around. Call me in a day or so."

"Please be discreet. You might alert the wrong person and put yourself in danger. Also, I'd like to maintain my cover as Mary Appleby."

I thought he hesitated a beat too long before agreeing. Then I thought of another question. "Do you know who inspected the test asphalt?"

"No," Phoenix said. "But Gambone mentioned several times that it was doing great, so someone's been looking at it. Check with him."

"Thanks. I will. And I'll call you soon."

I returned to the hotel. I was exhausted, but fired up by this reveal. Phoenix had promised to check with his fellow crewmembers, but I knew of one he wouldn't think to contact. It was ten PM here, but only nine in Illinois. I placed a call to Zeke Waggoner.

"Hi, Ms. Kincaid," Zeke said. "Have you had any luck figuring out what's going on with that Death Map of yours?"

"I've got a few clues," I said. "But nothing certain yet."

"I've been doing a lot of thinking about those days," Zeke added. "I haven't been able to come up with anything else that might help you."

"I was wondering if you ever took anyone to the job site after hours. Like, maybe if you were dating someone who had a child? Let the kid sit up on the equipment? I've heard some of the guys did that."

"No, I didn't," Zeke replied. "And I don't recall anyone mentioning that. But then again, I didn't hang with them much after hours. Didn't get close to anyone."

"Did you recognize any of the names of the victims in the Death Map article?" I asked.

"No, just the locations, is all," he said. "I did meet a few ladies on that job," he added. "I kept their names in my log book, by the name of the town. Hang on a sec."

He put down the phone and I waited.

"I don't have the article in front of me," he said a moment later, "but here are some names." He read off a list of ten names. He seemed to have been successful meeting women. As he recited off the names, I compared them to the ones in the article. No matches. The last name he read wasn't on the list of victims, but I knew it. I'd hiked with the woman in Dwight, North Dakota. She'd told me about a time when she and her husband were having problems and she had met a nice guy who was just passing through. I was filled with dread at the realization that Madeline McGuire had three children, including a boy. Were they at risk? How could I tell? My God. The clock was ticking.

Chapter 53

Charleston, South Carolina

I had left Raleigh for Charleston at the crack of dawn on Friday. Stormy weather contributed to a stressful flight. My head was killing me by the time I let myself in Harry's front door. I thought by this time he'd have left for the office, but he was still home and called out to me. I paused, but couldn't think of a way around it. I found him sitting in the living room, feeding fruit to Jay-Jay.

"Morning," I said. "Thought you'd be long gone for the day."

"Court was canceled this morning. How'd it go in Raleigh?"

"Good. Found out some interesting stuff."

"Hello, Lila, Hello, Lila," Jay-Jay squawked.

A tray of apple slices sat on the end table and I passed one between the metal slats. Beak snatched the fruit, claws gripped the horizontal bars; unblinking eyes surrounded by fluttering wings. Bird tension detectors working.

"I hoped I'd catch you. Want to talk?"

I didn't want to talk. I wanted to focus on actions. I needed to focus on actions. It kept me from thinking too seriously about depressing things. Like Ellen. Like Mike. Like Harry.

"Have a cup of coffee with me, at least. Sit down." He had a carafe and an extra cup on the coffee table. He was prepared. Harry had an agenda, and I didn't want to go there.

I took the cup of coffee and sat down. I didn't need more coffee, my pulse raced fast enough.

"I know I promised I wouldn't bother you," he said. "But I'm worried."

"It's going well. I've got a couple of interesting angles on the Death Map that I'm following up."

"I'm not worried about the story. I'm worried about you. You've wrapped yourself up in this to the point you've disconnected from everything else. Have you even thought about Sophia in the last few days? Visited Mike? Spoken to anyone about anything other than your investigation?"

He might as well have slapped me in the face. "How dare you?" I said, jumping to my feet. "You have no idea what you're talking about. I'm doing all this for Ellen and Mike. For Sophia, too. Have you ever thought it might be my way of dealing with the horror of the whole situation?"

Jay-Jay began frantic fluttering. Squawking louder. The pounding in my temple magnified the noise. I raised my voice above the din.

"Besides, I don't need to justify myself to you. None of this is about you, Harry." I was ranting and I knew it. Not enough sleep, too much sadness, too much horror. I couldn't stop myself. "None of this is about you and me. That was over long ago. Forget us. You dreamed of a family, well, it won't happen with me. It can't. I can't have kids. You should have moved on by now." I whirled around and stormed upstairs, the afterimage of Harry's shocked face etched in my brain.

Chapter 54

I couldn't calm down. Why had I let Harry get to me? I should have known better than to stay at his house. What was I thinking? I needed to put him out of my mind and re-focus on my investigation. I had every right to focus on the investigation. I paced the room like a caged rat. That image rammed my mind back into gear.

Sven Peterson had studied the effect of the neurotransmitter-like molecule on caged rats. He showed that exposure to ARP 2728 caused behavioral changes only in juvenile, male rats. Now, the same chemical turned up in juvenile, male children who demonstrated extreme behavioral changes, exactly like those young rats.

But how did those kids get exposed to the chemical? ARP 2728 could be a component of the test asphalt. The negative result from the state lab didn't rule out that possibility because Dr. Sims had had problems with the solvent. I could trace a trail from Frank Travis at Amalgamated Recovery Products sending the material to Sven Peterson in Toronto for testing, then from both men to Grant Montallvo at Manchester Chemicals.

But four to six years was a big lapse in time between when the asphalt was put in place and the killings I'd found. I tried to get the time frame to work out. Suppose the chemical was in the asphalt and slowly leached out to contaminate the environment. Perhaps the behavioral changes required a threshold level of exposure. But the water and soil results didn't support that idea.

I tried a variation of the aerosol theme. What if the asphalt actually did contain ARP 2728, but the boys needed to be nearby, to breathe in the fumes? And with boys being boys, maybe, if not brought there by one of the crew members, they went there to play on their own. But that didn't sound right to me, for a couple of reasons. One, boys usually played in pairs or groups, which would mean several kids would be exposed at the same time. I didn't have any evidence of multiple kids affected from one location. Two, as Phoenix Morgan had pointed out, if it was in the asphalt, potentially thousands of people, especially the work crew, would have been exposed. So why would only a few boys be affected?

I hoped Phoenix would have luck with the guy who suggested taking kids to the job site. If I could show that each of the kids had been to a job site . . . but right now, I only had proof of one: Mike.

Another possibility worth thinking about was that someone, like the inspector, could be deliberately releasing the chemical and exposing children along the same route as the test asphalt. Some sicko intent on harming the kids, or perhaps some sicko with a political agenda, wanting to implicate the companies involved in the test asphalt project. I wondered if any groups or individuals were protesting the test projects.

If Frank's formula for the new asphalt actually contained a dangerous byproduct, who would know about it? Sven said he'd reported it to the Canadian Department of Energy. What did they do with that information? I found a number for the department and reached a very polite woman who took down the particulars and promised to check their records from that project and get back to me. Shouldn't take but a day or two.

Also, Sven reported the results to Frank at ARP. Frank, of course, was dead, but what did he do with that information? He'd worked for Amalgamated Recovery Products, so possibly someone else there, like a technician or a boss, had access. I remembered the sympathetic secretary, and I paused in my mental analysis long enough to give her a call.

When I reached the ARP secretary, she remembered me as Mary Appleby. I expressed my condolences and shock over the death of Ms. Chesney and thanked her for putting me in touch with Brian Reese.

"Did you meet him?" she asked. "He was killed in that explosion, too."

"Yes, that's why I'm calling. Brian told me that right before Frank died, he received some bad news about tests on a formula he was working on. Frank was worried it would trash the whole project."

"Really?" she said.

"Yeah, well, I was wondering if you could check the records and see if you can find out about those tests? They were done at University of Toronto, I believe."

"Frank told this to Brian?"

I couldn't be sure what Frank had told Brian. I thought it was true, and I was fishing for proof that the test results that were worrying Frank were the same results that had worried Sven Peterson. I sidestepped the question. "Now they're all dead," I said, "the only way to confirm this is to get someone within the company to look into it. I'm sure you must still have Frank's files stored somewhere?"

She was vague, but took my number and promised to look into it if she had time.

Frank had been in the process of moving to California, going into business with Grant Montallvo, so Montallvo might know about the test results. Manchester Chemicals, where the same Grant Montallvo was now CEO, was in California and had hired Dr. Peterson, presumably to gain control over his research into ARP 2728. That meant there were people in the research labs there who might know.

Dr. Peterson had left behind his suggestion that I look more closely at Grant Montallvo, and now seemed like a good time to interview the man. I called Manchester Chemicals, but couldn't get past his executive secretary. So, I tried an online search for a home address or phone number. He was listed, with an address in an affluent suburb of San Francisco. Just as the corporate website had said, he had a wife named Skylar and two daughters. Maybe I could get to him through the home front. I dialed the number and spoke with his wife.

This time, I identified myself as Dorothy Adams, a freelance reporter with an angle on an article I hoped to sell to a San Francisco-based parenting magazine. I claimed they were doing a series on local residents and their different parenting styles, and that I'd heard through the grapevine that Mrs. Montallvo was doing an exemplary job raising her family. My readers would be fascinated to learn her secrets.

Mrs. Montallvo seemed reluctant at first and asked for some references. I pretended to be a novice reporter but promised to let her read and approve the article before I submitted it for publication. She put me on hold. After what seemed like an eternity, the woman came back on line and agreed to meet with me late the following afternoon for an interview. I asked if I could meet the whole family.

"Oh, I'm sure my husband will be out of town. He travels quite a bit, you see. The daily responsibility for the children is mine."

"That's fine. Thanks, Mrs. Montallvo. I'm looking forward to meeting you." I hung up. That was easy. I formed a picture in my mind of a bored housewife, craving attention and excitement, willing to place her hopes on an unknown reporter. I dialed the airport number from memory. I lucked out again with a seat on a direct flight leaving in two hours. Enough time to pack; too little time to leave Harry much of a note.

Chapter 55

Friday: En Route to San Francisco, California

I settled into my seat on the plane and tried to organize my whirlwind of thoughts. I refused to think about that little outburst with Harry. Instead, I sent a long text to Clunie, catching her up on my investigation. Then I reviewed the notes of my conversation the previous evening with Phoenix Morgan at the Italian restaurant in Raleigh. It brought to mind some interesting questions. Who had planted the idea in Morgan's mind to take the kids to visit the job site? Was Jack Gambone, the foreman, aware? Surely there were safety regulations and liability issues that would make Gambone ban this practice. I needed to place a follow-up call to Phoenix and a call to Gambone. I checked my watch. By the time I reached San Francisco, the crew would be finished at the job site for the day. I made a note to try to reach Phoenix at the Days Inn.

I also needed to speak to the big guy at Meyers Construction, George Meyers, to see what he knew about the elusive road inspector. As the owner of Meyers Construction, George Meyers should have contact information for Sky's-the-Limit Evaluations, how frequently the inspections were done, and what the results were. It was worth checking to see if there was a correlation between the inspection dates and the dates of any of the killings.

I scribbled down these thoughts. Phoenix Morgan knew my true identity. But I needed to remember to maintain the Mary Appleby persona when speaking to Gambone and

Meyers. If they hadn't noticed a connection between the Death Map and the test asphalt locations, I didn't want to bring it to their attention. Both Gambone and Meyers were in a good position to inadvertently mention my investigation to the responsible party, be it Montallvo, the inspector, one of the construction crew, or an as-yet-unidentified party. Too many people had died because of this investigation. I didn't intend to be one of them.

Realistically, they might not have seen the Death Map article. So far, only two people had raised the possibility of a connection between the construction project locations and the Death Map killings. I didn't think Phoenix would point it out to anyone, and Waggoner was safely out of the loop.

I would never be convinced that the explosion at California Dreaming was accidental. I knew Harry also believed it was intentional, and that it indicated my investigation was getting too close for someone, and that I was a target. While I agreed that Ms. Chesney and Brian Reese had been targeted, I didn't think anyone knew that I'd intended to be at that meeting; however, my questions to Ms. Chesney about Frank could have triggered the event. Chesney had set up the meeting with Reese, and someone else knew about it. Someone else was willing to go to extremes to keep both Chesney and Reese from talking. Was that someone Montallvo?

As much as I hated it, I couldn't entirely dismiss Harry's concerns, even though I'd introduced myself to Chesney and Reese as Mary Appleby. Even if Chesney had run to someone about the questions I'd raised regarding Frank, that person only knew about a nosy Mary Appleby. I'd given my real name to the police after the accident, but they weren't concerned that I was supposed to have been in the restaurant when it blew, so how would anyone else find out about me?

What about the inspector from Sky's-the-Limit? I would think that if someone traveled regularly to the locations along the test asphalt route, they would have noticed the connection to my Death Map. Assuming, of course, they had read my article. Should I assume he knew my real name and would be suspicious of any inquires? I had to make that assumption.

My headache was returning. Too many unknowns. I put away my notes and popped a pain pill. Sleep sounded like the right cure at the moment. My thoughts drifted of their own accord to Harry about the time I was nodding off. Once, I had planned on never seeing him again, and here I was staying at his house, trying to keep interactions with him strictly neutral, but somehow stirring up old feelings. I had done the right thing five years ago. Why hadn't he married someone by now, gotten on with his life?

I slept the sleep of the drugged and didn't awaken until I was roused by the flight attendant asking everyone to fasten seatbelts prior to landing. The headache was gone for the moment, and I had good luck at the airport renting a car and finding a room for the night. Things were looking up.

In my hotel room, I placed a call to the Days Inn in Raleigh and reached Phoenix in his room.

"Phoenix, Lila Kincaid here."

"Hi, Lila," he said. "Glad you called. I've got some information for you."

I picked up my notepad, ready to take down the information. "You sound chipper," I said. "What you got?"

"Good news. I asked around like you wanted, kind of casual-like, to see if anyone ever took a kid to the job site," Phoenix said. "Well, I found a guy named Hank who admitted to it. Another mother-son thing. Hank couldn't recall their last name, and was hard pressed to come up with first names, but finally remembered the woman was Anna and the son was Kyle."

I felt goose bumps erupt, remembering Anna and Kyle Bennett.

"Where was that?" I asked. "Did he remember the town?"

"No. Only their names. But I looked at that list of victims in your article, and those names aren't there. That's gotta mean there's no connection, don't you think?" he asked. "I mean between me knowing those women and what ended up happening to them."

Concern came through loud and clear.

"Could be," I said. "Did you talk to everyone?"

"Yeah. Hank was the only one to admit to it. You don't know how much better I'm feeling that nothing happened to those people he knew."

Mother and son, victims of an explosion. Coroner suspicious. I had not included their case in my file of the Death Map killings due to lack of evidence. It was probably no more than an unfortunate accident. But if this was the same boy who visited the job site with Hank, maybe I should tell Phoenix. Keep him asking questions.

So, I told Phoenix about them. Asked him to see if Hank recognized that last name, or if he remembered Linton, North Dakota.

"Hell," he said, so quietly I almost didn't hear. I gave him my cell phone number. I could have contacted Hank myself — he was on my list of Meyers Construction employees — but I wanted to push Phoenix to reveal who had originally suggested the idea of taking kids to the job site. Manipulation, plain and simple. I felt justified.

I redialed the Days Inn number and asked for Jack Gambone, not sure if he was staying at the same motel as the rest of the crew. He was registered, but not in his room at the moment. I left a brief message that I needed information on the inspection results. I left Mary Appleby's info and hung up. I knew it was a long shot. Gambone was on a job location and the information I wanted was most likely in his office, if he had it at all. I might as well call the office myself.

Meyers Construction's main office was in Texas, a closer time zone to San Francisco. The office was currently closed, but I left a message similar to the one I'd left for Gambone, with an additional request for specific dates and locations of the inspections and the name of the inspector in each instance.

Then I called down to the front desk for a wakeup call at eight in the morning. Hopefully, a response from Gambone or Meyers would arrive by then.

I shut off my cell phone and collapsed across the bed. I was feeling the effects of a full day of traveling, on top of my injuries. I was supposed to wait another hour before taking the next dose of pain meds, but I wanted to get to sleep early and it would help. Tomorrow would be a busy day and I'd need my wits about me. I took the pill, turned the TV news channel on low and promptly fell asleep.

~*~

The room phone rang with my wakeup call and I stumbled into the shower. After several cups of coffee and breakfast at the hotel's restaurant, I felt somewhat back to normal. I returned to my room, checked emails and phone messages. Harry had called my cell several times last night and once this morning. I tried to reach him at home, but he must've already left for work. I left a quick message and was about to dial his office number when an email from Meyers Construction came through on Mary Appleby's email. I'd have to call Harry later. The message from the construction company showed that Sky's-the-Limit Evaluations was located in Oakland, practically next door.

Mr. Meyers had sent the address and phone number, dates of inspections, and results. The name of the person who actually went on-site to do the inspection was omitted, but a quick call to the business's office number should give me that information.

I studied the inspection dates. The inspections were done annually, during the months of July and August. Forty locations were examined visually, digitally photographed, and laser analyzed for cracks, fissures, and moisture content. The locations were coded, and I didn't have the key to decode. A personal visit to Sky's-the-Limit rather than a phone call would probably net better results. They should be open by now. I checked MapQuest for directions and headed out.

I found the office of Sky's-the-Limit Evaluations without any problem. The reception area was tiny and sparse, and the secretary at the front desk played Texas Hold'em on her computer. Not a busy place, it seemed. I introduced myself and asked to speak to the person who handled the inspections of the Meyers Construction road project. The secretary asked if I knew the job number. I checked my copy of the report and provided the number. She minimized the game and opened a file on her computer. She found the case number and squinted at the document that opened up.

"That's odd," the woman said. "I can't see a name mentioned anywhere."

"Is the manager or owner of the business here?" I asked.

"No. I'm the only one here. I enter the data from the reports that come in the mail and send the final version out to the client."

"Who's your boss?"

"Mr. Montallvo. But he never comes in."

"Grant Montallvo?" I asked. "From Manchester Chemicals?"

"No," the secretary replied. "Glenn Montallvo."

"Glenn? That's impossible."

"Of course, it's possible. He signs my paycheck."

"Have you actually met him?" I asked.

"No," the woman said. "It's not all that strange. He's living in Texas somewhere and never comes to California. We handle everything through the mail, by phone with his

302

secretary, or through email."

"Surely someone comes in to check up on things."

"No. It works out quite well, actually. I'm a very independent worker."

"Look, I need to speak to Mr. Montallvo," I said. "What's his phone number?"

"I'm not supposed to give out the number," she said. "But I'm authorized to answer questions. What else would you like to know?"

I suddenly had a weird hunch. I leafed through my notebook and came up with a number. I showed it to the secretary.

"Well, if you already had the number, why did you ask me for it?" she said. "I've got better things to do than play twenty questions." She maximized Texas Hold'em.

"Sorry to bother you." I put the notebook back in my bag, leaving it open to the page with the contact information I'd shown the secretary. Now why, I wondered, would the ill-fated Ms. Chesney, formerly at Amalgamated Recovery Products, pretend to be speaking for the long-dead brother of the CEO of Manchester Chemicals?

Chapter 56

I arrived at Grant Montallvo's family residence at four-thirty, the appointed time. Mrs. Montallvo, a beautiful, petite blonde with a cheerleader smile, answered the door looking stylish in black Capri pants and pink sleeveless sweater shell. The string of pearls added a rich touch. She proudly introduced her two daughters, Isabella, five, and Evelyn, four. The girls dressed alike in frilly pink-and-white dresses. Their blond curls glistened in the sunshine.

Mrs. Montallvo insisted I call her Skylar, and we began with a photo shoot. I positioned Skylar and her daughters in front of the house and took several outdoor shots. Then we moved into the living room, where I took more photos and started the interview for my "article."

I asked about educational activities for the girls, choice of school, sports, play time with other children, favorite places to shop for clothes and toys, health care, and diet; everything one would expect for an article on a model parent. Skylar eagerly answered the questions and then I suggested the girls change into swimsuits for photos by the pool. The giggling girls ran out of the living room and I steered the questions to Mr. Montallvo.

"And where does your husband work?" I asked.

"He's president of Manchester Chemicals here in San Francisco, but he's also the owner of a small company in Texas and divides his time between the two places."

"So, when you said on the phone yesterday that he travels quite a bit, you meant to Texas, then?"

"Yes, mostly. We both lived there before we were married, but now he spends the majority of time here and travels to Texas one or two days a week."

"You're from Texas?" I asked. "You don't have the accent."

"No," she said with an easy laugh. "I'm originally from California. I have a degree in chemistry, and was working in Midland when I met Grant. We started our family right after moving here. I'll return to work when the girls are older."

I wanted to ask more about Grant, but I couldn't ignore this lead into the woman's career past. Any reporter doing a story on Mrs. Montallvo would jump at that introduction.

"You gave up a career as a chemist for your family?" I asked. "That's a big sacrifice."

"Oh, I wouldn't say gave up. On hold would be more accurate. I have a job at Manchester Chemicals anytime I want."

"You worked for Manchester Chemicals, also?"

"Well, not exactly," she said. "But they're following up on some of the earlier research that I did with another company. I do a bit of consulting for them from time to time, and I have an open offer to go full-time as soon as I'm ready. And it's not because my husband is CEO."

"Marvelous. A successful career and a successful family. And you should be proud of how you keep everything together, being alone so often. I guess the girls miss him a lot, make a big deal of his homecomings? Or are they used to his being gone so much?"

Skylar chuckled. "Of course they make a big deal out of his homecoming. They simply adore their father. Why, last week he spent Monday and Tuesday in New York City and brought home the nicest gifts." She fingered the pearls at her throat. "Then a quick trip to Midland a couple days later. That's where he's gone today, I believe."

"Too bad," I said. "I'd enjoy meeting the man behind the

happy family." A man who had apparently been in New York City the day of Buzz's death and the *Morning Star's* fire, and then in Midland the day of California Dreaming's bombing.

"Well, I told him about this interview. He hates missing it."

At that moment the phone rang. Mrs. Montallvo rose in one fluid, graceful motion. "Excuse me, please," she said politely and left the room.

I went to the fireplace mantle and studied the family portrait. Cute picture of the wife and kids with the handsome father.

Skylar returned a few minutes later, smiling warmly.

"Can you believe it? That was Grant," she said. "He's had a change in his schedule and is still in town. He suggested I bring you to his office for a few pictures and an interview. I hope you don't mind."

I panicked. The security guard at Manchester Chemicals might recognize me and blow my cover. The only ID I had for Dorothy Adams was a business card. The guard would want to see something more substantial, like Ms. Adams' non-existent driver's license.

"Um, are you sure? What about the girls?"

"Oh, no problem. I'll drop them off at gymnastics class. They were willing to skip it today for this interview, but they really want to go. It starts at six. We can still make it."

Right on cue, the girls came running down the stairs. Their mother raised her hand and they abruptly slowed to a walk.

"Change of plans," Skylar said. "You're going to gymnastics after all. See how quickly you can change into your leotards." They squealed in delight and ran back up the stairs.

"A picture of them at gym class would look great in the article," I said. "I think I'll snap a few photos of them before we drive over to your husband's office."

As a stall tactic, it wasn't too bad. Maybe I could figure out what to do when we reached Manchester Chemicals. Actually, this late in the day, it would surely be a different person at the security desk than on my previous visit, and they might not check my ID if I were escorted by the CEO's wife. Or I'd say I accidentally left my license at the hotel and hope they didn't think about calling the car rental company. I relaxed a little. I could pull it off. Maybe I could ask for a tour of the facilities, including the research labs.

The kids stormed downstairs dressed for gymnastics. I gathered up my stuff and preceded them outside. I headed for my rental car parked at the curb.

"Do you mind driving us?" Skylar called from the front door behind me. "I can catch a ride home with Grant after the interview."

"Sure," I said, "it's a compact, but we can squeeze in. Lucky you girls are little things," I added as they giggled and clambered into the back seat. "Buckle up, now."

Skylar directed me to the gymnastics studio. I photographed the girls while their mother made arrangements for them to be watched after class by the parent of one of the other students.

There were three instructors and about fifteen students. I introduced myself to the instructors and took down their names and details on the school. Isabella and Evelyn eagerly performed a series of stunts. They were natural showoffs. It was "Miss Adams, watch me. Miss Adams, watch me," over and over again as I snapped away. Maybe I would go ahead and write the article. They were cute kids. If I ended up with a case against Grant, people would be interested in his family life. I marveled that his children were so normal. It must be due to their mother's influence.

Then Skylar tapped my shoulder. "Surely that's enough," she said. "Grant's probably given up on us."

"Okay," I said. "Thanks, girls. See ya later."

Death Map

They waved good-bye and somersaulted across the room.

I pulled out of the gymnastics parking lot into heavy traffic, without much of a plan. I remembered the approximate location of Manchester Chemicals from my last visit when I interviewed Dr. Peterson, but I pretended to have no clue.

"So, which way?" I asked.

"Turn left at the third light and get on 280 South."

I followed the directions. Almost immediately, I saw the sign for the exit to downtown San Francisco.

"Next exit?" I asked.

"No, stay on 280," Mrs. Montallvo said.

"You sure?" I asked. "I thought Manchester Chemicals was downtown."

"Just follow my directions."

Skylar's voice had a harsh edge I hadn't heard before. Maybe my driving made her nervous.

The next green road sign said San Jose, 48 miles. I was confused. Surely we were headed the wrong way. I wished I'd studied my map of San Francisco a little closer. "I think we made a wrong turn," I said. "There's a map in the glove box."

"Shut up and go where I tell you."

My heart jumped at her tone of voice and I glanced toward her. Then my heart sank at the sight of the small, ladylike pistol pointed in my direction.

Chapter 57

I couldn't take my eyes off the weapon, traffic be damned.

"Watch the road," Skylar Montallvo said, giving the gun a little wave motion toward the front of the car.

I forced my eyes back to the interstate. "What the hell are you doing?" I asked.

"It's pretty simple. Do what I say and you won't get hurt."

I gulped and nodded vigorously, still staring at the road ahead. "No problem. Whatever you say."

Mrs. Montallvo didn't answer. I kept driving, wondering what the hell this meant. Why would a nice upper-class mother of two do something this extreme? There was nobody to pay a ransom for me. I didn't think I'd done or said anything to give myself away. Even if Mrs. Montallvo suspected I wanted to investigate her husband, this was an extreme response. Maybe she was just insane.

After about twenty minutes of mental despair, I calmed down a little. Whatever was going on, the woman wasn't likely to shoot me while I was driving along the interstate. But I couldn't envision an escape at eighty miles per hour. I needed to exit somewhere, and soon. I wondered how far Mrs. Montallvo intended me to drive, or even if she had a plan. Maybe I could talk my way into stopping for gas. Somehow manage to get away from her then.

"We need gas," I said. Not very creative, but true.

I felt the gun barrel press into my ribs as the woman leaned toward me to check the gauge. We drove in silence past the next two exits. Ten more miles sped past before we approached another Gas, Food, and Lodging sign. Plenty of time to wonder why this was happening.

"Get off here," she said. "There's a station a block to the right."

I stopped behind a van at the bottom of the ramp. Traffic flew along the busy crossroad; we sat there for several minutes before the van could pull out onto the road. I wondered if maybe I could jump out or something. But I'd never get out of my seat belt before getting shot. I tried to think of anything at all I could do to get out of this jam, but my mind seemed to be moving like mud. I thought of the tape recorder in my purse. My spirits rose and my mind latched on to the idea of turning on the recorder. At a break in the traffic flow, I edged the car forward very slowly.

"Speed up a little," Mrs. Montallvo said. "You'll attract too much attention."

I hit the brake suddenly, throwing my captor forward into the dash. At the same time, I reached into my purse and pushed a button, hoping it was the right one.

The gun went off, sending a bullet through the roof of the rental car. I screamed. "Don't shoot," I yelled. "My foot slipped is all. Don't shoot, please." I gulped and broke into a sweat when Mrs. Montallvo placed the gun next to my temple.

"Don't let it slip again."

"Okay, okay." I shook so badly I wasn't sure I could drive at all. "I'll try. Please, that gun's making me too nervous to drive."

Mrs. Montallvo lowered the gun to her lap, but kept it pointed at me. I glanced left and right. The cars flew by in both directions, and three cars waited behind us on the off-ramp. There were no pedestrians to be seen, but I could only hope someone in one of the nearby cars had heard that shot.

However, no one came to my rescue. No one paid the slightest attention to me except this crazy woman.

"Drive," she said, in a voice that harbored no alternatives.

I drove. I merged into the next opening in the traffic. I prayed for the approach of flashing lights in my rear-view mirror, but none appeared. All the cars around me had the windows up and probably had the music playing and air conditioning blowing. No one had heard the little gun go off.

The next traffic light changed to yellow, then red. Again, I stopped the car. The gas station loomed ahead on the right. God, why couldn't I think? I'd never been in a situation like this before. Now might be my only chance, and the light could change back to green any second. Maybe I would have a better chance to escape at the gas station? There were cars in line at the pumps, people standing around pumping gas. Much easier for someone to hear a gunshot, so maybe this maniac would be slower on the trigger.

The light changed and I pulled into the gas station, queued at the pump behind a small red pick-up. It was now or never.

I stared a long time in my rear-view mirror. Hoping I had some acting skills, I played the tried-and-true movie trick of glancing furtively over Mrs. Montallvo's shoulder to attract her attention. As I hoped, she couldn't resist glancing behind her. I snapped open the seat belt and flung open the door.

"Bad idea, Ms. Kincaid," my captor said seconds before the world disappeared.

Chapter 58

Unknown Date; Unknown Location

I couldn't move my arms. I couldn't open my mouth. My head pounded. There was no blessed loss of memory as in the movies. I remembered every stupid move up to the minute of my disastrous attempt to escape, and the bash to my head. I should've been patient, waited until one of us got out to pump gas.

I messed up.

Bad.

I didn't think my head could hurt so much, but pain meant life. I didn't know if that constant background roar came from my head or my surroundings. I eased open my eyes and looked around. It was night. I was tied to a chair, and I was wet and cold. Slowly, my brain began to process what my senses detected. I smelled ocean brine and felt water droplets spray across my face. The deafening roar meant nearby ocean crashing onto rocky shore or bluff. I was outside, probably on a deck or patio, because I could feel the decorated grillwork of wrought iron beneath my fingers. For all I knew, I'd been unconscious for hours, and could be miles from where I'd been attacked.

I'd made a tactical error in assuming Mrs. Montallvo had acted alone. There's no way that petite woman could have managed to get me from the car to this chair by herself. Grant must be around here, wherever here was. He could have been waiting for us near that exit. Maybe he'd been waiting to pump gas.

And hadn't Mrs. Montallvo called me Ms. Kincaid? Yes, I was sure of that. But how had she known my identity? I realized with a sinking feeling that I had seriously underestimated Grant Montallvo. He must have been expecting me to show up, warned his wife, had a contingency plan. No wonder it had been so easy to get an interview with her. How had he duped the woman into helping get rid of me?

Suddenly, the chair tipped back. I hadn't heard any approaching footsteps. I let out a yell but tape across my mouth restricted my sounds to a gurgle. No one could have heard me, anyway. I could barely hear myself above the constant roar of the ocean and the pounding of my heart. The chair and I traveled rearward. I tried to wriggle sideways to see where I was being taken, and by whom, but to no avail.

The chair was pulled roughly through a doorway. My hands, tied to the armrests, banged into the doorframe and the skin tore loose across the back of my knuckles. My curse rattled around in my thoughts. An overhead light clicked on, and I quit struggling. I was facing the sliding glass doorway and could see a little bit of where I'd been. The circle of illumination reached far enough to reveal pieces of a smashed camera, undoubtedly mine, littering a wet balcony. I felt as broken as the camera.

A man's face suddenly appeared inches in front of mine. I jerked my head back in surprise, then glared at him and issued grunting complaints. I recognized Grant Montallvo from the family portrait I'd seen in their living room.

"She's awake," Montallvo said.

"Finally."

Mrs. Montallvo's voice, still harsh, issued from somewhere behind me, out of sight of the reflecting glass. I took my eyes off the man and craned my head around looking for his wife, my two-faced kidnapper. The limitations of my bindings kept Mrs. Montallvo out of sight. I took in my surroundings instead. I was in an old-fashioned, country style kitchen. I could see antique cabinets and an ornate stove, a big wooden chopping block as a center island, with copper and brass cookware hanging from an overhead ring. Right out of a country design magazine layout.

"I didn't think I hit her that hard," Mrs. Montallvo said.

Grant Montallvo reached toward my face and yanked the tape off my mouth.

"Jeeze," I yelled.

"Sorry," he said.

"What the hell's going on? Why've you tied me up?"

"See," Mrs. Montallvo said, coming into view on my left. "She won't stop asking questions. We've got to get rid of her."

I tried to sit still, studying Grant Montallvo. I began to shake, the combination of fear and damp cold betraying me. "You . . . you . . . you must be the in . . . infamous Grant Montallvo?"

He sighed heavily. "Yes. I'm sorry, Ms. Kincaid, but my wife is right. You ask too many questions."

"It's what I do. I'll keep asking my questions until I get some answers."

"For God's sake," Mrs. Montallvo said. "Look at your situation, little girl. We don't have to answer anything. Tape her shut again, Grant."

"No, Sky," Grant said. "I want to find out what she knows and who else knows it."

Skylar Montallvo huffed loudly, crossed her arms, and stepped behind me, disappearing from view.

This was bad. My stomach bottomed out somewhere around my numb rear end. I'd never experienced this feeling before, but it reminded me of a bout of diarrhea coming on. They were going to kill me. They really were. And not a soul knew where I was. There was no rescue squad coming. I kicked myself for not getting word to Harry about my plans.

Then I remembered my tape recorder. I glanced down

at my chest and felt a minor lift in spirit. The strap of my purse still draped across me. It had a six-hour tape, but how long had I been out? Surely not that long. I looked around for a clock, but couldn't see one. Maybe, at least, Montallvo'd get convicted of my murder if I could get him talking, get a confession on tape. Provided, of course, someone found both my body and the tape.

"You can't kill me," I said suddenly. "Killing someone is not as easy as it sounds. It takes a lot of guts."

He laughed and stood upright facing me. "That's right," he said. "Guts. I've got the guts to do what needs to be done."

"What makes you so sure?" I asked.

"Experience."

Okay, he likes to brag. "What experience?" I asked. "Killing Brian Reese?" I tried for a derogatory snort, but it sounded rather pathetic with a shiver in the middle. "Setting a bomb is not at all like what you'll have to do to me."

"Reese *and* Chesney," Montallvo corrected. "And you're right. I don't get nearly the same satisfaction."

"As when?" I asked, wondering how long he'd keep talking.

"Seriously?" Skylar interrupted. "This is ridiculous, Grant. Stop it."

Again, I tried to twist around for a look at my attacker, to no avail. "How could you drag your wife into this?"

I heard Skylar Montallvo laugh. "Oh, he didn't drag me into this, honey. It was the other way around."

Chapter 59

I couldn't have heard that right. My kidnapping was Skylar Montallvo's idea? It threw my conceptions into a jumble. I couldn't come up with a response other than "Huh?" Reporter of the Year here.

"You actually don't know much, do you?" Grant Montallvo said.

Maybe I didn't know as much as I wanted to know. "Yes. Yes, I think I do," I said anyway. "I know you stole a formula for weather resistant asphalt from Frank Travis, caused Frank's death, and used the asphalt, knowing it was dangerous."

Skylar made a sort of sniffing noise. "That formula wasn't stolen and it wasn't Frank's. At least not entirely," she said. "You stink as an investigator, Ms. Kincaid. It's time we do the world a favor and help you retire from the field."

Talk about a critic. I'd found them, hadn't I? Even if I didn't understand everything, I'd found enough that Detective Turner and Harry and Clunie and Dr. Sims could continue along my trail. I clung to that thought.

"I even told you I was a chemist working in Midland and you still didn't get it. Frank may have helped, but it was *my* discovery." She moved into my line of sight, her pretty cheerleader smile now an evil smirk.

"That's right," Grant said. "And the three of us — Sky and Frank and I — bought out Manchester Chemicals to produce the asphalt on a large scale. I own Amalgamated Recovery Products, you see. Technically the formula for the asphalt belongs to me." He lifted his head and smiled at his wife. "Sky will disagree, but it's true. And Frank's death was purely accidental. He didn't have to die in order for us to get that formula, if that's your theory."

"Of course, he did," I said. "After he sent the product out for safety testing and it failed dramatically, he wasn't going to let you use it. He had to die."

"We know nothing about any outside testing," Grant said calmly. "We conducted all the tests ourselves. The product is totally safe."

"Then why hire Dr. Peterson, if not to control his research on the asphalt? And now he's dead, too. Awfully convenient for you, isn't it?"

"Peterson was a loose end," Grant said.

"Shut up and just get it over with, Grant. She knows too much."

The change in Grant's expression was astonishing. His look of concerned innocence transformed into one of lunatic delight.

"As always, sweetheart," he said, "you are absolutely right. I think it is time to bid farewell to nosy little Ms. Kincaid."

Chapter 60

My heart pounded furiously. I had a crazy thought that I might die of fright before Montallvo had a chance to do me in.

Think Lila, I scolded myself. *Think, and you might still get out of here.* I closed my eyes to blot out his image and tried my voice again.

I forced myself to take a deep breath, try to steady my nerves. "I easily found out about the formula, about Frank, and about Buzz," I said. The voice was working as long as I didn't look at his face. My hands shook, though.

"Ah, Mr. Bradley. Buzz buzz," Montallvo said, stepping back from my face. "I'm impressed, Ms. Kincaid. She's a pretty good investigator after all, darling." The sudden change in his voice from deadly serious to conversational gave me the feeling that the whole scene was staged, unreal. "Of course, you realize I didn't kill him," Grant continued. "He was mugged."

"You hired the muggers," I said. I opened my eyes and glared at him. My loathing for the man momentarily outstripped fear.

He laughed heartily. "Why, Ms. Kincaid. You can't prove that accusation. What slander! I should let you publish that and sue your paper. Then who would believe anything you say?"

"Okay," I said. "I'll bite. What else might I say? Maybe something about the miracle of having the long-dead Glenn

Montallvo in charge of Sky's-the-Limit Evaluations?"

He laughed even harder. "You don't know what a kick I get out of that."

"How did you get Chesney to go along with it?"

"Enough talk," Skylar said.

"No," I said without taking my eyes off Grant. "You want to know what I know. I know more than you think."

I continued, encouraged by his unexpected silence. "I know that in addition to bombing California Dreaming to either eliminate Brian Reese, Ms. Chesney, or both, you were responsible for bombing Buzz's car and burning out the *Morning Star* offices trying to get rid of any evidence that could connect you with the murder of Buzz Bradley."

"Ha," he laughed. "That's a lot of bad stuff I'm supposed to've done. Let's see, I read about the *Morning Star* attack in the paper. But I don't know anything about a car bombing. Nope, nothing about that."

"You lie," I said. "Those guys who were injured in the *Morning Star* attack were decent guys. Buzz was a fellow reporter helping me on this story. You won't get away with any of this."

"And your proof?" he asked.

I took a gamble. "Buzz backed his files up onto the Cloud. Everything is still there. How do you think I tracked you? Buzz had everything well documented. When the police see those files, you'll fry. And you were in New York at the right time."

He looked thoughtful for a moment, and then laughed quite merrily. My heart sank.

"Nice try, Ms. Kincaid," he said. "You know, a hired killer is so easy to find. Try any run-down bar and wait around. Someone with an urgent need for cash will eventually show up. There's never any question and no way to trace anything back to me. But I digress. I met with this Buzz Bradley and he had no inkling of what was going on. In fact, I doubt if he had any clue why those thugs descended on him. You, on the other hand, know way too much."

"I know your asphalt formula caused the deaths of all those kids and their families," I said. "And you know it, too. I've got proof you knew it was dangerous years ago. You, Mr. Montallvo, you are responsible."

"No, I disagree with you there," he said. "Those kids may have had a problem that made them susceptible to a chemical. It's their disease. I can't be expected to have any control over that."

"You didn't have to market the stuff."

I didn't see the blow coming. Grant's fist slammed into my jaw, knocking my head backwards. I fought the blackness that threatened to engulf me and forced my eyes to stay open, terrified by the fury which was seared into his face.

"You sound like Frank," he said, volume crescendoing. His voice was an echo of the muffled roar of the surf. Grant straightened up suddenly and began to pace the kitchen floor. Every muscle in his six-foot frame was tense. His hands were still clenched into fists. "Frank couldn't understand. It's all in the economics of the situation. Why can't you people see that? Every great endeavor has collateral damage."

I lifted my chin and glared at Grant. "They were only children," I said. He must have broken my jaw; it hurt so much to get out the words. "Why can't *you* understand? Children. They hadn't even begun to experience life and you ruined them."

He stopped pacing and smiled at me.

"I have, haven't I?" he said. "Too bad for you, but there's still no proof."

Again, his sudden smile chilled me. *Psychopath. Narcissist. He was the center of the universe, and nobody else even counted as real.*

"You're CEO of the company which made the test asphalt," I said.

He clapped.

"And," I continued, "my chemist can link that asphalt to a chemical found in kids that lived near the testing sites, whether you kill me or not, and your millions or billions, whatever, in road surface contracts will be gone."

I suddenly had a chilling realization. Senator O'Connell. He could have murdered Senator O'Connell over those same government road contracts. I didn't have a chance in hell to appeal to his conscience.

He didn't have one.

Chapter 61

"Shut up," Grant Montallvo said, his eerie smile morphing into a malicious glare. "Nothing dangerous shows up in the asphalt once it hardens."

"Grant," his wife said, "don't say any more."

"Stop worrying so much, Sky."

"Sky?" I asked, another realization dawning. "Oh, my God, you're Sky's-the-Limit Evaluations?" I couldn't believe I'd missed that connection.

Sky Montallvo laughed. "Maybe she's slow, but she gets there. Now end it, Grant, for good."

"You did the inspections," I accused. "Did you poison those boys with ARP 2728?"

"Ah, the brightest star on the block dims a little," Sky said with a sardonic laugh. "No, the asphalt was the culprit, as you suspected."

"My wife is correct. It's time. Besides," he continued, flashing a smile over my head in the direction of his wife, "my plan is foolproof."

My fear increased with his increasing pleasure.

"At first," he raised his eyebrows at me, "I intended to burn your body with this house. But," he stretched out his arms and waved his hands around in the air, "it's such a grand place. It'd be a shame to torch it."

I swallowed and stammered, "People know I interviewed your wife today. What about everyone at gymnastics class?" I strained my neck to turn towards Sky. "People at the gymnastics class saw me, spoke with me. Your daughters saw me."

"They saw Dorothy Adams," Sky said calmly. "No problem."

Damn. She was right. Anyone looking for the parenting article on Mrs. Montallvo by Dorothy Adams would be told it'd been cut or didn't sell or some such excuse. They'd think Dorothy Adams was a lousy reporter.

They'd be right.

No one I interviewed as Dorothy Adams would think twice if they saw an announcement about the death of Lila Kincaid. I momentarily had a brief hope someone would make the connection if my photo ran in the *Morning Star* or online. I twitched involuntarily.

Grant stretched out his arms again to indicate the house. "I'd hate to destroy this beautiful place. I'll have such great memories of tonight. It's up for sale, you know. Maybe my company will buy it. It'd be perfect to house visiting scientists or executives or . . . hey, we could have our Christmas party here."

"Yeah," I said. "Lovely."

"So, I've moved on to plan B. You're a reporter, you'll like this. See these?" He picked up a manila file folder from the kitchen counter top and opened it, giving me a look inside. I could see three sheets of paper. He poured them out on the kitchen counter. I tried to focus on the objects, but from my angle I could only tell that there was a newspaper clipping taped to each sheet. I couldn't read the headlines but wondered if one was my Death Map article.

He chose one and held it up for me to see. The headline read "Movie Mogul Accused of Kiddie Porn Connection."

"What's that got to do with me?" I asked.

He didn't answer. Instead, he held up the second sheet. The headline read, "Missing Children Spotted in Movies." Then he quickly replaced it with the third sheet of paper whose article headline read, "Violent Death of Boy Investigated — No Connection to Movie Mogul." Montallvo was watching me with a pleased look on his face.

"Don't you get it?" he said. "This house belonged to that very same movie king. See, I plant these articles on you, kill you, throw you over the cliff, and everyone thinks you were sneaking in to gather evidence for a story and fell to your death. Perfect."

"You're insane," I said. "No one will buy that cock and bull, especially not my editor." But I thought it sounded good. It was exactly the kind of story I might look into.

"We'll see," he said.

He grabbed my chair and dragged it back out onto the deck, tearing the skin on my knuckles again in the process. The stinging mist assaulted my face and my hope plunged with the temperature. Montallvo continued dragging my chair until we left the circle of kitchen light behind and reached the opposite side of the deck. He tipped my chair forward near the edge until my face touched the balcony railing. In the pitch black, I imagined a cliff dropping precipitously to the ocean below.

Montallvo switched on a flashlight and shined the beam off the balcony. My imagination was pretty damn accurate. A steep rocky cliff dropped off rapidly toward the ocean. The narrow stream of light illuminated a hillside thick with sharp rock faces, each glistening with moisture. Cold mist from the deafening waves compounded my fear and sent the chill deeper into my bones.

He clicked off the flashlight and threw the bluff back into darkness. Suddenly his breath burned my cold ear with promise. "It's a long, rough way down, little girly."

Chapter 62

He righted my chair, clicked on the flashlight again and found a rock that was within easy reach through the railing. He picked it up and waved it in front of my face.

"See," he said, yelling now to be heard above the ocean's roar, "you gotta look like you hit your head on those rocks over and over again."

I frantically tried to pull my arms free of the damp ropes, which only dug tighter into my wrists. Panic edged its way into my mind. The man meant business and I suspected that he could pull it off and no one would be the wiser. I wiggled my ankles, trying to loosen the rope holding my legs to the chair.

"You know," he continued, with a leering in his voice, "after a fall like that you should be pretty bruised and banged up. So, I intend to make sure you look the part."

He dropped the flashlight and raised both arms to swing the rock at my head. I closed my eyes and continued to struggle against the ropes around my ankles. My body tensed to receive the blow just as one foot slipped from its tie. Grant swung the rock and I kicked upward with my freed foot. I connected solidly with his groin.

His blow grazed my shoulder. It hurt like hell, but Grant was doubled over, his face nearly level with my lap. My anger swelled another notch and I kicked again with all my might. This time I caught him under his chin and felt a surge of satisfaction. He stumbled a few steps backwards, slipped on the wet wood floor of the balcony, fell and didn't move.

Through the light from the flashlight beam I saw liquid oozing from beneath his head. He was out of the picture for a while. Maybe forever.

Relief flooded through me. I let out a laugh that would've sounded slightly hysterical had it not been immediately and forever engulfed by the ocean's roar. The creep had cracked open his own head, not mine. I had a chance after all. Then, just as quickly, I remembered Skylar.

I tried to scoot the chair so I could watch the doorway for her appearance. The woman would eagerly finish the job her husband had bungled, and she had a gun. I struggled with the ropes. My second foot came free easily, but my wrists wouldn't budge. With the chair attached to my wrists, I could only stand as far as a squatted upright position. I toed the end of the flashlight, making it turn around the balcony. I didn't see any way off except back through the doorway into the kitchen and I didn't like that option. I sat back down and worked on loosening the ropes around my wrists, thinking about my predicament. How long did I have before Skylar came out to check on the situation? Only a minute or two, surely; she was not a patient woman.

I thought I'd try to position myself on the other side of the sliding glass door and use the element of surprise. I stood up as best I could and carried the chair, hermit crab-like, to the edge of the circle of light which flowed through the kitchen doorway onto the balcony.

I could see Skylar Montallvo's shadow in the kitchen but couldn't tell if the woman faced the balcony or not. I'd be visible from the kitchen when I crossed in front of the doorway, but I needed to get into position on the opposite side soon. Any minute she would wonder what was keeping Grant. She would step out onto the balcony to investigate. I wanted to be on the opposite side of the pool of light when Skylar stepped through that door and looked toward the flashlight.

Death Map

I noticed that the circle of light from the kitchen didn't quite reach to the far edge of the balcony. If I stayed in those shadows, I might sneak by without attracting her attention. I scurried to the railing and inched along the edge of the light, all the while keeping my gaze fixed on the moving shadow in the kitchen.

I had traversed about three-fourths of the way when Skylar came into view. I halted in my tracks. As she squinted toward the doorway, my heart sank. How could she not see me? Skylar glanced at her watch, then again at the doorway. She took a step toward the door. I froze; trapped in the worst spot ever.

Chapter 63

With my eyes glued to the doorway, I saw Skylar pause again. I held my breath. The woman turned her head away from the door as if listening. She pulled her gun out of a pocket and disappeared from sight. I didn't understand what distracted her, nor did I care. I scuttled as fast as I could to the shadow on the opposite side of the door.

I positioned myself as close to the sliding door as I could without stepping into the circle of light. My tiny arsenal included surprise and a chair attached to my butt. And desperation. I crouched even lower than my forced squat position in order to spring myself backwards, chair first, toward Skylar as she stepped through the door onto the balcony. If everything went as planned, the chair would strike the woman, knock her to the floor, and I would be able to get the gun. It could work. Or not. But anything was better than sitting and waiting to be shot.

Minutes ticked by. My legs cramped and I straightened and repositioned myself as much as I dared. I couldn't imagine why she took so long; she should've come out long ago to check on Grant. In reality this wait may only have been a few minutes, not the eternity it seemed. I made a mental note to count seconds the next time I got myself in a certain-death situation.

When the door finally slid open, I held my breath. It was now or never. I poised to spring backwards, chair first, at the first hint of Skylar stepping through the doorway.

I saw movement out of the corner of my eye and launched myself toward it. I connected and the two of us crashed onto the deck. I hadn't counted on how much it would hurt to fall on top of the chair. My head was jerked backward when I landed and I knew I'd have whiplash if I didn't die. I looked around for the gun and was stunned to realize that the person I'd tackled was not Sky Montallvo, but a man.

The man was not moving but I kept the chair positioned on top of him. I expected Skylar to appear through the open deck doorway any second and finish me off. I'd lost the element of surprise.

This man must be a cohort. He lay face down and I was positioned so that my left hand was on his jacket pocket. I felt something solid, metallic through the fabric. He had a gun.

I reached inside the jacket pocket and my elation changed to frustration. Instead of a gun, I found a Swiss Army knife. Perfect. Well, it would be perfect if I knew how to operate a knife with my feet.

I couldn't give into despair now. Skylar could appear any second. I held the knife in my fist and slid my thumb along the blade edges. I found a ridge and pushed up and out with my thumb. The blade raised and locked into position. This limited success buoyed my spirits.

I soon returned to desperation mode when I realized the impossibility of slicing away the ropes tying my wrists to the chair. But the knife was a better weapon than a chair and my plan with the chair worked pretty damn good. I couldn't congratulate myself too soon though, because Skylar wouldn't hesitate to gun me down if she found me in this position. I needed to get back to the shadow.

In pushing myself back to my feet, I noticed the bulge of a wallet in the man's hip pocket. I struggled around to get it. I pulled out the wallet and let it fall open. I gasped at the photo on the California driver's license. A slow smile spread across my face. I now had the proof in my hand that Montallvo's cohort murdered the scientist who first discovered the dangers of ARP 2728. Dr. Sven Peterson didn't die in a car accident.

He was murdered by my prisoner!

The man moved beneath me. I readied myself to jab the knife into the soft skin of his neck and finish off the killer once and for all. My hand shook in spite of my determination. The man twisted his head toward me and I yanked the knife back in confusion.

"Dr. Peterson," I yelled over the roar of the ocean. "I thought you were dead."

Chapter 64

The shock of seeing Dr. Peterson return to life, so to speak, energized me. I rolled my chair off him and let forth with a flood of questions, trying in vain to compete with the ocean's noise.

"What are you doing here? How did you know I was here, of all places? And what about that car wreck? They said you were dead."

Peterson sat up and rubbed his head. "Are you all right, Ms. Kincaid?" he yelled.

I nodded and pointed my head toward the kitchen, raising my shoulders. "Mrs. Montallvo's in there. She has a gun."

"I've taken care of her," he said. "Give me the knife."

I looked at the knife, suddenly unwilling to relinquish my only weapon.

"It's okay, Ms. Kincaid," he said. "I only want to cut those ropes."

"How did you know I was here?" I asked again, tightening my grip on the knife.

"Let's go inside," he said. "It'll be easier to talk." He stood up slowly and walked inside, leaving me standing on the balcony. I looked around; Grant Montallvo was still out cold, no immediate threat. I was still tied to the darn chair and dripping wet. I edged toward the open door and peeked inside.

Peterson stood in the center of the room, facing me, holding empty hands outstretched before him. Sky's gun was on the center kitchen block, out of his immediate reach. And best of all, there she sat, tied to a kitchen chair, glaring at me. I felt a huge weight lift from my shoulders and warmth spread through my body. Peterson was one of the good guys. I stepped through the doorway, still clinging to the knife and half scooting, half carrying the chair. The ocean's roar diminished with my fading fear.

"Where's Grant?" Sky said. "What's happened to him?"

"Out there," I motioned my head toward the balcony and let Dr. Peterson take the knife. He cut away my bonds and the chair banged to the floor. I rubbed my wrists, my neck, my aching calves.

"I'll check on him," Peterson said. "Are you okay for now?"

"Yeah," I said. "Thanks."

"Get that gun: keep it pointed at her," Peterson said, and then walked back out onto the balcony.

I followed as far as the doorway, where I could keep an eye on both Peterson and Skylar. Dr. Peterson leaned over Montallvo's prone form and checked for a pulse. "He's alive, but I'd better call an ambulance," he yelled.

He left Montallvo lying on the balcony and returned to the kitchen. He picked up the phone, listened. "No dial tone. My cell's in the car."

"Wait a minute," I said, trying to catch my breath. My entire body quaked uncontrollably. "I really need to know why you're not dead."

Dr. Peterson pulled off his fleece hooded jacket and smiled. "Here, take this." He slipped it around my shoulders. It swallowed me up and I relished its warmth.

"Thanks. Now, please? The story?"

"Okay." He glanced at Skylar Montallvo. She glared at us with eyes of glacier blue. He looked back at me. "But the quick version for now. My brakes were tampered with, my car went over a steep cliff, and most of it ended up in the ocean.

Only parts have been found so far. I was thrown clear, so I decided let them think they succeeded. Convinced a friend at Manchester to do some snooping for me."

"But what are you . . . hey," I called after him as he walked out of the room. "How did you know to come here?"

"Sorry, no time for more, we need the ambulance. I'll tell all in a minute. I promise."

Sky Montallvo stared fiercely at me from the confines of her chair. "How badly is Grant hurt?"

"Don't know," I said. "He'll probably wish he were dead once he has to face kidnapping and attempted murder charges. Not to mention charges associated with the test asphalt." I wondered exactly what those would be. I could use Harry's legal expertise about now.

Harry. He was going to be furious. That made me feel a little bit better.

Dr. Peterson returned a few minutes later, carrying his cell phone, a blanket and a bottle of water. I leaned against the kitchen's center island and Peterson draped the blanket around me.

"Now, drink," he said, giving me the bottled water. "It'll ward off hypothermia."

"What?"

"Trust me. Canadians know these things."

Chapter 65

The blanket felt great and the water did seem to help. My shivering slowed to an occasional shudder. My cramps subsided. I lived. Even better, I had one hell of a story.

"The ambulance is about twenty minutes out," Dr. Peterson said. "The police should be here before then. Want to call anyone?"

"Yeah," I said, taking the phone. I dialed Harry's number, got his voice mail, and said sorry I left in such a rush and I'd call him later. Then I dialed Dan McLeish's cell number.

"Hey, Dan," I said. "I'll be sending in some good stuff on the Death Map case. No time to talk now, police are on the way." I shot Peterson a grin as I hung up the phone. "My editor," I said. "I drive him crazy."

I returned the phone and turned serious again. "Now, please explain how you found me? *I* don't even know where I am."

"We're on the coast, about twenty miles south of Monterey," Peterson said. He rubbed his big hand across his thick mane of hair. "You can't imagine how relieved I am to have this nightmare over. I hated letting people think I'd died in that crash. But, hell. I don't like being used."

Mrs. Montallvo let out a scornful laugh. "You let yourself be used. You're pathetic."

I wouldn't have been surprised if she'd spit on the floor.

"Shut up, woman," Peterson said. "You look pretty damn pathetic, yourself, at the moment." He turned his attention back to me, anger slowly receding from his eyes.

"Who?" Mrs. Montallvo demanded. "Who betrayed us?"

Peterson ignored her. "My friend located a copy of the report I sent from Toronto to Amalgamated Recovery Products about ARP 2728. In Montallvo's records. Dated, of course, long before I began work here."

"That confirms my theory," I said. "Frank told Montallvo about your results and wanted to abandon the formula because it was too risky."

"I don't know about that part," Peterson said, "but remember I told you how they persuaded me not to publish my results? Well, my friend discovered that by the time I wanted to publish, Montallvo already had a lot of money tied up in the asphalt project and negative results would have ruined him. He needed control of my research. So, he bought me out."

I heard the note of regret. "But you couldn't have suspected what he was doing with ARP 2728," I said.

"I suppose that's true enough. I didn't get suspicious until you scheduled the interview with me. Then, when I started asking questions, things got weird. I still can't believe they tried to kill me."

"How did you figure out I was here?"

"Early today," Peterson said, "my friend contacted me about a memo her boss had inadvertently left lying sort of open on the lab bench. Actually, she spotted my name and pulled it out of a pile and read it. Montallvo warned her boss about your earlier visit to my office and that you were interviewing Mrs. Montallvo today and might try to gain access to other Manchester personnel. Your picture was attached."

Another shudder slipped through me. "I was afraid his security would catch on to that little slip-up in my credentials the day I visited you. But I used a different name today. How'd he figure it was me?"

Another laugh from Mrs. Montallvo. "We knew you'd be coming."

I frowned. "I still don't get it."

"I don't know, but he has an excellent security department," Peterson said.

"Mary Appleby in Midland," Sky said, giving a snort. "Who were you kidding? We'd circulated your photograph. Chesney knew who you were as soon as she saw you."

"Anyway," Peterson continued, "I thought I'd catch up with you after your interview with Mrs. Montallvo. I'd just found a place to park where I could watch their house when you drove off with her and the kids. So, I followed." He rubbed his forehead. "I didn't expect it to get so rough."

I suddenly remembered my tape player. I yanked open my purse. The green light was on.

"I got it all on tape," I said. "What with the memo and the same chemical showing up in the blood, we've nailed him. You do have a copy of the memo, I hope."

"Yep," Peterson said. "Have it right here." He patted his hip pocket. The sound of sirens peaked in front of the house.

"And we've got her, too," I said, nodding toward Skylar Montallvo. "She runs the outfit that did the annual inspection of the asphalt after it was placed.

"She claims the chemical was in the test asphalt all along," I continued, "but it's not detectable after it solidifies. She also claims to be the one who originally discovered the formula for the new asphalt. She's in this as deep as her husband."

We heard the knock at the front door.

"I'll go let in the cavalry." Peterson patted my shoulder and left the room.

"I hope the ambulance gets here soon," I called after him. "I don't want Montallvo to die this way. I want him to get the chair."

Chapter 66

I was back in a hospital ER again. Too many recent head injuries. Grant Montallvo was here somewhere, too. A nurse ignored patient privacy regulations and whispered in my ear that Montallvo had a broken nose and needed stitches across the forehead and was yelling to high heaven for his lawyer. His wife had been taken straight to lock-up.

After an MRI, the resident on duty assured me that all I needed was rest and a little TLC. She released me and I returned to my San Francisco hotel.

Harry was pacing the lobby. He looked pale and drawn, and I knew why.

"Lila," he began, but I butted in.

"I know, and I'm sorry. I should have told you, or somebody, where I was going, but, Harry, I had to move fast." I did a double take. "How did you know?"

He sighed. "Peterson had my number on the back of your business card. He called as soon as he thought you were in trouble."

I watched his face carefully. "And you flew right out?"

His expression gave away nothing. Damn lawyer tricks. They must take a class in masking emotions. "I thought you might need a friend."

I smiled. He was still a friend. "I did it," I said. "I found out why."

I gave Harry a huge hug. And accepted his hug back.

Harry was able to get a room on the same floor, and that comforted me. I wasn't sure how well I'd sleep after this whole ordeal — the kidnapping, the assault, the narrow escape from a killer — the ER doctor had cautioned me about post-traumatic symptoms. But right now, I felt elated. Mike — the Mike I knew — was vindicated. It made the whole dreadful series of events worthwhile.

I entered my room and pulled Mike's picture from its position on top of my computer, gave it a big kiss and stuck his smiling face back in place. I opened a new Word file and began to write up the day's events for the *Morning Star*. I finally crawled between the sheets for some much-needed sleep as dawn was breaking over the eastern hills of San Francisco.

Disturbing dreams kept me tossing and sleep-deprived. Harry came by about noon bearing coffee and bagels, and turned the TV to CNN. My story in the *Morning Star* was big news and reporters were scrambling to fill in details. The facts were being retold and confirmed — the SDS discrepancies, the chemical in the kids' blood, the bizarre change in the boys, the lies, the greed. Speculation on the personal histories of Grant and Skylar Montallvo filled the airwaves. Interviews were held with fellow employees and neighbors.

Dr. Peterson called, and then stopped by, carrying a vase of roses. I greeted him with a hug.

"I'm so glad you're here," I said, taking the flowers and leading him out to the deck. I introduced him to Harry. "I didn't get a chance to thank you properly," I added. "I wish I could repay you somehow."

"Well, I'm enjoying watching the bastard get crucified by the press," he said. "Want to hear the latest?"

"Sure."

"Scientists and techs are lining up to testify about the research at Manchester. But there are a couple senior level people that can't be found."

"Not surprising," Harry said.

"Remember my inside source?" Peterson asked.

"The one that found the memo about my visit?" I asked.

"Yes. She found out that research into ARP 2728 has been ongoing for years since my stuff disappeared. Under laboratory conditions, the chemical can be detected in the hot asphalt and the surrounding atmosphere. She suspects that anyone along the route where it might be used would simply breathe it in to get exposed."

"Did she know for sure it was being used in the test asphalt?" Harry asked.

"She says she didn't know, and I believe her. So far, no one has admitted to knowing it had already been used in test plots. The good news is that once the asphalt has hardened it doesn't seem to have any adverse effects on rats and presumably the same is true for people. In fact, the chemical can barely be detected in the hardened stuff. At least that's the preliminary data. The government may still want to tear up those test strips."

"I don't see how it would even be a question," I said. "But people will argue anything. At least we can prevent any more from being used. I wonder how many kids remain out there as living time bombs waiting to explode."

"What do you think, Doc?" Harry said. "Any way to find them?"

"Maybe. Could be as simple as a blood test."

"And if the test's positive?" I asked. "What then?"

Peterson shook his head. "Observation is all we can advise right now. Might turn out that everyone along those routes has the chemical in their blood. That still won't help identify the few individuals that are negatively affected by the exposure."

"Negatively affected?" I asked. "This isn't a mere sore throat we're discussing. Those kids turned into maniacs and may never return to normal."

Peterson held up his hands in front of him. "Sorry, Lila. Unpardonable choice of words. I'm not trying to minimize the danger. It's frightening that we know so little about what the chemical does or how to neutralize it."

I thought of Mike and Ellen and all the cases I'd uncovered in the course of this investigation. According to Peterson, the horror could continue. Montallvo was still a threat, even from behind bars. I had a sickening vision of Montallvo relishing each new case as it hit the headlines — his evil eyes gleaming in satisfaction.

The next morning, I sat on the balcony, looking out over San Francisco Bay. The police interviews had ended late the previous evening and I was ready to go home. Clouds obscured the top of the Bay Bridge and the water looked cold and dark. Ugly. The color of the day matched my mood. Even my steaming Earl Grey failed to warm me. The search was over, I'd vindicated my godson, but a big hollow remained in my life. I missed Ellen more intensely than ever. I was still grieving; frustrated by the senselessness of her death. All the deaths. So many lives cut short.

I'd be heading back to Charleston later this afternoon, eager to explain this mess to Sophia. Figure out how to help Mike going forward. I might not have a time like this with Harry again and we were overdue for a long talk. I owed the man an explanation. He stepped out onto the deck then and stopped behind my chair.

"You did good, kid," he said, laying a hand on my shoulder.

I pursed my lips. Yes, I'd done well. But I couldn't have done it without him. Like those days back in college.

"We still work well together, Harry," I said. I reached up and placed my hand over his. "But. . . ." The phone rang. I sighed. I'd hoped that the morning would not get interrupted so soon.

"I'll get it," Harry said.

I heard his tone harden and I was filled with dread, knowing the risk existed for new sensational killings along those routes. I'd had enough. Whatever punishment was dished out to Montallvo would never satisfy.

Death Map

Harry called me inside. "It's for you," he said. "Detective Lang, Raleigh P.D."

Raleigh? I breathed a sigh of relief. Raleigh wasn't on the Death Map. That's where I'd been interviewing the Meyers Construction Crew. I took the phone.

"This is Lila Kincaid," I said.

"Sorry to bother you this morning, Ms. Kincaid, but your editor at the *Morning Star*, name of McLeish, gave me your number."

I waited. Dan liked to give out reporter's numbers.

"Do you know Phoenix Morgan?" he asked.

"Sure," I said. "I know Phoenix. What's this about?"

"What was his involvement in the Death Map killings?"

"Only peripheral. Why?"

"It looks like he thought otherwise."

"What d'you mean?" There was that sinking feeling again in my bowels. The gray day turned darker.

"Mr. Morgan was found this morning," the detective said. "Attempted suicide."

"My, God," I whispered. Phoenix — the picture of health, the sensitive womanizer, the man who dated Ellen. And I'd used him. Pushed him.

"Are you sure?" I asked. "I never thought . . . you said attempted. He's all right?"

"They think he'll pull through." There was a pause. "He left a note. It was addressed to you, in fact, in care of the *Morning Star*. We read it, of course. But I'd like to read it to you."

He read Phoenix's suicide note.

Lila — I read your article today. It's all over the news, what was in that asphalt. I took that little kid there — not for his fun — but just to impress Ellen. Just for me. God, I can't get that out of my head. I'm so sorry. God forgive me. Phoenix

I turned and met Harry's eyes. His widened in response, on alert for another disaster.

"We're investigating," Lang said, "but I thought you might have an idea."

"But that's wrong," I said. "He didn't know what was in the asphalt."

"What's wrong?" Harry asked. "You're pale."

"But that's wrong," I said, my voice catching.

"What's wrong?" Harry asked, moving to my side. "Lila?"

I hung up, relayed the news, then shook my head.

"It's my fault," I said. "He didn't know. I should've realized how he'd feel." I turned off my phone. No more calls today. I returned to the grayness on the deck.

Harry followed.

"It's too sad," I said, staring into my cup of tea. "Phoenix told me once that he liked the maternal side of women. I think he wished he'd had kids of his own. He must have been wracked with guilt, thinking about the effect on those boys."

"I can understand," Harry said.

I looked at Harry. He probably did understand. He'd always wanted a family. Deserved a family. We needed to have that talk.

"I've got a confession," I said. I couldn't look him in the eye while I talked, but I let it all out. Everything I'd kept from him. Everything I'd kept from Ellen. My disease. My battle. My loss. I didn't pepper it with self-pity — I was beyond that now. But Harry deserved to know.

He was supposed to have moved on. That's why I guarded my secret. He would have stayed with me out of loyalty, his own need for a family put aside forever. But a family was what he wanted more than anything, even more than he wanted me. He just didn't realize it.

Somewhere during my monologue, he took my hand in

his. This was exactly what *wasn't* supposed to happen. He was supposed to move on. Get on with his life. Have the family he deserved.

Then he was calling me a fool. Softly. In a broken, raspy voice. We sat like that for a long time, while the sky changed from gray to blue.

The Final Interlude

May: Charleston, South Carolina

Twelve-year-old Michael Jacobsen recognized his position — flat on his back in a hospital bed. He amused himself by staring at the light overhead, then shutting his eyes tightly to allow the reverse image to drift across his brain. The afterimage made him laugh.

He remembered stretching out face down on a floor, the cold tiles refreshing against his cheek. The cold sensation had been a vapor creeping through his skin and entering his mind, awakening astounding images. He wanted that feeling again and he knew there would be no pain.

He remembered the sharp instrument finding its path to his blood. He had swung his arms, the blood flying in a circle, creating a pinwheel, a beautiful red pinwheel.

But there was no blood right now.

He focused on the red sharps container on the wall. It called to him. There were other ways to find the blood.

CHARLESTON, SC: Michael G. Jacobsen (12), died this morning at Cedar Creek Recovery Center where he had been a patient following the stabbing death of his mother, Ellen P. Jacobsen (31) six weeks ago. The Jacobsen killing initiated the discovery of the *Morning Star's* notorious Death Map which again made headline news nationwide last night with the arrest of the Manchester Chemical executives responsible for release

Diana Catt

of the chemical found in young Jacobsen's blood. See full story on page 1.

About the Author

Diana Catt is an author, editor, daytime environmental microbiologist and business owner. She has 20 short stories appearing in anthologies published by Blue River Press, Red Coyote Press, Pill Hill Press, Wolfmont Press, The Four Horseman Press, Speed City Press, and Level Best Books. Her collection, *Below the Line*, is available on Amazon. She is co-editor of anthologies *The Fine Art of Murder* (2016, Blue River Press), *Homicide for the Holidays* (2018, Blue River Press), and *Trick or Treats: Tales of an All Hallows' Eve* (2021, Speed City Press). She is married with three kids, four grandkids, and four pets. You can find the author's website at www.dianacatt.com.

Made in the USA
Monee, IL
28 June 2022

98723374R00203